Peter Watson

Peter Watson writes a weekly column for the *Observer* and also contributes to the *New York Times*. He is the author of five novels, including the best-selling *Crusade* and *Landscape of Lies*. He has also written five books of non-fiction, most recently *Sotheby's – Inside Story*, the best-selling account of fraud, deception and smuggling in the art world.

By Peter Watson:

Nonfiction
WAR ON THE MIND
TWINS
THE CARAVAGGIO CONSPIRACY
WISDOM & STRENGTH
FROM MANHATTAN TO MANET: THE RISE OF THE
    MODERN ART MARKET
NUREYEV
THE DEATH OF HITLER (with Ada Petrova)
SOTHEBY'S: THE INSIDE STORY

Fiction
THE NAZI'S WIFE
CRUSADE
LANDSCAPE OF LIES
STONES OF TREASON

Author's note

This novel is loosely based on actual events which took place in Sicily and New Orleans between 1879 and 1891, events that show how the Mafia left Sicily and became established in North America.

The chronology of certain events has been changed, to suit the convenience of fiction.

I am grateful to the New Orleans Public Library and the Historic New Orleans Collection for help with research.

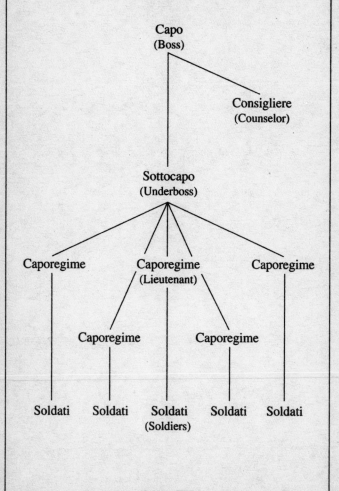

Structure of a
Typical Organized Crime Family

Capo
(Boss)

Consigliere
(Counselor)

Sottocapo
(Underboss)

Caporegime   Caporegime   Caporegime
(Lieutenant)

Caporegime   Caporegime

Soldati   Soldati   Soldati   Soldati   Soldati
(Soldiers)

Source: FBI

Contents

CAPO

PART ONE

—✦—

Soldato

1

"Sylvano, this is the most dangerous package you have ever carried. And the most valuable. If you are caught, and the package is opened, you will go to jail, despite your age. They might torture you, to find out where I am. You know that, don't you?"

Sylvano Randazzo nodded. The potential consequences of his actions were of no importance to him. All he cared about was that the man before him had addressed him as Sylvano. He hated the long version of his name. Everyone else called him Silvio.

"Good. Your youth is your best protection. It's one reason we've chosen you. But you are strong, so waste no time. Listen to an older man. Learn from his mistakes. Sleep as little as you can and you should be in Palermo the day after tomorrow. That's when you're expected. Anna Scafidi will meet you on the steps of the Church of San Domenico, at noon. She knows where the post office is, and it will be less suspicious for her to take the package to the bureau than a young man who can't read. She will write the address in her handwriting. Remember, the wrapping is as important as the package."

Silvio nodded again. That was the second time they had told him. Did they think he was an idiot?

"Wait until the package is posted. Then ride back at once. Is that clear? Do you understand?"

"Sono asino?" Silvio muttered under his breath. "Am I a donkey?" Of course he understood. Out loud he said, "Yes, sir." He was a tall boy, slender, good-looking in a swarthy way, with shiny Sicilian hair, black as olives. When he laughed, or glowered, the whites of his eyes flashed, like the belly of a fish glimpsed in a mountain lake.

The older man looked at him and smiled. "You get more like

your father every day." He reached out and put his arm on Silvio's shoulder. Suddenly he grew serious. "You have his eyes, that way of biting your lip—and, so I'm told, his brains. Your father used to say that only three things matter in life: brains, blood, and balls." He laughed. "He also said he didn't know which of these three is the most important. Maybe you'll learn the answer one day."

He paused, and let his arm drop. "And stop calling me 'sir.' If you perform this task well, Sylvano, I shall be 'Nino' when you return. We shall be comrades."

Silvio's chest swelled with pride. This was an honor indeed. Nino—Antonino Greco—was known all over Sicily. He was the most famous mafioso in the whole of Italy, noted even in Rome. Everyone had heard of "the Quarryman," as he was nicknamed, and it was said in the cafés of Bivona, their nearest town, that his deeds were reported as far away as London and America. He took his name from his abilities with explosives, learned in the quarries near Gela. His strength and decisiveness inspired people, but his fierce will, as combustible as dynamite, frightened them, too, and he knew it.

Sicily was a barren land, forgotten by God and by Rome. The harsh, bare mountains in the center of the island were visited only by the wind and the rare eagles who attacked goats and sheep from the direction of the sun so that their victims would be blinded. Deep, treacherous gullies cut through the landscape, where olive trees and meager oak trees struggled toward the sky, casting frail shadows across the boulders of dead riverbeds. The roads—tracks really—wound from gully to gully with dried horse manure often the only sign that someone had passed that way before. Despite this, the friends of the Quarryman, a hundred or more people who surrounded him, rarely went hungry. They ate fish, rabbits, lamb. They had eggs and wine. They had dammed a nearby stream and so had all the fresh water they needed. Though they lived in a remote hamlet in the folds of the Indisi range, behind Palermo, Nino was a provider, and now Silvio might join that select band who called him by the name he himself preferred.

"Now go," said Nino. "I expect you back after four nights." For a moment his face darkened. He had a full beard, and heavy eyebrows, and when he frowned the effect was chilling. "Do not fail me."

Silvio looked at him, then at his uncle, Bastiano—the man who had been his father for more than a decade, since his real father had been killed. No, he could not fail them. Bastiano Randazzo was Nino's *consigliere*, his counselor and right-hand man, but even so he owed everything to Nino. If Silvio failed, Bastiano would suffer, too.

His uncle looked at him without blinking. He was too proud to plead, but Silvio could read Bastiano's face. "Do not fail," the face said. "Please, do not fail."

Silvio hadn't expected rain. It was true there had been clouds gathering all afternoon, but as he clambered from his mule and took down his roll of bedding—and the package, of course—and lay under an old bridge in the Azzirioli gully, the drops began to fall in earnest, slapping hard onto the yellow stones of the bridge and shivering the silver-green leaves of the olive trees. Rain was unusual at this time of the year in Sicily, and he made sure the package was safe and dry.

After wolfing down a piece of salami and a chunk of bread, he tried to fall asleep, as he usually did, thinking of Annunziata. Living in the mountains, with Nino Greco and his "family," was in many ways exciting for a young man of seventeen. There is a word in Italian, *bivio,* which means a fork in a road. The small hamlet called Bivio Indisi was therefore at the fork in the road near the Indisi mountain. Nino had made it his headquarters some years before, after a landslide had cut off the hamlet from the outside world. From Nino's point of view, and the family's, Bivio Indisi was totally secure. Viewed from the Cammarata Mountains, the half dozen or so crumbling buildings looked as though they were carved out of Parmesan cheese.

But there were drawbacks, and Annunziata was one of them. Nino's daughter, she was Silvio's first love, and so far as he could tell, she loved him in return. The drawback lay in the fact that at some level everyone in Nino's circle was actually related to everyone else. Annunziata and Silvio were themselves cousins—their mothers had been sisters. Her mother had died in childbirth and Silvio's mother had been killed along with his father. The losses had been hard on the two cousins and given them an added bond.

Silvio hated to think back to his parents' deaths, but sometimes, late at night, he couldn't help it. It had been more than ten years ago now, but the memory was as vivid and as cold as a plunge in the Platani River. Five of them, two boys and three adults, were traveling on horseback between Filaga and Santo Stefano. Silvio's mother, Sylvana, rode ahead with his father, Lorenzo, and Aldo, Lorenzo's brother. Silvio hung back with Carmine, Aldo's son, his cousin. The boys' mules were smaller than the others, and slower, and in any case there were things Silvio and Carmine had to talk about that were no business of adults.

They had reached the bridge crossing the Capraria ravine. Silvio and his cousin sometimes played there, daring each other to balance on the low parapet with the deep gorge on one side. Lorenzo had been shot first—the side of his head simply flew away—but Aldo fell from his horse moments later, dead before he hit the ground. There must have been six guns at least, judging by the noise.

Silvio's mother—as a woman—might have been spared, as the boys were spared, but her horse had panicked and thrown her. Silvio watched helpless as her body hit the parapet. Her spine snapped—a sickening crack, like the sound of a huge cricket. Then she had fallen over the parapet into the ravine. Silvio dismounted and ran to where she had fallen. Everything had happened so quickly he was not yet in shock. He peered over the edge of the bridge. His mother lay fifty feet below as if she were hugging the boulder beneath her. Black blood disfigured the stone around her where her head had exploded as it had collided with the riverbed.

Silvio still shivered when he thought of it. He could still recall the stench of his own vomit as shock had racked his body. He had never returned to the bridge to play.

Although his grief had ebbed over the years, he was left with one secret, a devastating relic of that time. It had been a vendetta killing, everyone knew that, carried out by the rival Carculipo family, who fancied that Aldo Randazzo had interfered in their business interests, and had killed Renzo for good measure while they had the chance. Yet what still kept Silvio sweating at nights was that moments before the ambush he had seen a flash of sunlight between the trees, but had thought nothing of it. More important, he had *done* nothing about it. Of course, he soon realized that what he had seen, from his position behind his parents, was the glint of a gun. Had he been sharper-witted, he might have saved his parents and his uncle. He might have saved himself the life of an orphan. Nino had said he had brains, but Silvio knew that he hadn't thought quickly enough on the one occasion when it had really mattered. True, he had been only seven, but what difference did that make? Brains, blood, and balls. You were born with those.

As a result of the ambush, and the considerable sympathy that was shown for Silvio when he was growing up, he had been widely indulged by the family. But both Annunziata and Silvio knew enough to keep their feelings for each other secret. Nino and Bastiano would not be pleased to learn of those feelings. The Catholic Church had strict rules about that. Silvio or Annunziata might even be sent away, and that was unthinkable. The worst aspect of this package business, this test of Silvio's manhood, was that he wouldn't see Annunziata for four days. They had never been apart that long before, at any rate not since this feeling had grown up between them.

As the clouds continued to gather over the Azzirioli gully, Silvio finally fell asleep, his mind full of images of Annunziata's breasts. He had not seen them yet . . . not yet. . . .

The next day, the first sound he heard was the hiss of raindrops on the leaves of the trees. Rain was so scarce in Sicily that a shower was always good news, a proper storm even better. But Silvio could do without rain just now. The package had to be kept dry. He hadn't been told this in so many words, but he knew that it was going a long way, to England, and if the paper on the outside got wet, the post office might not accept the package. The wet could also damage what was drawn on the inside of the wrapping, and that would surely spoil the effect.

He had no raincoat—he didn't possess one—just the string bag that he wrapped around his body while he rode, and in which he carried his food and the money he had to pay Anna Scafidi. But the bag wasn't waterproof. After a moment's thought he decided to wrap the package in his bedding. It might get a bit crumpled but it would keep dry enough in there. Then he was on his way again. Bastiano had given him a watch for the trip, so he would know when it was noon, to meet Anna Scafidi, and although Silvio couldn't read, he could tell the time. From the watch he knew it was just after five.

The rain worsened. For Silvio, the best thing about it was that it brought out the smells of the island—the olives most of all, sweet and cloying, and the pines. Even the soil smelled, when it was freshly wet. When it rained in Sicily the rocks on the mountain-sides darkened. Within hours, small streams appeared from no-where, gurgling in hidden places. The birds kept quiet. One of those flash streams ran near where his parents were buried, in Cas-tronuovo. Not that he went there often; it made him too sad. The other good thing was that the rain kept the peasants inside; he saw even fewer people on the road today than yesterday. Given what he was carrying, he liked that. He told himself that everything was working in his favor.

He spoke too soon. Shortly after nine, he came to the Catala River. Here was a deep gorge with a narrow bridge, and as he came over the shoulder of the Parrino mountainside, he could see immediately that there were three figures on the bridge. They wore hats and gray-blue uniforms. *Sbirri,* as the local dialect had it: a term of abuse for the police.

Silvio reined in his mule. He had known something like this might happen. So far as the Italian government was concerned, the whole region of Sicily behind Palermo was infested with brigands and mafiosi. The locals felt differently. After nearly twenty years as part of the kingdom of Italy, they still didn't feel Italian, and resented the interference of the mainland, just as they had resented interference from outside for more than a thousand years. But for the time being, the outsiders had the upper hand. For one thing, they had the police, who mounted roadblocks like this one, hoping to trap someone unexpectedly.

Silvio got down from his mule and sat on a rock behind a tree, where he could see but not be seen. The hiss of rain was strangely comforting. He had to think. This situation was tricky. It required brains and balls. In other circumstances it would have been easy for him to have avoided the bridge. He knew the countryside well and could have cut across the mountains toward Cerruda and remained out of sight completely; but that would have taken time, more time than he could spare on this occasion. He had to be in Palermo by noon tomorrow. He was forced to stay on the road and cross the bridge. And he had to cross it soon. He needed a plan.

He bit into an orange while he thought. When he reached the bridge he would be searched. If the package were found it would be opened. When the contents were revealed he would be arrested.

The wrapping was a dangerous giveaway that would ensure he would be jailed. The object inside would never reach its destination and, being so sensational, would be blazoned over all the newspapers. More to the point, he would have failed.

The more he thought about his predicament the more he realized there was only one hiding place on a mule. He nodded to himself, stood up, threw down the remains of his orange, and removed the package from the bedding. He opened it and folded the paper carefully, then put it in his pocket for the moment, to keep it dry. What was inside the package was small and still a little smelly. He held the object in one hand, fighting to overcome his disgust. With the other hand he took hold of the mule's tail.

The three *sbirri* were smoking, sitting on the parapet of the bridge and looking at nothing in particular, occasionally complaining about the rain. But they heard Silvio's mule soon enough. They got up, stubbed out their cigarettes, and one of them took out his gun.

Silvio didn't falter but rode right up to them. Rain dripped from his hair.

"Get down," said the policeman with the gun.

Silvio got down.

"Strip the mule," the leader said to the others. "Saddle, bridle, everything." He had brass decorations on his shoulders—elaborate brass buttons. He must be a captain.

One of the other two men held the mule by the head while the third started to unstrap the saddle.

The captain put his gun back in its holster. He was small but broad, with a round face and a barrel chest. He lit a fresh cigarette.

"Now you," he said, picking bits of tobacco from his tongue. "Who are you, where are you coming from, and where are you going?"

"My name is Silvio Randazzo. I'm coming from Bivona and I'm going to Palermo."

"How old are you?"

"I will be eighteen next month."

"Isn't that a little young to be traveling on your own?"

Silvio puffed out his chest. "I'm a man."

The captain grinned sourly. "And still a virgin, I'll bet."

Silvio blushed, as if Annunziata herself had said it, and the captain cackled. Then his expression changed and his face darkened. "*Why* are you going to Palermo?"

"To see my aunt. My father—her brother—is ill. There was no one else to go."

"What is so important about your aunt?"

"She has money. For medicines."

The captain grinned again, slyly. He was thinking: What a pity we didn't intercept this boy on his way home, when he would have had some money on him. But that thought appeared to jog his memory, and he turned to his associates. "Well?"

The saddle was on the road, upturned, the bedding was unwrapped. The bridle had also been taken off and the bit removed from the mule's mouth. The third soldier held the animal by means of his own belt, wrapped around the creature's neck.

"Nothing here," the second man said. "Clean as a bishop's surplice."

"Search him, then," said the captain.

"Take off your shirt."

"In the rain?"

"Take off your shirt!"

Silvio did so and the second man took it from him.

"Now your trousers. And that bag wrapped around your waist."

The other policeman went quickly through the pockets of Silvio's trousers. In the bag he found the remains of the salami and some money. He pocketed the salami and held up the money.

"Put it back," growled the captain. "We're not the Mafia, for God's sake. That's petty change." He pointed at Silvio's legs. "Now your boots," he said.

After that they allowed Silvio to get dressed and to reassemble the bridle and saddle on the mule.

He gripped the reins and maneuvered himself onto the animal's back. He looked down at the men. "May I go now?"

The captain looked hard at him. "Bivona. That's Quarryman country. Where the English priest was kidnapped."

"Yes," said Silvio. "Everyone's talking about it."

"Have you ever met this man, Nino Greco, the Quarryman?"

Silvio shook his head. "No. But I wouldn't tell you if I had." The captain frowned until Silvio added: "I'm more afraid of him than I am of you."

"One more question," said the captain, stepping closer. "Why have you braided the tail of your mule?"

Testardo come un mulo! The stubborn pig! Silvio began to sweat. He was so nearly on his way; now this. He fought to remain calm, to speak as casually as possible, desperately hoping his voice was under control. "I didn't do it. My sister did it, two days ago. We did it to all the mules, to celebrate my father's birthday. That was when he was taken ill."

The captain moved again, to stand behind the animal and inspect the braiding. He lit another cigarette and picked more tobacco from his tongue.

"Everything happened so suddenly," said Silvio. "There hasn't been time to undo it." What was going through the mind of the captain? Had he seen something?

Suddenly the rain gusted and the *sbirri* began to think about shelter.

"Go," said the leader to Silvio, who immediately kicked the mule into action.

The captain called after him, "I had my first woman at sixteen." And he cackled again.

Silvio rode for half an hour, to put as much distance between himself and the police as he dared. But it was still raining and he didn't want his precious, awesome object to get wet. He led his mule off the road and threaded his way through the trees until he could not be seen by anyone passing. He dismounted, went round to the rear of the creature, and began to unbraid the tail.

Harriet Livesey pulled back the net curtains and looked out at the July morning. A fresh sun splashed across Cadogan Gardens. In normal circumstances, this would have filled her heart with joy, but not now. Deep inside, she hoped she might see her brother getting down from a carriage, signaling the fact that this awful business was over. But there was no one other than the postman on the far side of the gardens. London could not be the same until her brother was safely returned.

She sighed and made her way downstairs for breakfast, taking Rhum, her highland terrier, with her. He skittered down the stairs ahead of her, his fur a blur of white against the mahogany paneling of the stairwell. He had been such a comfort since her brother had been kidnapped two months ago. In the breakfast room, at the front of the house on the ground floor, the table was laid for two, on her instructions. She would not abandon her brother just because he had been seized by some tawdry Sicilian thugs. A place was set for Henry at all meals, as a symbol of Harriet's faith that the affair would all end well, and to show that the household was ready to welcome him back at any moment.

"Good morning, Edna," she said to the young woman who stood by the sideboard.

"Good morning, miss," the maid replied, dipping slightly in a small curtsy. A priest's family was not aristocracy, but Father Henry Livesey had a good private income since his elder brother, a soldier with the Wessex Regiment, had been killed in India.

"I'm not hungry, Edna. Just tea, please."

Before she picked up the morning paper, she glanced around the room. In Henry's absence she was in charge and was determined that the house should appear spick-and-span on his return, whenever that might be. Nothing had changed in the room since the previous day, of course. Those two damned pictures still dominated the wall opposite the windows. They were damned because one of them was a landscape, which ironically showed a valley that Henry owned at Fontana Murata in Sicily, a valley that contained valuable sulfur mines. They were the reason for his journey to Palermo and beyond, the journey on which he had been kidnapped. The second picture was by Sir Thomas Lawrence, a portrait of Henry and Harriet's great-grandfather, General Sir James Livesey, whose campaigns for Wellington had founded the Livesey fortune. The picture was unexceptional but it *was* a Lawrence, and in a routine valuation made by Christie's about three months earlier, just weeks before Henry had left for Italy, it had been valued at four thousand guineas. By another bitter irony, that was more or less the sum that the Sicilian brigand, Nino Greco, was asking for her brother's return.

Edna brought the tea and set it on the table. Rhum sat near his mistress and looked up expectantly. Sometimes he was fed scraps of whatever she was eating. Not this morning.

Harriet had been in favor of paying the ransom. What was one painting here or there? Unfortunately, the family solicitor, William Baldwin, who had power of attorney over Henry's effects in his absence, thought otherwise. Baldwin had been outraged by the demand and had brought in the local member of Parliament, Sir

Rupert Farrar. Farrar had raised the matter in the House of Commons, and after that payment was impossible. The foreign secretary spoke from the dispatch box in the House, criticizing the failure of the Italians to protect travelers in their land, and his comments had been widely reported in the newspapers. For Harriet then to have quietly paid the kidnappers would have smacked almost of treason. But for all Farrar's and the foreign secretary's huffing and puffing, Henry was still missing. The Italian government had promised help, but that was all it had been, so far as Harriet could see—promises.

Harriet was opening the *Morning Post* when the doorbell rang. In the early days, she had responded to unexpected arrivals at the front door with excitement, as if it might be Henry. She no longer felt that way. In any case, this sound was not entirely unexpected. She glanced at the clock on the sideboard—ten-fifteen. Probably the mail delivery.

She drank some tea and scanned the newspaper, then there was a knock on the breakfast-room door. Venables, the butler, appeared.

"The post, miss."

Harriet waved to the sideboard.

"No, miss." Venables stood his ground and Harriet looked up sharply. He held the silver tray forward. "It's a package from Italy. A Palermo postmark."

Harriet set down her teacup. She swallowed, then wiped her lips with her napkin, stood up, and took the package. Venables left the room. He was right, though: the package had been posted in Palermo two weeks before. Harriet's name was written clearly in blue ink, printed by what appeared to be an uneducated hand: some letters were in capitals, some were not. It was tied by string but not sealed with wax.

Of course it was from the kidnappers. She was in no doubt. Should she send for Baldwin, or the police? Even as she thought this she was already turning over the package and pulling at the string. Why a package? What could be inside? The first communication had been a simple note: one page. She removed the string and fumbled with the paper.

At first she didn't recognize what was inside. Then her body seemed to register the truth before her brain did. She felt the blood draining from her face, and a crawling sensation at the back of her neck. She became short of breath and tears forced their way into her eyes. Then she uttered a short, involuntary scream, and fainted.

The package fell from her grasp and landed beside her on the carpet. Rhum was for a moment alarmed by his mistress's fainting but was soon more interested in the object she had dropped. He sniffed at it but hadn't touched it by the time Venables, hearing the commotion, rushed back into the room.

Venables recognized the object as quickly as Harriet had.

It was a human scalp.

2

Nino Greco was in his late thirties but still a very fit man. The muscles on his thighs and forearms were as hard as the bark on an oak tree. The skin that stretched over his body was smooth; no wrinkles yet. His eyes were dark and deep, like the waters of Lake Arancio. He had been born in Campobello, near Licata, but his mother had died giving birth to him, just as his common-law wife, Tomasetta Priola, had died giving birth to Annunziata. Such deaths were far from uncommon in Sicily. Nino's father, Fermo, had been foreman at a quarry near Gela, and when he was thirteen Nino was taken there to work. All went well for two years. Then it turned out that Nino's father was the chief supplier of explosives to the local Mafia. The explosives used in a bank robbery at Catania had been traced to the Gela quarry and Nino's father had been charged, convicted, and imprisoned.

For the three years that his father was in jail, Nino was kept on at the quarry and learned the trade. He was taught how to make explosives, where to place them to dislodge the right amount of rock, how much was needed to create a particular effect, how fuses worked, and much else.

When Fermo Greco came out of jail, the Mafia looked after him. He couldn't go back to the quarry, so he was found a job as a *guardino*, collecting protection money in the olive groves around Licata. For three years Nino enjoyed the only steady, stable time he had ever known—would perhaps ever know. His father was a hard man, too, but he had a sense of duty where his son was concerned. He gave Nino a number of tips about explosives. No less important, he took his son to Palermo, where they savored the life—the nightlife especially—of the port, with its bars and brothels.

15

Fermo and Nino were to some extent protected by the fact that they were cousins, the junior branch, of the Priola family. The Priolas owned several large steamships but could only avoid labor problems in the docks with a little help on the side. Although the Palermo Priolas were a rich, prominent family, behind the legitimate shipping and transport business there was a less respectable enterprise run by some of their relatives.

At the age of seventeen Nino had been initiated into the delights of sex in the notorious Via Scina in Palermo. On one weekend, two of the Priola brothers had been especially solicitous, providing Nino with several *puttane*, as the women were called, and with copious amounts of the thick Sicilian red wine of which the young quarryman was becoming very fond. Exhausted, hungover, and feeling pleased with himself at having had four women in the course of the day, he had passed out.

When he came to, there was a man in the room. An unpleasant-looking individual with a long nose and crooked teeth, he had begun by asking if Nino had enjoyed himself.

"What's it to you?"

"Because, my friend, nothing comes free. You had the time of your life yesterday. Now it's your turn to pay."

Nino had panicked. "Pay? But I'm only seventeen. I work at a quarry. I don't earn much—"

"I know who you are and what you do."

"But . . . but, we're family, sort of."

"Yes, I know that, too. *I'm* family, believe it or not."

Nino looked at the man. He could have fought his way out of the room except that he didn't have any clothes on. It was only then that he realized he couldn't actually *see* his clothes. They weren't where he had left them. Someone had removed them. He was suddenly very frightened. The day before, the night before, had been a setup.

There was total stillness in the room until at length the other man smiled. "I see you now understand."

Nino lapsed into a sullen silence. The other man was not in the least bothered by this. He lit a cigarette, taking his time about it, breathing smoke into the stale air of the room.

"You're an explosives expert. You have access to certain substances we want."

"Who is 'we'?"

"You're seventeen: old enough to know what not to ask. Just listen. In a moment I'm going to give you your clothes and I'm going to take you outside. I'm going to take you to a building, a bank, here in Palermo. Inside that building I will show you a door. It's a metal door to a room-sized safe. You have to work out how much explosive is needed to blow the door. The door and nothing else. Then you have to get that amount of explosive for us."

By the time the man had finished, Nino was shaking. This was a carefully thought-out plan. His mind was working fast, but again he lapsed into silence.

The other man let the silence linger, appearing to enjoy his cigarette. Then he said, "Don't get mad, and don't sulk. Do this job well and houses like this"—he gestured at the walls around them—"can be yours for the asking."

He let a small pause elapse before going on, in a brighter tone. "We've been watching you. You're good, maybe better than your father. When he employed you, on our instructions, neither he nor we knew how you would turn out. It was a good investment."

He stubbed out his cigarette and stood up. "Nino, your father is as much a part of all this as anyone. Accept it. Now let's go!" He turned his head and shouted, "Beppo!"

The door opened and another man stood in the doorway. He was holding Nino's clothes. The man who had been doing the talking gestured forward, and the clothes were thrown onto the bed.

Nino had gone through with the first set of instructions reluctantly, and only because his father was so obviously in danger. But the bank job had been a glorious success, so successful that he had received more lire than he earned in six months at the quarry. By now he was addicted to the brothels of Palermo and had spent everything he made from the bank job within a matter of weeks. Nino was soon as enthusiastic a robber as anyone else. Before he was eighteen he had supplied the explosives for four major bank raids. He enjoyed the thrill, he enjoyed the earnings, and above all he enjoyed the whorehouses.

And that of course was his undoing. What eighteen-year-old quarryman could afford the fleshpots of Palermo? It wasn't long before he was visited by the *sbirri*, wanting to know how he found the money to visit the brothels of Via Scina. His answer—that he was a successful gambler at the Foro Biondo—was difficult for the *sbirri* to disprove but he did not convince them either. From then on he was watched, and followed.

A year later a gang war broke out on the docks of Palermo. Hitherto the labor gangs had been controlled by the Priola family, who looked after the gang leaders so long as Priola ships were unloaded first, and quickly. Sicily exported oranges, lemons, and olives to France, Britain, Holland, and America. There being no way to keep the fruit cool, speed was all-important. When, therefore, the owners of a new steamship line, the Orestano family, concluded a contract with some independent orange growers near Platani, the Priola organization was threatened. The Orestanos wanted rapid service, too, and used the same docks.

The important figures in the docks were the *mandatori*, the middlemen who put the fruit and the customers together. These were hereditary positions, passed from father to son and always run by the local Mafia. Until that point most of them had been under the protection of the Priola family. When two *mandatori* were found garroted—the traditional Sicilian form of strangulation—the Priolas' reputation as protectors of the middlemen was threatened. Other *mandatori* immediately began to hedge their bets, putting Orestano fruit together with their better customers.

A response was called for—one that was swift and far more terrible than anything the Orestano family would ever contemplate: a response that involved explosives.

Nino was well aware that he was still being followed by the police, but he had long ago established a routine whereby others in the family could buy off any *sbirri* in an emergency. For a few hours at least he was able to evade his "shadow." The explosives were duly delivered, and the next day the Orestano warehouse went up, raining oranges—or rather the remains of oranges—over the docks. As a countermeasure, it was highly effective. The only problem was that not only oranges were blown up. Two people were killed.

The deaths made it inevitable that the police would now search out Nino. The chain of events was circumstantial but too strong to be overlooked this time, and the police, now desperate for an arrest, would not bother about lack of evidence. The evidence would come later.

And so Nino went underground. It was not generally known that the sister of the abbot at Quisquina was married to a Priola.

The family did not advertise the fact; but occasionally the blood-line came in handy. Nino spent two months at Quisquina, dressed as a monk, until the warehouse business had died down.

However, he couldn't stay in the abbey forever and he needed money. Cattle rustling provided the answer at first. Tunisia was a ready market for cheap Sicilian meat, and stolen cows were cheaper than any other kind. The risk was minimal, and specially adapted boats or barges regularly left Sicily's southern shore with anywhere from twenty to forty cattle.

But Nino could never escape the fact that he had helped to kill several people. This gave him a notoriety that he never sought. On one occasion when cattle were in short supply, he and a few friends raided a quarry near Chiaramonte to steal yet more explosives. These were used to attack the railway between Messina and Palermo, which was then just being built. They ransacked the wages wagon and took away a load of dynamite used for blasting. His notoriety grew.

By now Nino had established a new base for himself at Bivio Indisi, after it had been cut off by a landslide caused by volcanic activity at Mount Etna. The *bivio* had been completely abandoned and Nino and his followers simply moved in one weekend. It was overlooked by the Indisi and Catera mountains, near where two ridges joined. The road from Filaga, which disappeared under the landslide, could be observed. Any other approach involved a two-day trek across mountains. It was as secure as an eagle's eyrie on Mount Cammarata.

Nino was hard and ruthless, but he was clever, too. He realized from the start that he had to have a power base. To get that, a Mafioso in Sicily needed not only strength but style, and that is what Nino had to acquire. In the cities and towns the Mafia leaders had protection rackets: they took a share of almost everyone's profits or income in return for fighting their battles. Nino had his links to the Priolas in Palermo, but they couldn't be used too often or too obviously. He needed to stand up for himself. That was when he had hit on his own form of *malavita*, as the underworld was called.

The Church of the Redeemer, in Erice, was soon robbed of its Tintoretto, a mournful *Madonna and Child*, and quickly ransomed back. This might have been an unpopular crime had not Nino made it his business to distribute much of his profits to the peasants in the area where he lived. He also gave some of the ransom from the theft to the monastery at Quisquina. The crime was a double-edged move on Nino's part. As well as establishing his popularity, it brought him protection, since the beneficiaries of his largesse would never divulge where he was living. And it gave him a quasi-political status. The Quarryman's robberies were seen, by the local population, as a form of protest. In supporting the peasants, he was seen as criticizing the Italian government for its neglect of Sicily.

As a result, Nino had soon attracted all manner of acolytes and hangers-on, many of whom were themselves refugees from justice. "A dog is not a dog without its fleas" was how the cardinal archbishop of Palermo had put it. Quite a few of these people were relatives in a distant way. Some brought their wives and families. Soon they were a "family" of nearly a hundred. In time, the Quarryman's family became more settled. Twice a year perhaps, they would plan some spectacular raid, then retreat to the remote complex of old farm buildings that had become home. There they cultivated what land they could, but mainly lived off what they hadn't given away—until the next raid.

The police made occasional forays against Nino, operating at the insistence of this or that politician, as often as not from mainland Italy. These forays never succeeded. Nino always knew when the police were coming for him, thanks to the shepherds and the system of whistled warnings they had devised. Sometimes he vanished; sometimes the platoons were ambushed and the survivors sent back the way they had come. Over the years the Quarryman's reputation rose; he not only seemed invulnerable to attack, but his occasional distribution of largesse brought him a larger and larger following among the peasants and tenant farmers on the hillsides.

Then Taddeo Panero, an Italian judge, was sent to Sicily to clear up Mafia crime. Two suspected mafiosi in Palermo were arrested for extortion, and Panero seemed to have convincing evidence. It was the first step in his cleanup campaign. What Panero did not know was that one of the suspects, a doctor, had delivered two Priola babies: he was therefore protected. The explosion that rocked Panero's hotel had all the hallmarks of the Quarryman's work. The judge was not just killed but dismembered. A report in *Corriere di Palermo* said that his head was recovered more than fifty feet from his hands. In the upside-down world of Sicily, this added to Nino's stature and put the Priolas in debt to him.

It was soon after this time that Nino, now in his mid-thirties, came to be respected as a Don, not just a feared leader but a respected dispenser of favors and of justice. The nearest town to the *bivio* was Bivona, and Nino sometimes went there to dine, or to use the brothel. The police in the area had been paid off, so it was safe for a night or two at a stretch. Once it became known in the *malavita*, the world of the mafiosi and their friends, that Nino was in Bivona, people began to come to him with their problems.

In the early days a young schoolteacher had approached him. She reported that the school piano had been stolen, so there was no music in the school and daily worship was impaired. Nino had nodded, and whispered, "*Sono un uomo accomodante.* I am an easy man to deal with." He found the piano, had it returned, then broke the fingers of the two young men who had taken it. However long they lived, they would never be able to make music. The elemental justice of this maneuver endeared Nino to the locals. Word spread that no one who came to Don Bivona for help went away empty-handed.

It was his political status that eventually led him to the idea of kidnapping an absentee landlord. These were extremely unpopular people in Sicily; although they lived elsewhere, they often milked the land of its resources. That the landlord chosen was an English priest was more or less accidental—as was the taking of an American artist who was not a friend of the priest's but just happened to be traveling with him. They had been kidnapped one day on their way from Valledolmo to the sulfur mines near Fontana Murata, which the priest owned and the artist wanted to sketch. Unfortunately for them, the Quarryman had planned a spectacular coup to demonstrate once again to the people that he was unquestionably the Don.

The Café Bivona, on the town's main square, was not a grand affair like some of the cafés in Palermo, but it was the best that Bivona had to offer. There were a few tables outside, where Silvio had always sat after his rare visits to the church on the opposite side of the square. He had always been aware that some sort of business went on in the back of the café, but now, for the first time, he was finding out exactly what it was.

Since Silvio's return from Palermo, his mission successfully accomplished, Nino Greco had taken to him as if he were his own son. He had loved the fact that Silvio had hidden the priest's scalp and the wrapping paper in the braided tail of the mule. "That took brains and balls," he had said, putting his arm around Silvio's shoulder and hugging him. "We know you have the blood." And he had moved his young protégé out of the house in the *bivio* where the children lived, installing him in the quarters where the single men lived. He had given him his own mule *and* a gun. Bastiano was teaching Silvio how to shoot.

Best of all, Silvio had been allowed to accompany Nino on this visit to Bivona, a visit Nino now made every Sunday in the company of half a dozen bodyguards. Two of those men, Silvio knew, were stationed at the entrances to the town, on the main road. Two more were seated here at the café, at tables outside. And another two, of which Silvio was one, were sitting at tables adjacent to Nino's. In Silvio's case, this had obviously been arranged so that he could watch and learn.

As they had sat down Nino reached forward to a jar of olives, took one out, and held it up. "See that?" he said gently. "Soft on the outside, hard in the middle. That's how a man should be, a leader. Remember that." He smiled, and slipped the olive into his mouth.

For the past hour Nino had received a stream of visitors. Silvio had never heard his uncle referred to before as "Don Bivona" or "Capo," as all the visitors addressed him. They had been respectful, arriving one at a time and speaking in low voices so that none of the business carried forward to the tables on the piazza.

The first man in the café this morning was Calogero Lanzone, a farmer who complained to Don Bivona that the farmer upstream from him had dammed the Simeto River, preventing enough waters from reaching the Lanzone pastures. Plants had withered and sheep and goats had gone dry. Could anything be done?

Nino said he felt sure the other farmer would see reason. Then he paused.

Nino was a good listener, Silvio decided. He sat perfectly still while people outlined their troubles, his hand over his mouth maybe, or resting his chin on his fist. But he never took his eyes off the person talking to him; he studied their faces, his gaze unblinking. He was forcing them to be truthful.

When he spoke he never raised his voice. Before he said anything he would always drum his fingertips on his lips. The ring on his little finger would sometimes catch the light. Unlike most people, Nino was comfortable with pauses. Now he waited for the other man to speak.

Lanzone then announced that a relative of his was in the police at nearby Cammarata. He could vouchsafe that if ever Don Bivona needed help there, this relative would oblige. . . .

Nino drummed his fingers on his lips again. He must have judged this an appropriate response, for he now assured Lanzone not to worry. His waters would be restored to him. Then he spoke the words that, before long, Silvio would come to associate with Nino. *"Non e il sangue di gallo"*—"This is not cock's blood." Silvio knew that at certain churches in Sicily the statues of saints would sometimes "bleed," from their sorrows for mankind, and be bandaged. The blood-soaked bandages would then be sold, for a lot of money, as holy relics that might work miracles. In fact, the whole business was faked; the blood was cock's blood. Nino was saying that his promise was real, no pretense.

Lanzone required no explanation. He simply thanked Nino and left.

Another person who approached the Capo was Maria Camastra, a middle-aged woman whose daughter, she said, had been made pregnant by the son of Luca Mancuso, who owned a vineyard in Borgo Regalmici. The son, Gaetano, was refusing to marry Maria's daughter, thus dishonoring the family.

Nino hesitated: a difficult problem. Luca Mancuso was a rich and powerful landowner, *un pezzo grosso,* a big shot. And surely Maria Camastra's daughter had been foolish.

Yes, said Maria, but she was only eighteen, and did not Don Bivona also have a daughter of eighteen?

The point hit home. Nino paused.

Then Maria Camastra announced that she was a cleaner in the mayor's office in Santo Stefano, the regional capital where the police headquarters were located. Might it not be useful for the Don to have a pair of eyes and ears in such a sensitive spot?

Nino nodded and whispered, "I am an easy man to deal with." Maria Camastro smiled back. Nino said he would speak to Luca Mancuso. "No cock's blood." Maria Camastra was satisfied.

But Silvio's biggest shock came when Frederico Imbaccari

entered the café. He was the manager of a bank in Santo Stefano, a small man but expensively dressed in a silk shirt and elegant shoes. He offered Nino a basket of oranges. Nino accepted but left them on the table.

"What may I do for you, Mr. Imbaccari? I'm flattered that a bank manager should call on me."

Imbaccari nodded. "I have a problem, Don Bivona. But I approach you not as a bank manager, rather as a man. Five years ago Vito Raffadali, a cousin of mine, bought land from me. He did not pay me any money at the time. The land was not planted and we agreed that Vito would grow orange trees and that when they began to bear fruit he would sell the oranges and start to pay me back. The trees are now mature, he is making money from the sale of oranges, but he refuses to pay me." He gestured to the oranges in the basket on the table. "He has threatened me and says that if I go to court he will tell my wife about my mistress in Cammarata."

"It's unfortunate you are so vulnerable. Vito Raffadali obviously knew about your mistress before he took over the land. He never intended to repay you."

Imbaccari lowered his eyes. "I realize that now."

Again, Nino let the silence hang between them.

"It is a matter of respect, Don Bivona. I would like the land back, because Vito has behaved badly, but am happy to let you have the crop of oranges for, say, five years."

Nino considered this. "Tell me about your wife."

Imbaccari looked sharply at Nino but then said, "She is a good woman. Very religious. She assists at the orphanage in Santo Stefano. We are happy. She knows nothing of Rosa in Cammarata but . . . that is only once a week."

Nino turned to Silvio. "You've been listening all morning. Now you understand what I do. Most of the people have simple problems, as you can see. The solutions are easy, once an agreement had been reached. But this . . . situation . . . is more delicate."

Was Nino asking for advice? He did take advice, occasionally. For example, he had got the idea to scalp the priest from an old friend, a mafioso who had been to America but been forced to flee home again. The man had returned full of tales about American Indians and their exotic war rituals. Silvio asked himself again: Was Nino asking for advice on this occasion? And from a seventeen-year-old? He was suddenly nervous. No, he thought on reflection, Nino wasn't asking for advice exactly, but he *was* expecting Silvio to react. That's why Silvio had been brought along this morning. Nino had known something like this might happen. It was, in its way, a test. He had been tested before, particularly when he'd taken the package to Palermo, but this was different. The other test had been about courage—balls. This was about brains.

He looked at the Don. He had to say something quickly. "Wouldn't it be fair," he whispered, "if the orphanage benefited in some way?"

Nino eyed him, then smiled and nodded. "You're right." Almost under his breath, half to himself, he added, "I can just hear your father saying that." For a moment Nino seemed lost in thought. Then he turned back to the banker.

"Very well. I'll speak to Vito Raffadali. I think I can make him understand. No cock's blood. You will have your land back. But I'll take only half your oranges, and only for three years."

Imbaccari blinked in surprise.

"I want you to give the other half, for the full five years, to the orphanage where your wife does such good work. And make sure they know that the proceeds come with my blessing. Is that clear?"

"Of course, of course." Imbaccari beamed. "A beautiful solution, if I may say so."

After Imbaccari had left, Nino turned to Silvio. "You did well. Maybe, *maybe,* you can take over from me someday. Remember that, but don't let it go to your head." He gestured out to the square, where Imbaccari had disappeared. "No one goes away *a mani vuote*, empty-handed. That's important." He reached forward and took an orange from the basket Imbaccari had left. He cut through it with the knife he always carried, and held out one half of the fruit. The color of the flesh was orange shot through with deep red. "Look," he said softly. "Listen to an older man. Learn from his mistakes. In Sicily, even the oranges bleed."

"Rhum! *Rhum!* Get down! I'm so sorry, Sir Rupert. He gets so excited by visitors." Harriet Livesey rose from her seat in the drawing room of Cadogan Gardens and lifted the highland terrier away from the baronet's ankles. Sitting down again, with the dog on her lap, she began to pour the tea. "Thank you for coming to see me, so soon after Prime Minister's Questions."

Sir Rupert Farrar nodded. "It is the least I can do, Harriet, as your friend and MP. I'm only sorry you couldn't be there yourself."

She handed him some tea. "How did it go, in the House?"

"Well, I think. It was quite full, and both sides were united. Gladstone raised the matter right at the beginning of business. The leader of the opposition has a deep voice, but he had to shout to make himself heard. And he spoke of his own and his colleagues' 'deep sense of outrage' at what you were made to go through. Members were very supportive, stamping their feet and shouting 'Hear, hear' all through what he had to say. Gladstone reminded the House that the Italian government had promised to help find Henry, when he was first kidnapped, and again when the first ransom note was received, but have actually *done* very little."

"Quite right," muttered Harriet. "I'm pleased he took such a strong line."

"Oh, but I haven't told you the best part," replied Farrar. "He even referred to the piece of paper the . . . the scalp was wrapped in. The one . . . with the drawing."

Harriet nodded, but looked away in distaste.

" 'This common criminal is toying with the British government,' Gladstone said. He slapped the dispatch box with his fist— quite a display for him. He said he wanted action from the prime minister, not more words. Quite a performance."

"But what did Disraeli do?" Rhum had quietened down and Harriet placed him on the carpet.

Farrar smiled. "Disraeli can be a pugnacious brute at times, but today he began gently, agreeing with Gladstone that you have been treated abominably. He even said he was revolted by what had happened, and, incidentally, he told the House that you have received a letter of condolence from the Queen. Is that true?"

Harriet nodded. "Her Majesty is most considerate."

Farrar held out his cup for more tea. "Well, as usual, the prime minister manipulated the House superbly. After he referred to the Queen, he hesitated. There was complete silence in the House. Then he said, quite quickly, 'Condolences are not enough.' Last Friday, he said, when he had first heard of this development, he had sent for the Italian ambassador. He had told him in no uncer-

tain terms, he said, that the Italian government had promised help
but actually had *done* nothing. It appeared that Rome had no
power over Sicily. He had then insisted that unless Signor Falfani
had an answer for him today he felt sure the Commons would support more direct action on our part."

Harriet looked intently at Farrar. "Such tough language," she
said softly. "How did the Italians respond?"

"I thought myself that this has all the makings of an interna-
tional incident," Farrar said smoothly. "Anyway, according to
Disraeli, Signor Falfani had been to see him again, this morning.
The ambassador had heard from Rome, he said. The essence of
the Italian response is that a regiment of the Lazio Brigade, num-
bering four hundred and eighty-four men and presently stationed
near Caserta in the south of the country, will be transferred to
Sicily before the weekend. They will disembark at Trapani, at
the western tip of the island, where their specific task will be to
capture the brigand known as the Quarryman and free Father
Livesey."

Harriet sighed. "How long has it been, Rupert? Nearly three
months? Three months of worry, sleepness nights ... But now
there's to be action. I suppose the Italians mean what they say this
time?"

Farrar set down his cup. "Your instincts are right, Harriet.
When the Italian ambassador came to see him, Disraeli told him
that his message seemed to indicate a readiness on the part of
Rome, at last, to acknowledge the seriousness of the situation.
However, Disraeli also told His Excellency that he had, in the
meantime, reminded himself of the Royal Navy's dispositions in
the Mediterranean. The Royal Navy! Can you believe it? Anyway,
Disraeli went on to say that we have the cruiser *Hook*, in Tripoli,
and the destroyer *Clarendon*, in Gibraltar. Telegrams had been
sent to each about an hour before the session, ordering them both
to Sicily. Harriet, my dear, they should be in Sicilian waters by the
weekend. Between them they have an able-bodied complement of
nearly three hundred men. The prime minister says he told Falfani
that unless the Italian government is as good as its word this time,
and the Lazio regiment really does arrive in Sicily according to the
timetable Falfani had promised, then Her Majesty's government
would give orders for the crews of the *Hook* and *Clarendon* to put
ashore and do the job instead. You can imagine how well that went

down with Falfani. Disraeli smiled at that point. Falfani assured him, he said, that such action on our part would not be tolerated in Italy but that in any case it would not be necessary, because the Roman government fully intended to act as it had promised.

"And there the matter rests, Harriet. The government will monitor the situation closely, and if it needs to take action, it will. Either way, my dear, this is the beginning of the end for Antonino Greco."

3

"Toto! *Toto!* Birthday boy, wake up!"

"Annunziata?" Everyone called him Silvio except Nino, who called him Sylvano, and Annunziata, who called him Toto, her private name since childhood. Why she did it and what it meant he had long since forgotten.

"Hurry," she whispered. "You're wasting time."

"What time *is* it?"

"Four. Four o'clock on your birthday. Everybody's asleep. Get dressed."

Silvio knew his room by now, even in the dark. He found his trousers and his shirt. He was lucky in a way. Many of the others in the *bivio* were forced to sleep with goats under the bed. The stench was unbearable but it was preferable to having the goats stolen. Silvio found his boots, but he didn't put them on, not yet. His eyes were adjusting to the gloom, and he could see Annunziata's outline by the door. She wore a long white skirt with a white blouse. She was fair for a Sicilian, and tall. Silvio knew her skin was the color of almonds.

"Come on, Toto," she urged, and was gone.

He turned left out of the bedroom doorway and went down the stairs leading to a yard, which was paved with stones. Annunziata was already waiting on the other side. Silvio paused. The yard was overlooked by several bedrooms, in two of which candles flickered. Whatever she said, some people were awake. He held on to his boots as, slowly, he edged his way around the yard, keeping to the shadows. But he made no sound, and very soon he was standing next to Zata, as he called her when they were alone. Here the rough ground began and he could put on his boots.

He tied the laces and stood up. As he did so Annunziata turned

and led the way across the ground, in among the olive trees. Both
of them knew the land here well, so Silvio had little trouble following. Indeed, he was almost certain he knew where she was
heading—a small grassy ledge, occupied by a few stone ruins that
had once been a temple in ancient times, when Sicily was ruled
from Greece. Because a small spring leaked out of the mountain
just here, there was enough grass to sit and enough tree cover so
that in daylight you could see without being seen. Mosses and a
few flowers also grew there in spring. They had discovered the
spot after following some goats there one day, when they were
both young children. By day you could look down on the *bivio* in
perfect safety. They called it their *giardino segreto*, their secret
garden. They often escaped in the early hours to watch the sun
come up over the Massa Carcaciotto.

Nino kept guards on duty all night, but both Annunziata and
Silvio knew where they were positioned, so they had no difficulty
avoiding the lookout posts. It meant making an occasional detour,
but the guards would undoubtedly have made them turn back
had they been spotted. Worse, their escapade would have been
reported to Nino and Bastiano.

But there were no mishaps, and after some forty minutes Silvio
scrambled onto the ledge slightly ahead of Annunziata. They both
turned on their backs and rested for a while, recovering from the
climb. They lay talking, looking up at the stars, which were just
beginning to fade as the edges of the day inched closer. How many
times had they done this in the past, talked while they watched the
sun come up, filling the mountainside with color? The early-
morning chatter of the birds was the only other sound.

"What time of the day were you born? Do you know?" Annunziata had a clear voice and a clear skin, but she smelled of the
straw mattresses they all slept on. Neither had risked washing.
Silvio thought her words gurgled like water over stones.

He shook his head. "I don't know. Does it matter?"

Silvio was not sentimental. He hated to look back. When he
did, all he saw was his dead parents. Bastiano and his wife, Smeralda, had worked hard at being Silvio's parents. They always
made a fuss of his birthday and saint's day. But nothing they did
could obliterate the raw fact that he was an orphan, less complete
than other children, inescapably alone and forever maimed by the

secret knowledge that if he had thought more quickly, acted sooner, he might have prevented his parents' deaths. Not even Annunziata knew about that. One day, perhaps, she would, after he had proved himself . . . but not yet.

Nino's comments that Sunday in Bivona had had a big effect on Silvio. You couldn't inherit the title of Capo; it had to be earned. But Nino had mentioned it, and that meant he thought Silvio might one day make the grade. He was his father's son, Nino's nephew; his blood was right. He had balls—his trip to Palermo had proved it. But did he have the brains? And what sort of brains did you need? He had been struck by the episode with the oranges in the café at Bivona. "In Sicily even the oranges bleed," Nino had said. Silvio reckoned he had a lot to learn.

Annunziata rolled over and looked at him. Her brown eyes were shadowy in the gloom. "I want to be sure it's really your birthday before I give you your present."

"In that case I was born a minute after midnight. But I don't see any present."

Annunziata eyed him. Then, without a word, she sat up and began to take off her blouse. A few pale strands of daylight slipped between the branches of the trees and threw soft shadows across her skin.

"Take your shirt off, too," she whispered. She turned toward Silvio but kept one arm across her breasts, hiding them.

He did as he was told.

"I visited that old *strega* near Cammarata yesterday," she said. The *strega* was a witch. "She gave me something to stop me getting pregnant. Now lie back and close your eyes."

He did. The grass under his back felt both cool and scratchy. Then he felt Annunziata moving.

"*Don't* look!" she hissed. "Promise?"

Silvio kept his eyes firmly closed. "I promise."

Then something touched his abdomen. It was very light and soft and he was being touched in two places. Still keeping his eyes closed, he could scarcely believe what was happening. But at the same time he did believe it. She had promised him she would surprise him on his birthday. Annunziata was leaning over him, allowing her breasts to hang down and her nipples to brush his skin. Where had she learned such a thing?

Silvio had never—not once—imagined that when he and Annunziata finally made love, she would take control. He had always imagined making all the moves. This was very different.

She crisscrossed his abdomen and chest, moving her breasts first one way, then another, but gradually moving up his body. Still he kept his eyes shut.

For a moment her breasts left his skin and he felt bereft. But then, as he had dared to hope, Annunziata allowed one of her breasts, its nipple, to brush Silvio's lips.

"Kiss me," she whispered.

He did so.

"Bite me. *Gently!* Bite me."

He bit, and a tiny moan hovered in her throat.

Silvio was confused. That moan seemed to tell him Annunziata was in pain when he bit her; but she found it pleasurable, too. He bit again. The same whimper was repeated.

Now Silvio opened his eyes and sought Annunziata's other breast. He pulled her to him and buried his entire face in her flesh. "Zata," he breathed. "Zata, Zata, Zata." It was like being immersed in the Sosia River, where they had bathed naked as children. Annunziata had been a favorite of his father's, too. He had called her his *passero*, his sparrow, because she had been so thin.

Annunziata allowed Silvio to feast for a while, then pushed him gently away. She stood up. Standing in front of him, without any hint of shame or modesty, she undid the fastening of her skirt and began to slide it down over her hips. There was little of the *passero* about her now. The daylight was strengthening all the time. To their right, and below them, the birdsong intensified. Annunziata did not hurry. She was wearing no undergarments. Silvio watched, still hardly believing that this was happening to him. Her thighs came into view, and the triangle of hair between her thighs. Then she let the skirt drop to her ankles and kicked it off. She stooped, rearranged the skirt on the ground, and lay back on it.

They had swum together as children, looked after the goats together on the slopes of Mount Catera. They had always sat together in church, received their first Mass together from Father Serravalle. They had bandaged each other's legs when they had fallen, been punished together for fishing from the dangerous cliffs of the Capraria gorge. They had told lies on each other's behalf. Now this.

Without standing, Silvio took off his boots and struggled out of his trousers. He slithered across to Annunziata and knelt above her.

"No," she whispered. "Not yet, Toto. Lie here." She indicated that she wanted him to stretch out next to her.

He did so, putting an arm under her neck. She pulled him to her and they began kissing. With one hand she stroked his chest then rubbed a finger across his belly.

Silvio was becoming intensely aroused. They kissed more passionately now, and Annunziata drew the back of her hand down Silvio's thigh. When she could reach no farther, she dug her nails into the flesh of his leg, and slowly began to draw them back up the inside of his thigh. Her nails hurt slightly, but to Silvio's astonishment, he found that he liked it.

When her hand reached his groin, Silvio broke off kissing. Now it was his turn to groan and whimper. He looked at Annunziata in the pale light. She smiled and kissed him again, closing her eyes. Now, *now* was the moment he had dreamed of. Gently he touched her thigh, enthralled by her smoothness.

Suddenly, below them and to their right, rifle fire barked several times in rapid succession, the echo richocheting back and forth along the Indisi *serra*. The blunt boom of shotguns answered the rifles, together with the high-pitched crack of revolvers. Birds flew squealing into the air. Voices screamed.

The moment he heard the bark of the rifles, Silvio leaped to his feet, but Annunziata was sitting on his trousers. "It's too late already," she hissed. "Get down!"

He saw the sense in what she said and fell to his knees. They both inched forward to the lip of the ledge where they had been lying. It was not yet five-thirty. The shooting had stopped as suddenly as it had begun and there was now a lot of shouting. Silvio could see the *bivio* but not much else.

"Look!" whispered Annunziata urgently. "Men in uniforms."

"Yes, I've seen them."

"A regiment from Italy?"

"Those aren't Sicilian uniforms." Silvio looked at Annunziata. "Someone led them here. They knew where to come. We've been betrayed."

That had to be true. All the nearby roads were guarded.

Someone must have led the soldiers across the mountains and through the cordon, someone who knew where the lookouts were posted.

As Silvio and Annunziata watched, the square courtyard behind the main house of the *bivio* started to fill with people. The open side of the courtyard was already occupied by a line of soldiers, barring any escape. Each soldier was armed with a long rifle and wearing the green-and-beige colors of the Lazio Brigade.

One by one, people Silvio knew were manhandled into the courtyard. He could see his uncle Bastiano and his aunt Smeralda; Andreo, who looked after the horses; Ruggiero, Nino's servant, who had a fine singing voice; Laura, one of the cooks; Elisavetta, the other cook; Pasquale, Paolo, and Gaspare, all children. Many others. They were being forced into the courtyard at gunpoint, some of them still half-asleep and half-naked. Silvio tried to count them—forty-one, forty-two, forty-three . . . He gave up. He could see Bastiano looking anxiously about the courtyard, possibly looking for Silvio himself.

"What are they doing now?" Annunziata asked gently, but Silvio had already noticed the movement.

"They're separating the men from the women—oh, *no!*" Silvio watched, horrified, as the men were lined up against a wall, *facing* the wall. "They're going to shoot them!" He started to get up again, but Annunziata pulled him back down.

"Sit still. You'll get killed as well. We need to watch. We have friends . . . elsewhere."

Annunziata was right. And in fact, the men weren't shot. Each man had his hands tied behind his back. Then his feet were tied, with enough rope between the ankles to allow him to walk. Finally, another long piece of rope was passed around the neck of the first man, then led to the neck of the second man, and on down the line. The whole process took almost an hour. All this time the women and children were kept separate on the other side of the courtyard. Silvio grew restless, though he realized there was little he could do.

After another half an hour there was a second flurry of activity. More soldiers appeared, this time escorting two men, one in black, with a bandage around his head, the other wearing what Silvio knew to be a white linen suit.

"The English priest," whispered Annunziata. "He's been found."

"And freed." Silvio was secretly pleased by that. He had not been happy with the kidnapping in the first place.

"And the American artist," added Annunziata. "They've given them one of our carts."

They watched as Father Livesey and the artist—a bearded, red-haired man called Thomas Forrester—were helped into the cart by two soldiers. Silvio was not the only one to have been impressed by Forrester's skill as a draftsman. Nino had not at first believed the American when he had said he was an artist, and had challenged him to make a likeness. The American had chosen Nino himself, and the result was so striking that Nino had used that paper to wrap up the priest's scalp in the package that Silvio had taken to Palermo.

Suddenly, from one of the houses in the *bivio*, three soldiers exited in quick succession. They turned back to face the door with their weapons drawn, and after a short delay a figure appeared. He was smothered in chains—chains that joined his wrists, chains that joined his wrists to his ankles, his ankles to each other. There was even a chain attached to his neck with a lump of rock on the other end, which the figure was being forced to carry.

"Nino!" breathed Silvio. Again, he would have leaped to his feet had not Annunziata held on to him tightly.

Nino's daughter spoke calmly. "They're leaving. We need to know which way they are going. Are they walking or taking the big cart?"

They watched in silence as a second and more cumbersome cart was wheeled into the courtyard and a mule made ready—the same mule Silvio had ridden to Palermo.

"Now we can go," said Annunziata, getting up.

"Shouldn't we wait till they leave?"

"They're taking the cart, so they need to stick to the roads. Which means they will either take the Palermo road at Prizzi or head for Trapani."

"Trapani? It's very small."

"But it's a port. They can sail to Rome from there. If they take my father to Palermo, there could be all sorts of problems. We have relatives and friends in Palermo—they must know that. Trapani would be easier from their point of view. Either way, at the speed they can travel they will need two nights on the road. We must go to the abbey. Come on, get dressed."

Annunziata was right. She had thought faster than he had. Faster and better.

She handed Silvio his trousers. For a moment the memory of what had taken place earlier flooded back, and Silvio brushed Annunziata's cheek with his fingers. Then he touched her breast. She looked up at him. "Toto, *caro*. An hour ago I would have given it to you. Now you must earn it."

The Benedictine abbey at Quisquina was a gray-stone building rising three thousand feet into the sky, about two and a half miles east of Santo Stefano and a good twelve from the *bivio*. Traveling on foot, over rough terrain for most of the way, Annunziata and Silvio did not reach the abbey until just after noon, by which time the sun was baking the stones on the hillside. Monks working in the olive and almond orchards below the abbey waved to the young couple as they completed the last climb of their journey. They were both well known at Quisquina.

In Sicily, as everyone on the island was aware, the church had long been suborned by the Mafia, so much so that no one any longer thought it odd. The church was, after all, an important part of life, and itself a form of control. The abbot of Quisquina, Father Ignazio Serravalle, had not been at all pleased when Nino had kidnapped a Catholic priest, albeit a British one, and an American artist into the bargain. But he had said nothing. He and Nino were related by marriage, and had remained good friends over the years, ever since Nino had hidden at the abbey after the Orestano warehouse explosion.

Two monks were standing by the main gate of the building, talking, when Annunziata and Silvio arrived. The travelers looked so tired and disheveled that they were shown straight into the abbot's study. Quisquina was off the beaten track and did not have many visitors.

Ignazio Serravalle was a small, neat man, with deep-set eyes and prominent cheekbones. Although he was clean-shaven, his chin was always dark from the sheer density of follicles. His hair had streaks of silver, like the trails left by a snail.

Father Ignazio kissed Annunziata and shook hands with Silvio. He insisted they drink some water before they did anything else.

Silvio had always been in awe of the abbot. He seemed so certain of his God. For Silvio there was no such certainty. How could there be a God who allowed his parents to be killed so young? Why did the church lay so much emphasis on the family when this God had allowed his—Silvio's—to be destroyed? He couldn't make up his mind whether religious people were lucky, or foolish. But at least Father Ignazio did not deliver sermons on the blessedness of poverty, as so many priests did. Nor did he visit women who failed to give birth every year, as so many of his colleagues did, demanding to know why these women were denying God what was His. Ignazio Serravalle was no fool.

"Now," said the abbot while they drank. "Why has Nino sent you? Is it urgent? You both look like chickens who've been chased by a fox."

They told him what had happened. His face registered his dismay, then his anger, but he heard them out in silence. As soon as they had finished, he was decisive.

"The Englishman must not be harmed further. It was a mistake to take him in the first place. The same goes for the American artist. The soldiers will take the Trapani road. You are right, Annunziata, Palermo is too big and your father has too many friends there for the soldiers to risk going anywhere near it. Which means that Nino and the others must be taken through Chiusa and Sambuca." He scribbled something on a piece of paper in front of him, a note to himself. Then he turned back. "You were right to come here. You have done well, though I will not ask why you two were not at home at five o'clock this morning." He smiled as they both blushed. "It was just as well for all of us. Now, go and bathe. We will give you something to eat. When you come back I may have been able to work out a plan. We must hurry."

An hour later, refreshed but scarcely relaxed, Annunziata and Silvio were back in the abbot's study, the chief features of which were a large fireplace and a blue-green tapestry that completely covered one wall. The abbot had with him two other monks, much younger men, tall and lean and clearly very strong.

"May I introduce Brother Benedetto and Brother Francisco."

They both nodded.

"We have been talking and I now believe there *is* a way for Nino to be . . . well, saved. There is a part for each of you to play in this plan, but it will not be easy. And you must leave very soon. But first I will explain the plan."

The weather had changed yet again. When Captain Ezio Fracci, of the Lazio Brigade, had first set foot in Sicily a couple of weeks before, the sun had been baking the rocks and the shimmer from the sea hurt the eyes. No more. Now it was raining and the tops of the mountains were smothered in cloud.

Still, this business would soon be over. He personally thought it had been demeaning for a distinguished regiment to be sent to this godforsaken hole to rescue a foreigner, moreover a foreigner who was an absentee landlord on the island. It wasn't the job of crack soldiers to arrest Italian civilians, even if they were criminals. But he had done his duty and now it was nearly finished. This time tomorrow they would be in Trapani and aboard ship. A few hours after that they would be at sea, en route for the mainland. Then the row between Italy and England would be over. Italy's honor would be intact.

The arrest had gone surprisingly smoothly. A certain amount of money had changed hands—naturally—and this mafioso hide-away had been divulged. The whereabouts of the Quarryman had been sought by the police for years, but Captain Fracci's unit had succeeded because he had obtained one vital piece of information unknown to everyone else. Through a special contact he had discovered that the local shepherds were on Nino's payroll and had a system of whistle alarms to warn of any approaching danger. Having plenty of men at his disposal, Fracci had simply removed two of the shepherds before his brigade had even set foot in Quarryman territory. His plan had worked. Greco's early-warning system had failed. Once the brigade had reached the *bivio*, a few shots had been exchanged, one of Fracci's men had been hit in the leg, and one of the Quarryman's people had been grazed in the head; but that was the sum of the casualties, and now Greco himself was trussed up like a wild boar. When it came down to it, these bandits were no match for a real army.

Progress was slow, of course. They had manacled Greco so heavily he couldn't walk. Consequently they had to use a cart, and the roads in these parts weren't good. They were now just skirting Lake Arancio, prettier than most of the scenery on this barren island but a difficult road nonetheless. Fracci was a northerner himself and couldn't wait to get back there. The poverty in Sicily appalled him. About a half mile back they had passed a *pagliaio*, a straw shelter in which a family of four were living. It turned out that the *pagliaio* was a seasonal dwelling built afresh every year by the family, who came here for a few weeks to collect frogs and snails at the edge of the lake. They sold them at the nearby market at Misilbisi: it was the only work they could find. In Trapani, Fracci had heard tell that in Sicily there were five able-bodied men for each job. He himself had observed the predawn labor auctions for construction projects—and seen wives scolding their husbands who returned home without having secured employment that day. Give him life in Lombardy any time.

Looking ahead, he could see they were coming to a *bivio*, a fork in the trail. One road led straight ahead, along the shore of the lake, the waters of which reflected the brown-purple hills beyond. The other road led off to the right, into the mountains. At home, near Milan, Fracci was used to the Alps and the deep-colored fir trees that grew halfway up them, like the beard on a monk. Here, the scraggy gray oaks gave out in the foothills, leaving the bare rock of the mountainside looking bony, devoid of all life save for a few eagles. When the sun shone, the glare from the white rock could give a traveler a headache in no time.

He saw the men in front of him stop at the bivio. What now? A sergeant was running back. Altogether Fracci's party numbered two hundred fifty people, about sixty mafiosi, the rest soldiers. The women and children from Bivio Indisi had been let go. The bandits and soldiers made a straggly line about a hundred yards long.

The sergeant arrived, panting.

"What is it?"

"We've reached a fork in the road, sir."

"I can see that. So?"

"The signpost doesn't agree with our map."

"How can that be?"

"I don't know, sir. Our map says that Misilbisi and Partanna should both be to the left, but the sign says Misilbisi is to the left, Partanna to the right."

"And we want the Partanna road, yes?"

The sergeant nodded. "And no point in asking the prisoners. They're bound to mislead us."

Captain Fracci bit his lip. It had been a condition of the guide who had shown them the way to Greco's *bivio* that he be allowed to disappear before the attack. Otherwise, he had said, he would be killed by relatives of the Quarryman. Fracci had been forced to agree.

"OK," he said to the sergeant. "Tell the men to have a short rest. Time for a smoke."

Fracci took out a narrow cigar from his tunic pocket, lit up, and breathed in the thick smoke. He sat on a boulder and took off his hat. This was going to be a difficult decision. Trapani was west and north of here, so either road went in the approximate direction. But that wasn't enough. Most of his men were traveling on foot and wouldn't thank him if he chose a road that added twenty or thirty miles to their journey.

"Look!" The sergeant was pointing. Down the road that led around the lakeshore, two figures could be seen coming toward them. One was dressed in the black of a priest, the other looked like a young woman. "They must be local."

"You're right," said Fracci. "Come on."

He got up and walked forward, past his men, who were sitting smoking, enjoying the rest; past the prisoners, who were making themselves as comfortable as they could, encased as they were in chains or ropes. Fracci walked toward the priest and his companion. The rain had turned the road to mud, brown as almond shells. He slithered about. As Fracci came closer he saw that the priest was quite young, too, about the same age as the woman. When about twenty yards separated them, he stopped and called out: "Father! Can you help me?"

The priest stopped. He looked surprised, but then smiled. "If I can, sir, if I can. What help is it you need?"

"You are coming from where, may I ask?"

The priest looked back down the road he had been walking along. "That way, sir, lies Misilbisi and Dragonara."

"And this other road, north?"

"Smaller, rougher. It is not always on the maps. But, unless I am mistaken, it leads to Partanna, Catalfini—and Trapani, if you go far enough. I have never been myself."

"Ah! I am grateful, sir. You are most kind." Fracci nodded his thanks.

The priest nodded back. "You could return the kindness, sir."

Fracci, about to order his men back on the road, turned to the priest in surprise. "I could? How, sir?"

"I see you have prisoners. You could let me bless them."

Fracci's eyes narrowed. "May I ask how long you have been a priest?"

"Certainly, and the answer is: not long. I am still a novice. This is my sister, who accompanies me to my monastery. Though I am still in training, does that matter?"

Fracci thought for a moment. These two young people looked harmless enough. He nodded. "Go ahead. Then we must leave."

The priest, followed by his companion, walked slowly along the line of prisoners, nodding to each one in turn and making the sign of the cross in benediction, until he came to the wagon carrying Nino Greco. There he stopped, reached into his pocket, and took out a small Bible. He held it aloft and slowly turned through half a circle, again facing all of the men in the line for a moment. As he did so he uttered his benediction: *"Quis einem peccat in eo quod cavei no protest."* He finished, turned back to the captain, bowed, and walked on.

The sergeant watched the priest and his sister walk a few yards and then turned back to his men, giving the order for them to move ahead.

Slowly they scrambled to their feet, put back their hats, picked up their weapons, and headed away from the shoreline, turning instead to the north: into the hills.

"I don't remember this gorge, do you?" They had been twenty minutes on the new road and the sergeant had dropped back again for a quick word with Captain Fracci.

"No, but then we cut across country on the way in. Why do you ask?"

"I don't know. This road seems a bit narrow. Primitive."

"The priest did say it was rough."

Slowly the sergeant made his way forward again, returning to the head of the column. The weather was still threatening.

The gorge twisted to the left. The sergeant looked up. Spindly oak trees, their barks covered in gray lichen—the color of the clouds above—leaned over the lip of the cliffs. Birds chattered, hidden in the branches halfway to the sky. He lowered his gaze: the riverbed was dry, just boulders and shingle and marooned driftwood. A few bottles. What looked like a shoe. The path here was overgrown—purple weeds hung out over the tracks and such horse manure as he had seen was very old. Not many people came this—

He grunted without meaning to. The curve of the valley had opened out into . . . a stone wall! Five hundred yards ahead, pale yellow rock faced him, scarred with streaks of brown and black. The sergeant looked from left to right, searching for the track, rising maybe to the hills beyond. No, he could see nothing. *The road was a dead end!*

He stopped. To his left was a metal contraption of sorts, though badly rusted. Beyond that were boulders, stacked neatly. To the right was a large wooden tripod, what used to be a crane.

The sergeant took it all in. These were signs of mining. This was a quarry.

The Quarryman!

No sooner had he thought this than a wave of warm air slapped into the flesh of his cheeks, and particles of sand and grit stung his eyes and filled his open mouth. As he coughed he sank to his knees instinctively, as an explosion boomed over him. With one hand he fumbled for his revolver; with the other he rubbed his eyes, trying to free the grit from beneath his eyelids. He coughed and spat the sand from his mouth.

It was a trap, that much was obvious, and the young priest had obviously been part of it. The sergeant tried to open his eyes, but the sting was too much and he closed them again. He began to crawl rapidly to his right, toward the dry riverbed where he knew there were boulders to offer protection. Captain Fracci had been outthought and they had been led up the wrong road, their escape sealed by a blast of dynamite that would have caused a landslide.

His elbow brushed a boulder and he turned and leaned his back against it. He rubbed his eyes again. His vision was blurred but the grit had worked itself free. A stone landed on his knee and he squealed in pain. Around him, dust filled the quarry and he couldn't see for more than twenty yards.

The chatter of the birds had stopped. Only the sound of falling rocks broke the silence.

The haze began to clear. He saw other men hiding behind other boulders. He looked back: the prisoners were standing in the open, abandoned by the soldiers, who had all sought hiding. They were corralled like cattle.

He had his revolver out now and he snapped off the safety catch. The haze was rising, thinning. But he still couldn't see the lip of the quarry. The smell of the explosive drifted on the wind. He heard men groaning. The haze lifted higher. His eyes were still watering, but he could see well enough now: the brigade, and the prisoners, were completely surrounded by high ground. Apart from the boulders of the dried riverbed, there was nowhere to hide. The famous Lazio Brigade was a sitting target.

The sergeant crawled farther into the riverbed, between two huge rocks, patched with gray-green lichen. As he did so, however, he heard the crack of rifle fire and bullets began zinging off the stones. He looked up to the rim of the quarry, searching for heads, the glint of steel, to aim at. He could see nothing and no one.

Yes! A flash of fire as shot left a musket.

He aimed, returning fire, kicking at the shingle, easing still farther between the boulders of the riverbed.

He heard someone grunt—and looked back, downriver, in time to see Enzo Collepietra, one of the brigade's soldiers from his own village, fall forward, his stomach blown out of him and plastered over a rock.

The sergeant began to sweat. They were under fire from both sides of the quarry. It was only a matter of time before they were picked off.

He heard other men squeal in pain. Fire was being returned, but spasmodically. Where was Captain Fracci? Had he been hit, or knocked out by the explosion?

The sergeant began to crawl back down the riverbed, hugging the boulders. The captain had been about a hundred yards back, near that final twist in the gully.

The sergeant's knees scraped on the rocks. He didn't look up. Twice he heard the crack of rock as bullets slammed into the boulders uncomfortably close. He passed two more of his men. One had had the side of his head blown away and his eyeball was hanging out. The other had had one of his hands ripped from his wrist and was sitting in the sand staring at it and screaming, blood drenching the trousers of his uniform.

The sergeant pressed on. Suddenly he saw Captain Fracci lying on the ground. He had been hit before he could reach the safety of the boulders; blood was oozing from his leg.

The sergeant looked up to the lip of the quarry nearest where he was. He fired off three shots in quick succession and then scrambled toward the captain, held him by the shoulders, and dragged him back toward the boulders.

"You're losing blood, sir."

"I'll be fine. How many men killed?"

"I've seen two. But there must be more. This riverbed won't offer protection forever. They're on both sides of the quarry."

"We have the better guns."

"But we can't see who to fire at—"

The sergeant stopped speaking. The quarry had fallen silent. The shooting had stopped as quickly as it had begun.

A few groans were all that could be heard, from men who had been hit.

"Captain!" a voice shouted from somewhere above. "Captain!"

Fracci lifted an arm, to acknowledge he could hear.

"Move your men into the quarry. Leave your prisoners and your guns where they are. Do as we say and your men will come to no more harm. Do you understand?"

Fracci was in pain and with one hand he tried to stanch the blood oozing from his leg. Even as he did this he quickly growled at the sergeant, "Order the men to fire."

"Is that wise, sir? We are—"

"While they are firing take some men and round up the prisoners. It's our only chance. *Get some hostages!*"

The sergeant looked along the riverbed. Men were crouched behind boulders looking at him, waiting for their orders. The prisoners were about fifty yards away.

He shouted. "Prepare to fire at will. . . . Fire!"

The din resumed. The sergeant scrambled forward until he reached the nearest men. "Sorengo! Limidi! Come with me." He nodded toward the prisoners.

The three men dipped between the boulders, working their way downriver until they were opposite the prisoners, who were shuffling slowly back toward the landslide.

Suddenly Sorengo fell forward against a boulder, his face hitting the stone, so that splinters of teeth broke off and ricocheted into the sand. The sergeant's gaze met Limidi's. Neither spoke.

The sergeant refilled the chamber of his revolver. The fire was now heavy from the lip of the quarry. "Ready?" hissed the sergeant. "It's our only chance."

Limidi nodded. "Ready."

The sergeant eased off his belly and crouched. "Now!"

He ran forward, low. As he straightened up he began firing about him, aiming where he judged the lip of the quarry to be. He heard gunfire but kept going. The prisoners were staring at him. Some tried to run but the ropes connecting their feet prevented it and a few fell.

The sergeant reached the prisoners. He ran into the middle of them, grabbed one of them around the neck, and pulled him toward the cart that held Nino Greco. He turned back. Limidi was right behind him, with his own hostage.

The sergeant waited. He couldn't see the people he was firing at, but they could see him, knew what was happening.

After a few minutes the firing died down and then stopped.

Limidi stood with his hostage at the back of the cart. The sergeant stood to one side. He still held the man he had grabbed by the neck, but he aimed his gun inside the cart, at Nino Greco. Now the negotiations would start. He waited for the voice that would come again from the lip of the quarry.

Silence.

Would any other men from the brigade risk open ground, to join him and Limidi?

No one did.

The silence stretched to a minute, two. Five.

Soldiers were groaning amid the boulders of the riverbed. But no one moved. Fracci's maneuver had half paid off. But what would happen now . . . ?

As he thought this the sergeant saw movement to his left and above him. He swung his revolver round, ready to fire. But it was a small object, with what looked like a tail. He watched, transfixed—and then horrified—as the object flew out from the lip of the quarry, seemed to hover for a moment, and then sank, accelerating toward the riverbed. Four sticks of dynamite, bound together with a fuse, landed behind the boulder where the sergeant was sure Captain Fracci lay.

Before he had time to double-check, the blast of warm air and the boom of the explosion rocked him on his feet. Sand and grit and stones again rose around him, clogging his eyes, his mouth, his nostrils. The man he was holding struggled, but the sergeant held on to him even though he was again temporarily blinded. He pressed the barrel of his revolver against the man's rib cage. The struggling ceased.

The air began to clear again. Limidi was still at the back of the cart, and still held his hostage. But the others had vanished in the dust of the explosion. All except Greco, who was still inside the cart.

The cloud of dust and sand lifted higher. Instinctively, the sergeant looked across to where Captain Fracci was, where the dynamite had landed.

He gasped. One of the boulders was no longer where it had been. And he could see Fracci. His throat tightened. The captain's body lay under a rock. He appeared to be missing an arm and his body was joined to his head at an unnatural angle.

There were more groans now and he could see three more uniforms lying lifeless near where the explosion had occurred.

The sergeant took in the scene. There would be no negotiation. He knew that now. Since the captain was dead, he was in charge and he still had men left—more than a hundred, maybe. But that wasn't the point. The point was: They were all hiding amid the boulders of the riverbed, beneath the gorge. Anyone who broke cover could be picked off, but if they stayed where they were, dynamite could be dropped on them at any time.

On the sergeant's face sweat mingled with grit and sand and dust. His eyes still stung. He was stung too with fear, shame, and embarrassment. The Lazio Brigade had been humiliated by a bunch of bandits, tricked into a trap by a child priest and his sister.

The sergeant looked back down the gorge. The prisoners were more than a hundred yards away now, beginning to clamber over the landslide.

He had three hostages—including Greco, the man they wanted back above all others—but they had made it plain they would not negotiate. The bandits would blow up his soldiers until he surrendered.

And if he didn't surrender? After they had killed his men, they would leave him to sweat. Without food, without water, without shelter. If he killed his hostages the bandits would kill him. If he didn't kill them but allowed all the men under his command to be killed, he would have to go back to the mainland as the only survivor out of one hundred and ninety men. How would that look? He preferred death.

No, he didn't, he told himself. He was a soldier and that involved knowing when you had lost. He couldn't win in this situation. That was obvious now. His duty was to safeguard the lives of his men who were still alive.

Still holding the hostage, he unbuttoned his tunic, using the hand that held the revolver. When he had his tunic open, he pulled the tail of his shirt out of his trousers.

"Limidi! D'you have a knife? *Quickly!*"

Limidi stared at him.

"Quickly! Your bayonet."

Using one hand, Limidi unclasped the bayonet from his rifle. He slid it across the floor of the cart.

The sergeant grasped it by the blade and, with his fingers, pulled his shirt over the point. He pulled until his shirt tore. Dropping the bayonet, he put his finger in the tear and pulled. A strip of shirt came away in his hand.

Using his fingers and his teeth, he wrapped the piece of shirt around the barrel of his revolver, formed a knot, and, again using his teeth, pulled it tight.

Then, still holding his hostage by the neck, he raised his gun above his head, waving his makeshift flag of surrender.

"You have no choice, Nino. You must leave the island. Your escape will have shamed, embarrassed, and infuriated the army. It's like you stole their virginity and didn't stay for the wedding. Now they will never rest until they find you. When they do, and they *will* find you someday, they will kill you. They will say you died resisting arrest. Believe me, I know. My brother is in the army." Father Ignazio Serravalle was in his room at Quisquina. He was helping the others to wine. "I think you should go to America."

Candles burned on the abbot's desk and, on the mantelshelf of the great fireplace, liquid wax was spilling onto the cold iron feet of the candelabra. Shadows flickered over the huge tapestry that dominated and darkened the room. The *tsk-tsk* of crickets could be heard through the open windows.

There were not many people in the abbot's study: Nino, now freed of his chains; the abbot's secretary, Luigi Garofali; Ruggiero Priola, from Palermo; Bastiano and his wife, Smeralda, who was also Nino's cousin.

Nino drummed his fingers on his lips. Then he turned to Bastiano. "What do you think?"

Bastiano wasn't drunk, but he was certainly the worse for wear. "Nobody is going to be safe, at least for a while. Nothing like this has happened before. We killed eleven of their men and injured thirty-three. That's a lot of blood. They'll wait for reinforcements, then come again. Not only must you go, Nino, but people—the authorities—must know that you have gone." He gripped his wine goblet and drank from it.

"Steady," whispered Serravalle, but Bastiano glared at him. He knew change had to come, but he didn't like it.

Nino turned to his cousin. "Smeralda?"

"Nino," she breathed, "you are my flesh. I don't want you dead. I don't want Annunziata to be an orphan. Holding the English priest was a mistake, I see that now. I'd rather look after Annunziata with you alive than with you dead. After a while she can follow you to America."

There was a silence in the room.

Nino leaned forward and took the wine bottle from the abbot. He drank heartily. The local wine was sour and he screwed up his face as he swallowed.

"America is a big country," he said. "Where shall I go?"

The abbot looked at Ruggiero Priola. Priola was a big man, balding, better dressed than the others. "Our families are related," he said to Nino. "Your grandmother was my grandmother's sister. In the past you have helped us, particularly when our business was threatened by the Orestano family. Now it is our turn to repay that debt. It is a matter of honor. As you also know, the Priola shipping line operates several steamers that sail regularly between Naples, Palermo, and New Orleans. The *Syracusa* leaves in six days' time."

"Six days! So soon?" Nino looked shocked.

The abbot spoke. "Nino, we have heard today that Rome has put up a ransom for you. Twenty-five thousand lire. That's going to tempt a lot of people. Not everyone in Sicily loves you as we do."

A grim smile briefly lit Nino's face. "No one must go empty-handed, eh?" He sighed. "But six days!" He looked across to Bastiano. "You will take over as Don. I would choose Gino Alcamo as your *consigliere*. Think you can manage?"

Bastiano nodded. "Thanks to you."

"Nino." It was Smeralda. "We shall miss you . . . and you will miss us, I hope. But . . . we . . . Bastiano and I think you should not go alone."

"What? Take someone else? Who?"

Now that Smeralda had made the first move, Bastiano was emboldened to speak. "You must take Silvio."

"He's just a boy! *Mezzomaturo*. Half-ripe. He'll be more trouble than he's worth!"

"Nino," said Bastiano, softly but firmly, "you have not thought about this as we have. First, it will be good for you to have a companion. Second, without you here, it will be helpful to have one mouth fewer to feed—"

Nino started to interrupt, but Bastiano held up his hand. "No, listen to me this once. You know the boy has talent. You yourself have been teaching him. He's very like his father. I heard you say he has the balls, the brains, the blood. Also, you owe your life to him. If he'd been in his own bed, he would have been captured like the rest of us, and unable to visit the abbot here and alert him to our . . . predicament."

"Yes, I agree, but—"

"Have you asked yourself *why* Silvio was not in his bed?"

When Nino shook his head, Smeralda butted in. "He was with Annunziata. They spent the night together at the old temple near Catera."

Nino's eyes widened and he gripped the wine bottle more tightly. "He has more balls than I thought. . . . I'll break—"

"Nothing happened!" cut in Smeralda.

"But it might have," said Bastiano quietly. "It might have. And with you away . . . who knows?"

"Their feelings for one another are unhealthy, Nino," said

Smeralda. "They are cousins. Peas from the same pod. Something like this is always a risk when you live as we do, away from everyone else. *You* need someone with you. *They* need to be separated. It is the right solution."

Now the abbot joined in. "He's a talented boy, Nino, and he's an orphan. He was eighteen last week. He's ready. He'll be a man by the time you get to America."

Nino looked from one to the other. "There is another way. I could take Annunziata."

"You could," said Smeralda, "but who's going to look after her when you get there? And while you're out attending to business she'll be in as much risk as if she stayed here. More so, probably. You have to find a place to live, you may even find a new woman, all the things men do in America. Be realistic, Nino—stop fighting us. We are your friends. Take Silvio, and send for Annunziata in a year. By then you'll be safe, you'll have a house, be rich maybe. Silvio and Annunziata will have forgotten each other. I am your flesh, Nino. I know you. You don't want Annunziata with you, not in the first months. Take Silvio."

There was another long silence, during which Nino occasionally drank from the wine bottle. He was breathing heavily.

At length he drained the wine and stood up, turned the bottle upside down, and held it by the neck, like a club. He brandished it at his cousin, then at Bastiano. "Very well," he said, his voice cracked with emotion. "I'll take Sylvano on one condition."

The others looked at him.

"He has to prove he's a man."

Still no one spoke.

"Someone betrayed us. While I was chained up, in that wagon, I heard the army captain talking. He was explaining to someone about our warning system. How did he find out about that? He was never specific, but he went on to say that someone in the regiment came from Borgo Regalmici and that this man played a part in capturing us. He'd acted as an intermediary."

Nino's eyes raked the room. "Now, who do we know in Borgo Regalmici who has a grudge against us, against me? Who is this canary who sang so loudly?" He glared from one to the other. "I will tell you. Luca Mancuso's son, Gaetano. He made Maria Camastra's daughter pregnant and then refused to marry her. I had a word with Luca and the wedding was set for next month.

Luca was understanding. But Gaetano must have thought that with me out of the way he wouldn't have to marry the Camastra girl after all."

He paused.

At first no one else said anything. Then Bastiano nodded. "And you want . . ."

"I want Gaetano Mancuso killed, Bastiano. And I want Sylvano to do it."

The main piazza in Santo Stefano was larger than in Bivona. The church was more impressive, more ornate, and there were two cafés and a bank, the latter closed because this was Sunday. In the afternoon, as it was now, sunshine filled the square, warming the stones of the wide steps that led down from the church.

Silvio had found some shade, in a small *calle* just off the square, where he could see the main doors of the church but where he was not conspicuous. He was not alone—three other men were with him. They were all older, more experienced than he. All had done before what he was to do for the first time today. Should he fail—God forbid!—they would ensure success.

Silvio was nervous. This business had blown up suddenly and he had barely had time to reflect on what was happening. He was both surprised and not surprised that he had been chosen. He had known, from the moment he had told Annunziata they had been betrayed, that morning in the *giardino segreto*, that Nino would want revenge. That was the way justice was done in Sicily. Silvio had also known, deep inside him, that he would at some point be required to do the sort of thing he was being asked to do today. It was inevitable, given the life he had been born to.

Now, however, he was beginning to see the various levels at which Nino's manipulative mind worked. At the same time as he was told to kill Gaetano Mancuso, Nino also told Silvio that he was to accompany him to America. The second piece of news was as big a shock as the first, and just as unpleasant. But he could see it made sense from Nino's point of view. It meant that Gaetano's killer was out of the way, virtually immune from any further revenge attacks. It also offered Nino a way of proving his loyalty and bravery. But most important, Silvio knew that Nino wanted Silvio away from Sicily. It was not hard to fathom. Obviously the

Quarryman had discovered that his daughter and Silvio were . . . well, closer than cousins should be.

Of course, the killings also achieved the elemental justice required by the Sicilian Mafia's code of *omertà*, silence. Gaetano Mancuso had contravened that code and so had to be killed. Everyone accepted that.

By tradition, revenge killings were the highest form of duty, for they had to be carried out in public, in order to achieve their full effect. They therefore carried the most risk.

The doors of the church opened and people began to appear. The service was over.

"Here they come," whispered one of the men standing behind Silvio. The man straightened up and threw his cigarette away. "Not long now." He patted Silvio's shoulder.

Silvio's mouth was dry. *Sono rettile?* he asked himself. Am I a reptile? Cold-blooded, thick-skinned, shadow-loving? No, far from it. His blood ran cold one minute, but sweat cascaded down his temples the next. He found himself thinking of the few things that had frightened him in his life. Diving off the cliffs into the Capraria River. Escaping a forest fire at Lanzone. Getting caught in a stampede of cattle at Campofelice. Nothing came close to this.

He watched the people descend the church steps. Young couples, old women, mothers with babies, chatting, laughing, a few men lighting up their pipes or cigarettes, relieved to be outside in the fresh air. Silvio didn't know Gaetano Mancuso—which should make what he had to do easier—but two of the men with him did. They also knew his routine: to stroll across the piazza after Mass and drink a vermouth at one of the cafés, idling away half an hour with friends, looking at the local girls.

"There he is," muttered the man behind him. "Dark blue suit, widow's peak, slightly buck teeth. Next to the man with a stick. See?"

Silvio did see. Gaetano Mancuso was tall, thin, good-looking, but already going bald. He had a swagger about him.

Silvio was thankful to note that Mancuso had no woman with him. Maria Camastra's daughter was nowhere to be seen— because, of course, Mancuso had no intention of marrying her. Had they been a normal couple, in love and happy in the usual way, she would have been here with him. For Silvio that made his task easier, too. Mancuso was a *mezza tacca*, beneath contempt.

Mancuso reached the café on the other side of the piazza. For a moment he stood talking to a group of men his own age. Quietly, two of the men with Silvio detached themselves and strolled into the square. Silvio watched as they approached the café separately and took their seats, ordering coffee. They would see to it that no one interfered.

The crowd in front of the church was beginning to thin and now Silvio's heart beat faster. What if something unexpected happened at the last minute? Would he be able to react quickly enough? He tried to moisten his parched lips with his tongue. He needed an audience, the bigger the better. If this went well today he would be famous—notorious—throughout Sicily. The more people there were to watch, the more successful it would be.

It would also be more dangerous.

"He's sitting down."

Silvio didn't need to be told. He needed Gaetano Mancuso to be seated for maximum surprise, for effect, and because it was safer that way. Silvio gripped the *lupara*, the hunting shotgun. He turned and looked at the other man beside him. They nodded to one another. Silvio was ready.

But no—Mancuso was on his feet again. He held a cigarette, wanted someone to light it. He chatted for a while, still standing. Silvio cursed. The crowd outside the church continued to thin.

Then a waiter brought Mancuso's drink and set it on the table. Mancuso strolled back to his place and sat down. Silvio couldn't hear what was said, but he could see that Mancuso was laughing. That made it easier, too. He was a cocky *puzzone*, this Mancuso. Silvio watched as he held the vermouth to his lips, swallowed the liquid, set the glass back on the table, then crossed one leg over the other, resting his ankle on his knee, lounging back in his chair, arrogantly surveying the piazza.

"Ready?" hissed the man at Silvio's side.

Silvio took a deep breath, nodded, and stepped out of the shadow into the square.

He forced himself not to hurry. He must not draw attention to himself, not just yet. He was an ordinary peasant, strolling through the town, come to enjoy the camaraderie of Sunday morning in Santo Stefano. His *lupara* would not draw particular attention. Almost all the men had one.

The crowd of churchgoers had moved away from the steps in front of the façade, but about half the people now stood in the middle of the piazza, a few yards from the café where Gaetano Mancuso was sitting. Silvio ambled through them. Children, playing, ran in and out of the throng.

He didn't want to hurry but he didn't want to delay either. As he walked past the crowd out of the corner of his eye he spied a face he thought he recognized. It looked like Luca Mancuso, Gaetano's father!

Silvio's throat tightened. No! But he couldn't think about that.

He kept his eyes forward. They were fixed on Gaetano, drinking his vermouth. He was still smiling. He always seemed to be smiling, this bastard.

Silvio reached the edge of the area where the tables were laid out. So far no one had paid any attention to him at all. He chose his route. He needed to be able to make an escape without running, without stumbling.

About half the tables were occupied. Everyone was talking at once. Silvio stepped between two vacant tables and halted. One or two people glanced at him, but with no real interest. That was about to change.

He stared at Gaetano Mancuso. The other man suddenly felt Silvio's eyes on him and looked up. At first there was a confidence about him, but that changed when Silvio's eyes met his.

Then, quickly, Silvio raised his *lupara* and at the same time uttered one word: *"Venduto!"* This was slang for traitor, someone who had sold out.

The shot ripped into Mancuso's chest and throat. People screamed as his torso seemed to cave in under the onslaught of the tiny pellets. His shirt turned a deep crimson, which soon began to blacken.

What people later remembered was that, in the complete silence that followed the single shot, there could be heard a terrible gurgling in Mancuso's throat as he struggled to breathe. Then the gurgling turned to a short, dry, rasping sound, and then it stopped.

At the moment when Silvio fired his *lupara*, the two other men who had been waiting in the café stood up and raised their guns to give protection. Now, swiftly but silently, Silvio placed his *lupara* on the table in front of the dead Mancuso. This was important. It showed that this was a Mafia killing, a revenge murder. Then he turned, threaded his way through the tables, and walked quickly back the way he had come.

4

If Silvio had ever felt worse than he did now, he couldn't remember it. Not when he had his worst toothache. Not when he had mistakenly stepped into a boar trap. Not when he'd been fighting Alesso Alcamo and they'd both tumbled into a campfire. He had never been to sea, and this first time, he fervently hoped, would be his last. It wasn't just that the Mediterranean was rough, though the waves were six feet high, or that the boat he was in was owned by a *vaccarro*, or cowman, which meant it was normally used for cattle smuggling between Sicily and North Africa, and therefore carried the dried ordure of God knows how many cows over how many weeks. No, Silvio had begun this journey feeling bad.

The Mancuso business had gone well. Nino and Bastiano had both been delighted by Silvio's performance. He had "made his bones," as they said in Bivona. He was no longer a boy, but a proper *soldato*. The others there that day had paid tribute to his courage; and the news—and manner—of Mancuso's killing had flashed around Sicily. The police were making a fuss, of course, but everyone else believed that justice had been done. Silvio's use of that word *venduto* had been understood by everyone: Gaetano Mancuso had got what he deserved.

But if Silvio had acquitted himself well, that didn't mean he was happy with the consequences. He realized it was easier all around if he left Sicily with Nino. Part of him was eager to see America. Who wouldn't want that? Like everyone else he had heard stories of the Wild West, the fantastic fortunes that were being made. But Annunziata was more important to him than America, and he was sick to his stomach at being parted from her. He had never known such a feeling.

Then there was the sheer injustice of it all. Everything, it seemed, had been decided that evening in the abbey at Quisquina, with Father Serravalle and the Priola man from Palermo. This gnawed at Silvio's belly. He and Annunziata had saved the day, for Christ's sake! People might not like the fact that she and he loved each other, but if they hadn't been doing what they were doing that night, that morning, who would have raised the alarm? *Testardi!* Who would have had the sense to go to the monastery and alert the abbot? Nino, and the others, owed Silvio and Annunziata their lives, certainly their liberty. Yet that debt was to be repaid by putting more than four thousand miles between them. It was enough to make anyone feel ill.

Annunziata's apparent acceptance of the decision only rubbed salt in Silvio's wound. On the night before they left, he had suggested that they revisit their secret garden, at the temple, where they had begun to make love on the morning Nino was captured. If they were going to be separated, let them at least enjoy one night. But Annunziata had refused. And rather coldly. She had seemed different ever since the meeting in the monastery, more willing to accept the decisions of their elders. Instead of making the most of their last few hours together, she avoided him. He didn't understand.

She had been there to see him off, of course. Like all the other women, she kissed her father, then Silvio, but chastely, on the cheek. As he held her, briefly, and smelled her skin, memories of their morning together came flooding back. The softness of her lips, the fine wisps of her hair, the curve of her neck—it was unbearable to lose her. He started to tell her that, was about to announce that he would not leave her, but she had drawn back, looked at him dispassionately, and handed him a package.

"Something to eat, on the journey."

Sono profugo? he had asked himself. Am I a refugee? He put the package in his bag. He was traveling with an old leather bag that had been given to him by Bastiano, who had said, "This was your father's, Silvio. I always admired it when we were boys, and he gave it to me on my twenty-first birthday. Now it's yours."

It took Nino and Silvio two days to trek across country to the coast, near Secca Grande. With so many troops out looking for Nino, they had to travel at night. Ruggiero Priola helped them to choose the south coast as the place to embark from. It was far from

Palermo and Messina, Sicily's two large towns, and much easier to avoid being spotted.

They found the *vaccarro*'s boat easily enough, beached in a small bay about three miles west of Secca Grande. The voyage had so far taken four hours, in very rough seas, and Silvio—and Nino, for that matter—were much the worse for wear. Silvio didn't dare even think of food, and opening Annunziata's package was out of the question. He sat on a bench at the rear of the barge and prayed that the seas would quiet down. Nino sat opposite Silvio. The *vaccarro* himself stood in the stern of the boat, steering by means of a huge wooden tiller. He had a crew of two who kept a lookout; the coast guards were active all around Sicily.

The seas did not quieten, but the constant rocking had one good effect: around four that morning, Silvio fell into a deep sleep. It was his usual dream, with one or two refinements. He was with Annunziata but they were children. They were out riding, on mules, near Vallelunga, when Annunziata's mule suddenly bolted. Silvio gave chase, and began to catch up. But, as always, just as he was drawing level a rock appeared and his horse stumbled, and he fell to the ground, screaming. Sometimes the screaming woke him. This time, as the horse crashed against the rock, Silvio saw that the rock had a face. The face of Gaetano Mancuso.

He awoke briefly at one point, to feel the hot sun on his face. He roused himself enough to take in the fact that the sea was still as unpleasant as before, that others in the barge, including Nino, were also sleeping, and he lay back down again.

The second time he awoke he was being prodded by the *vaccarro*. "Get up," the man said bluntly. "It's time."

Silvio swung his feet off the bench and sat up. It was dark but there was a full moon. In the far distance he could see land and, directly ahead, perhaps two miles away, there was a huge ocean-going liner, its white, green, and red livery sparkling under its own illumination. Nino came up to him. He looked different now, younger. He had shaved off his beard. But his thick black eyebrows still gave him an air of menace. "That's Levanzo," he said, waving to the dark landmass where a few lights flickered. Silvio knew Levanzo was an island off the western tip of Sicily, but he had never been there. "And that's the *Syracusa*," said Nino, turning toward the liner. "We'll be going aboard in half an hour. She's taking us to America."

"They're stopping the ship for us?" Silvio was impressed.

"This is the Priola line. Part of the family. We may have to hide for a bit, but we should be safe enough. And she's a proper liner, not just an immigrant ship."

Silvio had seen such ships before, at anchor in Palermo, but he had never imagined he would travel in one.

"Won't there be police on board? Won't they see us?"

"*Sbirri?* No. Government officials—one or two, I'm told. But they all owe their livelihoods to the Priola family. There's more money in it for them if they make it easy for us. After all, Italy wants to be rid of me. They're only helping." He grinned down at Silvio.

As they came closer to the *Syracusa* Silvio saw she had four funnels and five rows of windows in the hull. She was enormous. He also noticed that she was not actually stationary but steaming ahead slowly, just enough to keep her stable. A gangway had been lowered to sea level, and one or two heads poked above the railings at the edge of the deck—night owls naturally intrigued to know what this unscheduled rendezvous was all about.

The barge approached the *Syracusa* from behind. Three men stood on the small platform that formed the bottom lip of the gangway, two of them holding long poles with hooks on them. The third man wore a white uniform: an officer. Though the seas were calming, the barge rolled violently at times as it slowed to draw alongside the gangway. The *vaccaro* waved Nino and Silvio over to the starboard side of the vessel, ready to jump when they got close enough. "It's too rough to tie up," he shouted. "As soon as they get their hooks onto us, jump. They won't be able to hold it for more than a few moments."

Silvio picked up his bag and gripped it hard.

The two vessels edged closer. The men on the platform stretched out their poles, ready to clamp the side of the barge the moment they were able to. But then suddenly the swell struck them hard. It lifted the barge up and carried it toward the *Syracusa*. The barge hit the side of the liner about thirty feet behind the gangway, and Nino and Silvio leaped back from the gunwale to avoid being crushed. There was a loud thud, and the *vaccaro* let the wind out of his sails.

"I'm going to try it a little faster now," the *vaccaro* growled. "Sea's too high for a slow approach."

This time they accelerated toward the gangway as if they were going to sail straight through it. Nino and Silvio stood on the gunwale, ready to leap backward if the sea caught them unawares. A roll hit them when they were still about twenty yards from the *Syracusa*, but then, in the trough that followed, the barge accelerated still more until it was slightly ahead of the gangway. Then its sails were slackened deliberately, and as if by a miracle the barge slipped back through the water directly alongside the gangway.

Silvio went first, throwing his bag, then himself, at the officer on board the huge liner. Nino, perhaps because he kept hold of his bag, wasn't as quick. He tried to step onto the platform rather than jump, and in the moment that he hesitated, the barge was pulled away from the ship. The sailors were forced to let go. Nino realized he had to jump, but landed just short of the gangway and had to be grabbed and dragged aboard by the officer. Nino flopped onto the platform, panting, and glared at Silvio. Then he pushed past and strode up the gangway steps. Silvio and the two *Syracusa* crew members followed.

When they reached the top they were met by another officer and a small group of passengers, who stared at them in silence. The officer said two words to Nino, "Follow me," before he turned on his heel and pushed past the gathered crowd. Nino and Silvio were led along the deck toward the stern, through a doorway marked CREW ONLY, then down some stairs. At the bottom of the first flight they turned back on themselves and went down another flight. They descended four flights of stairs in all, the air getting steadily warmer as the *Syracusa* picked up speed.

Eventually, they turned left into a narrow corridor, and stopped halfway along. The officer opened a door and showed them into a tiny cabin, with two beds, a cupboard, a table and porthole. It was cramped, but they would have fresh air.

"We are two officers short this trip. Lucky for you, or it would have been the immigrant deck. Stay here. Those are strict orders from the captain. He will see you as soon as he can." The officer looked at Nino. "I will arrange for you to be sent something to eat. But you must stay here, for the time being. Is that clear?"

Nino nodded. "Is there a toilet?"

"At the end of the corridor. Use it as little as possible." Then he was gone.

Nino headed for the door. "I'll use the toilet first," he said. He went out.

Silvio opened his bag and started to take out what clothes he had packed. A couple of shirts, two pairs of trousers . . . he didn't have a lot. He also came across the food package that Annunziata had given him. He had all but forgotten it. It was wrapped in an old newspaper.

Odd. Annunziata had said it was food, yet the package felt solid. He hadn't noticed that before. Silvio unwrapped the paper and took out what was inside. It was a box, made of wood. He opened the box. Inside was a ring.

A set of knuckles rapped on the door and a voice could be heard in the corridor outside. "Gentlemen, may I come in?"

"Be my guest!" growled Nino.

A tall, cadaverous-looking man with a prominent Adam's apple appeared. His uniform was entirely white.

Nino and Silvio rolled off their beds and sat looking up at their visitor. Other crew members stood behind him.

"Gentlemen, I am the first officer. We are now in the Atlantic Ocean. We passed the lights of Gibraltar about three hours ago, as perhaps you noticed. The captain has instructed me to tell you that you may now be allowed outside your quarters, *but*—" He raised his voice as smiles spread across Nino's and Silvio's faces and they immediately made to move out of the cramped confines of their cabin. "*But* he would prefer you moved about the ship as members of the crew, as officers." He turned to the men behind him and held up a pair of white trousers. "We have some spare uniforms here. Please try them on. The captain would like to see you on the bridge as soon as you are dressed, to double-check that you look the part." Then he took more clothes from his men and threw a bundle onto Nino's bed.

"I'm not wearing any ridiculous uniform," Nino grumbled. "You all look like candles in a cathedral."

The officer's mouth tightened. "These are my orders, Signor Greco. The captain agreed to alter course to pick you up. He has kept you cooped up in here for your own safety. There was always the possibility that we might have been intercepted by a British naval vessel off Gibraltar. If passengers had seen you on deck, someone might have said something to the British and we'd all have been in trouble. You might have been taken off and, most likely, sent to England and hanged. But even now the captain is not prepared to have you roaming about the ship, where you might be recognized. If the Americans hear of it, they would not take kindly to such license. . . . Now—do I leave these uniforms here, for you to try on, or shall I take them with me, locking the door as I go? The choice is yours."

Nino glared at the officer. He clenched his fist. He had large, rather protruding ears, and when he was angry his jaw moved involuntarily, the movement spilling over to his ears. There was a red spot below one of his eyes. Finally he reached across the bed, picked up some of the clothes in the bundle, and tossed them at Silvio.

The officer smiled grimly and said, "Get changed and stay here. I'll be back in ten minutes to take you to the captain." He went out.

Silvio was more than thankful that Nino, on this occasion at least, had kept his temper. Their two days cooped up together had, perhaps inevitably, produced an intimacy that Silvio could never have imagined. It had fascinated and at the same time frightened him. All they could do while they were caged up was talk. Silvio had always known the bare outlines of Nino's life, but in the confines of that cabin on board the *Syracusa*, he had been spared no detail of the Quarryman's story. He desperately needed some fresh air.

And now he was dressed. There was a small mirror in the cabin, not sufficient for him to view his whole uniform, but he could see enough to know that it suited him. Nino was less impressive in his uniform—the close-fitting tunic made his head look enormous— but it would have to do.

They grinned at each other, then Silvio said, "Surely I'm too young to be an officer?"

Nino shrugged. "Let's hope the captain's thought of something. Otherwise, lie about your age."

There was a knock on the door and the real officer shouted, "Ready?"

Nino swung open the door and the two of them stood for inspection. The officer looked them up and down, sniffed, and then said, "You'll do. Follow me." He turned and marched down the corridor.

Much to Silvio's satisfaction, the officer first took them back on deck. The weather was fine, but a strong breeze was blowing from the southwest. The *Syracusa* was pitching as well as rolling. She was hundreds of yards long, with a metal deck. There was a strong smell of paint and the entire superstructure was made of metal. How on earth did she float? Silvio didn't want to think about it.

The first deck they came to, the lowest, was crowded, but as they mounted the stairways the other decks became progressively less so. Silvio caught sight of saloons, dining rooms, bars, but they kept climbing until they reached the top deck. Here it was really blustery. One last stairway brought them to the outside part of the bridge, which hung out over the edge of the ship.

At the top of the stairs, the officer stopped and turned. "Wait here," he shouted, to make himself heard. "I'll see if the captain is ready to receive you."

They stood on the edge of the bridge, their hair flapping in the breeze, gazing down to the sea. The *Syracusa* was moving through the ocean at about eleven knots, carving a wide green-and-white wake.

The door to the main part of the bridge opened and a man of about fifty beckoned them forward. The captain was a large individual, tall and wide, with a dark beard that ringed his face, and a huge stomach. He had a voice to match: big and booming.

Nino and Silvio stepped into the bridge, where the captain stood to one side. Three sailors, boys really, no older than Silvio, stood next to three separate steering wheels. Silvio had no idea these liners had more than one wheel. It made sense, he supposed, if one should fail in a storm.

"Come in and let me look at you," the captain said.

They stood before him.

"Hmm. Hardly perfect, but you're here at the request of Signor Angelo Priola, so we'll have to make the most of it. Quite frankly, it would have been better for me, for all concerned, if you two had kept out of sight for the entire voyage, but Signor Priola's daughter is on board, and she has requested that you both join her table this evening. Fewer questions will be asked if you appear as officers."

The captain turned and gave a technical instruction to one of the sailors. Then he turned back to Nino and Silvio. "If you are going to enjoy the benefits of the dining room, I expect to get some work out of you during the day. You, boy—how old are you?"

Silvio reddened. He hated being called a boy. "Eighteen, sir."

"You can work the immigrant decks. And you can help the doctor." He looked at Nino. "Do you have any skills, any training?"

Nino shrugged. "Explosives."

The captain frowned. "Yes. Stupid of me. I'd heard." He paused for a moment. "Not much use on board ship. But you look fit and intimidating. You can help patrol the casino. We occasionally have trouble there. Now"—he nodded to the officer who had led them from their cabin—"First Officer Breguzzo will show you where you have to go. One thing: you will be accepted by the crew. New people join the ship for every voyage and many of the lesser hands have unsavory backgrounds themselves. That's one of the many reasons people go to sea. I would, however, prefer it if you did *not* discuss your own situation. You are obviously going to have to enter America in . . . well, in an unorthodox way, and it is better if you keep to yourselves as much as you can. Clear?"

Nino and Silvio both nodded.

"Breguzzo will see that your breakfast and lunch are brought to your quarters. During the day I want you both working at your assigned tasks, from eight until six. That will keep you out of the way. In the evenings you may wear these uniforms and come to dinner in the main saloon—where I can keep an eye on you. Come and see me again the day before we arrive at New Orleans. Now—any questions?"

Nino shook his head. So did Silvio.

"Very well. Mr. Breguzzo, please show them to their workstations."

5

At first Nino and Silvio retraced their steps down off the bridge, then entered the main deck through a large set of double doors. Silvio was becoming aware that the ship was divided into a number of classes and that the higher the deck the higher the class of passenger—like the suburbs on the hills of Palermo. This part of the top deck, however, appeared to be devoted largely to pleasure. He was astonished to find that they were now on the balcony of a large hall, or saloon, as the captain had called it. The saloon was the height of two decks. Breguzzo led the way down a wide, curved, wooden staircase, with a magnificent ornate brass handrail. The balcony ran all the way around the saloon and on the lower level there was a grand piano, what looked like a small dance floor, and a number of dining tables. Was this where dinner was served? Silvio hoped so. He had never been to a proper restaurant, or to a dance, for that matter.

The saloon was empty, save for a couple of cleaners with mops and buckets. Breguzzo led the way across the dance floor to the far side of the room, where another set of double doors opened onto a corridor leading toward the stern of the ship. Silvio was astounded to see that this corridor was lined with shops—one selling books, another soap, a third selling chocolate. There was an entire room filled with books and a room where men were smoking. There was even a room where people could have their portrait painted. At the end of the corridor they turned left, but not before Silvio had time to glimpse through another set of doors a second restaurant, where people were still finishing their breakfast. He had no idea such luxury existed, still less that it existed on a ship. He wondered if the Via Scina had been like this.

They had arrived at a third set of double doors, smaller than the others but wooden and shiny, with two lamps above them. Silvio sensed that they were about to enter somewhere different.

Breguzzo went first. This was a smaller room than the saloon, with a much lower ceiling, picked out in patterns. At the far end was a bar, already open. There were also two roulette tables, a card table for a game he didn't recognize, and a fourth table with a dice pit. The casino.

Breguzzo was talking quietly with the barman, occasionally looking at Nino and Silvio. He beckoned them over. Motioning to the barman, he said to Nino, "This is Enrico. The bar is his responsibility. So is the casino. You report to him and do what he says. You keep out of everybody's way, unless there's trouble, and then you deal with it as tactfully as you can. Don't get familiar with the passengers. It's easier to be firm with them if you don't. Enrico will tell you who the difficult ones are. I'll come and see how you are getting on in an hour or two."

He took Silvio's arm. "You come with me."

They left the casino, went back down the corridor, past the breakfast room, and out onto the deck on the other side of the ship. Breguzzo turned toward the stern of the *Syracusa* and marched down the deck for some way. They came to a small door with writing on it. Breguzzo turned. "Can you read, boy?"

Silvio shook his head. "I'm not a boy."

The officer ignored the remark. "It says: 'The passengers of the first and second class are requested not to throw money and eatables to the steerage passengers, thereby creating disturbance and annoyance.' The same applies to crew. Clear?"

Silvio nodded again. He could never be a sailor: all these orders.

Breguzzo led the way through the door and down some stairs. With each flight, Silvio's heart sank. He was going to be cooped up again.

He was wrong, in a way. When they had descended so far down that Silvio felt sure they must be well below the waterline, Breguzzo opened a door—and immediately a flood of noise washed over the two men. But this wasn't machine noise. Silvio found himself instead in a huge gallery, with wooden bunks down each side and a wide passageway in the middle. The noise was a human one—people speaking, shouting, laughing, singing, crying even.

"Welcome to the immigrant deck," said Breguzzo. "Three hundred aspiring Americans, and the same number on the deck below."

"There's another one like this?"

"Oh yes. Some ships are entirely made up of immigrant decks, but not the *Syracusa*. You're lucky. You'll be able to get away from this at night."

Silvio looked around him in astonishment. These people— Neopolitans, people from the heel of Italy, Sicilians—must want to go to America very badly, or have been grossly unhappy at home, to expose themselves to such conditions. "Are they ever allowed on deck?" said Silvio as his nostrils began to take in the stench of the gallery.

"No. The ticket they buy is very clear about that. Access to the gallery only. They're all poor immigrants, don't forget. They're not interested in lolling about on deck, and they don't have any money to gamble. It's not perfect down here, but you can survive anything for a few days. You should know that."

Silvio did know that, but he was still shocked by what he saw. There was no mahogany or brass railing here, nothing shiny or plush, no shops or restaurants or dance floors. Simple fruitwood structures, with platforms for bunks at three levels, the lowest about a foot off the deck, the next four feet above that, and the top one the same distance above again. They were little better than boxes, the people packed in like so many oranges.

Every twenty bunks or so there was a little alcove with a table where families took turns eating. The air was clotted by little sulfur fires, which were used to add light whenever the passengers wanted to augment the newfangled electric light, which was very thin. Given that the mattresses were made of straw, anyone could see that the sulfur fires were potentially very dangerous.

Breguzzo strode down the central passageway, sidestepping children, crude toys, the odd bundle of luggage. At the far end of the gallery was a metal staircase with a metal railing, little more than a ladder really, which led them to an office overlooking the gallery. Breguzzo knocked on the door and, barely waiting for a reply, barged in.

Dr. Tolmezzo was a fleshy, bald man who wore steel-rimmed spectacles and a wing collar. He had soft hands with fat fingers stained by nicotine. When Breguzzo and Silvio entered he was just finishing examining a pregnant woman, whom he now ushered swiftly out, leaving her to negotiate the metal steps by herself. Breguzzo made the introductions and left again immediately.

Tolmezzo pointed to a chair and Silvio sat down. "So you are the Quarryman's nephew, eh?"

Silvio didn't know what to say. Hadn't he been told not to talk about it?

"Don't be coy," said the doctor. "The whole crew knows. I suppose it's for the best. They would have caught up with him somehow, sooner or later. It's easier to get lost in America, and New Orleans is one of the easier places in America to be invisible." He sat up in his chair. "Now, to work. Can you read or write?"

Silvio shook his head.

"You'll find both a help in America. Get started as soon as you can. Have you ever seen a baby born?"

Again, Silvio shook his head.

"A cow?"

"Yes."

"That might come in handy. We often get one or two births on a voyage like this, especially if it gets rough and people are thrown about. Are you the type that faints when you see blood?"

At that, Silvio had to smile. "Of course not."

"That's something. It's important being a ship's doctor. Under American law, the captain of a ship like this one is fined ten dollars for every person we put ashore who is dead. That's a lot of money, so the captain takes a particular interest in what we do. Now, the drill. It can be a tricky business. A lot of the time nothing happens at all, except for giving people a little camphor, or bismuth, for seasickness. Then, all of a sudden, trouble erupts—and you've got no backup. You have to diagnose, sedate, and operate all by yourself, usually with the captain standing over you while you do it."

He took off his spectacles and began to polish them with a silk handkerchief. "Can you count?"

"Yes. And I can tell the time."

"Hmm. I might teach you how to take a pulse. Now, I start at eight in the morning, seeing first-class patients. Around nine-thirty I see second-class passengers. At eleven o'clock I come down here. There are six hundred steerage passengers, so I may be attending to twenty or thirty patients a day. I remain here until lunchtime. After lunch I am in my office, which is in first class, writing up my notes. People know I am there and can send one of the crew for me if they need to.

"Before lunch, I shall want you with me at all times, to run errands, hold a baby perhaps, while I treat the mother, or to hold down a big man who's having a tooth out. After lunch, I want you in here, alone. I want to avoid this pit as much as I can, and you can come and fetch me if anyone needs me. You'll probably be fascinated by the mornings and bored in the afternoons. Not bad, considering the reason you're here in the first place. If anyone asks who you are, say you are the assistant medical officer. That should shut them up. I'll occasionally talk medical jargon at you, to impress on people that you have more training than you do. Just nod and smile and agree with me. Is that clear?"

"Yes, sir."

"Don't call me 'sir.' Assistant medical officers do not call medical officers 'sir.' Call me Aldo, or call me 'doctor.' Any questions?"

Silvio shook his head.

"Right. Now, sit over there and pretend to read one of these medical journals. We'll have more patients presently, I'm sure."

And so, for the rest of the morning, Silvio played doctor. He held bottles of iodine as Tolmezzo stitched the forehead of a young child who had fallen and cracked her skull. He was shown the yellow flag that the doctor had to give the captain to fly should cholera break out on board. He helped mix plaster of paris so Tolmezzo could set a leg that had been broken when its owner, an elderly woman, had fallen off her bunk. By noon he was hungry.

Just after one, Tolmezzo stood up. "Well, I'm off to eat. I want you back here at two sharp. Understood?"

"Yes, sir. I mean, Yes, doctor."

Tolmezzo made for the door. Then he had second thoughts, slumped back down in his chair again, and began rummaging in the drawers of his desk. "Hold on," he said. Speaking to himself, he muttered, "It's got to be here somewhere ... ah, yes." He pulled an object out of a drawer and handed it to Silvio. "Stick that in your top pocket. It will make you look like a doctor."

It was a pair of dental pliers.

* * *

When Silvio returned to his cabin he found that an orange and a plate of cold pasta had been left on his bed. There was no sign of Nino. He wolfed down the pasta and peeled the orange. It was red, and bled on his uniform. He had intended to spend most of his free hour on deck, enjoying the fresh air. Then he remembered the captain's warning to stay out of sight. Reluctantly he decided he would just lie on his bed. It was an opportunity to think about Annunziata. There hadn't been much chance in the previous days.

The ring Annunziata had given him had entirely wiped out any doubts he'd had since the change in her behavior. With the ring she was saying she loved him. More. In effect, she was proposing to him, giving herself to him, telling him she would keep herself for him until he was able to send for her. He suddenly realized that perhaps she had thought more about their separation than he had. It would also explain Zata's behavior—she had kept her distance merely to convince the others that it was all over between them.

Silvio took out the ring, which he had hidden in one of the pockets of his officer's tunic, and kissed it. He daren't let Nino see it, but he would keep it with him at all times. Annunziata made him forget his parents. She made him more like the man Nino had told him to become: soft on the outside, hard on the inside. Silvio knew that he and Nino wouldn't always be together in America. After a few months he would start out for himself. He would leave New Orleans, which meant nothing to him, and try another American city—New York perhaps, or San Francisco. Then, when he had settled, he would send for Annunziata.

Together they would live a normal life.

Together they would be happy.

"Are you the new doctor?"

Silvio shifted in his seat. This was the exchange he had been dreading for the past forty-five minutes, ever since he had come back from lunch. Two people had already been in with minor ailments, and had been easily fobbed off until the following day's surgery.

This time the door to the office was opened by a young man, no more than a boy really, like Silvio. Pale skin, large brown eyes, straight hair, black as the marble in Bivona church. A cheap shirt and trousers. A peasant.

"Er . . . no. I'm the assistant medical officer."

"You'll do. You've got to come. My brother's had a fit."

"What? Come where?"

"The next gallery down."

"You go back to your brother. I'll get the doctor." He stood up.

"No!" the other youth cried. Silvio was startled. "I went to the top deck first. He wasn't there. Come *on*! Please!"

Silvio didn't move. He probably knew less about medicine than anyone on the ship. What if he went with this youth and his brother died? Silvio might be blamed. Then everyone would know he wasn't an assistant medical officer at all.

"Please!" The youth was clearly frightened.

Silvio had seen fits, of course. Who hadn't? At Bivio Indisi dogs had fits and there were two people, one a child, the other a young woman, who had them fairly frequently—they were both the children of parents who were too closely related, or so it was said. Normally they were held down on their sides, and someone gripped their tongue so they couldn't swallow it and choke, until they came round. Usually that didn't take very long. Surely these people knew that much at least?

"Please!"

There was no way out. This youth wasn't going to leave the office without him. Silvio buttoned his jacket and opened the door. He would just have to play along.

The youth scampered down the stairs, doubled back on himself, then descended another identical flight of steep metal steps that Silvio hadn't noticed before. Sure enough, this led to a replica gallery below. Halfway along the passage a crowd was gathered by one of the alcoves. Sulfur fires had been lit to augment the electric light and there was a sharp, acrid smell. It was very warm. The youth led the way and the crowd parted to let him and Silvio through. In the alcove, on the floor, was a man of about twenty-five, stocky with curly brown hair. He was lying on his back with his eyes closed and his mouth open. His tongue was visible.

The youth told Silvio, "He hasn't moved since he passed out half an hour ago."

Silvio knelt by the man. What on earth was he going to do? He was watched, and now surrounded, by perhaps fifteen people.

"Is he still breathing?" the youth asked quietly.

Silvio lowered his head and placed his ear near to the man's mouth.

Suddenly the figure came to life. An arm was wrapped around Silvio, and a second arm pulled his shoulder to the deck. At the same time the man with the curly hair threw a leg over Silvio's torso, then sat astride him. The whole business had been a charade and a trap. In no time at all Silvio was flat on his back with the ex-epileptic sitting on top of him, grinning and whooping, riding him like a mule. The youth, too, was grinning. He had been a very successful lure. Why?

Silvio tried to struggle, but it was pointless. He might unseat the man sitting on his chest, but there were a dozen more in the crowd. He lay still, to preserve his strength. He would find out what was going to happen soon enough.

The man astride him snatched Silvio's white officer's cap from his head and put it on his own. Then he doffed it, saying at the same time: "Onofri Orestano, at your service. The name will be familiar, I hope."

It was. The Orestanos were the family who had tried to move in on the Priola organization. They were the people whose warehouse Nino had blown up all those years ago. When two of the Orestanos had been killed. Silvio lay very still now.

"You've disappointed us, Sylvano. My brother thought up this little game. But I said you'd see through it—you'd want to fetch Tolmezzo, and when Massimo said he'd already been to find the doctor, you wouldn't have believed him. Passengers from the immigrant decks aren't allowed on the upper deck—didn't they teach you that at medical school?" He shrieked with laughter.

He was right. Silvio should have spotted the flaw in the youth's story. He had only himself to blame.

"You are nothing to us, Sylvano—you understand that, don't you? You don't matter. We want Nino."

Silvio said nothing.

"He won't come down *here*, of course. We've heard he's locked away, doing a soft job in the casino."

"You'll never get to him." Silvio spat the words out. "He's too clever for you."

"Most of the time I might agree with you, Sylvano. But don't talk too big. This time we've thought things through—and we're going to borrow one of Nino's own tricks. Maybe we can't get to him on the upper deck, not without a lot of trouble anyway, but there is one way to ensure he comes down here."

Onofri Orestano looked down at Silvio and smiled, but it was a cold smile. He put his hand inside his jacket and took out a knife. "We're going to send him a scalp."

Sweat broke out on Silvio's forehead. He was suddenly as frightened as he had ever been. He could hear his heart beating against the deck. It almost drowned out the sound of the ship's engines.

He was tempted to struggle, to make it as hard as possible for Onofri Orestano, but he knew it would do no good, there were too many of them. He needed to think.

The others crowded around now, all grinning. They were about to watch some real sport. Two men sat on one of Silvio's legs, a burly redhead on another. A fifth man knelt on his left arm, a sixth on his right.

Silvio was crying now. He could neither speak nor think.

"Shall we pull the last bit of skin, rather than continue cutting? Make it quicker. Is that kinder?" Onofri sighed grimly, as if he were beginning to make even himself feel sick. "Okay. Enough talk. Make sure you've got him firm. He'll probably squirm like the devil."

Silvio felt the weight on him suddenly increase as everyone obeyed Onofri Orestano. It was as if he were being crushed into the deck. A seventh man, whom Silvio couldn't see, grabbed his hair from behind him and pulled his head down so that his skull was on the deck. Onofri was still seated astride him, pressing down on his stomach, polishing his knife. Silvio could just see him out of the corner of his eye.

"You know more about this than I do, Randazzo," crowed Onofri. "How long does it take to scalp someone? A minute? Five minutes? Half an hour? Do I start from the front or the back? The side maybe? How much bone do I take?"

Silvio couldn't speak. He was trying hard to think.

"Come on, Randazzo. How long did it take with that English priest? Did he scream? Was there much blood?"

Silvio felt the hard blade against his hair. He tried to scream, but the sound that came out was merely a sob. He felt Onofri slice through his hair and into his skin with the tip of the blade, and now he really did scream. Pain spread down his head like scalding water. Through the pain he felt the knife sawing backward and forward. It scraped against the bone of his skull. Pain billowed through his head and warm, sticky blood dribbled onto his neck.

Drying tears caked his eyes and the corners of his mouth. Mucus clogged his nostrils. He couldn't lose his scalp. *He couldn't!*

People were leaning forward to relish the damage. The knife sawed back and forth. The burly redhead sitting on his right leg was edging forward more than most. In his urge to see Silvio's scalp torn free—and the bloody bone below—he had temporarily shifted his weight. Though his head was being pressed to the floor, though blood and tears mingled at the edge of his eye, where the bridge of his nose formed a lip, Silvio could see along the deck—to the next set of straw mattresses, and a sulfur fire burning nearby. He saw his chance. He wouldn't get a second one.

Another stroke of the knife cut into his flesh. A fresh wave of hot pain flowed over him like blood on fire. He had never known such agony. And then a wave of anger spread over him, in the wake of the pain, and even hotter. Suddenly, and with a super-human effort, he arched his spine, forcing the man astride him to slide some way off him and to stop cutting while he regained his balance.

"Hold him!" shouted Orestano. "He's slippery, hold him!"

At the same time Silvio lashed out with his right leg, dragging it clear of the red-haired *malandrino* who was sitting on it. He aimed his foot at the sulfur fire.

The others had reinforced their weight on Silvio and he was again pushed down onto the deck. But he had hit the contraption the sulfur was contained in, and smoldering pieces like cinders had been sent flying across the gallery. Two landed on one of the mattresses, which immediately began to smoke, then crackle with flame.

Orestano, sitting on Silvio's chest, screamed: "The fire! Someone put out the fire!" He stopped cutting and looked back over his shoulder again. Flames had erupted in profusion from the straw mattress and were licking at the bed above. A black, acrid smoke began to fill the gallery. "Water!" shouted Orestano. "Someone get water." He might have stopped cutting but he hadn't budged.

Others began to move away, but not the men sitting on Silvio.

The bed above the first one had caught fire, and the smoke was spreading badly. People were beginning to cough.

"Hold him!" shouted Orestano. "Don't let him squirm."

But Silvio wasn't squirming. He was shouting. "Fire!" he yelled. "Fire! Fire! *Fire!*"

"Don't move!" screamed Orestano at the others. "Hold him!"

Now a third bed caught fire and the smoke grew denser than ever. Other immigrants, not part of Silvio's reception committee, were also shouting. Several people began to cough all at once.

Suddenly a bell rang, and Silvio heard running feet. The weight on his body began to ease. He saw now, from his position next to the deck, that three sailors had arrived. They carried buckets of water. Some of the men who had been sitting on him were trying to keep their bodies between him and the sailors, to hide what they were doing.

Now Silvio lunged again with his leg, and succeeded in knocking over one of the buckets of water.

"Hey!" grunted one of the sailors, and turned.

Silvio arched his body again, and screamed, "Help! Help!"

The sailor took in what was happening. So far as he could see, an officer was on the deck, being beaten up by immigrants. While all this took place the other sailors had managed to soak the burning mattresses in water. A mixture of black smoke and steam filled the gallery, stinging the eyes and clogging the nostrils.

"Get the duty officer!" the sailor shouted to one of the others. "Hurry up."

He stood in front of the people who were trying to shield Silvio from view. "Get out of the way," he ordered. "I *said*: Get out of the way."

Slowly, reluctantly, a few of the men moved. Others held their ground. Onofri Orestano still sat on Silvio, but he now had less support.

"Give me the knife," said the sailor, addressing Orestano. He held out his hand.

Defiantly, Orestano juggled the knife, tossing it so that he held not the handle but the blade. Then he threw it, aimed it, at one of the wooden supports of the bunks. It stuck, quivering, in an upright.

Then he lifted himself off Silvio.

Two more sailors arrived, and an officer. "What's going on here?" the officer demanded.

"These people tried to start a fire, sir," said the sailor who had rescued Silvio. "And I found them assaulting this officer. With a knife."

Silvio had clambered to his feet. Blood caked and matted his hair, ran down the back of his neck, and stained his tunic.

The officer stepped toward him. "Do I know you?" he said.

Pain throbbed in Silvio's head. His skull seemed about to crack. It was as if he had sulfur inside his brain. He didn't dare feel his head; he was terrified of the damage that had been done. He felt sick. Dimly he remembered what the captain had said, that people joined the ship every voyage. "I'm the new assistant medical officer," he gasped, swaying slightly. The acrid smoke on top of the pain made him feel very peculiar. "I help Dr. Tolmezzo."

"I think you need to see him yourself," said the officer, but Silvio never heard him. He had fainted.

6

Silvio leaned over the rail of the *Syracusa* and looked down at the ocean slipping by. The water was dark green, like cypress trees in shade. Nino stood next to him. Silvio's head was bandaged, and although Tolmezzo had dressed the wound, the pain still throbbed all the way through to the bone. At least there would be no permanent damage, the doctor had said. "Just a scar where only your barber is likely to see it."

Nino had been furious when he learned of the attack largely because of the lapse in security. The Orestanos had somehow found out in advance that Nino was to be onboard the *Syracusa* and had some of their *soldati* smuggled onto the ship, intent on pursuing the old vendetta. From now on, Nino said, Silvio stayed with him.

He demanded to see the captain and had returned with the news that for the rest of the crossing, he and Silvio would constitute one of the two-man night watches, patrolling the decks from eleven at night until six in the morning to make sure everyone was where they were supposed to be, that no one was falling or being pushed overboard, or breaking into someone else's cabin. They would sleep during the days, then begin work after dinner. It suited them and it suited the captain, since they would still spend most of the time out of the way of the bulk of the passengers.

"It's eight-fifteen," said Nino gently. "Do you still feel sick, or do you want dinner?"

After he had fainted, Silvio had spent the afternoon in bed.

"No, the sickness has worn off. I'm dying for a plate of pasta."

"Come on, then. Let's see what this Priola woman is like."

Nino led the way along the deck and they went inside. He pushed against the door to the saloon—and a world that Silvio had

77

never imagined opened up before him. Above the chatter of
people, he could hear a piano. A welter of colors greeted him—the
maroon velvet of ladies' dresses, the deep green of huge plants,
the white of linen tablecloths, the crystal of wine decanters. The
floor, apart from the dance area, was carpeted, the chairs were
upholstered in velvet, the walls were veneered in wood and
boasted huge mirrors in which Silvio could see that his new,
blood-free tunic was a shade too large for him. The ceiling was
gilded and the supporting pillars were inlaid with bronzed sea-
shells and topped by spread eagles. They were a long way from
the *bivio*.

"May I help you?" said a waiter. "Only selected crew are
allowed in here."

Silvio was too awed to speak, but Nino said, "Anna-Maria
Priola is expecting us."

"Oh. Very well. This way."

The waiter led them directly across the dance floor. Silvio's bandaged head was on full display. He wanted to run but didn't dare.

They approached a table set for eight that had two spare places.
A woman of about twenty-three rose to greet them. "Good evening," she said in a quiet but clear voice, and held out her hand to
Nino. "I am Anna-Maria. You must be Nino and this . . . this must
be Silvio." She shook Silvio's hand. "I had heard how handsome
you were, but it's always nice to have it confirmed in the flesh."
She gave him a warm smile.

Anna-Maria Priola was tall, with curly fair hair and a prominent
bosom, much of which was on show. And she was suffused by the
most delicate perfume. Silvio had never known a woman could
smell so wonderful.

"Nino, you sit next to me, please. Silvio could sit over there.
We'll talk later."

Silvio found himself disappointed not to be sitting next to
Anna-Maria. Although she was a total stranger, she was in theory
family, or almost. She was not beautiful in an obvious way, but she
had a face you wanted to look at, a face that changed all the time
and according to your point of view. Her nose was too strong, the
eyebrows too heavy, the eyes too knowing. But she carried her
body well. He studied the two women he would be sitting between: they seemed harmless enough—older, too old to be interested in him, and vice versa. One was fat, with a shiny skin. She

had dark hair that was pinned up but somehow tumbled down again. The other woman was even older, in her late forties maybe, but she was handsome, with high cheekbones and a perfectly straight nose.

They both welcomed him with huge smiles. After he had seated himself and a menu had been placed in front of him by a hovering waiter, the handsome one said, "Two questions, obviously. Your name and what happened to your head?"

"Sylvano Randazzo, but everyone calls me Silvio." He had already thought about the second question, which was obviously going to come up. He had decided it was best to make light of it. "I'm afraid I banged it in the lifeboat practice the other day. I cracked the bone, and tore the skin. I'll live," he joked, wondering where, exactly, Onofri Orestano was at this moment, and what he might be doing.

"What would you like to eat, sir?" The waiter had returned.

What could Silvio do? Unable to read, he stared blankly at the menu.

"Why don't you have the soup, and then I would recommend the veal." It was Anna-Maria.

"Yes, yes." He shot Anna-Maria a grateful smile. She nodded back. "I'll have the soup and the veal."

Gradually, as the meal passed, he began to relax. The handsome older woman was the Italian wife of an American politician in Savannah, Georgia, and she was returning from a visit to her mother in Naples. The fat woman was an Italian opera singer who was going to America on tour. As Silvio had hardly led the kind of life calculated to teach him about either American politics or opera, the evening could have been awkward. As it was, his own appearance sparked much of the conversation.

"Are you Sicilian, Silvio?" the politician's wife had asked soon after the soup was served.

"Yes."

"Then, seeing your head bandaged, I cannot help but ask what you think of the actions of your fellow Sicilian, the Mafia bandit, the Quarryman. Didn't he cut off the scalp of someone he kidnapped? Is it true that a lot of Sicilians support him?"

Silvio was aware that conversation had stopped elsewhere at the table. Both Anna-Maria and Nino were staring at him.

"It's true that a lot of Sicilians support him, yes. That's the easy part of the answer."

"Why is the other part difficult? You don't condone what he did, do you?"

Sono prete? Silvio thought to himself. Am I a priest? Why are they listening to me all of a sudden? Careful now. "I think that taking the hostages was a mistake. I think that scalping the Englishman was a bigger mistake." He could say that now with heartfelt certainty. "But crimes like this are not so simple. Sicily is different from the rest of Italy—actually, many Sicilians believe the island isn't part of Italy at all."

"It is true," intervened the opera singer, not a moment too soon, from Silvio's point of view. "Different operas are popular there— and they often cheer for the bad man, for instance the duke in *Rigoletto*. They do it just to be different and to show contempt for what is truly Italian."

"But the Quarryman, as they call him, is not a politician, he is just a common criminal," the other woman observed.

Silvio could sense Nino getting angry and realized he had to do or say something that would help them get away from this conversation.

"He's not a common criminal, surely. Whatever you think of his methods, he does give money and food to poor people. But tell me"—he tried to change the tone of his voice, to indicate he was changing the subject—"I read somewhere, in one of the Italian papers, that the Quarryman sent his portrait to England, and of course there's a portrait painter on board. Who has had their portrait made so far?" He turned to the politician's wife. "You are very beautiful. Hasn't he already asked you to sit for him?"

She smiled. "A pretty speech. When you get tired of the sea, you can always try politics."

Everyone laughed. The awkwardness had passed. Anna-Maria chose this moment to rearrange the seating of her table, moving the men around so that Silvio now sat next to her.

"Thank you for the help with the menu," he whispered.

"That's all right. Now you can do me a favor. Ask me to dance."

"I can't dance."

"Don't be silly. There's no such thing as not being able to dance."

She stood up and led the way to the tiny dance floor. Fortunately it was already fairly full and they were able to stand more or less still and simply sway in time to the piano. The music was lazy; Silvio fancied it must be American.

"Another reason for dancing is to get away to talk privately."

"About what?"

"You did well. You were very quick just now. Tell me, what are you going to do in America?"

"I don't know. I haven't thought about it. I didn't want to come, but I was made to." Silvio wasn't sure he should be saying all this, but it was too late now.

"You don't want to go to America? You'll *love* it. Why stay in Sicily? What's there?"

Something held Silvio back from mentioning Annunziata. In the cabin before dinner, while he and Nino were washing, Nino had told him that Anna-Maria's father, Angelo Priola, was a powerful man in New Orleans, *un pezzo grosso,* and that Silvio should do nothing to annoy her. On the contrary, they should both go out of their way to be nice to her, for if she recommended them to her father, they might soon get jobs in his business in New Orleans. It was a good sign that she had invited them to her table, Nino had said, and they should do nothing to jeopardize their good fortune.

"I know Sicily," Silvio said at length. "What's wrong with it?"

"You're running away, forced to run away. That's what's wrong with it. There'll always be violence in Sicily. It's too remote, too poor, too self-willed to be any other way." Suddenly she changed the subject. "Do you smoke?"

"Sometimes."

"I'll bet you've never smoked American cigarettes."

Silvio shook his head.

"What else have you never done? Are you a virgin in other ways, too?"

Silvio blushed and stumbled all at the same time. He thought of that *sbirro* the day he had taken the package to Palermo. People always seemed to be asking if he was a virgin. Did it show in some way?

Anna-Maria laughed. "Look, the party's breaking up. I've got to go back. Why don't you come to my cabin around . . . around midnight. We can have a smoke and talk some more. I daren't smoke in public. If my father got to hear of it he'd kill me. He hates it in women. Don't forget now—midnight. I'm in room 715." And she led him back to the table.

Silvio was of two minds about whether to tell Nino about his invitation. And he was of two minds about whether he should *accept* the offer. Wasn't he supposed to be on duty? And what about Annunziata? Anna-Maria had only asked him in for a smoke, but even so, he felt as though he would be betraying the girl he loved.

It was already past ten. After dinner the pianist had been replaced by a small band of four. The music had grown less sedate and the dancing more animated. Silvio had never seen anything like it. The captain, he noticed, had his pick of the women; they doted on his every word. He even played the piano at one point in the evening, to polite applause. At each end of the room there were coal-burning fireplaces, with marble mantels. Here and there geraniums grew in pots. Silvio was enjoying every moment, and was therefore dismayed when, just before eleven o'clock, Nino dragged him away. They had to wait at the foot of the steps to the bridge, where the two officers concluding the previous watch met them and gave them a report of their time on deck, before Nino and Silvio relieved them.

"All's well, except for cabin 717," said the senior officer. "One hell of a fight between husband and wife. So far it's only been words, but it could lead to more. Tread carefully."

They set off. This was much better than being assistant medical officer. During the day the sea had grown calm, but now clouds were beginning to obscure the full moon. The breeze, though warm, was freshening. The *Syracusa* began to rock gently. A few passengers were taking the evening air, strolling the deck. As Nino and Silvio passed the saloon the sounds of music showed no signs of slackening. Nightlife at sea, Silvio was learning, often went on until dawn.

Cabin 717, when they came to it, was as silent as a confessional. Either the husband and wife had settled their differences or they had killed each other. The adjacent cabin was 715.

"That's Anna-Maria's cabin," whispered Silvio. "She told me while we were dancing."

"Oh, she did, did she? What else went on between you two?"

It was dark, so Nino could surely not see that Silvio was blushing. But he seemed to guess. They had both come to a halt.

Nino drummed his fingers on his lips. Then he lit a cigarette. "Silvio," he said after a long pause. "The Priolas in New Orleans could be very important to us. How you behave with Anna-Maria is vital. What did she say?"

Silvio relayed what had been said on the dance floor—except for the part about his being a virgin.

Nino whistled. "She wants you. What a break! If we arrive in New Orleans with Anna-Maria sweet on you, we've got a real friend at court."

"You don't think I should go, do you? What about the patrol?"

"Silvio!" Then, more gently: "Silvio. Listen. This patrol means nothing to us. But Anna-Maria is a very rich woman. Her father's *un pezzo grosso*. This chance may not come again. I can do the patrol. You've seen for yourself, this is the easiest job in the world. Of course you must keep your rendezvous. Listen to an older man. Learn from his mistakes. I'll give you one tip."

"What's that?"

"Be about ten minutes late. That will show you're not too keen and she'll be growing nervous by then, thinking you're not coming."

In fact it was nearer half-past twelve before Silvio knocked on the door of cabin 715. At midnight the band in the saloon had taken a break and several passengers came out for a breath of fresh air. For a brief while the deck was as busy as the Via Scina in Palermo. Silvio didn't want to be seen entering the cabin.

Eventually the deck was cleared and he quickly took advantage of the fact. The sea was now quite rough and the deck moved beneath his feet.

The door was opened immediately. Silvio stepped inside. It was the first time he had been in a first-class cabin and he was astonished. It was about ten times the size of the metal box he shared with Nino; and where their box had flaky white paint on the walls, this one had mahogany paneling and mirrors. Where their quarters were lit by a naked electric light, this cabin had pretty pink shades in the shape of shells. Besides the sofa, in velvet, there were cupboards, a dressing table, a low table for periodicals, and a bar with bottles. There were even two other doors, which led to . . . what? There was carpet on the floor, and the window—a window, not a porthole—had lush red curtains.

Silvio was also struck by the way Anna-Maria had imposed herself on this room. She traveled with objects he would never have dreamed of carrying—since he did not possess most of them: framed photographs, a doll with a lace dress propped up against the cushions on the sofa, silk flowers, what must have been her own piece of red material that she had draped around one of the lamps to make the light softer and more interesting. A stack of books. He was out of his depth.

Anna-Maria had shut the door behind him. She crossed the room to the bar. "Tell me, Silvio, we know you've never smoked American cigarettes. Have you ever drunk champagne?"

"Yes." He was pleased he was able to show he had done something. "Nino bought some once. I was given a glass."

"One whole glass! My." She faced the bar and poured two glasses from an already opened bottle. She turned back and handed one to Silvio. "Now, for your second glass," she said, smiling, "but your first *real* drink, we link arms." She held her arm out and made him curve his around hers. "There, you see. And we both drink—to each other."

They drank. When they linked arms, their eyes were very close. Her eyes were brown but speckled, like lichen growing on a rock. "Don't sip it," Anna-Maria said. "Take a good swallow, or you don't get the full effect."

They drank a second time, and a third, then disengaged their arms. Silvio had enjoyed being close to Anna-Maria. She smelled so fragrant and her skin was so soft and milky that he wanted to touch her. He thought of Annunziata with a pang of remorse.

Anna-Maria refilled Silvio's glass, then arranged herself on the sofa. "Sit in that chair," she commanded. Silvio slumped down. As he took another gulp of champagne and set his glass on the low table between them, she took a silver cigarette case from out of her bag. The ship suddenly shuddered as it slid off a huge wave. Anna-Maria opened the cigarette case and held it out for Silvio. He took a cigarette. Then she said, "Why don't you unbutton your tunic? It's stuffy in here."

He held his cigarette with one hand and unfastened the top two buttons of his jacket. Again the ship gave a lurch.

She lit her own cigarette, then passed the matches to Silvio. Holding the cigarette gingerly, as though it might explode, he lit it. He set the spent match on the low table.

"Now," breathed Anna-Maria, leaning back on the sofa and crossing her legs, "this is what I call civilized." She smiled at Silvio. "Tell me, what are you going to do when you arrive in America?"

He shrugged, trying to hold down the awful feeling that had suddenly come over him. "That's for Nino to decide."

"Are you tied to Nino forever? Aren't you your own man?"

He looked at her sharply. He had a temper of his own, but it rarely showed when Nino was around: the older man was too unpredictable. "Yes, I'm my own man. But for the moment, our ties suit us both."

"My father is wealthy, and has position in New Orleans. He owns passenger ships and fruit ships. He controls the docks where the passenger ships land and where the fruit arrives. I am his only child. If I asked him to help you, he would." She looked at him, blowing cigarette smoke in his direction.

Silvio didn't know how to reply. Of course he wanted her help. So did Nino. In fact, Nino would kill him if he bungled this opportunity. At the same time he sensed that Anna-Maria had more to say but that a lot depended on his answer.

"I . . . I'd love to work for your father . . . but where would that leave us? Would I see more of you?"

Anna-Maria smiled. "A little too oily, Silvio, but flattering. And clever. I'll tell my father you're clever—and quick. I saw that tonight, at dinner."

Quick? He hadn't been so quick when his parents were ambushed.

She stubbed out her cigarette. "Come and sit over here." She moved along the sofa to make room for him.

He got up, not feeling at his best. He edged around the low table and sat down next to Anna-Maria.

"Good," she said. "Now, your next lesson is to light a cigarette for me. Women like that—at least I do."

Silvio picked up the silver box and held it open for her. She took a cigarette, leaning forward so that he could see the top half of her breasts. He lit a match and stretched out toward her. She put the end of her cigarette in the flame, leaning forward still more.

"Now the champagne," she said, drawing on her cigarette. "Finish your glass and pour us some more."

Silvio drained his glass. He got up and crossed the room. As he reached the bar he was gently thrown against it by the unsteadiness of the deck. That second glass hadn't helped. He definitely did not feel well.

Sono contadino? he asked himself. Am I a peasant?

He poured the champagne and took the glass back to the sofa. Again the ship heaved beneath him.

When he sat down, Anna-Maria leaned back, kicked off her slippers, swung her long legs around, and stretched them across Silvio's lap, lowering them onto his thighs. Greedily, she emptied her glass of champagne and set it on the table. Holding her cigarette near her mouth, ready to draw on it at any moment, she said, "How are you planning to enter the United States?"

"What do you mean? I don't understand."

"Of course you do. Or how innocent can you be? You and Nino are not exactly princes of the realm, are you? I didn't see you coming aboard at Palermo up the first-class gangway. You very nearly lost the top of your head before we were out of sight of Gibraltar. So you can't just walk ashore at New Orleans. You and Nino are going to have to work something out before we get to America. Illegal immigrants are put back on the boats they arrived on."

Silvio heard Anna-Maria, but he was no longer listening. The *Syracusa* was beginning to roll, pitch, and yaw all at the same time as the wind outside rose and the seas were whipped into a frenzy. His stomach appeared to be doing a dance inside him and he suddenly felt too ill to speak. He looked at Anna-Maria in horror. She was very feminine—fragile, soft, clean. He couldn't throw up in her presence, still less all over her.

Suddenly the ship lurched, the built-in furniture creaked and groaned, and the champagne bottle slid alarmingly along the bar. Silvio could wait no longer. He threw Anna-Maria's legs off his lap, put his glass down on the table, and ran for the door.

"Silvio!" his hostess called out. "Use the bathroom!"

But he hadn't realized that one of the other doors led to a bathroom, and in any case he wanted fresh air as well as the opportunity to vomit somewhere on his own. He reached the door, pulled it open, and jumped outside. Closing the door behind him, he ran toward the stern of the ship. Suddenly the deck wasn't there as the *Syracusa* lurched again. Silvio was thrown against the wall of a ventilator shaft and fell to the deck. He crawled to the edge of the ship, grabbed hold of the railing for support and, opening his mouth involuntarily but with relief, threw up into the void.

Annunziata was upset, screaming with rage. No, wait, she wasn't. She was smiling. Or was she? It was so difficult to tell. She was drunk—yes, that was it, uproariously drunk. She was on a dance floor, a bottle of champagne in one hand, a cigarette in a holder in the other. She was swirling around, but each time she revolved, there was a different man in her arms. Dark, fair, tall, taller, each one more handsome than the last. Wait! One of them looked like the Orestano man who'd sat astride him. They *all* looked like Orestano. Some of them kissed her neck—she liked that. She looked stunning and she looked happy. Silvio felt himself begin to sweat and tremble. It was time he put a stop to this nonsense. But he knew, somewhere inside, that he couldn't move, that he was condemned to watch. He tried to shout, but the moment he opened his mouth, the nauseous feeling returned. Annunziata vanished along with the men she was dancing too close to. This was no better. The boat was rocking—but in an odd kind of way, back and forth, back and forth, in quick jerky movements.

"Silvio! It's five o'clock. I'm bored. How long can you sleep, for Christ's sake?" Someone was shaking him.

He woke up. Thank God. All those men had been a dream.

"Here, drink this. It's coffee."

Nino had found Silvio slumped across the deck, totally spent after bolting from Anna-Maria's cabin. He had carried the young man to the other side of the ship; the bar in the casino had a door for the crew that opened outward onto the deck.

The barman had opened the door. "We're on deck duty," whispered Nino. "Have you got something for seasickness?"

"Hold on," the barman said. In a minute he was back.

"What is it?" asked Nino, staring at what the barman had in his hand. It wasn't bismuth or camphor.

"A key. To the shower room, a few doors along from here. It's for senior crew, but I've been on this ship so long I've got a key as well. Have him take a shower for as long as he can bear it. Don't worry, there'll be no one else there at this time of night. Bring back the key when you're finished."

Nino had helped Silvio to the shower, then resumed his patrol alone.

Silvio had stayed in the shower for half an hour before he began to feel better, as he sweated out the champagne and shook off the stale odor of tobacco and vomit that hung about him. He remembered little of the rest of the night. He had dropped into bed shortly after six and had stayed there ever since.

"Drink the coffee. We need to talk." Nino's voice was harsh.

Silvio drank from the mug. The coffee was good. He couldn't remember feeling this well in days. The sea seemed fairly calm, too.

"You said last night Anna-Maria offered to help us," Nino said.

Silvio nodded. He didn't like Nino's brusque manner, but he had seen enough in the *bivio* to know that the Don could be rough where women were concerned.

"You left in such a hurry. Was she mad at you?"

"For leaving like I did?"

"No, mulehead. For not screwing her."

"What?"

"Why do you think she asked you to her cabin? God! Your naïveté is getting on my nerves, Silvio. Listen to an older man. Learn from his mistakes. This is important. She's a woman of twenty-three, a nice woman in some ways, a *puttana* in others, but the important thing is that she is her father's daughter and we— you—have got to please her. You're eighteen, that's old enough."

Silvio buried his face in the coffee mug. How much of what Nino was saying was designed to push Silvio into Anna-Maria's bed and away from Annunziata?

"Here."

"What's that?"

"What does it look like, *idiota*. Money. To buy Anna-Maria a gift—"

"What—?"

"Don't interrupt! Remember what I told you? An olive is hard on the inside but soft on the outside. You saw the shops. Buy her some chocolate, some silk flowers, fancy soap—anything. But buy her something that gets you back into her bedroom tonight and every night until we get to New Orleans. I want you to screw that woman and keep her happy all the way across the Atlantic Ocean so that she talks to her father as if we were the Pope and St. Peter themselves. Don't cross me on this one, Silvio. I know what I'm doing. And don't fail me. Do you hear?"

He heard all right. He had heard that phrase "Don't fail me" before.

"Two questions."

Nino glared at Silvio. "Well?"

"How are we going to get ashore? Anna-Maria asked me."

At the mention of Anna-Maria, Nino relaxed. "Don't worry about that. You'll see when the time comes. What was the other question?"

"The Orestanos. Anna-Maria says they'll come looking for us. Or, if they don't, they'll tell the authorities about us."

"I've been thinking about that, too. I don't know how many they are, whether all the people who surrounded you were Orestanos or hangers-on, keen to be associated with an attempt to get at me. But I do have a plan, which also depends on you getting back inside cabin 715 tonight. I'll tell you the details once you've succeeded."

Nino stood up. "Now, get dressed. It's time you went shopping."

Silvio knocked gently on the cabin door. Down the deck Nino watched, half-hidden behind a ventilator shaft.

"Come in."

Silvio closed the door behind him.

"Look." Anna-Maria had poured two glasses of champagne in wide-brimmed goblets. "They're not moving. The sea is as flat as a virgin's belly. I hope you're feeling well."

"I'm fine." Silvio smiled.

Nino had been right about one thing. The chocolates had done the trick. When Silvio had arrived at Anna-Maria's table in the saloon that evening, the moment could have been awkward. In fact, for a short while, things *were* awkward. She had been deep in conversation with the man on her left, some sort of businessman who knew her father, and neither looked as though they relished the interruption.

But Silvio had worked on his speech. "I'm sorry I was such a *contadino*, such a peasant, last night," he said. "I'm not used to champagne. I hope you can forgive me. I'm told these chocolates are the best on board. Perhaps they will sweeten the memory of what happened."

Anna-Maria had beamed. "It's more important to have good

manners," she had replied, taking the chocolates, "than knowing how to hold your drink."

He had been careful that night to ask her to dance—and not to leave it to her to ask him.

"One more thing, Silvio," she had said during the dance.

"Yes?"

"Chocolates taste even more delicious when eaten with champagne. Will you come tonight?"

"If you still want me to, I'd love to."

She had squeezed his hand.

Now, in her cabin, she handed him a glass. She crossed to the bar, where she had laid out several of his chocolates on a plate. "Here, try one. Drink some champagne, and then, while you still have the taste in your mouth, eat the chocolate."

He did as he was told and moaned with the pleasure of the experience.

"Come and sit on the sofa." She did as she had done the night before, kicking off her slippers and lifting her legs onto Silvio's lap. She laid the plate of chocolates on her own lap. "Help yourself," she said.

He took another chocolate. Last night she had made all the moves, asked all the questions. He had acted like a sullen mule. He realized that the most flattering thing for her would be if he took the initiative tonight.

He pointed to the books on the table. "You travel with those?"

"I love reading. Other worlds, other times. It's a way of meeting people you wouldn't otherwise meet—or couldn't meet."

He nodded. He had never thought about reading in that way.

"Tell me about New Orleans. What kind of town is it?"

She considered the question, nibbling on a chocolate. "Nothing like Palermo, for a start. The main feature is the river, the Mississippi. It's huge—not like an Italian river, all dried up for most of the year—but maybe a quarter of a mile wide. It's brown, dark brown—like when they burn the stubble on the slopes of Rocca Busambra—fast-running, very deep, and you don't swim in it because there are huge eels. Sometimes it floods badly, so in places a big mound of earth has been built along its banks, called a levee. New Orleans was once a French town, that's why it's called New Orleans—Orleans is a place in France. Some people still speak French and many streets have French names. Everything interesting happens in the French Quarter. That's where the markets are—coffee, meat, fruit, clothes—and all the gambling joints, all the whorehouses. And there's this new kind of music. Brass bands but different somehow."

Silvio sipped his champagne more slowly tonight. "Does your father live in the French Quarter?"

Anna-Maria smiled. "No, we live to the west, in an area known as the Garden District. All the houses have big gardens, with very lush vegetation. Not many of the streets are paved, and when the river floods—well, you can imagine the mud. In the summer it's very hot and humid. In the winter it can be foggy. Oh yes, and there's a carnival after Christmas. It's called Mardi Gras."

"What's that?"

"A kind of fair. Everyone dresses up in fancy costumes and parades through the streets with bands—there are a lot of Negro bands in New Orleans. They make their way to a big dance hall, where the costumes are judged and there's a big ball. I go every year."

"What costumes have you worn?"

"Oh, one year I went as a Spanish flamenco dancer, and last year I went dressed as a Greek goddess."

Silvio didn't really understand, but had to keep talking. "Tell me about the Negroes. I've never seen one."

"No, that's boring, and you'll find out soon enough. I want to hear your story. You killed a man."

He nodded. "A vendetta."

"What does it feel like, to kill someone?"

What had Nino said? Be soft on the outside, hard inside. Like an olive. "The man betrayed us. Someone had to do it. The killing was just."

"Why you?"

"I had to prove my loyalty, my courage."

"Why? Were they in doubt?"

He pointed across the room. "You can't learn courage in books. There's always doubt until you're tested."

"But you are a blood relative of Nino's. Wasn't that enough?"

It was then that he realized the answer to his father's uncertainty. "Brains, and courage, are more important than blood."

She eyed him. "I wonder if you're right. But you still haven't explained. What's it feel like to shoot someone?"

"I've only done it once. It's not as bad as seeing your parents die."

There was a silence in the cabin. Silvio couldn't read Anna-Maria's face. She held her glass to her lips but didn't drink. Then she said, "Take off your jacket and pour some more champagne."

Silvio went to the bar, but when he turned round Anna-Maria was nowhere to be seen. One of the doors, to the bedroom, was open.

Now what? Silvio had not dared wear Annunziata's ring, and it was only a matter of days since he had seen her. Could he be this unfaithful to her so soon? She would be missing him, thinking of him, just as he thought of her. She would never imagine that he had already met someone like Anna-Maria. He had never imagined it himself. He kept reminding himself that Anna-Maria was not as beautiful as Annunziata, but she *was* inviting, and interesting—all that reading, no doubt. And he couldn't deny he wanted to touch her, to bury his face in her flesh, to feel her naked skin against his. Then again, what choice did he have? Nino had made it clear what he wanted Silvio to do. No matter that Nino might have more than one motive for pushing him into Anna-Maria's bed; his argument was a good one. It *would* be difficult for them to find their feet in New Orleans and Anna-Maria's father was their best hope. The Palermo Priolas were family, but maybe they would feel their debt to Nino was discharged by his safe passage to America. And they had no debt to Silvio.

Nor could he entirely overlook the fact that these were near-ideal conditions in which to lose his virginity. An older, willing woman, champagne, their own cabin on an oceangoing liner. A week ago Silvio had never been anywhere more sophisticated than Palermo. The world of champagne, chocolates, and dancing was as alien to him as the Vatican.

Silvio slipped his fingers between the stems of the champagne glasses and lifted them off the bar. With his other hand he picked up the champagne bucket—the bottle inside it was still half-full—and walked across the cabin. He went through the open doorway into the bedroom. He paused only to bend his foot behind the door and kick it closed.

"I've got a plan."

Nino fell into step with Silvio as they patrolled the deck. They were walking toward the stern of the ship, past the kitchen. Though the weather was cloudy, it was warm.

"A plan for what?"

"Now that I've gotten you laid, it's time to strike back at the Orestanos."

Silvio could barely concentrate. Half an hour earlier he had been looking down at Anna-Maria writhing beneath him. He had found out what he'd missed that night on the hillside and it was even more glorious than he'd imagined.

"Listen to me, you mule. Tonight, while you were fucking your head off, I stopped by at the bar of the casino—remember the outside door last night where we were given the key to the shower?"

Silvio nodded. They had reached the stern of the ship. They crossed to the other side and began to walk forward.

"I sponged a drink off the barman, and while we talked I said you got lucky." Silvio shot him a glance, but Nino merely chuckled. "Now listen. Tomorrow night, when you're with Anna-Maria, I'll do the same thing. I'll add that from what she's been saying, you're set up for the rest of the trip."

"But—"

"Shut up! Listen to an older man. The barman knows who I am. All the crew do. I'm betting he'll sell the information to Onofri Orestano."

"What information?"

"That every night, between midnight and three, I am alone on deck. And that each night, around two, I stop by the casino bar for a drink and a smoke. One night, between now and our arrival in America, the Orestanos will come for me."

"How will they get onto the main deck?"

"Whoever sells them the information will also make sure they can get up here. Probably dressed as crew. There are two hundred crew on this ship—I know because I asked. They might all know *me*, but they won't all know each other."

"If fifteen come for you you're dead. There are no sulfur fires on deck."

"There won't be fifteen. From their point of view this has to be a quiet, clean job. If they make a mess they'll be handed over to the American authorities and put back on the next ship to Palermo. Or be tried in America. After all, this is a Priola ship and they are Orestanos. In any case, whoever sells the information about me won't want a whole gang on the rampage on the upper deck. That way his own job is at risk, if anyone found out who passed on the information.

"No, my guess is that the deal will be for two, three, or four of them, just a handful, to sneak up here, dressed as crew, then to try and surprise me, overpower me, knife me, and throw me overboard. Then they'll slink back to the immigrant decks, three or four anonymous people among six hundred. Everything will be hushed up. I wasn't on this ship when it left Palermo, so why should I be on it when it arrives in America?"

"I thought we were protected by the Priolas?"

"Only up to a point. They arranged for us to be smuggled aboard and have given us passage, but that's it. In their position they can't be seen aiding someone like me. If I get caught, or killed, they'll say they knew nothing about my being on board."

They were midships now and descended the steps to the deck below.

"This is the tricky part—but if it works it will be effective. Tomorrow night, you sleep with Anna-Maria, just like tonight. But after you're done, and *only* after you're done, you tell her my plan—"

"What!"

"Keep your voice down. Anna-Maria is family: a blood relative. We can rely on her. She would react like her father if I got killed, but if she can help stop it, or help beat the Orestanos, she will.

"Now listen. Tomorrow night, after you've fucked her, you tell her that from then on, you will go to her cabin every night as before. But until something happens, instead of fucking your brains out—and try not to put it quite like that—you will leave her cabin at precisely one-thirty. If you're being watched, as I expect you will be, whoever is doing the watching will wait half an hour or so after you arrive, to see that you really are staying awhile. But he won't wait forever because, if I'm right, and there are only two or three or four of them, he'll be needed for the assault on me. So at one-thirty, when your watchman should long since have gone to join the others, you leave Anna-Maria's cabin.

"I want you to check that no one follows you. Then take up a position outside the casino bar *but* on the deck below. There's a set of steps that connects the two decks; they won't expect you to hide there. Remain in the shadows as much as you can—*and listen*. As near to two o'clock as I can, I'll go into the casino bar. You may hear a scuffle, but in any case I'll call out. I don't know what it will be, but you'll hear. Then come up the stairs as quick as you can."

Nino paused, and Silvio interrupted. "How can you be so sure it's going to work out that way? They could jump us in the cabin—"

"We're only in the cabin in daylight. Only officers are allowed in that part of the ship. They need to make a quick getaway after they hit me—so their attack has to be on the open deck, which means it has to take place at night. If they attack both of us, they're bound to need four or more men, to make sure it works. That's too unwieldy a number. They'll attack me alone. Believe it."

Silvio still wasn't convinced. "What if there *are* more than four of them? It could happen, Nino, and then we'd be hopelessly out-numbered."

"It won't matter," said Nino. "When you hit someone, always hit them as hard as you can. Listen to an older man. I'm betting the Orestanos won't carry guns. They need to do all this in silence. But *you* will have a pistol."

7

Silvio had never seen so many officers' white uniforms all together in one place. They stood in three rows, behind the first-class passengers, and as Nino had put it, they looked like candles in a cathedral. In fact, this being Sunday morning, the saloon had been turned into a cathedral of sorts—or at least a chapel—for an hour or so.

Silvio had not been keen to attend the service. He rarely went to Mass in Sicily and he thought Nino was equally infrequent in his attendance. But this time Nino had insisted. Was it because Anna-Maria would be there, and Nino wanted to impress her? Or was there a side to Nino that Silvio wasn't aware of? He certainly seemed engrossed in the service, and knew all the Latin responses.

The saloon made a reasonable church, Silvio decided. The ship's chaplain stood by the piano, with a large cross on the sideboard behind him where the cutlery was stored. The pianist was the same man who played in the evenings, though he now wore a different expression on his face, more beatific. The captain, who clearly enjoyed the sound of his own voice, led the singing. Outside, the weather was glorious; but despite all that, Silvio did not feel well.

He had woken that morning without really wanting to. His talk with Nino the previous evening had depressed and frightened him. Too much was happening too quickly.

Until recently, aside from the death of his parents, nothing much of consequence had occurred in Silvio's young life. But in the past weeks that life had been transformed. Before his ride to Palermo, with that fateful package, he had lived the life of a boy. Now, only a few weeks later, he was heading for a different world, already an exile and a murderer. He was about to be involved in a vicious fight, where, it was as certain as could be, someone else would be killed. Yes, he had grown up as part of Nino's family, so he had been brought up to expect the unexpected. Still, he had never expected *this*.

Silvio looked about him. Not only the captain was singing lustily. They all were—Anna-Maria, the chaplain, Breguzzo, the first officer, Dr. Tolmezzo, Enrico, the barman from the casino, the opera singer. Even Nino.

Suddenly Silvio understood why Nino had insisted on coming to the service. He was frightened of dying in the fight. Or he was prepared to die, and was making his peace with God. Most likely, knowing Nino, he was asking for a few favors.

Why wasn't he more religious? Silvio asked himself. Was it really because his parents were dead? That's what he'd always told himself. No merciful God would have let that happen, surely. Or was there more to it than that? He looked at Nino out of the corner of his eye, then across to Anna-Maria. They both appeared to be unswerving believers—why couldn't he feel the same?

Maybe it *was* something to do with family. Anna-Maria had parents, Nino had Annunziata. Did that mean each had a sense of being part of something bigger than a solitary individual, of something that went before and would come after? Silvio suddenly stopped singing. He had never, not once, felt lonely. Until now. Until now he had only wanted to sleep with Annunziata for the pleasure. He had never thought of having children. If he was killed in the fight with the Orestanos, he would leave no one behind. The only way to make up for losing his parents was to have children of his own: he saw that now.

When Silvio entered Anna-Maria's cabin that evening, she was already in her nightdress, reading. She put down her book, gave him a peck on the cheek, and pulled him by his jacket toward the bedroom. "The champagne's in here."

He resisted, however. "What are you reading?"

"Something translated from the French, about a woman who takes Paris by storm."

"Who wrote it?"

"A Frenchman called Emile Zola."

"Can a man write about women?"

She eyed him. "Why are you so interested?"

"Why are you?"

"I told you. You can go anywhere with books. All over the world. Into the past. You feel things in books, sometimes, before you feel them in real life."

"Such as?"

She shook her head. "You're not here to talk about books, Silvio." She reached out and took his hand. Once in the bedroom, she began opening the champagne. He went to help but she shook him off. "I'll do this. You get undressed."

He unbuttoned his tunic and began to slide it over his shoulders.

"What's *that*?" She had spotted the gun in his pocket.

He had planned to tell her afterward, as Nino had said, but now that she had seen the gun he told her why it was there.

As he did so he noticed that Anna-Maria changed. She gave him his champagne, but then, taking hers, she walked away from him. She reopened the door that linked the bedroom and the cabin. She walked back and forth in the cabin, asking questions.

"Whose idea was this? How many times have you used a gun? How can you be so sure there will be only three Orestanos? How can you shoot them—the whole ship will hear the explosion. What would happen if Nino got killed but you lived? How do you know they will even accept the bait?"

The more questions she asked, however, the more Silvio realized that they weren't real questions, in the sense that she demanded a specific answer. Rather, Anna-Maria was rehearsing, for her own benefit, the risks of the venture. But the whole time *she was excited*. Last night she'd been eager to hear about his vendetta killing. Part of her was frightened, yes. But she seemed fired up by the idea of him as a gunman. Now she even went to his tunic, which he had dropped on a chair, and took out the gun. Silvio noticed that beneath her nightdress Anna-Maria's nipples were firm.

She came back into the bedroom and stood before him. Gently, she shoved him backward so that he sat on the bed. Then she pushed him flat, lifted her nightdress over her head and, completely naked, sat astride him.

Anna-Maria looked up and down the deck. "All clear," she whispered. Silvio stepped outside. It was the following night, cloudy, but with brief snatches of moonlight. It didn't take him long to reach the ventilator shaft he had earmarked as his hiding place. It was very quiet on board.

So far as Silvio could tell, no one had spotted him. The only problem was that the sea was beginning to get choppy and a light breeze had sprung up. That made hearing difficult.

He fingered the gun in his pocket. He might only be eighteen but guns had been part of his life as long as he could remember. He had seen countless animals slaughtered by *lupara*, and he had now seen—he counted swiftly—fourteen people killed by guns, if he included the Lazio soldiers shot in the quarry. And Gaetano Mancuso.

He liked guns. He liked their heaviness, their solidity, the very fact that there was no doubt about their purpose. He thought pistols and revolvers—revolvers especially—were beautiful, so clean, smooth, and shiny, with absolutely no waste about them. Rifles and shotguns he liked less. They were ungainly, he thought. . . . Footsteps were approaching. He stepped back into the shadows and held his breath.

Two women went by, two old women, obviously taking the night air before turning in. "Thank you for rescuing me from the casino," he heard one say to the other. "I'd already lost far too much and . . ." But the rest was lost on the breeze.

Time was passing. He didn't know how much exactly. He had been forced to give Bastiano's watch back to him and now didn't have one. If their lure didn't work on the first night, they had decided, then they had to join up again not long after two, when Nino had finished his drink at the casino. Nino had said he would come down the stairs near where Silvio was hiding. So long as there was no one around, they could join up there and then.

Sure enough, at about a quarter past two there was a clatter from above, and when it stopped, Nino stepped out onto the deck. He looked up and down the ship, then whispered, "Silvio!"

Silvio moved out of the shadows.

"Did you see anyone?"

"No, just two old women who'd lost at the casino. You?"

"No. But I made a discovery. Tomorrow is the barman's night off."

"So?"

"My guess is this: The barman sold us out. He won't want to be anywhere near when the trouble starts. He wants to be able to say he was safely tucked up in his bunk. He wants an alibi. My guess is they'll come tomorrow night."

It was a nerve-racking day. At least it was for Silvio. Nino seemed to take it in his stride easily enough, sleeping all morning, cleaning the gun that Silvio would use, singing in the shower down the corridor.

Silvio spent a lot of the time daydreaming about Annunziata. Now that he'd slept with Anna-Maria, he was—well, if not yet a man, well on the way to it. There were things he could teach Annunziata now, little ways he could bring her pleasure. That morning on the mountain ... the morning the *bivio* had been attacked, he had been surprised at the pleasure she had shown when he had bitten her nipples. How could he have been so naive! Anna Maria had shown him much more than that, and now he imagined himself showing Annunziata, imagined her moving on the straw mattresses of the *bivio*, moving and moaning in a way that, even as he gazed out to the empty sea, thousands of miles from her, made him aroused.

Of course, he didn't mention any of this to Anna-Maria, when they danced that night during dinner. Instead, he brought her up to date on what had happened the night before.

"That makes sense," she said, when Silvio told her about Nino's theory.

"You seem used to this sort of thing."

"You never get used to it, Silvio, but you see it. It goes on in Palermo, it goes on in New Orleans, why shouldn't it go on aboard ship on its way between the two?"

"Aren't you ever frightened?"

"Of course I am. I'm frightened for your sake, I'm frightened— a bit—for Nino's. But I'll give you a tip, Silvio, from a woman who ... well, who's had her ups and downs. Never, *never,* show your fear. Always remember two things: not to underestimate your opponent, and that he is probably just as frightened as you but is maybe better at concealing it. It's the same with women; the more frightening you find them, the more nonchalant you must appear."

"Are women always a man's opponents, then?"

She grinned. "If it does happen tonight—and I feel that it will—and if you win, come to cabin 715 afterward. I've got a small supply of something that makes sex even better."

"What's that?"

"I'll tell you once you've earned it."

It was rougher than the previous night. Silvio had been on mules that gave a smoother ride than this ship. And it was darker. He was well hidden behind the ventilator shaft and had been standing in position for more than twenty minutes, or so he judged. But he would have a problem hearing any commotion on the deck above, and the ship was rocking so much that anything might happen in a fight.

Silvio was apprehensive, to put it mildly. He was tall and well built, but he knew that older men had filled out and were more muscular than he was, at eighteen. He knew he was nimble, but he had never really experienced prolonged pain, and if he was knifed in a fight, he was worried how he would react. He might let Nino down; or himself.

The wind gusted and the *Syracusa* dropped suddenly between two waves, creaking all over the place. Silvio wondered about those creakings. Was this ship as safe as—

That noise! Was it running feet, on the deck above? He strained to hear. They had both accepted that Nino couldn't just call out "Silvio!" the moment something happened. Silvio needed to take the attackers by surprise. But was the attack already happening? He couldn't be sure.

He leaned forward. Was that a thud he heard? A grunt? More running feet? He ventured out from behind the ventilator. He had to hear better. He stood at the foot of the staircase.

Then he heard a scream. It was muted, but it was definitely a scream. Nino had been cut!

He took out his gun and leaped up the stairs. They faced forward and the scream had come from toward the stern. He turned, the lower half of his body concealed by the stairwell. Yes! He could see Nino clearly, holding what looked like a chain. Nino had his back to the wall of the lifejacket store, and the three—there were three—Orestanos stood facing him with their backs to Silvio. Swiftly he took off his shoes. Silence was needed now. He moved as quietly as he could toward Nino and the others. The ship was rolling badly—thank God he no longer felt seasick.

He slowed as he neared the group. What was he going to do? Suddenly the ship rolled again, and the middle one of the three Orestanos was thrown backward—right onto Silvio. It happened too quickly for him to dodge, and without thinking, he raised the gun and brought it down on the other man's head. Or he would have done, but the ship continued to roll and he was thrown off balance. The barrel of the gun struck the side of the man's head, forcing him to the ground but also making him cry out.

The other two turned—and the man on the right, a quick thinker, immediately lashed out with his knife at Silvio's forearm, the one holding the gun.

The blade made contact just below the elbow—the knife slicing through the flesh to the bone. Pain exploded in Silvio's arm, a tide of boiling heat. He grunted and squealed at the same time. And dropped the gun.

Saturated in pain, Silvio was nonetheless aware that Nino was swinging his chain at the man who had wielded the knife. He slapped him around the ankles, pulled, and upended the man onto the deck.

But the third man had made a dive for the gun. Silvio was paralyzed, rooted to the deck. All he could do was watch through his tears as Nino reached down to the man Silvio had hit over the head and snatched his knife. As the third man picked up the gun, Nino slid the knife inside his tunic sleeve. Silvio was close to being sick.

"Basta!" shouted the man who had the gun. "Enough." It was unnecessary. Silvio was holding the slit in his right arm with his left hand, crying and trying to stanch the flow of blood. The pain just wouldn't stop and made even his gums ache. Nino stood still.

The man who had been chained by Nino now knelt to the man whose skull had been cracked. He was beginning to come around. "Onofri! Onofri! Quickly. We have their gun."

This seemed to work, for the other man, the biggest of the three and the man who Silvio realized had cut him down in steerage— Onofri Orestano—looked up. He transferred his gaze from Nino to Silvio, then to the man holding the gun. He grinned.

Unsteadily, Onofri Orestano stood up. The ship was still rolling. He grabbed Silvio. "Stand over there," he growled, shoving him roughly toward the wall next to Nino. Then he looked around the deck. "My knife! My knife! Where the fuck is it?"

Silvio managed to gasp, "I kicked it overboard. You won't cut anyone else with that." It may have been the greatest lie of his life. Or the last one.

The big man took a step toward Silvio, raised his arm, and slapped him hard across the face with the back of his hand. He was wearing a ring and its edge bit into Silvio's cheek. But this move coincided with another roll of the ship and Onofri Orestano was unbalanced, falling to one side. For a moment the gunman's eyes followed the other man's fall. In that moment Silvio heard Nino grunt and saw his arm swing forward. Moments later he gasped as a knife punctured the gunman's chest, cracking his breastbone. The man let out a wail of surprise, fell to his knees, dropped the gun, and pitched forward onto the deck.

This time Nino was the quickest on his feet. Silvio could still only watch through his pain as Nino leaped forward, picked up the gun, and turned it swiftly on the others. They froze. "Over there," Nino said to Onofri, indicating that he wanted the two live Orestanos to stand together. Then: "Silvio! Here, by me. Quickly!"

Silvio didn't respond immediately. He couldn't. He was fighting a desire to throw up. It was as if someone was pressing a sharp, hot sword to his bone without any respite.

Nino addressed Silvio again, but in a quieter voice, "Not long now, Silvio, I promise. No cock's blood. Hold on. I'm going to move the others to the stern of the ship. I want you to drag the dead man behind me—as fast as you can. It's important. Do you understand?"

"Yes." He managed barely a whisper. Nino might not have heard. Silvio nodded instead.

"You two," hissed Nino, using the barrel of the gun to indicate the stern of the ship. "Move."

Through his tears, Silvio watched as the others glared at Nino. But after a moment of defiance they shuffled in the direction he wanted. With his left hand Silvio grabbed the dead man's collar and began dragging him along the deck. There was a big stain on the man's chest, but he had stopped bleeding. The knife still stuck out, where it had become lodged. Like the price tag on meat in a butcher's shop.

Silvio lagged behind the others. He watched as Nino moved closer to the Orestanos—too distant for them to lunge at him with any hope of success but close enough to fire with accuracy if they tried any tricks.

But there were no tricks, and soon they had reached the stern of the ship.

Silvio heard Nino shout, "Stop! Stand there!" Then he saw him indicate the ladder that led to the sternmost lifeboat on this deck. Nino now simply waited, without speaking or moving, while Silvio caught up. One moment Silvio was sweating, the next he was shivering. The pain in his arm was as intense as ever. "Put the dead man there," Nino said to Silvio, nodding toward the ladder. "But don't get too close to these other vermin. Then come and stand near me."

Silvio did as he was told. After he had let go of the dead man, he could at least nurse his bad arm with his good hand. He seemed to be losing a lot of blood. Through the pain, he heard Nino address the Orestanos again. "Get in the boat."

By now the realization of what Nino was planning had dawned on the Orestanos. "No," said the big man, Onofri. "You'll have to shoot us instead."

"And if you shoot," said the other one, "the whole ship will hear." He grinned. "Go ahead, shoot."

For a moment they all stood there. Silvio was close to being sick again. He didn't care if Nino shot them. He had to lie down.

"Think about this, *mezzatacca*," said Nino as quietly as he could in the wind. "Am I going to let you live, or remain onboard, to fuck up my arrival in America? No. You can either die now, here, this very minute. Or you can take your chances in the lifeboat. The choice is yours. I'm going to count to five, and then I'm going to shoot. One . . ."

The Orestanos' grins had faded. They looked at each other.

"Two . . ."

Silvio's head was swimming. He was growing dizzy.

"Three . . ."

Onofri Orestano knelt down and grabbed the clothing of the dead man. "Get in the boat," he said to the third man.

"But—"

"Four . . ."

The third man suddenly clambered up the ladder as Onofri lifted the body onto his shoulders and began to follow. As he rose, the other man, who was in the lifeboat now, took the dead man from Onofri's shoulders and pulled him onboard. Then Onofri Orestano climbed over the lifeboat's gunwale.

Silvio couldn't hold out much longer. The fingers of his good hand were sticky with warm blood. He had to be sick and he had to lie down.

"Quick!" hissed Nino. "Silvio, take the gun."

Silvio hesitated.

"Take the gun!"

He let go of his arm and held out his good hand. His sticky fingers closed over the gun.

Quickly, Nino ran to the derricks that supported the lifeboat. He operated the levers that swung the vessel out beyond the edge of the *Syracusa*'s deck. He then found another lever and jerked on that. At once the cable that supported the lifeboat began to play out. The boat began to descend.

At this, the Orestanos began to shout and scream. "Help! Help! Save us! For the love of God, Nino. Help!"

Nino took the gun from Silvio. Sweat and tears mingled on Silvio's cheeks. There was the taste of vomit in his throat. He didn't move as Nino rushed to the edge of the ship and pointed the gun at the Orestanos. They fell silent.

The lifeboat hit the water. The cold black sea was very rough by now. The boat was immediately tossed one way and the other, like a fly on the end of a fishing line. Silvio stared down without moving. It became clear to the Orestanos that they must disengage the cable. With the *Syracusa* steaming through the water at ten or eleven knots, and pitching and rolling, the lifeboat was being pulled against her hull, the cable going slack and tightening alternately. The smaller boat might break up in no time.

Silvio and Nino watched as the big man fought with the cable, disengaging first the stern link, then the bow link. He looked up as the lifeboat began to slip behind. Nino waved, but Silvio couldn't move his limbs; he just stared through his tears into the darkness. The sea was so high, and the gloom so dense, that the lifeboat soon vanished.

Nino turned. "They've gone. Now let's see to your—"

But Silvio was lying on the deck.

* * *

Annunziata had a gun. She pointed it at him and screamed, "Don't ever come near me again! Fuck whoever you want, you're such a sophisticated man of the world now, Sylvano Randazzo. See if I care!" Annunziata *never* swore. Now she took the gun and held the barrel upright, closing her fingers around it, moving her hand up and down, as though the barrel were a penis. She laughed. "Is that what Anna-Maria does, Toto?" She laughed again. "But is she as pretty as me?" Then she took the gun and aimed it at Silvio. "Good-bye, Toto," she said, laughing. "No lifeboat for you." And she fired.

Silvio screamed, but no sound came. He tried to dodge the bullet but suddenly realized he was tossing and turning—and sweating—in bed. In the cabin.

"Ah!" said a voice. "You're awake."

Silvio groaned and turned over. Instinctively, his left hand went to his right arm.

"I stitched and bandaged it," said the doctor. "You'll live, though we were worried for a while. You lost a lot of blood, which is probably why you fainted. I gave you a sedative. That's three times I've treated you, Silvio, in three days. I'd say you were unlucky."

"What . . . what time is it? And where's Nino?"

"Ah . . . it's five o'clock, in the afternoon. You've been out for sixteen hours. As for Nino, as you call him, I'm afraid you won't be seeing him for a while."

"What! Why not? What's happened?"

"The captain is aware of what you did. Lifeboats dropping into the water make a lot of noise. You can imagine that he was not, shall we say, jumping with joy at the news. He ordered that the ship turn back—"

"Did they find them?" Silvio was suddenly scared all over again.

"We steamed in a large circle, in heavy seas, during the hours of darkness, from two-thirty to five. Then we spent two hours in daylight crisscrossing that part of the sea where they should have been. But no, we did not find them—and don't look so pleased with yourself: the captain lost three passengers and nearly six hours. He is going to have to explain that without reference to

Nino and you, since you're not supposed to be on board. It will
cost him money."

"But why can't I see Nino?"

"Use your head. You've both caused so much havoc on this
ship you are confined to your cabins. Because you were injured,
you were left here. Some small hovel has been found for Nino.
You're both locked in and will remain that way until it's time to
put you ashore in four days' time."

Dr. Tolmezzo stood up. "So get used to it. I'll come by twice a
day, to dress your wound and watch out for any infection." He
knocked on the door and Silvio heard a key being turned in the
lock. A moment later the doctor was let out, and the door locked
behind him.

Silvio stared at the ceiling. So: the Orestanos had been seen off,
but at a price. On the whole, he thought, the price was worth
it, given that the alternative was unthinkable. But the whole
episode, which had ended well for the moment, nonetheless
showed that Nino had made some implacable enemies. Nor would
it end here. In time, the Orestano family would hear of what
Nino—and Silvio—had done, and there would be retaliation. It
would take time, but it would come. So much for America being a
fresh start.

He thought about Anna-Maria. She had been waiting for him
last night, with the promise of yet more sexual favors. Would she
be angry with him for not coming? He couldn't believe so. She
must have heard what had happened to him.

Should he get a message to her? Yes. He got off the bed, but at
once felt dizzy and sat down again. His head cleared and he stood
a second time. The *Syracusa* was fairly steady, and the rough
weather of the previous evening seemed to have died down. He
went to the door and tried the handle. It was definitely locked
on the outside. He banged on the door itself with the fist of his
left hand.

There was no response.

He banged again.

Still nothing.

He gave up. There had been someone outside while the doctor
had been with him. Was the guard permanent? If there were any
more Orestanos on the ship, and they found out where he was
being held . . . It didn't bear thinking about.

He lay back on his bed. He had only just awakened, but he felt tired again. He closed his eyes.

For God knows how long he slept, wakened, slept again. Twice when he woke it was dark, but on the third occasion it was light, so he must have slept through the night. From time to time his arm hurt, and once he noticed a tray of food just inside the door. Cold pasta and a glass of beer. He ate and drank greedily.

By the time he could sleep no more, it was, he judged by the light and the position of the shadows, late the following day. That meant there were three nights to go, if he'd correctly remembered what the doctor had said. For hours Silvio lay on his bed. Someone had left a newspaper on a ledge in the cabin wall. Silvio couldn't read but he could look at the engravings. One showed a mammoth gun, a cannon of some sort. Was this a report of some war? he wondered. But the sight of the gun made him think back to the fight with the Orestanos.

Silvio was beginning to realize that he did have brains. When he had pretended he had kicked Onofri's knife overboard, he had shown an ability to think quickly. It was true there were other occasions, too—such as when he'd fooled the *sbirri* who had questioned him about the mule. His quickness of mind had been such, in effect, that others had believed him. Say something quickly enough, and confidently enough, and people will believe you. Was that what brains was really about?

At the same time he wondered whether he had Nino's sheer brutality. Was he as hard on the inside as he told himself? Could he, Silvio, have fired that gun at the three men standing on the deck? Or if they had begun to clamber out of the lifeboat at the last minute? He doubted it. Could Nino? Oh yes.

They were different. The differences were becoming clearer as this voyage progressed. It was worth bearing in mind once they arrived in New Orleans.

His arm still hurt from time to time, but he played it up as worse than it was so that the doctor kept coming. This was the only company that Silvio was allowed. The doctor told him that the immigrant galleries were rife with gossip about the treatment of the Orestanos. Tolmezzo was of the opinion that no one on board ship had the guts to take on Nino—or Silvio, for that matter—but that the moment the ship docked at New Orleans, it would be different. The vendetta would be resumed.

That apart, the doctor had little to report. A woman in the lower immigrant gallery had given birth to twins, some chickens kept onboard as fresh food had escaped and caused havoc on the boat deck, a man had lost his house, gambling at the casino. One immigrant had developed typhus fever and been isolated. For Tolmezzo, the voyage was scarcely out of the ordinary.

Silvio couldn't sleep, but lay awake, thinking. He thought of his father. Had he lived, what difference would it have made? His father would not have let him leave Sicily, that's for sure. His father might have been Capo instead of Nino. They would have stuck to cattle rustling. There would have been no kidnappings, no Lazio Brigade, no betrayal, no vendetta, no exile.

Was America so exciting, so wonderful as everyone made out? He suddenly became very homesick.

Some hours after dark that night there was another knock on the door. Silvio raised himself on his elbows—to see Anna-Maria being admitted by the man outside. She was dressed in a long pink silk dress and long white silk gloves and she carried a bottle of champagne and two glasses. The door was closed behind her, and locked.

"How did you manage this?"

"You look terrible. Kiss me."

He got up and did as he was told. Not having had the option before, he suddenly realized how badly he needed a drink. It was the first time he could recall that he had ever felt a need for alcohol.

She started to open the champagne. With his bad arm, he obviously couldn't do it. "We're not far from America," she said. "In America, money is what counts. In America, money is more important than sex. You can buy anything. A thousand lire, in the right pocket, opens doors."

With his good arm, he took the opened champagne bottle from her and began to fill the glasses. "I'm sorry I couldn't keep our last meeting."

"You're forgiven. Provided you make up for it now." She started to take off her dress.

Silvio removed his own clothes, but as he took a step toward Anna-Maria she said, "All your clothes."

"I'm completely naked."

"Everything," she said, nodding to his arm.

"You want me to undo my bandage?"

"I want to see your wound." She looked him straight in the eye.

Dumbfounded, but considerably aroused by the sight of her body, Silvio unpinned the bandage and began to unravel it. Layer by layer he unwound the linen strip until at last the gash was revealed. There was a line of black thread, all but obscured by the purple blood beneath the skin and a number of yellow patches at the edge of the purple. He had not seen this himself, at least not since he had been on deck two nights before, and he didn't like it. The view made him feel ill.

"Seen enough?" he said brusquely.

"What a scar you're going to have. What a badge of honor." Then she smiled at him. "Put the bandage back," she said, her voice barely more than a whisper. "Then you can do anything you want with me."

She visited him for two more nights. Each time, she told Silvio, the price for opening the door went up. "But I can't sleep unless I'm fucked first."

"I don't like women who use bad language," Silvio replied.

"Bullshit, as the Americans say. You've only ever had me, so don't start laying down the law. In any case, I only talk dirty in the bedroom—and you'll find out soon enough that's what most men like. Now, I've got a message from Nino. Tomorrow is our last night at sea, and you and he are being taken off before we get to New Orleans. You're to meet Dr. Tolmezzo after breakfast in the morning. Be ready, with your bag packed. Are you listening?"

He nodded.

"So this is our last night, for the time being. I brought you something." She handed him a card.

It was an engraving of the Church of the Annunciation in Palermo.

"What's this?"

"It will take you longer to get to New Orleans than it will take the *Syracusa*. I'll be home the day after tomorrow. When you arrive, come and see me. The butler will answer the door. Give him that postcard and say you're expected. This way, if you are arrested, there is nothing to connect you to my name. Also, you will have changed *your* name. Send me the card and I'll know it's you."

"What's a butler, and where do you live?"

"Ask Nino what a butler is. And ask anyone in New Orleans where Angelo Priola lives. Everyone knows. Come around four in the afternoon. *Don't* bring Nino, not the first time. Are you listening?"

Silvio nodded.

"Now," she said, "tonight has to be something special. What haven't we done?"

Sono pervertito? Silvio asked himself. Am I a pervert? He had no idea.

"Lie back," she said. "Lie on the bed." When he had done so, she knelt by the bed and took his penis in her hand. She lowered her head over his groin. "Now, some men think this is even better than talking dirty."

"Sit down, both of you. Here, and here." Dr. Tolmezzo's office, on the first-class deck, was small but comfortable. Silvio and Nino had been summoned there just as Anna-Maria had predicted.

The doctor lit his first cigar of the day. "I have been asked to look after your immigration into America. You are a . . . shall we say *unusual* couple, but we are going to try something that has worked before. Thanks to your treatment of the Orestanos, we are three passengers short of the number that should be onboard. However, because the Orestanos were dressed as crew when they attacked you, they left their papers belowdecks. We have found them."

He held up two sets of documents that had been on his desk in front of him. They were colored a pale pink.

"The captain has decided you will both, for the time being, change your names to Orestano."

"I'm not doing any such—"

"Of course you are, Nino. Hear me out—you'll see how neatly it all fits in. In the first place, we can give you correct papers, which is saying a lot. In the second place, it means that the captain needs to account for only one missing person rather than three. One is normal on a voyage like this, but three would have needed some explanation. It also means the captain has to pay only ten dollars instead of thirty, no small thing."

Nino muttered under his breath. It sounded like the beginnings of an earthquake, but quickly died away.

"Now, I'm going to give these to you. Nino, you become Lorenzo Orestano—and Silvio, you become Livio Orestano. You stay that way for as long as it takes. However, there is a problem with these documents. The physical descriptions of the Orestanos don't fit you two. Lorenzo was heavier than you, Nino, and Livio was fairer than Silvio. Which is where I come in.

"Before we get to the main port of New Orleans, about two miles to the south, we come to quarantine. We're now just passing somewhere known as Eads Jetties, the southern tip of the Mississippi delta. That means we are a hundred miles from New Orleans. From here we take Southern Pass to the Head of Passes, where we reach the river proper."

"What's quarantine?" Nino growled belligerently.

Tolmezzo puffed at his cigar. "Quarantine is a form of hospital. We have to stop the ship, and an immigration officer and a doctor will come aboard. They tour the ship and can go anywhere they choose. If they see someone who looks ill, they haul them off the ship into quarantine, where that person remains until he or she recovers, or dies. It's a simple but effective way of ensuring that infectious diseases do not enter America.

"It is also my responsibility, as ship's doctor, to draw to the authorities' attention any of the passengers on board who I know are sick. We usually have one or more on a ship this size and this trip is not out of the ordinary in that sense, since one of our passengers, as I think I told Silvio, has developed typhus fever. Now, I propose giving you two a dose of a powder about two hours before we reach the quarantine station. The powder will make you feel feverish, with a high temperature, and you'll come out in a rash. It will also make you dehydrated, so you'll be thirsty. It's not very pleasant, but those are an approximation of the symptoms of typhus fever."

"What! I don't like the sound of this."

For once, Silvio agreed with Nino.

Tolmezzo batted away the cigar smoke that hung in the room. "The effects will last for only twelve hours. Enough to make sure that you are taken off the ship and put into a hospital, along with the man who really has the fever. I will tell the doctor who comes aboard that I have had you in isolation for three or four days, as I have the real patient, and no one will be able to contradict me. Your immigration papers will be visible, stuck in your pocket, so in these circumstances it's extremely unlikely that anyone will come near you during the inspection of the ship, and so no one will read your papers, to discover that you don't fit the description.

"You'll be taken ashore and placed in an isolation ward for a few days, during which time you'll make a steady recovery. Now listen to me carefully here because the quarantine hospital has very strong security, so if at any point anyone realizes you are faking your symptoms, you'll be in a pretty hopeless position. After a few hours ashore your temperature will come down again and the rash will fade. *However,* although you can do nothing about your body temperatures, I want you to pretend that you still feel feverish, weak, and thirsty. In actual cases of the disease, after several days the patient reaches what we call a 'crisis.' At that point, if he's going to recover he will fall into a gentle sleep, and wake up some hours later with the fever gone, but still very weak. Obviously you must keep faking the symptoms so that no one becomes suspicious, also so that very few people will come near you.

"As well as appearing dehydrated, and so forth, I also want you to be very tired, lethargic, in a stupor, sleeping all day." He smiled through the cigar smoke. "I don't imagine that will be very difficult. Again, if you sleep all day you will be behaving as if you are still ill, and no one will bother you."

He tapped some ash onto a metal tray on his desk. "All clear?"

Both Nino and Silvio nodded. Neither was exactly thrilled by what lay ahead.

"You will remain in isolation for perhaps ten to fourteen days, until you show signs of recovery. Then you will be examined a second time by immigration. They will insist on seeing your papers but, with luck, will still not risk coming too close to you.

"Now, here comes the clever part. There were three Orestanos who attacked you, which means we have a spare set of papers, those belonging to Onofri Orestano. The captain will say that Onofri died of typhus fever here on the *Syracusa*, and I shall agree with him. Onofri Orestano, we shall say, was buried at sea, and in view of the fact that he died of an infectious disease, all his belongings were buried with him. This will be accepted.

"Once the *Syracusa* reaches New Orleans proper, I shall contact one of our people there who will find someone—a friend—who fits the description of Onofri Orestano, as set out in his immigration documents. He will then come to visit you in quarantine. As I said, security is very tight, and only blood relatives are allowed to visit. The fact that the name on his papers is the same as yours will be enough.

"On his first visit, I want you both to be very lethargic, still weak. This will enable whoever we send to appear shocked at your appearance. This is important. He will remark, in a vague, not too obvious way, to the doctors and any immigration people who may be around, that you both look terrible, that you, Nino, have lost a lot of weight, and that you, Silvio, are still sickly looking. He will repeat this on a subsequent visit. With luck, this will mean that when you are judged to be recovering, and your papers are inspected more closely, if they *are* inspected closely, the authorities have been, so to speak, 'primed.' They will expect 'Lorenzo' to have lost weight and for 'Livio' to look sickly. Am I still making sense?"

Again both his listeners nodded.

"Good. We're almost through. You will be allowed to leave when you are clearly on the road to recovery and are without the symptoms of fever. You must remember to act as though you are genuine immigrants who came to America of your own accord and are looking forward to starting a new life here. Also, get your story straight. You are supposed to be brothers, so you have to know about each other—birthdays, nicknames, the sort of thing brothers would know about each other. The immigration people might just ask you questions to satisfy themselves that you are who you say you are. They have enormous powers.

"The man impersonating Onofri Orestano, whoever we choose, will come to the hospital every other day and, at some stage, will be allowed to take you away with him. And that's it. I gather everything is paid for, so all you have to do is remember how to act ill."

For the next twenty-four hours Silvio tried not to think about his forthcoming ordeal. When the powder was finally administered, the drug took about half an hour before starting to work, and

Silvio began to feel dreadful. Nino and he were taken to a cabin on the second deck that he had never noticed before. It had four bunks in it. At first Silvio sat on one of the lower bunks and stared out of the window. The *Syracusa* was now in the mouth of the Mississippi and he was having his first glimpse of America. It was very flat and sparse, except for the occasional wooden fort that went by. There was more life on the river itself—countless other ships passed them, causing the *Syracusa* to rise and fall in their wake and making Silvio feel even worse. Eventually he lay down on the bunk.

By now he was shivering one moment and sweating the next. His shirt was damp and clung to his shoulders. His body felt as if it were on fire, and his skin prickled and burned. He suffered in silence, but Nino let out a series of little grunts. It passed through Silvio's mind at one stage that, in fact, Tolmezzo had misled them, that the doctor was himself in the pay of the Orestanos and that he had poisoned them.

But then Silvio felt the vibration from the engines change as the *Syracusa* slowed. Soon it stopped altogether, and after a moment he heard voices. Some of the time the language was Italian, at others a tongue he didn't know—which he presumed was English. Then the light in the cabin darkened, as people—presumably immigration officers and the quarantine doctor—looked in through the window.

There was a short delay, and the cabin door opened. Tolmezzo appeared. "I have two stretchers for you here," he said quietly. "You are being taken ashore, to the quarantine hospital." This was all done for the benefit of the quarantine doctor outside, on deck.

The stretchers were carried ashore, where the sailors handed them across to four men whom Silvio presumed to be nurses. Nino and he were taken into the building, a red-brick affair three stories high, with a slate roof. They were carried down long corridors painted pale green and eventually placed in a room with two beds and a window from where they could see the river. Then they were left alone. Fortunately there was no sign of the third passenger, the man who really had typhus fever.

For hours they lay there. At times Silvio slept. He was woken once by voices, a second time by a candle being brought in. A man who was presumably the doctor peered at them but didn't touch them. Then, in the middle of the night, when it was inky dark, he woke up and knew the worst was over. He had stopped shivering and was no longer exhausted. For the rest of the hours of darkness he lay thinking of Annunziata. He imagined her mouth closing over his penis the way Anna-Maria's had done two nights before. The sight of it, disappearing into her mouth as she cradled his testicles in her fingers, had fixed itself in his memory, as had the feeling of her tongue flickering around the edge of his foreskin. It was not only the pleasure, but the feeling that he was getting more out of the act than Anna-Maria was. She was giving him a gift, to mark his arrival in America, but she was also offering him a lure; she had saved this for their last night on the *Syracusa* to tempt him back for more, to ensure she saw him again.

He became aroused all over again as he thought about it. Despite the pleasure, he had been aware of a certain danger. The act brought back a memory that, years ago, someone in the *bivio* had killed himself by putting a gun in his mouth and—

Anna-Maria must have known what he was thinking, for she had broken off what she was doing and murmured, "Don't worry. I won't bite."

Annunziata had a more beautiful mouth than Anna-Maria. Her lips turned out more, the color of almond shells rather than almonds proper. Her jawline was more marked.

He tried imagining what her mouth would be like wide open, how it would change their relationship once she had done it. Anna-Maria had spewed his semen into the palm of her hand and massaged his testicles. "Now lick me," she had said.

She was right. He was growing to like her coarseness in the bedroom. Would Annunziata ever be the same?

If they made it safely into New Orleans, how soon could he send for her?

The next day was the beginning of the dangerous phase. Both Silvio and Nino were back to normal but they had to pretend they were still seriously ill. Lying on his bed, day after day, when he wasn't tired, was harder than Silvio had expected. Sounds came from outside the hospital, sounds of activity from the river, sounds in the corridor outside their room. Voices in that strange tongue that he knew must be English.

Whenever they were visited by the doctor or a nurse, Silvio, who practiced his shivering during the interminable hours when they were alone, would put on what he hoped was a convincing display. Nino would resume his groaning.

One day they were visited by someone else, a dark-haired, sallow-skinned man, who accompanied one of the nurses. Silvio, like Nino, lay on his bed trying to understand the English until this new man said, in Italian, "Lorenzo, it's me, Onofri, don't you recognize me? You look terrible. How are you feeling? Do you need anything?"

Nino groaned, then muttered, in case anyone else spoke Italian, "Onofri, thank you for coming. Water."

Water was brought and the man calling himself Onofri said, "I'm sorry you're still so poorly, Renzo. Maybe you'll be over the worst soon. I'll come again tomorrow. Bye, Livio."

That night Silvio and Nino decided it was time they should appear to have reached the crisis point in their fever. The next morning they started to show some improvement. When they received visits from the nurses, they felt it was safe to ask for proper food. That had been a problem: both of them had felt ravenously hungry, but because they were not supposed to have an appetite, they had been given only sips of liquid nourishment. Consequently both were genuinely weak.

"Onofri" visited them every other day. When they had been in quarantine for nine days, he translated something the nurse had said in English. "The immigration people are coming tomorrow. If you're cleared I can collect you the day after." He didn't say anything else. As Tolmezzo had pointed out, it was possible that one or more of the nurses understood Italian.

That night they lay quietly on their beds, going through the details of their lives as "brothers." They had decided to invent as little as possible. Given their age difference, they had to be half brothers, but with the same father, so they had the same name. They went over birthdays, the way their father had been widowed, their local church, where they bought their guns, the illnesses they'd had as children, why one of Nino's teeth was missing, when they had stopped sharing a bedroom at home, and much, much else. They had fallen asleep rehearsing their performances.

When the immigration officers arrived, Silvio was surprised to find that their first act was to move him out of the room he shared with Nino. One officer led him to another room down the corridor that was similar to the room he had just left, except that it contained chairs rather than beds.

The immigration officer had another man with him, who suddenly said, in Italian, "Leave your documents just inside the door. Then go and sit at the far end of the room." This man was clearly the interpreter.

Silvio did as he was told. He was then left for about half an hour, alone. He guessed they were asking Nino questions and would then come and ask him the same questions, to see whether the answers of the "brothers" matched. This was the crunch.

After a while he heard footsteps approaching. Then the two figures reappeared. The immigration officer, wearing gloves, held the immigration documents. He sat down and read what was written. For a few moments he scanned the details, every so often looking up at Silvio to check what was written. It was unnerving.

At length he said something. The translator spoke. "The document says you are fair-skinned. You are not fair."

Silvio had anticipated this question and had his answer ready. "Have you ever suffered typhus fever? That document also says I weigh two hundred pounds. I don't expect I weigh that now."

The interpreter spoke to the immigration officer.

A short silence.

Then: "What is the name of your father?"

Silvio began to sweat. The fact that they were asking these questions meant they were suspicious. Had they been tipped off? If he and Nino failed today, they would be put back on the *Syracusa* and be in Palermo by the end of the month.

At least he could answer this question. It was part of the routine he had worked out with Nino.

"Ignazio."

"When is your brother's birthday?"

That was easy, too. "March the second, 1852."

"Does he have a nickname?"

"Not really. I think my parents called him 'Zozo' as a baby, but now it's just Renzo."

Another short silence.

"What work did you do in Sicily?"

They had thought about this, too. "I spent some time in the orchards near Bagheria, picking oranges and almonds. But there was not enough work to employ everyone. That is why I—we— came to America."

Then: "You have a bad scar on your right arm. It is not mentioned in the documentation and is clearly new. What caused the injury?"

Christ! This was something they hadn't thought about. And such an obvious question, too! What was he to answer? He couldn't say he was wounded in a fight on the ship. His brain reeled. He couldn't take too long about his answer either. What would Nino say if they asked him? Had Nino already been asked? Silvio had to think quickly, but he had to think systematically also. Nino would not tell the real story, of course, or anything like it. He would say that the injury had occurred before they boarded the *Syracusa*. They were supposed to be brothers and they were supposed to be orchard workers—yes, that was it! The orchard. There was an orange orchard near Bivio Indisi. But how would he have injured his arm? The oranges were picked by hand and the greatest danger lay in falling off the ladders.

The immigration officer was looking at him. Silvio must answer. He'd have to risk it.

"I fell off a ladder picking oranges. I caught my arm on the ladder as I fell. No one was there to help me at the time."

There was an exchange between the officer and the interpreter. Then the interpreter looked back at Silvio. "Your brother said it was an almond tree you fell from."

Silvio had the sense not to get flustered by this slight discrepancy but to make light of it. "My brother wasn't there. I told you, I was on my own. We have orange orchards and almond orchards everywhere in Sicily. Obviously Renzo thought it was almonds, but he's wrong, it was oranges."

Another exchange between the interpreter and the officer. Silvio tried to appear unconcerned but his heart was thumping away inside his rib cage, like a bird flapping its wings. He brushed his good hand through his hair as a way of covering his face.

A moment later the immigration officer stood up and placed Silvio's pink document on the chair where he had been sitting. The interpreter stood also. "As soon as the doctors say you can be discharged medically, you are free to go. Wait here a moment."

Silvio nodded, not daring to speak. Thank God they hadn't noticed the scar on his head! They hadn't come close enough. He remained seated as they went out. He listened as their footsteps retreated down the corridor. He was in America!

8

Harriet Livesey put down her teacup and pointed to the Lawrence portrait on the wall. "I wanted to pay the ransom. It would have meant losing that picture. But the solicitors wouldn't hear of it. Once the matter had been raised in the Commons—well, my hands were tied."

It was Henry Livesey's first morning back in England and he and his sister were enjoying breakfast together in Cadogan Gardens, as she had always promised herself they would.

Livesey had a bandage around his head, and there was a slight bloodstain seeping through. For the first time in months he was eating his favorite breakfast, kidneys and bacon.

Harriet helped herself to the toast. "I had a letter from the Queen, you know. Offering her condolences. Most kind."

Henry nodded. "The prime minister told me."

Livesey had reached London the day before, when he had received a summons from Disraeli, who wished to see him at Downing Street. After that, Livesey had dined at his club, so this was the first real conversation he had had with his sister.

"What else did Disraeli say?"

"I think he mainly wanted to see how I had coped with the kidnap. He was anxious to let me know that the Italian government had acted only after he had goaded them into it. What he did say, though, was that he had heard from the Italians that Greco—the Quarryman—has left Sicily. After the ambush, when all those soldiers were killed, and Greco rescued, the regiment of the Lazio Brigade was reinforced. The government in Rome was livid that their forces had been belittled by a bunch of bandits and sent a second regiment to support the first. It would have been only a matter of time before Greco was caught again. According to Disraeli, the Italians think he has gone to America."

Harriet pushed the toast rack toward her brother. "When are you seeing the doctor?"

"Noon."

"And afterward . . . would you like a holiday, Henry? It's been such an ordeal. I thought maybe Scotland. Glenesk, perhaps—"

"No!" Livesey was vehement, and for a moment Harriet was taken aback.

"I'm sorry, my dear. I didn't mean to shout. But no, no holiday." He set down his knife and fork. "You don't . . ." He started again. "You don't realize how this . . . ordeal, as you put it, has affected me. I can't relax now, or not yet anyway. There would be no point in going to Scotland, given the way I feel. I'd be on edge, and that would make me foul company. I can't just forget what's happened to me. No amount of pretty scenery can erase the past weeks and months. Parts of Sicily are very beautiful, but that sort of beauty is marred for me, perhaps forever."

"Henry, no!"

"Unless, *unless* . . ." He raised his voice. "Unless I can do something about Greco." He picked up his fork and stabbed at the remainder of his bacon. "I intend to see the Italian ambassador in London. I've a few ideas about how I might go about finding Signor Greco." He waved his fork at his sister. "He may have forgotten this whole episode, but I haven't."

Never in a million years would Silvio have imagined his first proper vision of America. He had anticipated seeing a low coastline, some exotic trees perhaps, strange animals, or some unusual buildings indicative of the new world. Much to his surprise, on the day after their interview with the immigration official, he and Nino were led by 'Onofri Orestano' north, away from the quarantine hospital along a mound of earth topped with oyster shells. This was called a levee, and it took them toward the New Orleans docks. "When it rains," said 'Onofri,' "the top of the levee never gets muddy. When we reach the city, you'll see that the same can't be said for the streets."

All the rivers in Sicily were in deep gorges, and dry for much of the year. The Mississippi could not have been more different. Here it must have been more than a quarter mile wide. It was deep and fast-running, gushing millions of gallons of brown water down to the sea every minute. The levee itself stood way above not only the river but the flat countryside. As he looked Silvio grasped the central fact about New Orleans: the city was *below* river level! That's what the levee was there for—to keep the river in its place. Amazing.

"Stop here a moment," said 'Onofri,' reaching a bench on the levee. "I'll point out the main areas of town in a second, but first a few home truths." The man held out his hand. "I am no more Onofri Orestano than I am the Pope, as you both know. My real name is Francisco Faldetta. I specialize in welcoming the more . . . unusual immigrants to America."

They all shook hands. Then Francisco turned and gestured toward the city. "That's New Orleans. Straight ahead are the docks—see the wharves and warehouses, and the masts and smokestacks of the steamers? Beyond that, with the red roof, is the French Market—fruit, clothes, coffee, meat, oysters. Behind the market is the French Quarter. That's where everything happens. I'll be taking you there, soon as we reach the docks. And that," he said, sweeping his arm even farther left, "is the Garden District, where the rich people live."

An hour later they were in the middle of the docks watching the bales of cotton and barrels of oranges being unloaded. The docks were built into the levee hereabouts, and on leaving the wharves, Francisco, Silvio, and Nino were forced to climb *up* the levee. When they reached the top they could look down on the other side, where the city was spread out below them.

Immediately in front, as straight as a ruler, was a wide road, with rails down the middle and horses pulling carts.

"Canal Street," said Francisco. "There used to be a canal there but they filled it in. New Orleans is wedged between the Mississippi and a big lake, Lake Pontchartrain. Lots of canals link the two waterways so the fruit can be moved quickly. Fruit and cotton transportation are the main businesses here. Fruit comes in. Cotton goes out. Fruit goes rotten quickly, so it has to be shifted fast. The labor gangs on the wharves are well organized."

He led the way down the levee. The crowds were as bad as in Palermo.

"What are these rails for?" Silvio asked.

"For the streetcars. You want to go from one part of the city to another, and you don't want to walk or get wet, you pay a penny and take the streetcar. When it rains, or the river floods, the roads get very muddy. But not the rails. The horses can pull them even when the mud is ankle-deep." He laughed. "As it often is."

They walked up Canal Street, away from the river. Silvio was struck by the mass of wires everywhere.

"Telephones," said Francisco. "The coming thing. You talk into a tube, your voice goes along a wire and comes out the other end, maybe miles away. Eerie."

Most of the buildings were three or four stories high, Silvio noticed, and built of wood or brick. He had imagined New Orleans would be more like Palermo, with stone-and-marble palaces. The pavements were covered with balconies in many cases, making the shops and bars they were passing dingy and dark. But there was an astonishing variety of shops. Werlein pianofortes, Eadows wallpapers, Gay and Le Fanu's furniture, Stevens firearms: Francisco read them out, and translated.

"Okay, we turn right here," he added. "Basin Street. You'll see that at the end of this street there's a huge basin, a sort of inland harbor where the Girondelet Canal ends and the barges are moored. This canal goes to Lake Pontchartrain."

"Is this the center of town?" asked Silvio. "Is there no church?"

"Yes, it's the center, and there *is* a cathedral, closer to the river, on Chartres and St. Peter's Street. It's called St. Louis's."

"Why is it called the French Quarter?"

"Shut up, Silvio," hissed Nino. "Fucking questions."

"No, that's okay," said Francisco. "New Orleans is a strange place. We go down here, Bienville Street." He turned back to Silvio. "First it was conquered by the French. Then the Spanish took it but the French snatched it back. The Americans bought it from the French in 1803. Something known as the Louisiana Purchase. Anyway, this part of town still seems French. French names for streets, the French Market, people speaking French, French buildings—look." He pointed forward to where a house with a wrought-iron balcony, painted in green, stood out over the pavement. Silvio could see other, similar balconies repeated farther down the street.

Just then they heard a piano playing. They stopped to listen.

"Welcome to the *vieux carré*," said Francisco. "That's French for the 'old quarter.' This is why the streets are crowded. This is why New Orleans is the second biggest city in America, after New York. The river brings the fruit and cotton, the fruit and cotton bring in a lot of money. The French Quarter helps people spend what they earn. You can't count the bars and brothels, the restaurants and gambling joints, the fortune-tellers and cornet bands. It's a wild town."

"What are they, cornet bands?" Silvio liked the sound, loud, and the rhythms, very fast.

"There's a new kind of music here. Small brass bands, sometimes with piano or drums. Negro bands, white bands, quadroon bands."

Silvio remembered that Anna-Maria had talked about a new music in New Orleans. But something still puzzled him. "What's a quadroon?"

"Come *on*," hissed Nino. "For fuck's sake."

"One more block," said Francisco. "Then we're home." They crossed Conti Street and, after another fifty yards or so, turned into a little alley. A door off the alley led to a small garden. Across the garden they climbed an outside staircase to a balcony, where a middle-aged woman was watching them. She had black hair and wore a long black dress.

"Tomassina," said Francisco, "don't just stand there. Some wine for our guests . . . Don't worry," he said, turning to Nino and Silvio. "Tomassina knows who you are, and you aren't her favorite persons. But she'll get used to it. I'm being paid for this. Please sit." He indicated a table on the balcony. They sat down.

Tomassina brought a jug and some glasses, and chunks of bread with sliced tomatoes on them, doused in olive oil. It was very welcome.

"You can stay here," Francisco said. "In my sister's room. She'll sleep with Tomassina, and I'll sleep in the living room. For two weeks. But by then you'll have seen Angelo Priola."

Nino looked at Silvio, but spoke to Francisco. "How soon can he call on Anna-Maria?"

"You know Anna-Maria?"

"He fucked her on the boat over."

Silvio reddened.

"Then I hope Priola never finds out, Nino. For his sake."

Nino grinned. "Fathers don't like their daughters being messed with, do they?" He looked Silvio straight in the eye.

Silvio glared back.

Nino turned to Francisco. "Anna-Maria seems to have fallen for him. She invited him to call on her and said she'd help with her father. What should we do? Where do they live?"

"On Chestnut Street, in the Garden District. Nice house. I suggest that, in the first place, Silvio call on Anna-Maria when we know her father isn't home. If he is, and spots you, he's liable to turn ugly. He's only got the one child, so you can imagine how precious she is to him."

"How can we tell when Priola isn't at home?"

"Not too difficult. I know for a fact he'll be at Mattie Marshall's tomorrow, between four and seven. That's a whorehouse he has a stake in, on CustomHouse Street. There's a big poker game there every Tuesday, and Angelo Priola always plays. You can wait for him outside Mattie's, watch him go in, then know you've got three hours of safety."

"What about the mother?"

"Drinks. By four she'll be in her room with a mint julep and deaf to the world."

"Why does she drink?"

Francisco looked surprised, then nodded. "Of course, you've never met Priola. I tell you, Nino, if you were married to him you'd drink, too. He's like one of those bantam fighting cocks they have in Palermo. Small, stringy, immaculately turned out. But he knows how to draw blood."

That night Francisco took them on a tour of the *vieux carré*. Silvio had seen nothing like it in his life, and even Nino, who prided himself on being hard to impress, was astounded.

By evening, they were no longer Nino Greco and Silvio Randazzo. They had discussed changing their names on the *Syracusa* but not done anything about it.

Francisco insisted, however. "You must learn English in America," he told them as they were enjoying another glass of wine before they left the house. "Learn English but pretend to speak it badly. Then the Americans will underestimate you. It's good advice. Also, Nino, you were not exactly a nobody in Sicily. I heard what happened. You must change your name."

And so Nino became Nino Grado, and Silvio was Sylvano Razzini.

They started that night at Annie Merritt's, on CustomHouse Street, then took in Fanny Decker's, a few doors away, Madge Leigh's, where there was dancing, then Mattie Marshall's, ending up at Lulu White's octoroon house, known as Mahogany Hall, on North Basin Street. Most of these were three-dollar houses, save for Lulu White's, which, with its cut-glass chandeliers and wood paneling, was a five-dollar house.

They each took a woman at Annie's and again at Lulu's to end the evening. Silvio had no idea where the money was coming from but didn't care. In between women, they drank and listened to some of the new cornet bands, Sylvester Conant at Fanny's, Professor Bonfant at Madge Leigh's, the Tio Brothers at Mattie's.

Finally, Francisco took them to the most unusual place of all. This was on Bourbon Street, which led off CustomHouse Street, and it was called the Old Absinthe House. The chief feature of this bar was a long line of glasses, some with green liquid in them, some with yellow.

"What's this?" muttered Nino suspiciously.

"This is the greatest drink in the world. Absinthe."

"What is it?"

"It's made from wormwood. Same base as goes in vermouth." Nino looked at him.

"It's a plant. Medicine. But it also turns out absinthe."

"Is that French, too?"

"Swiss. Swiss French."

Silvio stared at the line of glasses. Above each was a tap, part of a long pipe that ran the length of the bar. Water dripped—very slowly—from the taps, the drops falling into the glasses.

"Neat absinthe is green," said Francisco. "You add water slowly, so the drops 'kiss' the absinthe, and it turns yellow. Then it's ready to drink." He took one and handed it to Nino. He passed a second to Silvio.

"Be careful how you drink it," he said. "It's addictive. But in small amounts it makes all your troubles fade away. Beautiful." He took a glass for himself and raised it high. "To Nino and Silvio." He sipped the yellow liquid. "Welcome to America . . . and good riddance to Sicily."

Silvio lay in bed in the Faldetta house and listened to the early-morning noises of New Orleans. He couldn't sleep and all the drinks of the evening before had dehydrated him. He needed water. He got up and tiptoed out onto the balcony. He remembered where the kitchen was. The jugs were all empty, but he found an orange and, picking it up, began to peel. He went back to the balcony and sat on a bench. When they had been children, Annunziata and he had often competed to see who could unpeel an orange first, making sure the skin came away in only one piece.

He divided the orange into segments. As he slid one into his mouth he again found himself thinking of Zata's parted lips. He could still remember the moment when he stopped thinking of her as a girl. They had been looking after some younger children, and playing a game, which involved hiding. They had sneaked into a church and, when the younger children almost caught up with them, slipped into the confessional together, standing side by side, very close, remaining silent. He could remember Zata's familiar smell—straw, from the mattresses they slept on, the coarse soap they all used, the hint of the animals they shared the *bivio* with. He was a good bit taller than Zata by now, and that day, in the gloom, she was wearing a black dress with a V-neck. Standing close, he looked down to see the gently swelling slope of her breasts. She noticed him looking and whispered, "I know what you'll be confessing on Sunday, Toto."

Then a younger child had burst in on them and the spell had been broken.

But the following Sunday she had waited for him after Mass, and after confession. "Well?" she had asked as he came down the steps. "Did you confess?"

He shook his head. "It's not a sin to think."

"Yes, it is, Toto. I think about you that way, a lot."

He stopped and looked at her. "And did you tell Father Serravalle?"

"No. We're too alike, you and me, Toto. Father Serravalle would only spoil it."

"Spoil what?"

"Come to the olive press after dark tonight. I've got a cigarette. You can kiss me."

They had met as arranged. They had smoked the cigarette and Zata had shown him how to kiss with his mouth open. She had known more about such things then than he had, but now . . . now he had the experience. Finishing his orange, he listened to the hoot of a steamer casting off, the occasional whinny from a horse, the din of a band still playing in some far-off bar even at this hour. New Orleans was obviously more sophisticated even than Palermo, but he felt a long way from Sicily. If he had been in the *bivio* now, he could have gone down to the river, or cleaned some guns, or peeled some potatoes, or visited the traps, looking for rabbits. He was suddenly homesick.

But he couldn't go home. Nino and the Orestanos had seen to that. He had to get used to it here. He got up and walked back to bed. If he couldn't go back to the *bivio*, he'd have to bring the *bivio* to New Orleans. And that meant Zata.

"Father Livesey, I am most grateful that you could spare the time to come in today. I see that your head is healing. It's small consolation, I know, but at least there were no complications."

Henry Livesey shook hands with the Italian ambassador, Pasquale Falfani. The ambassador was a tall man, from Milan, and very elegant. He wore a pale linen suit and a wing collar, hardly a combination an Englishman would wear, but somehow he got away with it. The embassy was elegant, too, a huge house in Belgrave Square with the ambassador's office on the first floor overlooking the gardens in the square itself. The room had deep crimson curtains and, if Livesey was not mistaken, a portrait of Garibaldi.

Livesey's letter to the ambassador had elicited a fast response. In fact, Falfani had written, he himself had been on the point of contacting Livesey. He had asked the Englishman to attend the embassy on this very day, for an introduction to someone of importance. So far, however, there were just the two of them in the room.

As Livesey thought this the door to the room was thrown open and another man was shown in. He was a tall, red-faced individual, bald but with a ring of gray hair around his head. The ambassador and the new man shook hands, then Falfani turned to Henry. "Father Livesey, I would like to introduce you to Mr. William Pinkerton."

"Pleased to know you, Father," said Pinkerton, shaking hands. Livesey was surprised to note that the man's accent was American.

The three men sat down. After coffee had been served by an assistant, the ambassador began. "Father, Mr. Pinkerton is the son of Allan Pinkerton, who, as you may know, is a Scot who emigrated to America and founded the famous private detective agency. The Pinkertons and the Italian government have agreed to cooperate in a secret investigation which will, I can say, be close to your heart. We have received information that Nino Greco—the Quarryman—has escaped Sicily and fled to America."

Livesey set down his coffee cup. "Yes, I'd heard."

"I'm afraid the information is no more precise than that." The ambassador smiled ruefully. "These south Italian mafiosi have their own misplaced code of honor and a law of silence, which prevents them from talking to the proper authorities. So, although I am certain that our information is correct, I have no details as to how Greco entered America or where exactly he is.

"In any case, the Italian government has retained the Pinkerton Detective Agency to help trace Greco, and if and when we find him, we intend to arrest him. This, of course, is where you come in. Naturally, there are no photographs of Greco—they hardly have such inventions as the camera in the wilds of Sicily—but you do have a likeness of him, a good likeness by all accounts.

"Now, Mr. Pinkerton has been in London on other business but returns to Chicago—his firm's headquarters—in three days' time. What we would both like to know is whether you would be willing to spare your drawing of Greco so that Pinkerton may have it in America. Greco's exploits in Sicily were so notorious that we feel he must surely have changed his name. But he cannot change his appearance, not by much, anyway. If Pinkerton should come across him, or someone they think is him, it would help enormously to have a good likeness, to make sure we have the right man."

"We have agents in all the main American cities," said Pinkerton. "We're in touch with them all by telegram. We can act very quickly—"

"There's no need to go on," interjected Livesey. "The man humiliated and mutilated me! In a cupboard at home, not a mile from here, I have the remains of my own scalp and a drawing of the man who cut it off. I can't go near that cupboard but I can't throw those things away, either. I just can't bring myself to do that." He looked distraught. "I'm a priest, a Catholic priest. I know the Bible backward. As a Christian, I'm not supposed to think about revenge, an eye for an eye and all that. Let me tell you:

I can think of little else. I can't turn the other cheek. I *refuse* to. Maybe I'm not suited to the priesthood, but oh yes, I want revenge. I want revenge so badly I can taste it. I want Greco to suffer like I suffered. I want him humiliated like I was.

"So yes, ambassador, you may have your drawing."

The Priola house was made of wood, on two stories, and at first-floor level a balcony went all around the house. The balcony was carved with a delicate tracery and the woodwork was painted a brilliant white. Baskets of flowers hung from the exposed beams that supported the roof, the baskets alternating with lanterns. The garden, whose main feature was an enormous eucalyptus tree, was lush almost beyond belief, with succulent greenery everywhere and the sound of water flowing. It was surrounded by a high wall into which were let a pair of wrought-iron gates where Silvio now stood. He pulled a knob that, somewhere between the gates and the house, sounded a bell.

Silvio had been dispatched to Anna-Maria in a taxicab, paid for by Nino. But from here on he was on his own.

A Negro appeared from the front door of the house. He had close-cropped silver-gray hair and a slight stoop. He was wearing a gray apron. He walked up to the gate but didn't open it. "Ye-e-e-s?"

Silvio took out the card, the view of the Church of the Annunciation, which Anna-Maria had given him on the *Syracusa*. This was the tricky part. He had been coached in what to say, in English, by Francisco. "Please give Anna-Maria card. Here is Silvio."

The black man did not immediately accept the proffered card. "You know Miss Priola?"

Silvio didn't understand what was being said, but smiled anyway.

"Do you speak English?" the Negro asked.

Silvio smiled again. "Anna-Maria, please." He pushed the card through the gate railings.

Just then Anna-Maria herself appeared on the balcony, at the side of the house.

"Anna-Maria!" Silvio called out. "Anna-Maria." He waved the card.

She looked startled, then recognized him and waved. She

turned and headed for the stairs, stopped, and shouted something down to the Negro, something in English, Silvio guessed. The Negro opened the gates and Silvio stepped inside.

In no time, Anna-Maria appeared through the front door on the ground floor and walked quickly toward him. Now she said something else to the Negro and he headed off, back into the house.

Instead of kissing Silvio, as he half expected, Anna-Maria put her finger to her lips, gesturing him to be silent. Then she beckoned him to follow her deeper into the garden. They walked past some lush green bushes with orange flowers, a couple of miniature palms—he'd seen those before, in Sicily—and suddenly they were in a little clearing with a stone bench.

"Banff will bring us some lemonade," said Anna-Maria. "Father is away, playing poker in the French Quarter, but some of his men are in the house, for a meeting tonight. It's better we talk out here."

Just then the Negro reappeared with a jug and two glasses, and Anna-Maria waited while he set them on the bench. She said a few more words in English to him, and he again disappeared. She poured the liquid and offered a glass to Silvio.

He took it and drank it. It wasn't champagne. It was very sweet.

"So, you made it. You are in America."

He smiled. She was wearing a white dress and had her hair up, tied by a white ribbon. She looked less Italian, somehow. Her skin and lips shone. Briefly he described what had happened since she had last seen him, dwelling only on the fact that he had thought a great deal about her; he did not say he'd thought only about her body.

She laughed. "That was good," she said. "One of the best I've heard. You hear all sorts of stories in New Orleans, about how people come in, hidden in barrels of salt, or in crates of fish, or rolled up in carpets. But it was clever to have yourself put in quarantine. My father will like that."

"That's one reason I've come, Anna-Maria." He had thought carefully about this exchange, and decided it would not do to say he had come *only* in connection with her father. "Maybe you and I could go dancing—I saw a wonderful dance place last night. And you did say your father might be able to help Nino and me." He explained about the name change.

"Where are you staying?"

He told her.

"Was this dance hall near there?"

He nodded.

"You mean Madge Leigh's. That's a whorehouse. I'm not allowed there."

He raised his eyebrows and she laughed. "Just because I'm not allowed doesn't mean I don't go! My, you've a lot to learn—about life in general and New Orleans in particular. Have some more lemonade." She held out the jug.

Then she grew more serious. "I've already mentioned you to my father."

"You have?"

"Yes, but don't get excited. I mentioned in passing that the great mafioso, Nino Greco, was aboard my ship, traveling incognito, with one of his lieutenants."

Sono tenente? Silvio asked himself. He supposed he was. "And?"

"He just nodded. But nothing escapes my father. My problem is that I have to think of a way to bring you up in the conversation. I can't say you came here this afternoon. He'd go mad if he thought you and I had . . . you know. You certainly wouldn't get a job then. In fact, you'd probably have your balls cut off."

Silvio felt an urge to leave, as quickly as possible.

"What I need to do is mention Nino again, in such a way that it gives Father an idea, and then he thinks it was *his* idea."

Silvio smiled.

"This is what we'll do," she said, appearing to make up her mind. "I'll think of something to tell Father when he comes home this evening. Later people are coming for dinner, and cards—my father loves cards. Around ten, I shall say I'm going to bed. Half an hour later I shall be able to slip out. It will take me another half hour to get to Madge Leigh's. I'll meet you there at eleven."

He nodded, finished his lemonade, and made to move. He definitely didn't want to be here when Angelo Priola arrived home.

"One thing," said Anna-Maria as he stood up. "If I do this for you, what are you going to do for me?"

He looked down at her. She was smiling.

Suddenly he laughed. "Don't worry," he said. "I went to Annie's last night, and Lulu's. There may be one or two things I can teach *you* now."

* * *

The two cornets blared out in unison. Underneath them the trombone pulsed a steady beat. Over and around them the piano swooped like one of the seagulls Silvio had seen following the *Syracusa*. This new music fascinated him. It was so brisk and he liked the strong rhythms. He longed to move his body in time to the beat.

The music was only one aspect of Madge Leigh's that held his attention. Everything, from the engraved mirrors at the back of the bar to Baptiste Moret, the fat Negro playing the piano, from the corsets worn by the girls to the oysters heaped on the bar counter, from the carnival masks that adorned the walls to the comings and goings of couples up and down the stairs . . . he was fascinated by all of it.

Then there was the drink. Silvio, who had drunk only local wine before leaving Sicily, had acquired a definite taste for champagne aboard the *Syracusa*. Here at Madge Leigh's he noticed that no one drank champagne, certainly not the men. There were a few wine drinkers, but most of the men drank either beer or something called rye whiskey, which, he understood, was made from a special kind of grain. He hated it, but had ordered one because everybody else did. It tasted like soap.

One of the girls came up to Silvio. She had creamy skin, black hair, and brown eyes. Brown lips. Close up, her face had freckles, like the marks on the trout in Lake Arancio. She said something in English. He just stared at her. She tried a second language, French perhaps. Silvio just stood and smiled, but she stormed off.

Francisco laughed. "You've got to learn English, Silvio. She called you handsome. Said this was a five-dollar house but you could have it for three. Can't afford to miss a chance like that. Incidentally, she's a quadroon—remember you were asking? Part European, part Negro. Great coloring, huh?"

Silvio blushed. But Francisco was right; the girl was beautiful, that skin especially.

He looked up at the clock near the bar. It was ten past eleven and Anna-Maria still hadn't turned up. He was growing edgy. If she didn't show, Nino would blame him. To take his mind off Anna-Maria he tried to concentrate on the dancing. It appeared that some of the women were paid for dancing with the men. That was new, too.

"There she is!" Nino pointed.

Anna-Maria, wearing a cape, was standing inside the main door, searching the room with her eyes. Silvio drew her attention by waving. She smiled and came toward them.

"Well—?" Nino started to say, but Silvio nudged him.

"There's no champagne here, but what else would you like? Bourbon?"

"Yes. Lovely." She looked around. "Ah! Bruno and Baptiste. Great band." She waved to the pianist, who waved back.

Silvio handed her a drink. He felt very nervous.

She drained it in one gulp. "Well," she gasped, catching her breath. "You're in luck. I overheard my father talking to his friends, or at least the people who work for him. He has trouble on the luggers' dock."

"What sort of trouble?" Nino, Silvio thought, was just a little too aggressive. He was a bit like one of those bantam cocks himself.

"The only kind there is. Exactly the same kind of trouble as in Palermo. My father has been running the labor gangs, the roustabouts who unload the fruit and oysters and load the cotton, but another family is trying to move in. Things are getting rough. Some tough action is called for. I heard Father listing the people he thought could do it. I mentioned your name." She looked at Nino. "I said you'd been on my boat, incognito, and that I'd also heard you made it safely into New Orleans. He told one of his employees, Teresio Alfatti, to go and look for you."

"Why didn't you say you were seeing us tonight?"

Anna-Maria shook her head. "I'm his daughter, *stupido!* I don't get involved in business. And in theory I'm not allowed in here." She pulled her cape around her. "Now, I had hoped to be able to stay a little longer, but if Alfatti is looking for you two, I don't want to be here when he arrives. My father would soon be told." She turned to Silvio. "Walk me to Canal Street. I can catch a cab there. It won't take long."

She led the way out to CustomHouse Street, walking as quickly as the crowds on the sidewalk would allow. Silvio eventually caught up. She spoke out of the corner of her mouth as they hurried along. "There's something I wanted to say, out of earshot of that *asino*."

"You mean Nino."

"Well, I don't mean Madge Leigh, do I?"

Silvio was silent.

"First, learn English. You'll never get anywhere in this country unless you do. You're stupid if you don't. The other thing is: Get out of Nino's shadow as soon as you can."

"What!"

She stopped on the sidewalk and turned to face him. "Silvio, you're now in New Orleans, the second city in the greatest and fastest-growing country in the world. You have a good brain but you haven't learned to use it yet. You've got to think for yourself. Once you do, with your looks, you could do almost anything." They moved on and came to the corner of CustomHouse and Dauphin streets and stepped off the sidewalk into the dust. They crossed the street and remounted the sidewalk. "Nino is a violent, unstable man. *Miope.* Shortsighted. Stay with him, and sooner or later, and very probably sooner, you will be in trouble. Or, more likely, dead."

They came to Canal Street. "I can get a taxi here," she said.

"When can I see you again?"

"In a few days, after what's going to happen has happened. I'll know where you are and will send for you. But remember what I said, Silvio. Learn English and dump Nino. Otherwise your life may be a short one."

"Francisco! Are you awake? Francisco." The voice called up in Italian to the balcony from the courtyard below. "Francisco Faldetta!"

Silvio, still in bed, looked at Nino. Nino gestured for him to keep quiet, at the same time finding the gun in his trousers, hung over a chair. "It could be the immigration department," he whispered. "They could be on to us."

They both watched as Francisco ambled to the balcony.

"Yes? What? It's early. Who are you?"

"It don't matter who I am, Francisco. Have you got two *malandrini* hidden up there, two Sicilian guests who came over recently on the *Syracusa*?"

Francisco turned his back on the other man. "You're crazy," he shouted over his shoulder. "Go back to the whore you slept with last night." It was a good performance.

"You see them, Francisco, tell them Angelo Priola wants to meet them. Tell them Angelo Priola has a job for them. Tell them

Angelo Priola thinks they are tough *malandrini* from Bivio Indisi. You and I know they are cowards, though, eh? They hide and whisper, like chickens when the fox is near. Tell them, Francisco. If you see them." He turned to leave.

"Stop!"

Nino stood on the balcony, in his underwear. "You are looking for me."

The other man grinned. "So. The Quarryman. Mr. Explosives. You don't look like dynamite to me. More like—"

"Say what you have to say, and go." Nino had shown the other man his gun. "This is no cock's blood."

The grinning stopped. The man stared at the revolver. "Noon today. The luggers' wharf. Priola will be in his office. It has a flag-pole with an American flag and, below it, an Italian flag." He turned away.

"Stop!"

The man turned back.

Nino rested his gun on the top of the balustrade. "I haven't dismissed you yet. What is your name?" The menace in his voice was unmistakable.

"Teresio Alfatti."

"Well, Alfatti, next time you run errands for Mr. Priola, do so with more courtesy. Is that clear?"

The other man said nothing.

Nino picked up the gun. Speaking very quietly, he repeated, "Is that clear?"

Still the other man didn't speak.

Nino cocked the gun and took aim.

"Yes."

"Yes? Yes what, you *mezzatacca*?"

"Yes . . . sir."

Nino put down the gun. Now he grinned. "See how easy it is to learn some manners?" He waved the man away.

Back in the bedroom, Silvio at last allowed himself to breathe again. He remembered the warning Anna-Maria had given him the night before.

Silvio stood on the corner of Basin and Canal streets and enjoyed the rain. He had never seen clouds so low as they appeared just now, almost within reach. He marveled yet again at those fine balconies on so many of the buildings. Not only did they look good, they afforded shade when it was sunny—and were now offering dry shelter when it rained.

It was a quarter of an hour before midday and Silvio was waiting for Nino, who was getting a shave and haircut. Despite his tough talk and general lack of manners, Nino was sprucing himself up for this meeting with Angelo Priola. He had even bought a clean shirt.

Silvio, no less than Nino, was intrigued about meeting Priola. Everybody seemed frightened of him, even Anna-Maria, who, on the *Syracusa*, had seemed without fear.

Nino came out of the barber's shop. He stopped on the sidewalk and lit a thin cigar. With a clean shirt and tidy hair, he seemed quite transformed. He turned into Canal Street and set off for the docks, dashing from balcony to balcony, to avoid getting soaked. Silvio ran after him.

The rain made no difference to the activity at the docks. The loaders, ships' crew, and immigration people all wore coveralls, and some had large floppy hats. Silvio counted two passenger liners, seven fruit vessels, and fifteen steamboats. The area of the dock opposite the end of Canal Street was known as Picayune Pier, but in general the piers did not have numbers or names, since few of the stevedores—the roustabouts—could read. Instead, all locations had a sign taken from a deck of playing cards. Everyone knew what the queen of spades or the jack of diamonds looked like.

Nino and Silvio climbed the levee near Picayune Pier and looked down. Nearby, a large white ship with a yellow-and-red flag was unloading melons, pale green. The rain lashed down now and a mist had settled in. The far bank of the river, a quarter of a mile off, was almost obscured from view.

Nino and Silvio made their way past several gangs of roustabouts unloading oranges and bananas. Sure enough, at the near end of a pier marked with a jack of clubs, there was a small flagpole, near the top of which flew the American flag. Just beneath it was the green, white, and red tricolor of Italy. Through the rain they suddenly heard the noonday "gun." This, Francisco had told them, had been a real gun many years ago; now it was a steam hooter farther upstream.

Nino ran down the levee. Silvio followed.

A man in a large overcoat and a wide-brimmed hat was standing outside the door to the office. Nino announced himself, and the man, after frisking them, stood to one side. They were expected.

Inside was a room with three desks and a small gate that led to an area with a much larger desk. Two men were there, one seated at the large desk, the other looking out of the window at the rain and the river. The man standing was about thirty, thin, with a sallow skin. He had receding hair and high cheekbones and wore a suit and a stiff collar. The other man was older, thicker set, with a full head of dark hair and a bushy mustache. He wore a frock coat, which showed off his cuffs to advantage, and expensive-looking boots. His fingers were curled around a cigar.

"Sicily could use some of this rain, huh?" he said by way of greeting. "I'll bet you're missing the smell of olives, figs, the sound of bells, the taste of fettuccine." He smiled. For some reason his voice made Silvio think of chocolate. "I'm Angelo Priola. This is Giovanni Nogare."

They all shook hands.

They sat down and Priola fiddled in the drawer of the desk he was sitting at. He took out a bottle and some glasses. "Whiskey?"

The others nodded.

He poured and they drank. Priola wiped his mouth.

"Tell me, Nino, how is Ruggiero? Still boxing, eh? Still chasing everyone else's wife?" He grinned. "And Calogero's? Some restaurant! Is their tagliatelle still the best in Sicily? I remember it, I really do, even after all these years."

"Still the best," replied Nino, smiling back. "Ruggiero spends more time there now than chasing women." He tapped his stomach. "He's putting on weight." He paused. "How long you been here, Angelo? Ten years? Twelve?"

"More! A lot more. I came over in 'sixty-four, on the *Rometta*. What a hellhole she was. I was thirty-five. Fifteen years it has taken me to build this business, and now they are trying to take it away. Like the cholera, they suddenly show up on my territory. *Mine!* Before you know it, the disease is everywhere." He glanced briefly at Silvio, then back at Nino, and refilled their glasses. "Tell me, Nino, how many people you killed?"

"Enough." Nino swallowed the whiskey.

Priola looked at him hard, all the while drawing on his cigar.

At length, he went on. "Nino, I have a problem. You can help, maybe. Until now New Orleans has been a quiet town. We Sicilians have controlled the fruit trade, and the oyster trade, and that has given us a strength here. I got nine ships at the moment. Two liners, sailing mainly between Sicily and America, and seven other ships, importing fruit, some from Italy, more from South America. The *Syracusa* is one of them.

"People, with one or two exceptions"—here he smiled—"are not a problem. Nearly all have papers and they unload themselves. The liners bring people to America and take cotton back. It works. Fruit, my friends, is different. Fruit is delicate, fruit is fragile, it begins to decay the minute it is picked. That is the opportunity and the problem. People like fresh fruit, the fresher the better. The fact that it goes bad so quickly means that it's pricey, and that demand continues—you can't store it or lock it away to be eaten later on.

"It also means fruit has to be moved quickly at all stages of its journey. And that means the business is wide open to sabotage. Someone takes it into his head to interrupt the flow, that soon gets expensive for us. For me."

"And someone is doing just that?"

Nodding, Priola drained his whiskey glass, wiped his mouth again. "Until now, I've had control of the labor gangs who unload the ships, the roustabouts, and we've had years of peace. They get a wage I can afford, and if anyone else tries to import fruit, either they accept my gangs and pay me a small commission or their ships don't get unloaded and their fruit rots on the dock. It's as simple as that. It suits everyone. It keeps Sicilians in work—and let me tell you nearly all the Italian immigrants in New Orleans are Sicilians. Also, with the money I'm making I'm beginning to have some political clout in this town. So—better prospects for all Sicilians."

"But . . . ?"

"But, as you say, someone is trying to change all that. Someone is trying to take me on."

"Who?"

"I'll get to that. I want you to have the full picture so you know what the job entails. The trouble began on the piers upriver from Canal Street, when a few Sicilians from near Solunto moved in, one at a time. Eventually they formed a group, large enough to intimidate the other labor gangs on those piers. Their first move was not to pass on the commission I was due for the unloading of another company's ship. We're not talking big money, but it was an important change, and pretty soon the entire docks knew about it."

He helped himself to more whiskey. "The next move was the murder of my foreman. Officially he fell into the river late one night after a few drinks, but I saw the body and he must have been drinking with a broken glass, because his throat was cut. Garroted. As a result of that, all the other gangs in that part of the docks threw in with this new group. Now they had complete control of the area upriver from Canal Street, and they refused to unload my ships. Word got around, and now the other fruit importers are unloading their fruit upriver, paying a commission to the new group and lifting their hind legs on me. My reputation and my income have been hit, hit bad."

"But you've still got the area downriver of Canal Street?"

Priola nodded. "But last week there was a fire in one of the warehouses on Old Levee Street. Arson. A lot of cotton went up and one of our night watchmen was roasted to death. Couldn't get out of his office."

This time Nino said nothing. Priola poured more whiskey, though Silvio hadn't finished his second glass yet.

"As I keep saying, we've had peace in New Orleans for years. I'm not a violent man. I'm a businessman. *Ma non sono lombrico!* But I can't stand by and watch these *malandrini* take it all from me. These Soluntese need to be hit, Nino, and hit good. I want my piers back. I've helped create this goddamn town and I'm not having it stolen from under me now. I need a spectacular job here, and soon. Something cunning. The fox eats while the wolf howls, eh? I don't care who you have to hit, or how many, but I want those labor gangs back in line and the other fruit companies in my pocket."

"And if I do this?"

Priola drank more whiskey and again wiped his mouth. "Whatever. I'll give you your own ship, if you like. Or a half share in one of the whorehouses in the French Quarter. Madge Leigh's or Sally Levy's. You'll have all the money, all the girls, all the booze you could want. And respect."

"Would I be number two to you?"

Priola looked at Nogare, then back to Nino. "Not yet, Nino. If we were back home, Giovanni would be my *consigliere*. You know what they say in Sicily: greed swells the belly but narrows the mind. I'm a generous man, I will reward you well. But let's take our problems one step at a time."

Nino was silent, and Silvio thought he was about to get moody. But all he said was: "I'll need some money now, somewhere to live, a few men, and some technical help. I don't know where to find explosives here."

Priola looked at Nogare. The younger man spoke for the first time. "I'll give you whatever money you need." He tossed a bundle of notes onto the desk. "Here's a hundred dollars to begin with. As for men, how many do you need, and when? We have four hundred, maybe five, in the labor gangs. All Sicilian. Let me know. I am here, in this office, every morning. As for explosives, I'll look into it. This is not quarry country, but new railroads are being blasted all the time. As for living quarters, we have something special—a boat."

"A boat? Not another—"

"No, no. Don't worry. This boat isn't going anywhere. There's a very nice flat-bottomed houseboat moored to the end of this pier."

"What's wrong with the French Quarter?" Nino scowled at Nogare.

"Everything. Think about it." Nogare tugged at his shirt cuffs. He obviously cared about his appearance. "Once this business gets started and people figure out who's behind whatever you make happen, you aren't exactly going to be the most popular man in New Orleans. If you lived in the French Quarter, you would be hard to protect. On a houseboat, where the only access is by pier or the river itself, you are much safer."

Nino didn't like it, but he could see it made sense. He drained his glass.

"Now," said Nogare. "Bodyguard—"

"I've got one." Nino nodded his head in Silvio's direction.

"Are you sure he's old enough? Can he shoot?"

"He'll do."

Nogare looked at Priola.

The older man said, "Nino, this is a tough town—"

"He'll do."

Priola shrugged. "If you insist. That's most of the details sorted.

Now let me tell you who you're going to be doing business with."
He wiped his mustache.

"Two brothers, Alfredo and Giancarlo Cataldo. Giancarlo is the
clever one, the fox. Alfredo is older but less wily. Giancarlo is
about forty-five and comes, as I say, from Solunte, near Bagheria.
Began collecting protection money in the fruit market there.
Bagheria is run by the Liotta family, as perhaps you know. Giancarlo rose in their ranks, but not being a blood Liotta, his prospects
were limited. Until he married into it. He was promoted again, not
only because of his marriage but also because he killed the head
of the Freemasons in Solunte, who was trying to 'reorganize' the
fruit market.

"I tell you, Giancarlo had a bright future back home in Bagheria, but although I called him clever, he did one stupid thing.
Refused to keep his dick in his trousers. Two years after his marriage to Giulietta Liotta, he knocked up the wife of an orange
farmer who was under Liotta protection. The farmer went to old
Francisco Liotta and asked for justice. The old man liked his son-
in-law but could not refuse the farmer—too much honor was at
stake. Giancarlo was given a choice: he could either leave Sicily
or be killed."

Nino, showing impatience, shifted in his seat.

"I'm giving you this background, Nino, because I don't want
you to underestimate Giancarlo. I'm telling you he is clever,
furbo, cunning, and he had a future in Bagheria until his dick went
to his head. In Bagheria he got used to having money and power,
and I can tell you that he wants them again. He will expect
someone to come for him; he knows I will retaliate. It is up to you
to surprise him, outfox him."

"Where does Giancarlo live?" Nino asked.

"On Burgundy, between Hospital and Barracks Street," replied
Priola, looking at Nogare, who nodded. "It's an area of town
known as Little Palermo. His weaknesses, apart from his family,
are colored women and bourbon. At times he can't get enough of
either. Most nights, I'm told, he passes out on top of one of Lulu
White's quadroons at Mahogany Hall."

"But he'll have a bodyguard," Nino replied. "That's too obvious. We'll have to think of something else. What else can you
tell me about him?"

Priola looked at Nogare. "Giovanni?"

Nogare shrugged. "I've heard he's very superstitious. He has his fortune told every day, through the cards. He never does anything unless the cards tell him it's safe."

Nino smiled at Priola. "And you call this guy clever?"

9

Annunziata had not been to the abbey at Quisquina since that day, weeks before, when she and Silvio had rushed to alert Father Ignazio Serravalle to the Italian soldiers' capture of her father. She had been sent this time with a message for the abbot.

The journey across the Serra di Leone and the Pizzo Stagnataro had brought back memories of the night when she and Silvio had so nearly made love. She still vividly recalled the smell of the moss in their *giardino segreto*, the crystal clarity of the stars, her own behavior in taking the lead, Silvio's confusion and delight. Then there had been that terrible interruption and their breathless dash to reach the abbey. Annunziata frowned to herself as she thought back.

It had been a shock when those events had led to her father's and Silvio's departure. But she had hidden her tears. As Nino's daughter, she had learned early on to hide her feelings. She had realized, long before Silvio had, that he was being taken away for a reason, and she was the reason. Nothing she could have done, nothing *they* could have done, would have made any difference. On the contrary, they would only have made the situation worse. She had realized, even if Silvio hadn't, that they had to think long-term. She would follow him to America. There they would be freer to go their own ways, in a new country where the Catholic Church had less power over people's lives.

So she had behaved coldly toward him, to quell their elders' suspicions—as if she had learned her lesson. But she had also given him a ring. Silvio could wear that without her father knowing what it meant and it would always remind him of her, of her love for him. And how she loved him! That had not dimmed in the weeks since he had been gone.

The corridor where she was waiting was cool. There was a smell of candle wax, and a carved wooden Madonna stood at the end, under a light. Annunziata liked Quisquina.

The door opposite her opened and Luigi Garofali came out. "Father Ignazio will see you now, child. You may go in."

Annunziata didn't like the way Father Luigi looked at her, and she loathed being called a child. But Father Ignazio was different. He got up from his desk, kissed her on both cheeks, and invited her to sit down. He closed the door, shutting out Father Luigi. Then he sat on the edge of his desk and looked down at her. An ivory cross hung over the front of his dark brown habit.

"Now, Annunziata, what have you got to tell me?"

"Elisavetta Scalice has had a baby girl. They would like you to baptize her, and ask for a date." Both Annunziata and Father Ignazio knew that this request was not quite what it seemed. It was true that Elisavetta had given birth and that the daughter would be baptized by Father Ignazio. But Nino, and now Bastiano, traditionally used christenings, weddings, and funerals to hold gatherings with the abbot, to plan ahead. Annunziata's visit was the announcement of such a meeting. It was for Father Ignazio to set a date.

He went round his desk and took out a diary. He flipped through the pages. "Let's see. Not this week, and not next. But . . . the Saturday after that. The twenty-third. Can you remember that, Annunziata? Or shall I write it down?"

"No, it's all right. I can remember." What was so difficult about remembering a date?

He stood up. The meeting was at an end.

But she still sat there.

"Annunziata?"

"Father, will you hear my confession, please?"

He smiled. There was no priest in the *bivio* where Annunziata lived. He was pleased that a young woman like her was so religious.

"Of course, my child. Come and kneel near me."

She walked around his desk and knelt by his chair. "Forgive me, Father, for I have sinned," she whispered.

"How long has it been since your last confession?"

"More than a month, Father." She hesitated. "It has been difficult, Father. . . . It still is. . . . When I last came to see you, with

Silvio Randazzo, you . . . you said you would ignore why we were not with the others when they were captured." She paused.

"Yes, Annunziata?"

"We were together, Father." It came out in a rush. "We were together—and I . . . I took the lead."

Father Ignazio looked straight ahead. "What happened?"

"Nothing happened. *Nothing!* I swear. But I wanted to. I still want to. Very badly at times. This is what I have come to confess. I think all the time about that night. About Silvio."

The abbot said nothing for a while, until it was clear that Annunziata had finished. But he was thinking hard. These young people, they were so grown up and confident part of the time, yet at other times so at sea. Annunziata's confession was welcome. He saw a way out of a dilemma.

"Annunziata, for your penance I want you to devote prayer three times a day to Gabriel. It was he, you remember, who announced to the Holy Mother that she was to bear the infant Jesus. I want you to marvel at the miracle of birth, its precious nature. Do you understand?"

Annunziata nodded.

"Very good. You have my blessing, child. Now get up. You may go. We shall give you some water and some fruit before you leave."

"Thank you, Father." Annunziata got to her feet and walked back around the abbot's desk. She crossed to the door.

"Oh, Annunziata," said Father Ignazio, as if an afterthought had struck him.

She turned. "Yes?"

"Confession is always good for the soul, but I think that on this occasion I am free to tell you something that you appear not to know."

She looked at him, puzzled.

"You are obviously very much in love with Silvio."

She said nothing but reddened slightly.

"I think it may help if you understand why Silvio went to America."

"My father needed a companion."

"Yes, but it was more than that."

"What do you mean?"

Father Ignazio put on his best smile. "This will come as a

shock, my dear, but, you see, Silvio *asked* to go. He *wanted* to go.
I'm not an expert on these matters, but doesn't that suggest he
never loved *you*?"

Silvio bit into a banana and gazed across the river. When he had
heard they were going to live on a boat, he had been as doubtful
as Nino, but after his first night he was beginning to change his
mind. It was not exactly luxurious, yet it did have more space than
most living areas in the French Quarter, and the view couldn't be
bettered.

There were now three of them, Nino, Silvio, and a man of about
twenty-five, called Garcia Furci, tall, with crinkly black hair and
huge, strong hands. Garcia was to work nights. Silvio would protect Nino during the day, but at night, while they slept, they both
needed a bodyguard. Garcia was a Sicilian from Trapani but had
been in New Orleans for five years and spoke passable English.
Having been one of Priola's own bodyguards, he was not overjoyed with his new assignment. Still, he knew better than to question it.

Silvio and Garcia were sitting together on the small deck. There
was a bowl of fruit between them, and two mugs of coffee,
brewed by Garcia. Nino had not yet appeared, though it was
already eight-thirty.

"How long do you think this business will take?" Garcia asked.
He had put his gun on the table.

So Garcia knew about the plan. Silvio wondered how many
others knew. "It's early days," he replied. "And I don't ask Nino
what he's thinking. He keeps his thoughts to himself until it's time
to go. What's the English for 'river'?"

Garcia stared at him. "I'm not a fucking schoolteacher," he
growled.

Silvio shrugged. "How long did it take you to learn the
language?"

"A couple of years. I began working in a shop, a grocery store
run by an Italian. I swept up, but I could listen. You find it comes
if you're a good listener."

"I need to learn, and fast," Silvio said.

"There *is* a school, you know, on Claiborne Street. A lot of
immigrants go there. But it costs money."

Silvio reflected that he was being paid now. At least he assumed he was. Nino had been given that bundle of notes by Nogare. He, Silvio, must remind Nino to give him his share. Tricky.

Garcia finished his coffee. "Time for me to go. When shall I come back?"

Silvio weighed the question. "Around eleven. Not before. I'm not sure what's going to happen today. This is our first proper day as . . . well, on this boat."

Garcia got up. "Eleven it is, then. *Ciao*." He climbed down from the lugger, onto the small jetty where the boat was moored. He was soon out of sight.

The minute he had gone, Nino appeared. "Make me some coffee," he said gruffly as he sat down and reached for some fruit.

Sono schiavo? Am I a slave? Silvio asked himself, not for the first time. But he did as he was told. When he came back, and placed the coffee in front of Nino, the older man grabbed his wrist. "Silvio," he hissed menacingly, "we need to talk. Freshen your own coffee and come back. Be quick!"

Silvio was back in no time. He sat down across the table from Nino.

Nino swallowed what was left of Silvio's banana. "So, the first part is finished. We're in America, without being caught. We have a job and some cash. Therefore, my friend, it's time for a little plain speaking. Listen. You are a child no longer, and pretty soon we're going to find out just how much of a man you are. Killing the Mancuso boy·was easy compared to this job. How's your arm?"

"It's mending."

Nino drummed his fingers on his lips. After a while he turned to Silvio, frowning. "The first thing for you to learn is this: Trust no one who is not part of our family. Brains, balls—and *blood*, remember? Priola is family, Nogare is not. Anna-Maria is family, Garcia is not. Never, and I mean never, discuss our plans with anyone who is not family. If Garcia asks you again, just say it is family business. He will understand."

Nino paused, then said quietly, "Second, never discuss our plans with anyone unless I am present. In anything we do, only you and I will know. We will both know everything and we will both know exactly the same. Two heads are better than one. That way, mistakes might be avoided. If anyone tells you anything that seems relevant, and I am not there, you can never know if it's a device to drive a wedge between us. So you ask them to repeat it to me, in your presence. Clear?"

Silvio nodded, though he thought Nino was being hard on him.

"This is going to get rough, Silvio, before it goes away, if it ever goes away. I'm not cock's-blooding you. Believe me, before it's over you're going to need someone to rely on—and we only have each other."

He paused again.

"Third, I'm going to teach you about explosives. I don't know yet exactly how we will hit Cataldo, but explosives will be used. I'm relying on you, Silvio, not because you've come to America with me, and because we've shared ... well, you know what we've shared. I'm relying on you because you are family. A blood relation. I repeat: never trust anyone who is not family, no matter how reliable they appear. If they are not family, you can be sure they will have some other member of their *own* family they are being loyal to, before you. Always remember that."

Nino drank his coffee slowly. "One last thing. Although you are family, Annunziata is my daughter, my *flesh*. I know all about the two of you. Put her out of your mind. She's your cousin and you can never have her."

He made a fist, then uncurled one finger and pointed it at Silvio, very close to his face. "This is not cock's blood either. If I find out at any time that there's anything between you and Annunziata, I shall kill you more easily than I kill Giancarlo."

Over the next days Silvio saw a side to Nino that he'd only glimpsed once, onboard the *Syracusa* before the fight with the Orestanos. Nino stopped drinking, he forgot his food, and although he traveled about New Orleans at great speed and seemed relaxed, he retreated into himself.

The explosives proved less of a problem than they had thought. Priola's employees reported that an entire shipload had arrived from Lisbon and was awaiting onward passage up the Mississippi to Memphis, for railroad blasting. A favor was called in, and the dynamite appeared in the lugger late one night.

Giancarlo Cataldo himself presented greater difficulties. He appeared to spend most of his days on the wharves. He spent his nights, five out of six, at Lulu White's Mahogany Hall, where he had dinner followed by a woman. But Silvio and Nino also noticed that Lulu White's was heavily guarded when Giancarlo was there. Giancarlo had *two* bodyguards, and each was armed.

On the few nights Giancarlo wasn't there, he was home with his brother, his brother's wife and children, on Burgundy, near Hospital. He was heavily guarded there, too.

But it was this schedule that made Nino so thoughtful. Giancarlo might be heavily guarded but he was a man of routine.

After nearly two weeks Priola asked to see them and they met, as before, in the office on Picayune Pier. Nino reported no progress but said he wasn't worried. It had taken him three weeks to arrange the Palermo-docks job. Priola was slightly more bothered because he said he had heard that another fire was already planned for one of his piers. The hit on Giancarlo couldn't be put off forever. "I thought you were a fox, Nino," he growled. "Show your cunning."

The breakthrough came, ironically enough, in the most heavily guarded place after the wharves themselves—at Lulu White's. Assiduous reconnaissance by Silvio established that Giancarlo always arrived late, ate dinner around ten, with huge amounts of wine, then retired upstairs with one of the girls, *always to the same room*. After an hour of exertions, according to the gossip, he usually passed out, and the girl came downstairs again. Giancarlo therefore spent several hours, alone and unconscious, in that one room. The guards remained in position downstairs, in the saloon and outside. If some way could be found of getting into the right room beforehand, without being noticed, Nino and Silvio would have a chance.

They decided to take it in turns. Nino would go with a woman one night, Silvio the next. However, they took their women upstairs a good hour and a half before Giancarlo arrived. As a result, they were back downstairs half an hour before he showed up.

There were fifteen rooms upstairs at Lulu's and it was not until six nights had elapsed that Silvio, who was "on duty" that evening, was finally taken to the room that Giancarlo used. Inside, it was very basic—a bed, a chair, a mirror on the wall, a washstand with a china basin, and a couple of towels. The only refinements were a bedside lamp with a red shade, which gave the room a warmish glow, and a rug.

Silvio's problem, now that he was actually *in* the room, was to get the girl out again so he could be alone there for a few minutes.

He had given some thought to this. After he had taken off his shoes and his shirt, he smiled at the girl, reached into his pocket, and took out some money.

"I feel lucky tonight," he said, trying out a phrase he'd heard often enough.

She was a tall girl, blond. She smiled back.

Silvio held out ten dollars. "You make three plays for me. Roulette table. Your three lucky numbers, okay? I lose, you come back and make me happy. I win, you buy champagne, we drink it together."

After the many nights spent at Lulu White's among the girls and the punters, Silvio had by now picked up some English. He found he could understand much of what was said, even though he couldn't speak more than a few words himself.

The girl took the money. "Yo' sure yo' got enough to pay me if yo' lose?"

He dipped into his pocket again, brandished more bills in front of her nose.

She appeared mollified. "Ah gon' look forward to that champagne." And she left the room.

Immediately, Silvio crossed to the window and threw it open. It overlooked a dingy alley that Nino and he had reconnoitered. There was never any guard here, only at the main door to the whorehouse and at the foot of the stairs, inside.

"Nino!" he called softly, peering into the gloom.

"Here," a voice responded.

Quickly, Silvio unwound the thin rope that was wrapped several times around his waist. He lowered the rope to the ground, retaining hold of one end.

Nino moved out of the shadows, grasped the other end of the rope, and started to tie something on it. Then he tugged the rope twice, and Silvio began hauling it back up. As he pulled, a bundle of dynamite came into view. Now came the tricky part. Nino and he had studied the beds at Lulu's and they were all the same, built the same and laid out the same. The base of each bed was about a foot off the ground, and large lace covers hung down over the sides of the mattress, reaching almost to the floor.

Nino had designed a package of dynamite sticks that could be slid under the mattress. The most difficult part was hiding the fuse, a long black wire that had to be led from the explosive around the edge of the room, under the carpet to the window, up the wall and outside, down to where Nino was waiting. To help conceal it, Silvio moved the chair from the bedside and placed it by the window. He was able to hide another part of the wire behind the washstand, but there was no escaping the fact that a length of wire that led from the carpet to the washstand was clearly visible. They would just have to hope that Giancarlo arrived tonight too drunk to register anything other than the woman with whom he was about to pleasure himself.

When the wire was hidden as well as it could be, Silvio flopped down on the bed. What a bonus it would be if, on top of killing Giancarlo, they should also win at the tables.

The blond girl returned to the room just two minutes later— empty-handed and glum. She shook her head. "No luck, honey. 'N' ah was sho' lookin' forward to the champagne."

"What about me? I lose ten dollar. *Allora,* take . . . your clothes off."

Would the girl spot the wire? She was far from drunk and she seemed to be staring at it right now. But then she turned, took off her shoes, hoisted her dress over her head, stepped out of her underwear, and sat on the bed. She put her hand on the inside of Silvio's thigh and smiled. Immediately aroused, he began to unbutton his trousers.

He thought of Anna-Maria. Wait till he told her he had fucked someone lying on a bed of dynamite.

Slowly, Silvio was acquiring a taste for whiskey. He was standing at the bar of Lulu White's, discreetly watching Giancarlo. In the last three quarters of an hour, Silvio had downed three shots of Jack Daniel's; if he wasn't careful he would soon be drunker than the man he was supposed to be keeping an eye on. *Sborniato,* as they said in Sicily. Pissed. Drunk as the wind. He asked the barman for a glass of water.

Giancarlo Cataldo was a big man in a small frame. He had a wide mouth, a flat nose, and dark, receding hair. But his eyes were large and missed nothing—Silvio had to be careful that his quarry did not notice he was being watched.

Cataldo had arrived in Lulu White's about an hour before and had been playing cards ever since, getting steadily drunker. He drank wine, and by Silvio's reckoning was already on his third bottle. His voice had grown louder, he laughed more readily at the jokes told by others at the table. Despite the booze, he seemed to be winning the game.

Silvio was growing nervous. About ten minutes before, Cataldo had looked around the room and beckoned to a girl. His chosen companion for the night was thin, with large breasts. She went over to him, bent down to listen as he said something in her ear, and then disappeared. If previous evenings were anything to go by, he had just ordered dinner, which would be served upstairs, by the girl. Sure enough, a few minutes later the game broke up and Cataldo rose and walked toward the door. This was normal, too; he would converse with his bodyguard outside for a few moments, then retrace his steps to the staircase at the back of the room. Silvio was able to keep his back turned the whole time during this chain of events: he could follow Giancarlo's movements in the mirror on the wall behind the bar.

Cataldo stuck to his routine, climbing the stairs slowly, taking the remains of the wine with him, holding the bottle by the neck. At the top of the stairs he turned to his left, then left again, back along the gallery, stopping at the third door on the right. He was behaving exactly as he should do. A few moments later the girl reappeared, carrying a tray with food on it.

Silvio now knew he would have the most nerve-racking wait of his life. In theory they could have blown up the room right there and then, as soon as Cataldo was inside it. Once the explosives were detonated, anyone near the bed would be killed; and swift action would minimize the risk of Giancarlo spotting the telltale wire. But that would kill the girl, too, and although Nino hadn't been too bothered about that, Silvio had dissuaded him. It was pointless to make more enemies in New Orleans than they needed. If it ever got out that they had killed one of Lulu White's girls, they would have two sets of enemies *and* have all the whorehouses in the city closed to them. Even Nino didn't want that.

So now Silvio had to wait for Giancarlo to eat his dinner, fuck the girl, and then pass out. As soon as she reappeared, the plan could go into action.

Half an hour passed, three quarters, an hour. Silvio grew restless. If past evenings were anything to go by, the girl should be emerging any minute now. But so far there was no sign of her.

The bar was as busy as ever. Mahogany Hall had a new band,

led by the cornetist Theogene Baquet. In the early part of the evenings Baquet played in the Lyre Club Symphony Orchestra, but after ten-thirty he could be seen here at Lulu White's with his smaller Excelsior group, playing altogether hotter music.

Silvio's attention was drawn by Baquet's fingering of the cornet and for a moment he didn't notice that a girl—*the* girl?—was standing by his side. He had missed her exit from the room. Or had he? She was thin, with large breasts, but on reflection he couldn't be sure it was the same girl. He *thought* it was, but . . . The whole plan could founder on any miscalculation on his part. Nino would never forgive him, nor Priola, nor Anna-Maria. He had to settle this.

He leaned toward the girl. "Buy you a drink?"

She looked at him. "Sho'," she said, "but don' expect to go upstairs right away, honey. Ah only just come down 'n' ah *need* a drink." She signaled the barman to bring her a beer.

Her reply almost settled it for Silvio, but not quite. Although he understood her words, he could not be absolutely certain this was the girl he had seen go with Giancarlo, and until he was certain, nothing could happen. He began to panic but he couldn't ask her outright if she had been with Giancarlo. His questions would be recalled later, once the explosion had occurred. If it did occur.

The girl looked at him, and raised her glass. "Thanks, handsome." She swallowed. "What's yo' name?"

"Silvio."

"Yo' accent is—"

"Sicilian."

She nodded. "Thought so. That Cataldo is Sicilian, too. D'yo' know him?"

Silvio shook his head.

"He's very generous. Yo' generous?"

Sono munifico? Silvio wondered. Am I generous? He'd never had enough money even to pose the question. But his doubts had been resolved. She *was* Cataldo's whore. Yet he couldn't just cut off the conversation. He would draw attention to himself, and that would be remarked upon later.

"How much this Cataldo pay you?"

"Five dollars."

"I don't have five dollars—but I go get it. You wait here?"

"Don' worry, yo' bet' lookin,' 'n' younger. Yo' can have it fer three."

"I only got two." Please don't let her do it for two.

"Two's kinda insultin', sir. If yo' wan' to come back."

"Okay. Wait here. Back in five minutes. Three dollars, okay?"

She nodded. "Ah'll nurse mah beer fer ten minutes. But no mo'. Yo' ain't *that* han'some."

Relieved, he went out. He turned right out of the main entrance, rummaging in his pocket for cigarettes. At the edge of the building, he stopped, took out a match, struck it, and lit his cigarette. He waited a moment, puffing to make sure it was going. This was the signal to Nino, hidden in the alleyway at the side of Lulu White's—the signal that he could go ahead. When Silvio was sure his cigarette was lit, he sauntered off in the direction of Royal Street, toward the river.

Their plan was carefully timed. Nino would count to two hundred. By then, Silvio would be two and a half blocks away, near the corner of Chartres and CustomHouse Street, where Priola was playing cards.

Silvio passed Dauphine and Bourbon streets. At Royal he crossed to the other side of the roadway. At the junction of CustomHouse and Chartres he paused. In this area there were many balconies. He stopped under one of them and leaned on the metal pole supporting it. He looked for all the world as though he were enjoying his cigarette and taking the evening air.

Giancarlo Cataldo turned on the mattress and puffed the pillow. He groaned. He was fucking tired. There were some men, he knew, who were as stiff as a ripe banana skin after a few drinks, but he'd never had that problem. That whore tonight, for instance, had had trouble accommodating him at first, he was so big. A little more whiskey had done the trick. They had rutted like water rats after that, fucking to a standstill. Then they had finished the bottle, before she left.

Whiskey, he thought. It ran through him. He turned again on the mattress. He wanted to sleep—Christ, how he wanted to sleep—but right now he needed to take a leak even more. He swore under his breath.

Groaning, he heaved himself off the bed. There was a bucket in the corner and, naked, he crossed the room. He lifted the bucket and held it next to his thighs. Murmuring in pleasure, he voided his bladder. He placed the bucket back on the floor and turned back to bed. Out of the corner of his eye he noticed something he had never seen in this room before—it looked like a wire. His eye followed it. One end led from the carpet under the bed, the other end led up the wall and out the window. He frowned. What *was* this?

He knelt down and peered under the mattress.

The explosion separated Giancarlo's head from his body at the neck. His right arm was also dismembered and on the wall behind him blood, urine, and soot disfigured the wallpaper in a huge, vivid spray. Fluff from the mattress clung to any wet or sticky surfaces and the bucket was mangled virtually beyond recognition.

When people from downstairs eventually plucked up courage to venture into the remains of the room, they discovered that the body hair on Giancarlo's skin was all scorched. And his flesh smelled as if it had been cooked. His penis was never found.

"Nino, I want you to meet my tailor, Rocco Chivasso. Not a Sicilian but the next best thing, Milanese." Priola made the two men shake hands. "You, too, Silvio."

Priola ushered the tailor to the door. "Rocco, I'll be sending these two to you in a coupla days. Look after them, will you?"

"Certainly, Mr. Priola. It will be a pleasure." As he went out he closed the door behind him.

Priola turned back. "Sit down, gentlemen, sit down. Please. I thought it would be more comfortable, and more private, to meet here at my house than on the waterfront." He took out a bundle of notes and threw it at Nino. "Five hundred. Give the kid what you think he's worth. And keep anything Giovanni gave you for expenses."

Priola was obviously highly delighted with the events of the previous evening. "You did well, Nino. You, too, kid. That plan was so *neat*, so foxy. A real pro's job, hitting the one guy, no mess, no one else involved. I can quietly repay Lulu White for damage to her property. Very good. I'm very pleased. Ah, here's Giovanni."

Giovanni Nogare had let himself in without even knocking. He alone, it seemed, had that privilege.

"Giovanni," Priola said. "I've paid our . . . lieutenants here. A job well done. What have you heard?"

This morning Nogare looked as though he had just come from his own tailor. He was so spick-and-span he could easily have been mistaken for a lawyer or a banker or an accountant.

"The *sbirri* have rounded up a bunch of Sicilians. Some are our men, some are theirs. But Cataldo was Sicilian and the police are mainly Irish, so they don't give a damn for Italians in general and Sicilians in particular. They know who Cataldo was and that he wasn't exactly the Virgin Mary. They are probably saying 'Good riddance.' They figure it was some sort of vendetta to do with the docks and, since no one else was injured, don't see the need to get any more involved. As for the Cataldos, there's a meeting going on at their wharves right now. They know it's us who hit them, but they don't know who, exactly. Lulu White is livid that her premises were hit but grateful we spared her girls. So long as we repay her for the damage, and maybe push some extra business her way, she won't cause trouble. The most important thing is that these rains are causing the river to rise."

Nino and Silvio looked at each other in amazement. What relevance did that have?

Priola observed their bewilderment. "If it goes on raining to the point where the river breaks the levees, all manpower—army, police, fire brigade, and any able-bodied volunteers—will be occupied trying to repair the levees so that the damage is confined. The police will forget all about this foxy little killing. Pray for more rain."

"The real problem," said Nogare, "is what to do next. At some point the Cataldos are sure to retaliate, so do we offer to negotiate before they can organize themselves?"

"Who do we negotiate *with*?" asked Priola.

"Cataldo's brother." Nogare, who had been standing, finally sat down. "Who is a lot less cunning."

"What's our best way of making contact with him?"

"You don't."

There was silence in the room. No one had expected Silvio to speak unless spoken to.

Nogare turned on him. "Look, kid—"

"No, no," interjected Priola. "Let him have his say." He turned to Silvio and waited.

Sono sciacco? Silvio asked himself. Am I a fool? He wasn't sure exactly why he had spoken up, except that he saw the situation quite clearly. He *knew* what to do. "You'll get better terms if he comes to you, rather than the other way around."

"What makes you think he'll come to us?"

"He won't. You have to persuade him."

"And how do we do that?"

"Hit him again."

Again there was silence in the room. Priola exchanged glances with Nino and Nogare, then said softly, "Go on, kid."

"One hit signals we're fighting back after the knocks you have taken. But that's all. The fight here is not just for physical control of the wharves, but for the power over the minds of the men who unload the ships. All Sicilians. Therefore, you should do two things, both of which Nino taught me."

Nino sat up and looked harder at Silvio. Silvio looked right back at him.

"The first thing he taught me is to hit hard when you hit. We should try something even more spectacular than last night's job. The second thing is that at the same time we should give the ordinary men on the wharves a reward for being with us."

Priola rose, walked to the bar, poured four whiskeys, and handed them around. "I'm still listening."

"We have to act very quickly, for maximum effect. What I would do is kidnap one of Alfredo Cataldo's children."

The others were shocked. But Silvio knew they were also impressed.

"How would we get near him?" Nogare asked. "They're watched the whole time."

"How old are the children? They must be taken on walks, when they're surrounded by relatively few people."

Priola was nodding. "I like it. If they find their child has been taken by Nino, they'll be terrified of receiving an interesting body part in the mail. Yes"—now he was smiling—"it could work."

"I have a better idea," Nino said thoughtfully.

All eyes turned to him.

"They are Sicilians. There will be an elaborate funeral for Giancarlo Cataldo. Everyone will be there—except for very young children. They will be left at home. *That's* when we hit them."

"Yes!" Priola slammed his fist down on his desk. "They will want to get the funeral out of the way before they come at us. And that will make them careless!" His face lit up like a small boy's at a fireworks display. "Giovanni will find out the date of the funeral. He will also provide you with expenses, as before. Nino, you and the kid work out the rest of the details. Now, is there anything else?"

Giovanni said nothing. Nino shook his head.

"Yes," said Silvio.

They all looked at him.

"If this works, will you please stop calling me 'kid.' "

Silvio ran a finger down Anna-Maria's spine, and between her buttocks.

A sound gurgled in her throat. "I like that."

He passed the flat palm of his hand back up the skin over her shoulders and massaged her neck.

"More."

"Let's have a drink. The more we delay the second time, the better it is. Have you noticed that?" He got off the bed and crossed the room to the bar.

"The sooner we do it the second time, the sooner we can do it a third time."

Looking out across the Mississippi, pouring the wine, Silvio smiled to himself. It was midafternoon—broad daylight—and Anna-Maria had turned up unannounced. Nino had grinned when she arrived but soon made himself scarce. It was obvious what he thought: every time Silvio fucked her took him away from Annunziata.

He handed Anna-Maria her wine. "Sicilian wine, the best."

"Bullshit!"

"It is!"

"Bullshit! Sicily's a nice enough place, Silvio, but don't be blinded to its shortcomings. Have you ever tried French wine?"

"It's piss."

She sat up. "Next time I come, I'll bring some. You'll see. It's less harsh, more interesting. You're bright, *carissimo*, but you've a lot to learn."

"Who says I'm bright?" He thought briefly of his parents.

"Well, my father, for one."

Silvio looked at her sharply. "Oh yes? What did he say?"

"I heard him tell one of his men—that you had the brains of a bishop."

"When? When did he say this?"

"Couple of days ago. He also said you thought with your balls—it's a phrase he uses, it means you have character, courage, but a thinking kind of courage." Her expression changed. "Have you thought about what I said, about getting away from Nino?"

"That's not easy, Anna-Maria, not just now."

"Maybe not. But don't delay forever. I'm not joking, Silvio."

"I know. What does your father say about Nino?"

"That he understands violence, that he's willing to go one step further than anyone else, but that he can never be Capo outside Sicily, he's too much of a peasant."

Silvio fell silent. Nino had told him never to let anyone drive a wedge between them. Anna-Maria was doing just that.

She looked at him levelly. "It's not just Nino you have to put behind you, Silvio. It's Sicily. Something's making you look back, isn't it? Is it a woman?"

Silvio colored and Anna-Maria nodded. "I thought so. Your first love, eh? Poor you. What's her name?"

He looked away.

"Come on. What's her name?"

"Annunziata."

Anna-Maria let a silence elapse while she sipped her drink. "You'll forget her, you know. Oh, not for three months, or six months, but you'll forget her. Then, one day, you'll suddenly be shocked by the fact that you haven't thought about her for days.

"She's part of Sicily, Silvio, part of your youth. But you're a man now, with a future. You should use me to help forget her, to put Sicily behind you."

He looked at her.

"You're learning English, you must learn to read, learn how to think big, learn how to present yourself so people respect you. I can teach you some of that. I'm not just a body, you know. You never love anyone like your first love—nothing hurts quite so much as the first separation, but you'll heal. You don't want to heal right now, but you will."

She put down her wine and lay back on the bed.

"If you want, just this once, you can imagine I'm Annunziata."

                              * * *

Seven carriages were drawn up on Burgundy Street. The Cataldos
lived in the Little Palermo district of the city, between Burgundy
and Barracks streets. The carriages were all black, the horses with
black plumes woven into their manes. A Negro brass band stood
respectfully at the head of the procession.

Silvio watched from down the street. A small crowd had gathered to see the funeral of a man who had met such a spectacular
end, so there was no danger of Silvio being spotted or standing out
in any way. It was still raining and the streets were turning muddy.
Silvio had been drinking in Madge Leigh's the evening before
when he heard that a number of crevasses, or breaks, in the levee
had formed above New Orleans, at Bell's Plantation. The fire
department, several police forces, and many other volunteers had
been called out to help with the repairs. As far as he could see,
there were no police attending the funeral.

The coffin appeared from the entrance to the courtyard where
the Cataldos lived, carried by four strapping Negroes. Idly, Silvio
wondered why so many men were needed—or perhaps this was
for show. There couldn't have been much left of Giancarlo after
Nino's explosives had done their work.

Nino was farther down Burgundy, on the corner of St. Philip
Street, hidden in a carriage with its curtains drawn. These carriages were common in New Orleans, as Silvio had discovered,
used by women of finery who didn't want to be gaped at, or
robbed if they were wearing jewelry.

The coffin was maneuvered into the front wagon and the
mourners, led by Alfredo Cataldo and his wife, climbed into the
carriages. A man from Leclair's funeral parlor, dressed in a black
frock coat and a tall top hat, visited each carriage to ensure that
everyone was ready to start. Then he walked forward and gave the
leader of the band a firm nod.

The brass immediately struck up a dirge and began to move
forward. At the sound of the music, more people came to stare.
Silvio stood his ground as the procession went by. His job was to
follow at a distance, all the way to Metairie Cemetery. As the
youngest, fittest, and fastest runner among the small team Nino
had assembled, he was to watch for any deviation in the funeral
routine. If there was any move that could result in Nino being

surprised or trapped in the Cataldo courtyard, he would dash back to Burgundy Street to sound the alert.

The procession wound its slow way down Burgundy, turned right on St. Peter's, then left onto Rampart. The cortege made another right on Toulouse, which brought the coffin and the mourners to the basin, at Basin Street. All along the route the music attracted onlookers. Some of the men took off their hats as the procession went by. Others just glared, or even turned their backs. They knew what Cataldo had been and why he had been killed, and they shared the view of the police: good riddance. At the corner of Basin and Conti, the cortege passed Mary O'Brien's and the sound of the brass band was almost drowned by the early-morning session of Mike Gillin and George Filhe, who were already playing there.

As the procession went along it picked up a handful of extra mourners, who walked behind the carriages. These appeared to be mainly Sicilians, anxious to pay their last respects to a powerful man. They all knew, or thought they knew, that retribution for the murder was coming and they had to show allegiance.

After some forty minutes the mourners arrived at the cemetery. Cemeteries, Silvio already knew, were special places in New Orleans. Metairie Cemetery was sited very carefully. Metairie Ridge was the only raised ground for miles around, and even this was scarcely fifty feet above sea level. In all other parts of New Orleans the soil was so waterlogged, so much a part of the great Mississippi delta, that bodies couldn't be buried; sooner or later the remains of cadavers simply floated to the surface. Even here, in Metairie, bodies were interred in sarcophagi aboveground. The appearance of the cemeteries, row upon row of small stone resting places, some elaborately carved or decorated with bright flowers, had given these places their nicknames: Cities of the Dead.

The Cataldo sarcophagus, Silvio was not surprised to note, was elaborately ornate. Giancarlo would leave one underworld for another in grand style.

Silvio still kept his distance. By now, Nino should be in the Cataldo house. The plan was simple. He was to arrive in the carriage, dressed as a priest. He would explain to the guard that he was a friend of Giancarlo's, from upriver, from Natchez, that he had been in New Orleans when the killing took place, and had rushed into the remains of the room in Lulu White's to try to administer the last rites. Alas, he had been too late. He was unable, unfortunately, to attend the funeral, as he was obliged to catch a steamer upriver, taking him home. But as a priest, he would like to do the next best thing to attending the funeral, he would like to bless a blood relative of Giancarlo. He had been told that Giancarlo's nephew, Ranuccio, was considered too young to attend the funeral: could he please bless the child? Underneath his cassock Nino carried a *lupara*, the traditional Sicilian shotgun, from which both the barrel and the stock had been sawn off. Once inside the house, the rest should be easy. An easy *raccolto*, as they said in Sicily, an easy harvest.

At the cemetery, the band had stopped playing and the coffin was being taken from the wagon. The mourners were stepping down from their carriages and gathering around the sarcophagus. Silvio noticed that two or three of them were girls from Lulu White's. A priest—a real one, Silvio hoped—stood ready to begin the ceremony.

Silvio edged away now. He pretended to be studying the inscriptions on the various sarcophagi, as if looking for one in particular. Gradually, however, he worked his way back to the main gate, where the flower sellers were located. From here he could keep an eye on the funeral, able to see if anyone suddenly detached himself from the group of mourners.

The plan, once the child had been abducted, was to sail up the Mississippi with him in a small lugger, a fishing boat used on the river and in the Gulf of Mexico. Two men and a woman, Sicilians brought in specially from Baton Rouge, had been chosen for this task. Afterward they would return to Baton Rouge and the child would never be able to identify his abductors. The lugger would sail upstream for as long as the negotiations between the Priolas and the Cataldos went on, putting ashore each evening to send a telegraph to Angelo Priola with further instructions.

Silvio had transferred his attention from the sarcophagi to the flower seller outside the cemetery, trying to guess her nationality. This was a game he often played since he had been in America. Suddenly he noticed a man he recognized running in the street. He knew where he had seen the man before—at Lulu White's. He was one of Giancarlo's bodyguards. The man was panting and sweating and had a wild expression on his face. Silvio turned his back on the man, quickly approached the flower seller, and bought some carnations. As he did so the bodyguard ran on through the gate and straight for the funeral party. Silvio eased himself away from the gate and began to head south, back toward town. But he still lingered; he wanted to see what happened.

The bodyguard approached the mourners. He sought out Alfredo and pulled him to one side. Their heads were bent together in conversation. Then Alfredo put his hand to his head and cried out. All the other mourners turned to look at him. Quickly, he dragged three men from the rear of the group and spoke to them urgently. They immediately sprinted for the gate. The other mourners were confused. Alfredo went to his wife and put his arm around her. He whispered into her ear, then she screamed, and sagged in his arms.

Silvio didn't dare wait any longer. The first three men were almost at the gate of the cemetery. As Silvio began to stroll south along Conti Street, Alfredo's men ran past him.

He dumped the flowers in the first trash bin he came to.

PART TWO

—

Caporegime

10

Father Ignazio Serravalle looked around the Church of the Madonna dell'Olio and beamed. This was a delightful little church where he had carried out many baptisms, weddings, and funerals. It was simple, built of the local Calandrella quarry stone, with two rows of columns supporting a terracotta roof and a small gallery over the main entrance. The windows were plain, the apse undecorated, and there was no art of any kind to alleviate the stark whitewash with which the interior was painted. But this sheer simplicity, among the olive and almond groves of the Casino mountain, was effective. The church was a jewel.

More to the point, for many of those present, it lay at the end of a simple track. No one could be surprised, or ambushed, in this church, and it was precisely for this reason that it was preferred by many of the local Mafia families in central Sicily. That, and the fact that it was only used once a year by the bishop, to bless the olive harvest in mid-March.

But the chapel was full today. Weddings were more important than baptisms and more pleasurable than funerals. As the singing came to an end, Serravalle brought his gaze back to the couple in front of him. Annunziata and Gino made a handsome pair, he thought.

"Will you please be seated," he said when the music stopped. He waited while they all settled themselves.

"I won't keep you because it's hot and we are all longing for some cool wine. But this is an important day for Annunziata and Gino—Signor and Signora Alcamo—and I think we should dwell for a moment on the big step they are taking. Marriage is the most beautiful thing we can do in this life, the union of one man with one woman, symbolizing the indissoluble bond between man and

God, the foundation of the church. Nothing we mortals do can approach the mystery that is God, but marriage certainly offers deep satisfaction, the chance to experience love in all its guises, the opportunity it offers for children, new individuals to glorify the Lord."

Father Ignazio himself derived considerable satisfaction from this marriage today. After all, it had been his comments—his falsehood, if he was honest, acting under the guidance of the Lord—that had caused Annunziata to turn away from the wretched Sylvano. It was a blessing, a divine spark, that had given him the idea to tell her that Sylvano had wanted to go to America. His remarks had devastated Annunziata; but that, he told himself, was in the short term. He, Ignazio Serravalle, had interpreted God's law properly. The relationship between Sylvano and Annunziata was unnatural, and that was that. It had taken Annunziata months to get over what the abbot had said, but she *was* over it, now, and much the better for having divested herself of all feeling for Silvio. Because Father Ignazio was an abbot, Annunziata had never questioned the truthfulness of what he had said. She had believed him implicitly.

And, he was pleased to note, she had gradually adjusted. It had taken time, but eventually she had begun to show an interest in other young men. They, of course, had shown an interest in her all along; she was a highly attractive young woman. For a time the abbot—and others—had been unsure which of the Alcamo brothers, Gino or Alessandro, she had preferred. When Gino asked him to get word to Nino, to ask if he might marry Annunziata, the abbot had been as pleased as everyone else. Privately he thought that Annunziata still looked sad from time to time. He suspected that deep inside she was still in love with Sylvano. Fifteen minutes ago, however, she and Gino had been married. Love no longer mattered. She was out of harm's way.

"I say to the young couple . . ." He raised his voice, for emphasis. "I say . . . remember that marriage is a sacrament, a holy thing. Treat each other with love, respect, and gentleness and you will be repaid many times over in good fortune, no matter what happens in the world outside." He smiled at the congregation. "Now we will sing a final, joyful hymn and after that we can all go out into the sunshine to drink and eat and sing and dance, and enjoy all those good things that God, in his mercy and wisdom, has provided."

As the people stood for the hymn Father Ignazio looked down again at the newlywed couple. Annunziata looked more beautiful than ever in white. He hoped she would soon have babies. With babies to love, she could put Sylvano behind her forever.

New Orleans, Silvio had decided, had very little in common with Sicily, save in one respect: rain was welcome. True, it turned the unpaved roads into quagmires, and if it went on long enough, the river rose and the levees were threatened. But showers cooled the air, kept the mosquitoes down, at least for a time, and brought out the scent of the bougainvillea that festooned so many balconies in the French Quarter.

Not that he was smelling the bougainvillea just now. Like many other New Orleans people, when it rained he took shelter in the French Market, which had a roof of terracotta tiles, supported on stone pillars. There he surrendered himself not to the scent of flowers but to the smells of the market—baking fish, tobacco, melons, pineapples, and above all, roasting coffee.

In the last six months Silvio's circumstances had changed more than he could ever have hoped. The kidnapping of Alfredo Cataldo's son had gone better than any of them had envisaged. It turned out that Marina Cataldo, Alfredo's wife, had nearly died giving birth to her only son, and as a result could have no more children. Barren as a biscuit, as they said back home. On being told of the kidnapping, she had become hysterical and insisted Alfredo accede to all Priola's demands. Being Sicilian, Alfredo was by no means used to taking his wife's views into account, but the boy was his only son, too.

Silvio had also gotten the psychology right. Coming so soon after Giancarlo's brutal death, and with the kidnapping and mutilation of the English priest in Sicily so fresh in everyone's mind, Alfredo was not about to take any risks. On condition that his brothels and gambling joints would remain under his complete control, he agreed to withdraw from the fruit wharves. The boy was returned unharmed. The beautiful part was that the New Orleans police were not even aware that the kidnapping had taken place. The Priolas and the Cataldos settled their differences entirely outside the law.

Priola, Nino, and Silvio knew this was only a temporary peace. The Cataldos would regroup and try to hit back, but meanwhile the vast mass of Sicilians in New Orleans, who did the bulk of the unloading and loading on the wharves, were now more afraid of Priola and Nino than of Cataldo. That was all that counted, at least for the moment.

Priola had been as good as his word. Nino and Silvio had been given control of the wharves, a small cut of the turnover, and free use of the brothels that were under Priola control: Madge Leigh's, Sally Levy's, and Frankie Belmont's. They had money in their pockets, new suits made to measure by Rocco Chivasso, and the respect of the men on the piers. In the eleven months they had been in America, they had picked up a lot of English. Silvio's teacher was a quadroon girl at Madge Leigh's whom he was becoming fond of. With her help he was also learning to read.

For Silvio, the only shadows in this existence were his thoughts of Annunziata. He had slipped into an easy relationship with Anna-Maria. She came to the lugger every Tuesday afternoon and they fucked for a couple of hours. She also read to him. He found he was interested in the books she had. He liked hearing about Paris and London and the Italy of the Renaissance. Other people, other times, could be so different and yet the same. It was fascinating and, in some strange way, comforting. His mother had liked reading; he remembered that now. There was little chance of Angelo finding out about Anna-Maria and Silvio; Tuesday afternoons he took confession, regular as clockwork, then played cards. Although Anna-Maria was not beautiful, Silvio had come to like the way she looked. She moved so well and enjoyed sex so much that he could really relax with her. Their Tuesday-afternoon sessions were perfectly satisfying in an uncomplicated way— cleansing almost. On the other hand, his love for Annunziata— lovely, unattainable, chaste Annunziata—was idealized.

The problem had been that his existence in New Orleans had grown settled. He was earning money, more than enough of it. *Caricato*, as they said in Sicily. Loaded. He had friends and acquaintances, far more than he ever had in Sicily, and he was only just nineteen. After the kidnapping he became Priola's favorite. He was even allowed to address him as Angelo.

The solution was clear: if he was to have Annunziata he would have to give up New Orleans, the wharves, Madge Leigh's, Anna-Maria, Rocco Chivasso's suits. He would have to find another town and start again. He simply didn't know if he could do that on his own, without Nino or Priola.

And then, one day in April, Nino had casually given him the news that Annunziata had been married the month before.

Nino hadn't been able to keep a smirk of triumph off his face. "I'm not cock's-blooding you," he said.

Silvio tried not to show any reaction at all. At first he refused to believe it. Despite his own muddle, he had been so certain of Annunziata's love for him. Especially after she had given him the ring. He had been in America less than a year and already their pact had dissolved into nothing. He had been unfaithful, and Annunziata had married.

Silvio had of course asked Nino whom Annunziata had married and been disappointed when he found out it was Gino Alcamo. Gino was a good rider, a good shot, cunning and excitable. But he was not a leader, and therefore nowhere near good enough for Annunziata. Yet she had sacrificed her virginity to him.

Silvio went on a drinking binge after that, sating himself on the girls at Madge Leigh's. For a few days, he even succumbed to the oblivion of absinthe. Then, after allowing himself several sober days of reflection, he tried to get word to Annunziata. Madeleine, the quadroon at Madge Leigh's who was teaching him to read, could also write. He told her what to say, in a letter, to ask Annunziata why she had gotten married, why she hadn't waited. He was too proud to describe his own feelings and in that way he knew the letter was incomplete. But in a way it didn't matter, because he had never received a reply. It took him several months to realize that no letter was coming. Once he did, he stopped carrying her ring. And he hadn't carried it since.

Silvio's only consolation was that he now didn't need to leave New Orleans. He could enjoy the pleasures of the city without any shadow hanging over him. He could put Annunziata behind him forever. He would never go back to Sicily, not now. It had all happened as Anna-Maria had predicted.

He was further comforted by the fact that, as it turned out, he had quite a good business brain. Perhaps it was because Nino and he now received a small share of the take at the wharves, but he began to develop a keen eye for the goods that shifted most quickly, and for which demand was growing. That was why he was at the market today. Sometimes a chance remark or encounter could be a useful guide to the fluctuations in trade. He had been in the French Market when he first heard a woman ask for oranges "but not blood oranges." These, of course, were the very red oranges that came from Italy, the ones Nino thought symbolized their way of life. "Even the oranges bleed in Sicily," he had once said. But they were clearly unpopular in America. It was difficult for a Sicilian to admit so much to himself, but Silvio wasn't sentimental. He made a recommendation to Vito, the foreman of the roustabouts, who then made a recommendation to the shippers, that blood oranges be avoided. As a result, their turnover in oranges last month had risen by twelve percent. In the French Market on another occasion he overheard a vendor shouting the praises of "European apples." Again, Silvio advised Vito to reduce their intake of South American apples and import more from Spain, France, and England. The turnover of apples had since improved by seven percent. Priola and Nino were delighted and now Silvio had three tailor-made suits.

Silvio could read numbers, and simple arithmetic was no longer a problem. He could also read all the signs and notices in the French Market. He knew from those when the itinerant dentist was expected. He had never needed him—not yet—but he sometimes enjoyed watching the show. He still couldn't read the bulk of the body type of the *Daily Picayune* or *The Delta* or *The Mascot*, though he could decipher most of the headlines.

All in all, apart from the news about Annunziata, life was good. He was no longer a clumsy virgin. He had learned to become a proper lover who could give pleasure to women as well as himself. Quadroons, he had found, were special. They were languid, voluptuous, succulent. They never made you feel you were paying for it. Their skin—a pale *caffe latte*—and their dark hair and eyes were a distinctive mix. Quadroons were of mainly European descent, but had one Negro grandparent. Madeleine, like Anna-Maria, was a few years older than Silvio, but unlike Anna-Maria, and although she was a whore, Madeleine managed to convey the impression that she was an innocent. She appeared genuinely fond of Silvio and let him do anything with her. He wouldn't marry Madeleine; he wouldn't even be faithful. But for a while she consoled him while he got over Annunziata.

"You gonna stan' there all day?"

Silvio realized that his mind had wandered. A big black woman, her arms full of peaches, was bearing down on him and he was blocking the way. He moved to one side, to the edge of the covered part of the market. As he did so he noticed a stack of crates of rotting fruit, which had been moved out into the rain.

"What are those?" he asked the vendor at the nearest stall.

"Shaddock," said the woman. "Can't give it away these days. That's the last lot I'm buying."

Silvio made a mental note to mention this to Vito. He had no idea why tastes changed. Sometimes there was an explanation, often there wasn't. But that tastes changed there was no doubt.

He looked at the shaddock, the large round fruit pale and pathetic in the rain. Then he looked at the rain, which was falling so hard the drops bounced back up again when they hit the ground. But he couldn't avoid the weather any longer. He had a rendezvous with Anna-Maria.

Anna-Maria put down the book. "That's enough about London for now," she said. "This Dickens is a bit gloomy, don't you think?" She pulled a sheet around her and took two cigarettes from her silver box. She passed one to Silvio and lit them both.

"I count you as one of my successes," she said, blowing smoke into the room. "When I met you on the *Syracusa*, you didn't know what to do. Now I love our afternoons. Fucking and reading, smoking and fucking."

"Who taught *you*?" replied Silvio. He enjoyed these lazy afternoons on the lugger just as much as he enjoyed his times with Madeleine. The bodies of the two women were very different, but that, surely, was the point.

"Never you mind. An older man, of course. But that's not saying much. I was fifteen." She exhaled more cigarette smoke. "Am I better than your quadroon?"

Silvio stopped smoking, and blushed. *Concime!* Horseshit! "How did you know about her?"

"Silvio! My father owns the place." She turned on her side, to look at him. "Well . . . is she good?"

"You're not jealous, I hope."

"I am if she's better than me."

"She's not better. Just . . . different."

"How? Tell me."

Silvio got out of bed and, totally naked, stood looking out of the

window of the lugger, across the river toward Algiers, the town on
the other bank. He watched as a steamboat put out from the wharf
where it had been tied up, bow end on. Steamboats left at all times,
but now, around four o'clock in the afternoon, was the favored
hour for many of them. If they left now they arrived at Baton
Rouge, the next town of any size upriver, in time for breakfast. It
always took the boats a few minutes to get up their full head of
steam and in the meantime the boat was swept downriver on the
current. The exercise could not be performed at the wharves
because from time to time steamboat engines blew up. Only when
it was almost out of sight around the bend did the boat start to
make headway.

"Silvio, tell me. How is the quadroon different?"

Sono sposo? Silvio asked himself. Am I a husband? Do I have
to explain? He knew he had to be careful. That much was instinctive. The last thing he wanted was for Anna-Maria to be jealous of
Madeleine. The truth was he liked them both and wanted the
arrangement to continue. Anna-Maria had a firmer body and was
more adventurous in bed, often taking the initiative. Madeleine
was more languid, more pliable, her body softer, juicier. Where
Anna-Maria was a leader, Madeleine was a slave. To say all that
might change Anna-Maria forever. But he had to give an answer
of some sort.

"She's there. I only see you once a week. I don't pay you, I pay
her. She makes no demands."

"And I *do*?"

"No! No." He was mishandling this. "No, you don't. But . . .
you're more of a personality, more forceful. You're more invigo-
rating. She's more . . . relaxing, I suppose."

"And which do you prefer?"

Christ, Anna-Maria wasn't giving up. But he knew he had to be
firm. He was learning how to deal with women. "I like both,
Anna-Maria. I need both." He turned to face her. "When you think
of that first man you had, what feeling comes over you?"

She smiled. "Ah! The first is always special. In some ways the
best."

"Exactly. Never forget that you were my first."

That, he could see, had pleased her. She threw back the sheet and beckoned to him. "Come here. I've thought of something that will really invigorate you."

He went toward her, but at that moment heard footsteps and movement outside. There was a sense of urgency about the noise and he quickly reached for his gun, in his jacket pocket.

There was a knock on the door. Three rapid taps.

"Yes?"

"It's Gaspero," said the voice. He was one of the senior roustabouts. "Sorry to disturb you, Silvio, but Nino sent me. You have to come right away. It's urgent. Vito's been stabbed. He's dead."

Ten minutes later Silvio was looking at the body. Vito had been garroted. There was a piece of wire around his throat, the traditional Sicilian method. The weapon had been left with the body, to show that the killer was also Sicilian. This was a vendetta killing.

"Where was the body found?" Silvio asked.

"In the hold of the *Goya*."

Silvio understood. Vito's killing achieved two things. Most immediately, it scared the management of the Spanish company that owned the *Goya*. They didn't want this kind of trouble, and in the future they would almost certainly use wharves owned by companies other than the Priola piers. Equally, the location of the killing showed that the Cataldos had infiltrated the Priola gangs. From now on, no one on the Priola wharves could trust anyone else.

Nino turned to Gaspero. He drummed his fingers on his lips. "What family did Vito have?"

"A wife, two boys."

"Give the wife this." Nino handed Gaspero a roll of dollars. "It will pay for the funeral and more. Ask her to come to me when the funeral is over. And make sure it's not too elaborate. We don't want to draw attention to this. We'll settle it our own way." He turned to Silvio. "Come with me."

He led the way up the boards of the wharf to the top of the levee, then set out along a path that ran the length of the raised bank.

It was the custom in the evening for New Orleans people to promenade along the levee, taking the air, nodding to other walkers they knew. In the case of Nino and Silvio, they were accompanied at a distance by two other men, their bodyguards.

They headed south toward the Mint and the Pontchartrain railroad. To their right, across the river, the lights of Algiers were just appearing.

"It would have taken at least three people to overpower Vito," said Nino. "It must have happened quickly, or he would have called out."

"Do we tell Angelo?" asked Silvio.

"No, not yet. He will only say he's paying us for protection. Now we have to earn it. How many men can we count on?"

"A hundred and fifty in each shift. Say four to five hundred."

Nino stopped and looked at Silvio. "How do we find the Cataldos?"

Silvio bent and picked up an oyster shell from the path. He threw it into the river. "There's only one way."

"How?"

Silvio picked up another shell and sent it after the first. "We have to set a trap, with bait."

Nino nodded, understanding immediately. "Me."

"No."

Nino looked surprised. "Who then?"

Silvio threw a third shell. "You are the better killer. The bait will be me."

They resumed their walk. At length Nino said, "I'm not sure I can let you take that risk."

"Give me a better idea, then."

More silence. Then Nino said, "Let's think of a plan first. Then decide who plays which part."

But Silvio had already been thinking. "We have to choose a time when normally we follow a routine. That's when they'll come for us. Now, I see Madeleine every afternoon when I'm not seeing Anna-Maria. But I'm always guarded on these occasions, and in both places, the lugger and Madge Leigh's. It would be difficult for a killer to get away. The same applies to you at Lombardo's. You have your shave every day, but you're always guarded."

They walked on for another hour, passing the Cotton Press and the Tobacco Press, tossing ideas back and forth. Any change of behavior on their part, they decided, would look suspicious and be ignored by the Cataldos. And they couldn't suddenly get rid of their bodyguards. They returned to the lugger with no plan formulated.

Over the next week three more Priola roustabouts were killed, garroted like Vito. Angelo Priola sent word that he was aware of the trouble and wanted it handled quickly, before it got out of hand. But still no plan emerged.

Then, two nights later, while he was watching Eugene Michael's Cabbage Band at Mary O'Brien's, Silvio observed two men gambling at the tables. They suddenly got into a ferocious argument. One accused the other of cheating and would not be placated. He threatened the other man with all manner of brutality if he didn't receive immediate repayment and an apology. The other fighter was in fact far too drunk to apologize to anyone, and both men were put out by the bouncers on the door.

When Silvio reached the lugger that night, he found that another Priola roustabout had been garroted.

As Silvio walked down the wharf and stepped onto the gangway to the lugger, Gaspero tried to stop him. "It would be better if you hold on here for a while."

"Why?" Silvio said belligerently. "*Sono disoccupato?* Have I been fired? I'm tired. I live here. And I need a drink—"

"Just accept what I say. Get lost for a while."

Silvio stared at him. Then, quietly, he muttered, "Get out of my way."

Gaspero didn't move.

Silvio's hands clenched. "Get out of my way. I won't say it again."

After a moment's hesitation, Gaspero shrugged and stepped aside.

Silvio trudged up the plank. He stepped on deck, threw open the door to his bedroom—and stopped. Two figures in the bed turned to face him. One was Madeleine. The other was Nino.

Silvio just stood there, so that Nino was the first to speak. "Silvio, listen. Listen to an older man. She's just a whore. I know you had a soft spot for her but—" He stopped as Silvio reached into his jacket pocket and took out his pistol.

"She may be a whore," Silvio hissed through clenched teeth, "but she's *my* whore." He turned to Madeleine. "And that's *my* bed!"

Madeleine looked crushed. "Silvio, I ain't been here befo'. Yo' never brought me. He said it was his room. I swear."

Silvio turned back to Nino. "What is this?" he screamed. "A game? Fucking my woman in my bed. You sick? *Pazzo?* Are you mad? You got some problem with me? You wanna fuck all my women, Nino? All of them? What is it? What is it with you?" He suddenly leveled his gun at the other man. "Come on! What is it?"

But Nino wasn't intimidated. He smirked at Silvio. "She's just a whore, kid. Don't get too attached. You gotta learn. Be like a man. She fucks for money. She's a three-dollar whore, not even a five."

"My bed, Nino. Why my bed? And don't call me a goddamn kid!"

"It ain't your bed. You work for *me*! You forgot that, didn't you? *You* do as *I* tell you, *kid,* and if I wanna fuck your whore in your bed, you gotta swallow it. This is my boat, *my* boat. Get that clear." He pointed a finger. "You been getting above yourself lately, kid, *ringalluzitto,* cocky, making all these *business* suggestions to Vito and Angelo. As if you were thinking, maybe, of taking over from me—"

The rest of their exchange was cut off from those watching and listening on the wharf as Silvio stepped inside the room and kicked the door shut behind him.

Gaspero held his breath. What Nino said was true; Madeleine *was* a *puttana*. At the same time everyone knew that she was Silvio's. As for Madeleine, she had to make a living. What would happen now? Maybe it was true that Silvio wanted to oust Nino. He was an ambitious kid, and bright. Everyone could see that.

Gaspero listened for gunfire but all he heard at first was more shouting. Then, suddenly, there was a huge crashing sound, as if furniture was being thrown around. Had Nino made a dive for Silvio? The lugger began to rock in the water as the two men rolled around inside the bedroom. There were more shouts and squeals from Madeleine. It sounded as if more furniture had hit the deck. Then the door opened again and this time Madeleine ran out, half-naked. She rushed down the gangplank and up the wharf, still screaming, clutching her clothes. A small crowd began to gather.

The shouting and cursing and crashing went on for some time. At one point a chair was thrown through a window, sending shards of glass everywhere. Gaspero winked at the bodyguard. This was one hell of a fight. *Una zuffa zaffe,* trading punch for punch.

At last, the sounds stopped and there was utter silence from the lugger. Was someone dead? Were they both dead? A few moments later the door opened and Nino appeared. His shirt was torn, there was blood on his face, and his hair went wildly in all directions. He was breathing heavily and sweating. He propped the door open, turned back into the saloon, and bent down. Still bending, he dragged Silvio's figure out onto the deck. Silvio, so far as Gaspero and the others could see, was virtually unconscious. He, too, had his shirt torn, there was blood on his collar and a swelling on his lip. One eye was colored deep crimson.

Nino dragged Silvio to the gangplank and then down it to the foot of the wharf. Then he went back onto the lugger and disappeared into the bedroom, only to return with a few clothes in his arms, a razor, and some cigarette cartons. These he threw on top of Silvio's body, which lay where he had left it, half in the Mississippi and half out.

Still panting heavily, Nino addressed himself to Gaspero but pointed to Silvio. He spoke in scarcely more than a whisper.

"He's out. He's lost it. No one points a gun at me, or screams at me like that. This ain't cock's blood. The kid's history. Don't let him anywhere near this boat again, or any of our wharves." He turned back to the lugger, but then had a second thought. "His dick went to his head and he fell for a whore. He's still a kid. We can do without that. From now on, he's on his own."

He staggered back to the lugger, slamming the bedroom door behind him.

Gaspero looked down to the foot of the gangplank, where Silvio began to stir. He groaned, put his finger to his lip, winced, touched his eye, winced again. He opened his other eye and looked at the people on the wharf, watching him. He glared back but didn't speak. He struggled to his feet, groaning and cursing under his breath. Then he knelt again to pick up his cigarettes and razor and clothes. Most of them were in the water. Then, slowly, still wincing in pain, he walked up the wharf to the top of the levee, and disappeared.

* * *

Silvio lifted the small glass to his cracked lips and downed his drink. He looked at himself in the mirror behind the bar of the Old Absinthe House. Through the flowery writing that was engraved on the mirror he regarded his appearance. *Sono mostro?* he thought. Am I a monster? In the days since Nino had thrown him off the lugger, he had cleaned himself up a bit, but his face still bore the marks of the fight. He felt the cut on his lip and still winced. The flesh around his eye had turned from crimson to black, to yellow, the color of overripe pears. No decent whore, let alone Anna-Maria, would want to come near him in this state.

He looked at his watch. Twenty minutes past midnight. Late; he had better go. He left a few coins on the bar and made his way, a trifle unsteadily, to the door. This was the fifth—or was it the sixth?—bar he had been in tonight, and he'd had a couple of drinks—or maybe more—in each one.

He stood outside on the sidewalk, adjusting to the gloom of the evening. He patted his jacket pocket, to make sure his gun was where it should be. Then he set off home.

Home? He grunted to himself. It was three days since his fight with Nino and there had been no word to come back. He had found accommodation in a shack on Dumaine Street, but spent most of his days in the bars—certainly all of his nights.

Silvio made his way along Burgundy, turned right at Orleans, left on Bourbon, headed two bocks east, and arrived at Dumaine. His shack was three doors along here. His gait was unsteady and uncertain. He reached the shack and stopped. Propping himself against the wall, he felt inside his jacket pocket, took out his gun, put it back again, then found his key. He searched for the key-hole. After a while he turned the key in the lock and let himself in.

Inside, he lit the gaslight, took out his gun, removed his jacket, rolled it up, and put it under the bedclothes. He went out the back, to where there was a patch of earth, and peed. That felt good. Then he went back inside, took off his shoes, turned off the gaslight—and then very quietly crept back out into the garden. He stood against the back wall, in the shadows, holding his gun. Outside in Dumaine Street, a late-night carriage rumbled by; in the distance, a ship's siren could be heard from the river. Somewhere, someone whistled.

Suddenly he heard the front door creak open and he was instantly alert. A moment later he heard whispered voices coming from his bedroom. He could wait no longer and whispered himself.

"Now!"

There was a short pause, during which he crouched and turned to face the wall behind him. Then there was a slight hissing sound, and suddenly the whole garden was illuminated as his room, his new home, exploded. Splinters of wood and glass showered over him as the bed, the gaslight, his rolled-up jacket and shoes, and the three men who had arrived to kidnap or kill him were blown to God knows where. In the brief flash that followed the explosion, he saw the grin on Nino's face.

They had done it again.

11

William Pinkerton stood on the steps of City Hall, on Lafayette Square, and looked about him. St. Charles Avenue, which ran east to west, was an important thoroughfare. Three lines of streetcar rails, the most luxurious hotels, the gasworks, and the French Opera House all lay along this one street. Pinkerton had not been to New Orleans before, but—so far—he liked what he saw. It was quite unlike other American cities, much more European. He looked at his watch and cried out in dismay. His sightseeing had gotten the better of him. His meeting with the mayor was scheduled to begin in four minutes, and if he didn't hurry he would be late.

Moments later he was being shown into the spacious office of Mayor James Milton. Milton was a tall man with a high forehead and a hooked nose. He rose, walked around his desk, and shook hands with Pinkerton. He then turned to another man in the room, who had a mustache and wide blue eyes. "This is David Martell, my chief of detectives. From what you said in your telegram, Martell might be the man for you."

Pinkerton and Martell shook hands, then they all sat down.

"Gentlemen," Pinkerton began, "thank you for seeing me. As you know, Pinkerton's is a private detective agency and I am here at the behest of the Italian government. I am presently engaged in a tour of several U.S. cities—New York, St. Louis, New Orleans, San Francisco—where the population of Italian immigrants, Sicilian immigrants in particular, is very large. The Italian government is especially concerned about its reputation abroad and is worried by the fact that in recent years, a large number of refugees from justice have sought freedom by immigrating, illegally of course, into this country.

"I have with me a list of some one hundred and ten criminals who are believed to have crossed the Atlantic, which I would like to leave with you. Many of them, of course, will have changed their names, but the list may be useful nonetheless.

"I'm also able to tell you that one especially notorious villain, Antonino Greco, may be here in New Orleans. As you may or may not know, Sicilians are a prideful people who allow themselves to be governed by this maddening code of silence, *omertà* as it's called—so information is hard to come by. However, I've been told by the Italian government that one of their informants has said that Greco *is* here in North America and is living in one of our big cities. All the informant knew was that the city where Greco is living has a name that begins with 'New.' New York, New Jersey, New Brunswick, New Orleans maybe.

"Now, if it should happen that you come across Greco, but aren't sure, then I have this, which may help." Pinkerton took out the wrapping paper with Greco's image drawn on it. "Here is the man we are looking for. I can't leave this with you—I have to show it to others—but if you have any luck I can always send it to you as a matter of urgency. With the latest scientific techniques, I may even be able to have some photographic copies made."

He sat back. "I hope what I say is of interest."

Martell leaned forward and nodded. "We have lots of dagos here, Mr. Pinkerton, most of them Sicilians. The worst problem is that they simply won't talk to the police. *Omertà,* you call it? I hadn't heard of that."

"A private code of honor. Rivals might kill each other, but they will never talk to the proper authorities. It makes our life very difficult. We in Pinkerton's have our informers everywhere—but not among the Sicilians."

"Well, I think something of that sort must be happening here in New Orleans," said Martell. "There was an explosion here just a few weeks ago. Three Sicilians were killed. But do you think we can find anyone who saw or heard anything? Nobody will talk, nobody at all."

He shook his head. "Look, we know that a lot of Sicilians work in the docks, unloading fruit. I'll make sure we keep an eye out there." Again he studied the drawing Pinkerton had brought with him. "He's tough looking, this Greco. To be honest, I hope to God he's in New York and not New Orleans."

* * *

"Hush up, now, ladies and gentlemen. Hush *up*, I say!" The barker waited while the crowd quieted. He glared at the people in front of him from the back of the wagon where he was standing.

"That's better," he cried at length. "Some people don't got no manners." The barker was a big man, with a barrel chest and weather-beaten skin. His Stetson hat threw a shadow across his face, wherein lurked massive, shaggy eyebrows. "All right. All right. Now we come to the main attraction of the day, the man you've all heard so much about—"

At this, there was a murmur from the crowd.

"Yes, people. The man who found the Lord one rainy night in Sherman is here in Memphis to entertain you. Chickering's Wild West Show *pree*sents with pride the person who—I can say without *fear* of contradiction—was once the *wickedest* man in Oklahoma."

The barker took off his hat. "The one! The only! The man whom the Lord has chosen to come among us . . . Colonel J. P. Gutelius! Yes!"

Applause broke out as the barker leaned down, held out his hand, and pulled onto the wagon another man, slighter built, with a wispy gray beard, a less imposing hat, a frock coat, and a string tie.

He beamed his smile at the people beneath him, bowed slightly, and raised his arms. "Let us pray!"

The people fell silent, lowered their heads.

Silvio looked about him. He had never been to a Wild West show before and wasn't sure what to expect. Until very recently Memphis had been a Wild West town, so he had been told. He and Nino had seen one or two cowboys on horseback in the streets, but maybe they'd been from the show, rather than real.

Nino and he were in hiding, while the Cataldo business blew over. Memphis was several days from New Orleans by steamer, they were staying in a hotel under assumed names, and Angelo had given them more money than they could spend. They'd had whores galore, were shaved every day, tried all the casinos, had been to the floating circus—on board a huge steamer—and even visited the Civil War battlefield at nearby Shiloh, though Nino had found that really boring.

"A-men," cried the colonel, finishing the prayers.

"A-men," called out the crowd.

"Good people, thank you for comin'. I ain't as young as I used t'be, 'n' I know Memphis is changin'. So today, I got somethin' special, somethin' wonderful, somethin' *dangerous*!"

"Yes!" cried some of the crowd. They knew what was coming. Despite the patter, they'd seen all this before.

Silvio craned forward to see.

"People! You're gonna see a horse—"

"Yes!" cried out part of the crowd again. "Yes!"

"But this ain't jes *any* horse, y'hear? This is a stallion, an *outlaw* stallion. A stallion which, if I were to take him back to Dade County in Kansas, or Cheyenne, Wyoming, or Sioux Falls, Dakota, would be arrested, and then shot. This stallion—which I call Old Spanish—is probably the most *fee*rocious horse that *ever* lived. He killed—he kicked to death, or trampled, or threw off at high speed—seven people. He killed James Cotton in the Dakotas, Hull Galloway in Independence, Ivar LaFollete on the Chisholm Trail. I never ride Old Spanish. I got more sense. But so long as I don't ride him, we're friends, him and me.

"You can all meet him presently." The colonel reached into his pocket and took out a handbell. He clanged it. "But first we got work to do."

"What now?" hissed Nino, obviously growing bored.

"Wait!" Silvio hissed in reply. He was intrigued.

A woman standing in front of them turned. "Hush now, you two. This is an auction. People bring things they don't need no more. The colonel sells them, for a small fee. You watch."

Sure enough, another woman had climbed on the wagon, carrying a violin.

"All right!" shouted the colonel. "Hush up now. This good lady has a violin. Seems her husband died and she don't need it no more." He stared down at the crowd and smiled. "Someone out there must need to make music—ain't no decent home without music. Let's start at five dollars, five dollars ... makita five, makita five. ... Oh, let's take the glory road, people!" He clanged his bell as someone raised a hand. "I got the five, makita six ... Six! Thank you, Lord, for the blessings of the day. ... The six ..."—*clang!*—"the seven ... and the lady makes it eight! Thank you, Mother. I'll ask Him to give you a double portion of grace. ..."

Nino had seen enough and moved away, slipping through the crowd. "A religious auctioneer," he said under his breath as they escaped. "Now I've seen everything."

Silvio was inclined to agree. At the same time he couldn't help but admire a clever piece of selling. He found himself wondering if there would be a market for an auctioneer in New Orleans.

They walked on. Past the shooting gallery and the blacksmiths, selling spurs. Silvio wondered if he should buy Anna-Maria something, a gift. Yes, but not spurs, he thought. Something more personal. He'd noticed a bookshop elsewhere in Memphis and he knew she loved to read.

The blacksmith reminded him that they hadn't waited to see the outlaw stallion. Annunziata had been kicked by a horse once, when they were children. Everyone in the *bivio* had been very worried for a while and she'd had a terrible bruise and walked with a limp for weeks. But eventually she'd made a complete recovery.

He didn't think so much about her now. But occasionally he couldn't help it. He remembered the bruise on her skin vividly. He remembered her skin vividly, too, the blemishes on her knees and elbows where she had fallen as a child, the fold of her eyelids, the lobes of her ears—none of these memories had faded when he thought back. Did that mean he still . . . ?

There had been a time when they were fishing from a boat in Lake Arancio when Zata had hooked herself. In casting her line, the crude, handmade fishhook had snagged her skin and become embedded behind her ear. Silvio had managed to work it free, but not without cutting the skin and shedding Annunziata's blood. She had been very stoic, but during the rest of the day they had caught several trout, and put it down to Zata's blood being on the hook. After that it had become their lucky hook and they always used it. He had brought it with him to America, though it was months since he had been fishing. He decided he must search out that hook when he got back to New Orleans.

"Look at this." Nino had stopped by a huge, pyramid-shaped tent. A sign read INDIAN MUSEUM.

Nino led the way in, paying the five cents' entrance charge for himself and Silvio.

Elaborate feathered costumes greeted them. Next to those were some moccasins, made of beaver pelts, according to the note

written on a card. Next came a map of where the various tribes—
Pawnees, Klamaths, Sioux, and Shoshonis—were located. After
that came a range of Indian weapons: bows, arrows, knives and
daggers, spears for fishing. Silvio had tried a spear once to catch
fish in Lake Arancio: hopeless. Annunziata had laughed at him.

Next came something he didn't at first recognize. It was about
the size of a hand and covered in hair. At first he thought it was
some sort of animal, or purse of sorts made out of animal skin.

Then he felt an itching down his spine and he nearly retched. It
was a human scalp.

"I'll have another six oysters, and some more milk, please, Hedi."
The New Orleans chief of detectives, David Martell, didn't drink
alcohol, but he ceded to no one his passion for shellfish. Every
night on his way home from the office, he stopped off at Dominick
Virgut's for dinner, and it was always the same: oysters followed
by chicken, washed down with milk.

He looked at the man across the table. Emmett Villard was a
sourpuss—he always looked as though he'd just had some bad
news—but he was a fine detective. He wasn't drinking *or* eating.

"Emmett, I asked you here because I have a special job for you
and I don't want anyone back at City Hall to know about it."

Villard sniffed.

Martell laid his hand on a sheet of paper next to his plate. "This
is a list of names, Italian names. All are men and all are wanted by
the Italian government—all, without exception, have committed
serious crimes. And all are here, living in America, on the run and
using false names."

The oysters arrived and Martell squeezed a little lemon juice on
them. He picked up his fork.

"You remember that bombing the other week?"

Villard nodded.

"There's a fight going on among the dagos in this town—
Sicilian trash mainly—and it's my guess that if some of the people
on this list are hiding out here, now is a good time to go looking
for them. If they're fighting among themselves, that can work to
our benefit—it should make information easier to come by.
People will be less loyal to each other."

He forked an oyster into his mouth and closed his eyes in

pleasure. He swallowed and then wiped his lips with a napkin. Like the tablecloths around the restaurant the napkin was printed with a red check on it.

"I understand you speak Italian."

Villard nodded. "My mother was Italian."

"Good. I want you to go undercover. Live in the French Quarter as an Italian, invent a background for yourself, get a job in a bar maybe, but keep your eyes open and your ears tuned in to all the gossip. I want a weekly report. We'll meet here—don't come to City Hall. Is that clear?"

"Sure. But . . . why are you suddenly leaning on the dagos?"

Martell was eating another oyster. He finished chewing before speaking. "There's an election soon. I hear the eyeties are backing Parker. If he wins, I'm out as chief of detectives. A scandal involving the dagos is just what we need."

He picked up another oyster and slid it smoothly into his mouth. As he chewed he picked up the list of names and handed it across the table.

"Welcome back," said Angelo Priola. "How was life on the Mississippi?"

Nino shrugged. "I don't like boats, but if you have to go on one, then the *Crescent City* is the one for me."

After a month in Memphis, Nino and Silvio were back in New Orleans. Angelo had judged it safe to bring them back and they were now living together on the lugger as if the fight between them had never happened—which, in reality, it never had. They had been called to a meeting at Angie's house and had entered by the back door.

"That was a foxy plan," Priola said, going to the bar and pouring the bourbons. "Was the fight your idea, Silvio?" The old man was learning that while Nino had the balls to blow people to pieces, it was Silvio who had the brains to concoct these diabolical operations.

Accepting his bourbon, Silvio nodded.

Priola gave him an appraising look. "Well, there'll be no more trouble from the Cataldos, that's certain. I expect you've heard that Alfredo was one of those killed?"

They both nodded.

"He didn't infiltrate your teams, of course, the way the others did. But he couldn't resist paying Silvio a visit. They were going to torture him"—he gestured to Silvio—"before killing him." He shrugged. "So that's both Cataldo brothers gone and the wharves are ours." He looked across to Nogare. "Which is just as well, because things are changing in this town."

He settled back in his seat. "There's an election due about a year from now and I'm backing one of the candidates for mayor— Harrison Parker. If our side wins, certain things fall into place, which is why I want to give you three here the general outline of what's in my head. Whoever is mayor of New Orleans heads the committee that selects the chief of police. If we can get the police on our side, we'll be like the family in Palermo. Police protection for our wharves would make them safer. See what I mean?"

They all grunted agreement.

"The current mayor, James Milton, has an Irish chief of detectives, someone called David Martell. They both own a piece of a restaurant here, an oyster bar called the Red Lantern. My plan is to replace them with people more . . . accommodating to our interests. But political campaigns are expensive. So, over the next weeks and months, I need much bigger profits from the fruit wharves. You won't have the Cataldos to contend with, but I still want some new ideas for those businesses." He looked around at the other men in the room. His eye settled on Silvio. "You're the idea man. Think of something."

Sono barbone? Silvio thought. Am I a poodle now? All he said was, "I already know what I would do."

Priola raised his eyebrows.

"You've got the wharves tied up, though you need more protection there. Where you can expand is in the bars and whorehouses. You need three shifts on the river, for loading and unloading. You also need an extra group of men—just to watch, to stop infiltration, and to check out anybody suspicious who is recruited. That makes four groups, or regimes."

"Tell me about the bars."

"You need a fifth group. We could operate it the way it works in Sicily, in the orange and almond groves. We let people operate their own outfits—bars, restaurants, grocery stores, whatever— but we receive a share of their turnover each week."

"Just like that?"

Silvio smiled. "I'm sure one or two will need a little persuasion. But only one or two."

They all looked at him.

"This has more advantages than you think. We get to earn more through protection *and* we 'ask' the shops and the bars to buy goods from our wharves. Also, it gives us eyes and ears all over town. If people pay us for protection and anyone else gets out of line, we know about it pretty quick."

Priola tried not to look impressed. "What's in it for you?"

"You give Nino the docks, you give me the French Quarter. You're still the Capo, Giovanni's still your *consigliere*. Nino is *sottocapo* of four regimes, I'm the *caporegime* in the Quarter. People will soon learn that the Priola family is properly organized in New Orleans. Like a family in Sicily. We're used to shifting fruit quickly. Our men take orders and move fast because otherwise the fruit rots. I'm saying we simply move that organization inland, to the Quarter. No one else is organized like us."

Priola turned to Nogare. "Well?"

Nogare shrugged. "He's right about protection. It works in Sicily. It could work here. But there's a big difference."

"Which is?"

"In Sicily, everybody is Sicilian. So far, in New Orleans, we have only moved among Sicilians. Which means the police are never involved. If we start the same rackets here, offering protection, we're going to run up against the Irish, the Germans, the niggers, everybody. Gradually, the police will find out more and more about us."

Priola looked at Silvio. "He has a point."

"Yes, but this is America. We can't *just* deal with Sicilians. Whoever they are—Poles, Swedish, Portuguese, French—if they think their store or workshop or bar will be torched, they won't be that eager to go to the police. Think of the rewards. You'll be able to buy the election, and the police will be on our side anyway."

"Nino, what do you think?"

Nino drummed his fingertips on his lips. "I think people in this town are frightened of us right now. Those who know. Those who don't know can be told. It's a good time."

Priola nodded. "I'd like to think about this. Silvio, as usual, has put his finger on something very clever. But Giovanni's point needs considering, too." He drained his glass. "That's enough strategy for one night. This was supposed to be a welcome-home party—and I've got a surprise for you." He smirked at them. "There's a new batch of girls at Madge Leigh's. Fresh flesh! Nothing like it, huh?"

They all drained their glasses and got up. In the hall, as they went out, Anna-Maria was walking by. She smiled at her father but gave Silvio a hard stare. Then she looked at his coat, lying on a chair. Silvio picked up his coat and put it on. He put his hands in his pockets and immediately felt a slip of paper. For the time being he left it where it was.

Nino and he left the house and got into the carriage that Priola had ordered. It was already dark, but when they reached Madge Leigh's, about fifteen minutes later, he gave his coat to the check girl but kept the paper. Silvio could read well now, so he had no problem with Anna-Maria's note. It said, "Tuesday, as usual. In the lugger."

Angelo Priola had been right. Madge Leigh's was stuffed with new girls, many of them quadroons. Silvio was intrigued. He liked fresh flesh, but he was also looking forward to seeing Madeleine again. It had been a month since he had been with her and he had yet to thank her for helping them fake the fight. Where was she? Was she upstairs with someone? Here was Madge Leigh herself now, working her way along the bar, chatting to her favorite customers. He would ask her.

Silvio ordered some wine and stood listening to the new band, named after its leader, the clarinetist Alphonse Picou. The music was slow and mellow.

Gradually Madge Leigh came toward him. Funny how no one ever shortened her name to Madge; she was always Madge Leigh—even, it was said, in bed. She was a small, birdlike woman with sharp features and a very precise manner. She was wearing a bright red dress, off the shoulder, and a necklace that he could only hope was made of glass and fake diamonds. If it were real it would surely be stolen from her before the end of the week. She needed protection, he thought idly.

"Welcome back, boys," she whispered, smiling and offering her cheek to be kissed. "Ah'd heard yo' were in town. No fireworks tonight, ah hope."

Nino shook his head. "We're here to try your new girls."

"That's mo' like it. They real keen, an' one or two of 'em are very young. Ah always keep yo' in mind, Nino." She grinned.

"I don't see Madeleine," said Silvio. "She upstairs?"

Madge Leigh's face hardened. "Maddie's gone, Silvio. She left mo' than a week ago."

"Gone? Why? Gone where?"

"Where, ah don' know, ah'm sho'. As to why, well, ah only own twenny percent of the joint. Mr. Priola owns the bigger piece. An', two weeks ago, he suddenly announces he's changin' all the girls. Good fer business, he said, though we was doin' well enough, it seemed to me, an' lots of people, like yo' all, had their favorites. But no, all the girls had to be changed. Men like fresh blood, he said, though if yo' ask me, that daughter of his had somethin' to do with it."

"Anna-Maria? Why you say that?"

"She ain't hardly never come to the club, but she was here las' week, makin' all sorts of suggestions, for new decorations, new lights, new food—'n' new women. Mr. Priola, as you mus' know, dotes on her. He always does anythin' she asks."

Silvio was furious. His mind went back to their last afternoon on the lugger, when Anna-Maria had questioned him so closely about Madeleine. He had tried to be careful in his replies, not wanting to make Anna-Maria jealous, but he had obviously failed. As soon as he was out of the way, she had gotten rid of her rival.

He finished his wine and ordered another. His indignation mounted. He became determined that Anna-Maria would not have things all her own way. He would find Madeleine and reinstate her at Madge Leigh's. The French Quarter wasn't that big. Or else he would go someplace else to sleep with her if Madge Leigh would not agree to take her back. After all, Madeleine had played her part well in preparing for the fake argument with Nino. And that had led to the success of their plans with the Cataldos. He owed her a lot.

He drained his second glass and ordered a third. As he gulped at it he thought angrily of Anna-Maria. Come Tuesday, far from having sex on the lugger, there would be a fight to rival the one he'd had with Nino. Except this time it would be for real.

The corner of Orleans and Dauphine streets was dominated by a large flower shop. A big sign outside in gold letters read

DONOVAN'S GARDEN. Silvio and Gaspero stepped inside. A man came toward them. He was thin, with a pale skin.

Silvio spoke first. "I'm looking for Mr. Donovan."

"I'm Patrick Donovan."

"Ah, good. Mr. Donovan, I represent certain business interests in New Orleans. A group of friends who hate all the bombings and knifings and garrotings that have been taking place in recent weeks have decided to do something about it."

Donovan stared at them.

"The police have obviously not had much success at either stopping the violence or catching the criminals, otherwise what I am proposing wouldn't be necessary. But we—my friends, that is—feel that we have the answer."

"And what might that be?"

"An arrangement. A contract, if you like. My friends will guarantee peace, a quiet life in the area, complete safety for you to carry on your business in the normal way, and you—along with all the other businesses in the neighborhood—will pay a small proportion of your turnover for this service. *Una tassa particolare,* as we say in Sicily. A private tax. Nothing that will hurt, you understand. Just enough for my friends to be able to meet their overhead for offering this service. You understand?"

Donovan threw back his head. "I understand very well, you greasy dago. You're offering a protection racket. Well, you can hurry back to whichever stone you crawled out from under, and go play with yourself. I'm not paying protection to you or any of your so-called friends—more slimy Sicilians, I'll wager. This is a decent neighborhood and I've got a good business here, built with my own hands and with no help from wops like you. So get lost." He shouted, "Do you hear? Go back to your own kind with all those other eels in the river."

Silvio didn't move. He just stood, staring at Donovan. Then, instead of leaving, he strolled around the shop, looking at the blooms, the dried flowers, the miniature trees. He stopped and looked down. "What's this?"

"What does it look like? Ice."

Four blocks of ice stood slowly melting in a shady spot.

"Why have these got flowers in them?"

"It's the fashion. You wouldn't know, I'll be bound, but society hostesses put ice on their tables, in trays, to cool down their dinner parties. The flowers make the ice look pretty, and at the end of the evening the ladies can take away a fresh bloom as a gift. Not everyone eats with their fingers, like in Little Palermo."

This Donovan was becoming tiresome.

"Think carefully about my offer of an arrangement, Mr. Donovan. You can always find me at Madge Leigh's. I won't come here again."

"Make sure you don't. Now go spread your slime someplace else!"

Again Silvio stood his ground. For a moment or two he and Donovan remained staring at each other. *Sono anguilla?* Silvio thought. Am I an eel? Eels wriggle. He wasn't wriggling.

Silvio stooped down and picked up one of the ice blocks. It was heavy, but he managed to lift it above his head. Then he let it fall onto the stone floor. With a dull thud, it smashed into a thousand pieces.

"This better be good, Silvio. Mrs. Priola is jealous of Sundays. Only day she sees me, she says."

"Nearly there," replied Silvio. "Up Orleans to Rampart." He led the way as Nino and Angelo followed. They had been lunching at a restaurant called the Court of Two Sisters, on Royal and Toulouse, so it wasn't far.

As they approached Rampart, however, the normal street noises began to be overwhelmed by a regular rhythmic thumping and chanting. Farther north it got louder still, until, as they turned the corner, the beat drowned out all other sound. They stopped and stared.

"I'd heard about this," breathed Angelo after a while. "But I ain't never been. They're all niggers."

In front of them, in the square, hundreds of Negroes were dancing. Dancing and chanting, dancing and slapping hand drums, dancing with their eyes closed. Some beat their hand drums with bones, others wore black top hats, battered and broken, still others had paint smeared on their faces. All were in a frenzy.

"Okay," growled Angelo. "Okay. So this is voodoo, Congo Square on Sunday. I'd heard of it, now I've seen it. So? We ain't niggers."

In reply, Silvio pointed diagonally across the square. "She's the reason we are here, Angie."

They saw a woman, a black woman with long black hair, and a black dress with a white lace collar and cuffs. Her hands were held by women on her right and left as she swayed from side to side in time to the beat. Her huge eyes were closed.

"Widow Milan," said Silvio. "The most powerful woman in the city."

At this, Angelo turned to look at him. "How come?"

"She's a voodoo queen. *The* voodoo queen, in fact. They say she even put a spell on her old man, and he disappeared."

"So? What's it to us? What do we want with niggers?" Nino had drunk a lot of wine at lunch and his belligerence was never very far from the surface.

"Let me ask you both a question," said Silvio. "Do you believe in voodoo?"

Angelo couldn't understand where this was heading. "I'm a Catholic, for Christ's sake. I go to confession every Tuesday. Voodoo is for ignorant niggers."

"Nino?"

Nino looked across the square. He didn't appear as convinced as Angelo. All he said was, "I guess not."

They both stared at Silvio.

"You call me the idea man," he said to Angelo. "You said you wanted something foxy. Well, here's an idea. The niggers are the biggest group in the city. Bigger than the Sicilians, bigger than the Portuguese or the Germans. Now the niggers are free, hundreds of them—thousands—are moving into the city. And the only thing that bothers them, gets to them, is voodoo."

"What are you getting at?" Angelo's tone had changed.

"The docks are expanding. We're already taking on people who aren't Sicilian. Blacks, quadroons, Creoles. Say we pay Widow Milan a little visit, have a talk with her."

"To say what?"

"Come *on*, Angelo! She knows she's a phony. She's a goddamn hairdresser by day! She sells curses and charms and they work—or don't work—by hit or miss, pure chance. Say we had an agreement . . . so that when she delivers her curse . . . it works. Think how much *her* power would increase. But *we* would actually be controlling *her*."

Angelo regarded Silvio with astonishment. "You think that could really work? You sure she has all that power?"

Silvio pointed across the square. "There's your answer. She fills this place every Sunday, and there are illegal meetings all over the bayous on other nights. If we control her, we have a big say over the niggers. Don't forget she could even put a jinx on the Cataldo bars and gambling joints. All they need is a few 'accidents' that she had predicted."

Angelo looked at Nino. "What you think?"

"There's more 'n' more nigger shop owners, music joints. It'd save a lot of manpower if they bought lucky charms from her, rather than paid protection direct to us. It would confuse the law, too." Nino punched Silvio lightly in the shoulder. "The kid's smart, Angie."

He ducked as a hard right hook was returned in his direction. Silvio still hated being called a kid.

Normally, on Tuesday afternoons, after Nino had made himself scarce, Silvio opened the wine in time for Anna-Maria's arrival and drew all the curtains. Not today. Today, he waited in the saloon, fully clothed.

He heard her footsteps as she came aboard. He followed her sounds as she went to his bedroom, opened the door, called out his name, then walked around the deck looking for him. First she went to the other side, in case he was smoking, looking out over the river. Then she went to the galley, in case he was preparing some food. Finally she approached the saloon and opened the door.

"*There* you are! Why are you sitting in here? And why are you still dressed? We don't want to waste a moment." She put down the book she had brought to read to him, but then she took in the expression on his face. "What is it, Silvio! You seem angry—why?"

He blew cigarette smoke in her face. "You got rid of Madeleine."

She colored. "I did not—"

"You're blushing, you liar. Madge Leigh saw you in her club last week, changing everything: decorations, food, the lights—and the girls. You tried to disguise it, didn't you? Hoping no one would notice. But all you wanted to do was get rid of *one* girl."

"Silvio, she was a whore!"

"I liked that whore. That *whore*, as you call her, helped Nino and me flush out those Cataldos, helped your father regain control of these wharves, which in time will help him finance his political campaigns. That whore has done more to keep you in fine clothes and booze than you've ever done for yourself."

"Silvio, I'm sorry. I didn't know—"

"Yes, you did. Don't play innocent with me, Anna-Maria. *La Beata Vergine.* We both know it's not true, and on this boat at least, it won't work. You're a jealous, scheming bitch and you've been found out."

"You should be flattered I'm jealous."

"*Sono bambino?* You want everything your way. With you there's no room for anyone else. What I did with Madeleine *never* interfered with anything I did with you—until you let it."

"That's not—"

"We could have gone on the way we were for months, years maybe. But you had to spoil it." He stubbed out his cigarette. "If I can't have Madeleine, I don't want you either. Go fuck someone else."

She gripped the back of a chair and swayed slightly. Then she took control of herself and straightened up. "Be careful what you say, Silvio. Don't treat me like Nino treats *his* women. Remember who I am. You mustn't speak to me like that."

"I'll speak to you the way I want. I liked Madeleine, and I'm going to find her."

"You're pathetic. She's a quadroon whore. A nigger whore!"

"No! You've already forgotten what I said. She helped us. And look how you've repaid her. I tell you, Anna-Maria, it's you who's the whore." He paused, then spat. *"Puttana!"*

She glared at him. Her eyes narrowed and her lips closed. He registered a look on her face that he had never seen before. A mean and dangerous look.

"I won't take that from you," she hissed. "Just because you can read and write now, and know one fork from another. Just because you know what to do with that thing between your legs doesn't give you the right to speak to me like that. Don't underestimate me, Silvio. Just because my father made you his *caporegime* doesn't mean you can treat me like one of your *soldati*. If you want a fight I'll give you one." She picked up her book from the table. "And I fight like I fuck. Dirty!"

With that, she turned on her heel and went out. He listened as the sound of her footsteps disappeared down the gangplank.

"Come in, chil'. What kin ah do fer yo'?"

Silvio sat on the stool in front of Widow Milan. He had heard fantastic tales about her house on St. Ann Street. They said it contained a twenty-foot python, mummified babies, the skull of her dead husband, and two altars, one for bad luck and one for good luck. In fact, the room was small and hot and smelled of some sort of incense. Small bags hung everywhere. These, Silvio had been forewarned, contained charms, allegedly composed of dried lizard, bat's wings, owl's liver, small pieces of flesh from the bodies of black people who had committed suicide. He didn't believe a word of it.

Tonight Widow Milan had on a white turban, huge earrings, and several necklaces made of shells and beads. She wore no rings on her fingers but a bright scarlet sash at her waist. The skeleton of an alligator jaw sat on the table between them.

Silvio wasn't frightened exactly. He certainly didn't believe in voodoo mumbo jumbo, not at all. But the fact that so many people *did* believe it meant he had to tread carefully. The basis of Widow Milan's power might be phony, but her power was real.

"Yo' got an achin' heart, chil'? Yo' in love? Yo' need a *gris-gris*?"

A *gris-gris*, Silvio knew, was a charm, good or bad, according to need.

"No, ma'am."

"Then what yo' wan'? Speak, chil'. Hurry now."

"Friend of mine came to see you the other day," Silvio said. "Name of Nino. Said his girl was acting up. Throwing herself at other men. You sold him a *gris-gris* for a dollar, said it would work. That my friend's woman would come back. She hasn't."

"Yuh gotta give these things time, chil'. Time."

"I had another friend come here. He had a fever. His *gris-gris* cost a dollar-fifty. A dollar-fifty! He's still sick."

"What *is* this, young man? I don't discuss no other folk who comes here. That's my business. Now, yuh wan' a *gris-gris* or what?"

Silvio smiled. He took out his gun. "This is my *gris-gris*," he said softly.

Widow Milan stared at him.

He pointed the gun at her and cocked the hammer.

"Lordy," she breathed.

He grinned. "If I was going to shoot—there's nothing you could do. None of your charms or spells or trances would save you, would they?"

"Ah'd git yo' from beyon' the grave, though."

Silvio put the gun down. "No, you wouldn't. You don't have that power, lady. You don't have no power at all."

She narrowed her eyes. "Be careful, chil'. Yo' know what yo' sayin'?"

"I sure do. But don't worry. I'm not here to break your power. I'm here to make a deal."

She cackled. "Ah don' do no deals with no white boys. I don' need to. I'm Widow Milan."

"You haven't heard the deal yet." He fingered the gun again.

"The way I see it, you work as a hairdresser during the day. You listen to white folk's tittle-tattle, catch up on the news, and back here you turn that knowledge into predictions. Lots of black people believe you because you're dressed up in beads and shells and surround yourself with weird things. But the truth is: You're wrong as often as you're right, maybe more."

He paused, waiting for her to contradict him, but she didn't.

He put his gun away. "Now, how about this for a deal? Next time you have someone who comes to see you and wants something bad to happen to someone, you tell me. Me and my friends will arrange for an accident. Understand? We'll make it look natural, an argument maybe, a fire, whatever. But something bad will happen. Think about that. In no time at all, your power will be greater than ever. People will truly fear you. They will say Widow Milan can really put the *gris-gris* on someone. You'll be richer than ever, famous—and feared. That's what you like, isn't it?" Silvio could see he was right. Her eyes were glistening. "Now, in exchange for this . . . backup . . . you occasionally have to help us."

"How d'yo' mean?"

"Nothing bad. One time we might ask you to tell all the nigger folk to do this rather than that. Not to unload a certain ship maybe, because it's jinxed. Not to buy their booze in certain liquor stores, because it's watered maybe. Not to work on certain construction

sites because the ground is cursed in some way. Simple things."
He smiled at her.

She stared back at him. For a moment she seemed to mumble,
in a language he didn't recognize. Was she putting a spell on him?
He reached for his gun again. "I'm not scared of you, Widow
Milan. All your *gris-gris* ain't worth one bullet."

She stopped her mumbling, and sighed. "Who is yo', young
man? Yo' the devil?"

He looked at her, as if he were considering the idea. Then he
started to chuckle. "Yes, ma'am, indeed. That's exactly who I am."

They were both laughing now. "You can tell folks that tonight
you had a visit from the devil hisself." He pocketed his gun and
stood up. Looking down, he suddenly stopped laughing. "I'll be in
touch," he said.

Father Ignazio Serravalle took the baby in his arms. The infant
gurgled a few low squeals but fortunately did not object further.
The abbot stepped closer to the font near the rear of the nave. As
usual the plain simplicity in the Church of the Madonna dell'Olio
was working its magic on the people assembled. They stood quietly, waiting for the ceremony to begin.

The abbot made the infant safe in his arms, looked up, and
beamed at the people around him. To an extent, on this occasion at
least, his smile was false. By rights, the gathering for this baptism
ought to have been bigger. But a cholera outbreak on the island
had limited travel. There had been many deaths already. People
were frightened.

Only two dozen relatives and friends of Annunziata and Gino
had turned up, including one or two Priolas from Palermo, who,
after the baptism, would no doubt give him news of America.

"Will the parents stand here, please?" Father Ignazio pointed to
a space by the font. "And the godparents here. Thank you. The rest
of you can just gather 'round." He ran through the service quickly
because the infant was becoming more skittish.

The abbot had been delighted when Annunziata had given birth
to a baby boy and had immediately agreed to perform the baptism.
He had heard rumors that her marriage to Gino was not turning
out especially well, but the birth of the child seemed to contradict
that. He had been surprised to find that the boy's names were to be
Antonino Sylvano, but there was nothing he could do. Surely she

was not *still* carrying a torch for Sylvano Randazzo? He had been gone two years now. The abbot could only hope the birth of the young Antonino Sylvano would come to replace the other Sylvano in Annunziata's affections. She certainly appeared to dote on the child.

After the service there was wine and salami and goat's cheese back at the *bivio*. The abbot immediately sought out Ruggiero Priola, who had come all the way from Palermo especially for the ceremony. "You bring news, I hope," Father Ignazio began.

"I do," said Ruggiero, "though I fear it is not all good. Nino and Sylvano are now with Angelo, my cousin. They have changed their names, are settled, and are safe. Nino is sending money back—through us—though only Don Bastiano knows this. Angelo says that Silvio has the gift." Ruggiero tapped his temple. "He has brains, that boy. He sent a letter to Annunziata." He grinned. "But we intercepted it." Then his features darkened. "But in Palermo we also know that the Rome government is beginning to stir. They have sent a list to America. More than a hundred names. Many of our friends are on it. So are Nino's and Silvio's. We are planning to alert them."

The abbot nodded. "And tell me," he said. "The cholera. How is it?"

"Bad. More than seventy people in Palermo have died. And it's spreading. There have been cases in Bagheria and Alcamo."

"Don't tell people here," replied the abbot. "A christening should be a joyful occasion. We don't want to spoil the happiness of Gino and Annunziata."

Patrick Donovan swayed slightly as he made his way along Royal Street. He had drunk too much tonight. The oysters at the Red Lantern were always good, but he shouldn't have had the extra half dozen or the wine that went with them. Still, what harm could half a dozen oysters do? It was his birthday, for Christ's sake.

Not that it was still his birthday, strictly speaking. Midnight had come and gone more than an hour ago. He stumbled as he missed yet another loose plank in the sidewalk. Careful.

He stepped into the road. It was muddy, but he felt safer. He reached the end of the block and turned in to Orleans Street. He stopped, bewildered. A crowd of people blocked the roadway. But it was past one o'clock! New Orleans was a late town but not this late—

All of a sudden he saw—beyond the crowd and above their heads—some sparks flying upward. At almost the same time his eyes focused on the smoke, darker than the night, and his nostrils took in the tang of burning. *Something was on fire!*

Already, he was running. He slithered in the mud, but he didn't care now. He reached the outskirts of the crowd and pushed past several people. The crowd grew denser and he was forced to elbow his way forward. He had to see where the fire was.

He lifted a child out of the way, despite the protests of its mother. Then, all of a sudden, he could see. He could see flames. He could hear crackling as wood was consumed, as glass broke. The smell of the fire filled his nostrils and smoke began to smart his eyes. But he felt a sense of relief. It wasn't his shop on fire.

It was a shoe shop about three doors away, an old-fashioned cobbler's owned by a German. Donovan's woozy head had cleared immediately at the first whiff of danger and he refocused now on his German neighbor, whom he could see standing in the road, obviously grief-stricken.

Donovan went up to him. "Hans? I'm sorry—I really am. What happened? Was it electrical?" The newfangled electrical light in New Orleans was always causing problems.

"This wasn't electrical," hissed the German. "Someone started this fire, deliberately."

"What! How do you know?"

"Those dagos told me there'd be trouble if I didn't pay them protection."

Donovan stared at him. "But . . . you can't be certain it was them."

Even as he said this Donovan realized how stupid he sounded. He looked along the street to his own shop, three doors away. He was next.

"I'm looking for a girl named Madeleine. Tall, dark, well built. A quadroon. Does she work here?"

Silvio's English was improving all the time, but on this occasion at least, it didn't help. The woman behind the bar shook her head. "Nevah 'eard of 'er."

There were countless bars and brothels in the French Quarter, most of them on CustomHouse, Burgundy, and Bourbon streets. Silvio's task was made slightly easier by the fact that Madeleine was a quadroon. Not all houses accepted girls of color, so there was no need for him to waste time in all-white houses.

He had been looking for three days with no luck. He glanced at his watch: it was nearly ten and he was hungry. He would try one more whorehouse and call it a night. Madge Leigh's was only a block from where he was now and he was due to meet Nino there at ten-thirty. He should make it easily.

The next place was Carrie Freemantle's, reputed to be part owned by Harrison Parker, the man Priola was sponsoring as mayor. Silvio knew that in his political campaigns, Parker had promised to clean up the French Quarter, but he doubted if those grandiose plans would come to anything. It was just an empty claim designed to land a few votes from the Southern Methodists and Baptists who lived in the suburbs.

Silvio mounted the steps of Carrie's and pushed at the door. The bar had a nautical theme, with fishermen's nets and stuffed fish festooning the walls. Behind the bar was a huge glass tank with live lobsters and crayfish.

He ordered a bourbon, leaning against the bar for a moment. It was usually easy to tell who the madam was in any house. She was invariably older, had obviously once been stunning looking, and now wore a colorful dress that enhanced her bosom, holding out the prospect that, for favored customers, the madam might oblige.

In Carrie's, Silvio had no problem locating her. She was a striking redhead, probably fifty, and wearing a vivid green dress that exposed her neck, shoulders, and the upper third of her breasts. She was flirting with various men and playfully hitting them with a fan.

For perhaps ten minutes Silvio watched as she worked the room. But she had noticed him, too, and the fact that he was watching her. She suddenly crossed the room and walked straight up to him. "You should learn to keep your eyes to yourself. You make me feel naked."

"In your case that's nothing to be ashamed of."

She smiled, flattered despite herself. "You're new here. I would have noticed someone as handsome as you. Who do you want? Young, old, black, white, one, or two?"

"Let me buy you a drink first. It's better not to hurry these things."

She acknowledged his politeness, then nodded to the barman. He would know what to bring.

When the drink arrived, they toasted one another.

"I like redheads," he said. "Green suits you."

Again she smiled. "Not so fast. I don't even know your name, and *I* decide who I sleep with."

"I can wait. I'm still not twenty-one. You can call me Livio."

"Well, Livio, if you're as good with your dick as you are with your tongue, you'll be very popular here. Like to see some girls now?"

"Yes and no," replied Silvio. "In fact, there's a particular girl I'm looking for. A quadroon called Madeleine."

Carrie stiffened. "What do you want with her?"

"So she *does* work here?" Silvio was part excited and part relieved.

"She *did*!"

"What do you mean, *did*?"

"She's in jail."

"What!"

"She stole a client's watch. He was so drunk she thought he wouldn't notice, but he did. Called the police and they arrested her. She was carted off last Thursday. I heard she stands trial in a couple of weeks."

"But she's just a child."

"Serves her right. We charge good prices here and the girls are well paid. There's no need to fleece the customers, even if they are drunk."

Silvio's mind was in a whirl. What had come over Madeleine? He had been drunk countless times in her company and she had never stolen from him. When she had worked in Madge Leigh's, she had been well liked by the customers and by Madge Leigh herself. Something drastic must have happened to bring about this change.

He looked at his watch: ten-twenty. He had to keep his appointment with Nino. In any case, the prison would be closed to the public by now. But he would find her in the morning, to see if there was anything he could do. She badly needed to see a friendly face, of that he was sure.

He took Carrie's hand. "I'm afraid I can't stay now—but I'll be back. As I said, I like redheads." He finished his drink, paid, and went out.

Madge Leigh's was crowded. Whatever Silvio felt about the change of personnel at the club, he had to admit that the new band was really hot, and was attracting more and more customers. So was this new drink someone had invented, brandy and bitters, a "cocktail" as it was being called. He threaded his way through the crush to the back. After Priola had decided to go along with Silvio's idea for reorganization, it had been agreed that, although Silvio would continue to sleep on the lugger for safety's sake, he would use the back room at Madge Leigh's for his daily head-quarters. People knew where to find him, could leave messages there, he was protected still, he could take his meals there. It made sense. Nino and he had dinner at Madge Leigh's most nights, before the big card game started—it was no longer confined to Tuesdays and Thursdays. Priola sometimes joined them, with Nogare.

When Silvio reached the back room Nino was already there. Stella, one of the girls, was sitting on his knee and had her tongue in his mouth. When Silvio entered the room he shoved her away. "Okay, we'll eat," he said. Nino had finally found a woman he liked, but he could still be cruel on occasions.

As Silvio sat down, Nino poured him some wine. "Madge Leigh just came by, with a message. Seems that Donovan dropped in. He's agreed to your terms."

Silvio nodded. "I thought he might."

Silvio drank the wine Nino had offered. "Things going well with Stella?"

Nino made a face. "I have to slap her around once in a while. To keep her in line. But she's a good kid—and can she cook!"

Silvio never understood why Nino found it necessary to hit women, but he said nothing.

"Now," said Nino. "I have some bad news."

"How bad?"

"Bad enough. Vito Liotta has been seen in the Quarter."

Silvio stopped drinking as Nino nodded knowingly. Vito Liotta was the son of Francisco Liotta, the Mafia Don in Bagheria, the father-in-law of Giancarlo Cataldo. The Liotta family was one of the most influential in the Sicilian Mafia. Vito's presence in New

Orleans meant that the easy times were over. Liotta had arrived to mastermind the fight back.

Nino nodded again as the news sank in for Silvio. "It was going to happen, sooner or later. At least we know who we're dealing with."

"What do we know about him?"

"A cruel bastard. He once pulled the fingernails out of someone he was interrogating. And clever. He killed the Bagheria chief of police and they couldn't lay a finger on him."

Silvio stared at Nino. This was life. The moment you thought you were settled, the world turned.

Stella burst back into the room with their dinner, two plates of crawfish boiled with pepper, and sweet corn. This was hardly Italian food, still less a Sicilian dish, but both Nino and Silvio had fallen for the New Orleans delicacy. Stella placed a bottle of wine and a huge empty bowl—for the crawfish shells—between them.

Nino waited until she had gone out again before proceeding. "Liotta alone doesn't bother me. He ain't got the power here he has in Sicily. But he'll obviously team up with the Cataldos, what's left of them. There's a family link between them, just as there is between us and old Angelo. Vito's smart. He can provide leadership and brains; they can provide muscle and local knowledge."

"So what do we do?"

"This time, little nephew, the answer is obvious, even to me. We hit Vito before he's settled, before he has a chance to get organized and come at us."

"And how do we do that? Where's he living?"

"I don't know, but Gaspero and some others are trying to find out."

Nino bit into his food, picking up the crawfish shell with his fingers. Silvio did likewise, but thoughtfully. He didn't like the sound of this. Of course, he had always expected the Cataldos to regroup at some stage, and he and Nino had their own men secretly in place in the opposition's camp. It was costing a fortune but it might now pay off. That must have been how Nino learned about Liotta in the first place. There was little the Cataldos could do without Nino and Silvio knowing about it right away. But Liotta's arrival was a surprise—and a good move from the Cataldos' point of view. Silvio had to admit it.

Just then the door to their room was thrown open a second time. Thinking it was Stella come to take their plates, Nino, who was still eating, looked up, ready to shout at her to clear off.

But it wasn't Stella. It was Angelo, and he looked extremely angry.

"Angelo—" began Nino.

"Shut up!" hissed Priola, striding across the room, to stop and stand over Silvio. "Get up, you little runt," he muttered menacingly.

Silvio wasn't sure what "runt" meant, but it obviously wasn't flattering. He got to his feet. What was all this about?

Without warning, Priola lifted his arm and slapped Silvio across the face. It was a hard slap, with all the force of his considerable weight. Added to that, Silvio wasn't expecting it, so he was knocked off balance and fell across the table, sending the cutlery and plates and crawfish all over the floor.

Priola bent over Silvio and slapped him again, less hard this time but still hard enough to hurt.

Silvio covered his head with his arms as Priola picked up the chair Silvio had been sitting on and crashed it over his head.

"Nano!" he cried. "Runt! Runt!"

"Angie!" Nino screamed. "What the fuck—?"

"Taci! Shut up!" shouted Priola as he searched around for something else to hit Silvio with. There was nothing, so he took off his shoe and started hammering on Silvio's skull.

"Have you been fucking my daughter?" he yelled. "Have you? Have you?"

Priola was still beating Silvio with his shoe, although Silvio had now crawled into the corner of the room.

"I asked you a question, runt. Have you been sleeping with Anna-Maria? Answer me! Yes or no?" He stood over Silvio, breathing heavily and holding his shoe in his right hand.

Nino wiped his face with his napkin. He had never known Angelo Priola this angry. It was something to see.

Gradually, Silvio took his arms away from his head. He, too, was breathing heavily. His head felt sore and his lip was swollen where the heel of Priola's shoe had caught it. He was still bestraddled by the other man.

Their eyes met. Priola rubbed the sweat off his cheek with his free hand. He sniffed. "Well? Yes, or no?"

Silvio put his hand to his lip. It was sticky with blood.

"Yes, or no?"

"Yes," Silvio said softly.

He ducked as more blows rained down on his head, but he crawled quickly across the floor and hid under the table. Probably he could have stood up to Angelo Priola, but sheer brute strength was not what this was about. Anna-Maria was the jewel in Priola's life.

Priola didn't follow Silvio under the table. Instead, he was talking to Nino. "When did this all start, Nino? Come on, I want to know. The runt's going to pay. He's too foxy by half. When did it start?"

Silvio held his breath while Nino answered. What would he say?

"I don't know, I'm not his keeper—"

"The fuck you don't know! Anna-Maria recommended you to me. Does that mean you met on the boat?"

Nino's silence proved that the answer was yes.

"Jesus! So it's been going on for two years. It's only a wonder Anna-Maria hasn't been knocked up." He sighed heavily and kicked at Silvio under the table. Then he slumped into one of the chairs. "Give me a drink."

He seemed to be calming down, but Silvio remained where he was. Angelo Priola could explode again at any time.

Priola swigged his drink.

"Silvio's a bright boy—" Nino began, trying to help.

"No, he's not. He's twenty, a man. And he's behaving like a man who's just discovered his dick and thinks he can stick it wherever he likes." Now his temper was rising again. "Well, he can't. He can't fuck my daughter and escape the consequences." He was fuming again now.

"What consequences?" Nino asked. "You yourself said she ain't knocked up."

"Anna-Maria wouldn't fuck just anybody. She must like the runt!" He poured himself another drink. "No, Nino, it ain't right. The runt's a man and is going to go through with this like a man."

"What do you mean, Angie? Silvio ain't a bad kid."

"He's not a kid. He's always telling us he ain't a kid. Well, he's right. He's a man and he's going to behave like one." He raised his glass to his lips and finished his bourbon in one gulp. "I'm not having my daughter disgraced. This ain't Sicily, but it ain't Africa either. We do things here like we do in Palermo." Again he kicked at Silvio under the table. "He's going to marry her."

12

Silvio had never been in a prison before. Normally he was as superstitious about prisons as any of his kind, and normally nothing would have made him go near New Orleans Parish Prison. But he had promised himself he would help Madeleine.

The Parish Prison was on Treme Street between Orleans and St. Ann, not far from Widow Milan's. It was a four-story, block-sized stone building, with two bell towers above the main entrance porch. It was one block away from the Basin and three from the Catholic cemetery. The guard at the door had directed him to an office just off the main corridor on the ground floor. There he explained whom he had come to see, and was told that the women's section was on the third floor. There was a staircase at the end of the main corridor.

Inside the prison, the dominant sensation was the smell, a strong disinfectant, no doubt masking numerous other odors. Silvio ran up the stairs. On the first two floors he saw corridors leading off in either direction, closed off by gates made of huge iron railings. Off the corridors he could see large barred cells, each one with a window. There were half a dozen prisoners to each cell.

Like everyone else in New Orleans, he had heard stories about the Parish Prison, how it was really two prisons, one for the rich and one for the poor. Anyone who was rich could send out for the best food and the best wine and dine every night in comfort, visited by friends and relatives. All the newspapers were available, and even girls from CustomHouse Street. But if you were poor it was very different. Prison food was not just bad, it was rancid. The bread was moldy, it was not unknown for the gruel to have maggots growing on it, and people had died from drinking the water.

There was no fruit. Silvio had little doubt which sort of prison Madeleine was in.

He reached the third floor. Anyone could come and go in the prison provided he or she had a good reason. But the regime was extremely arbitrary. Pickpockets could be punished by hanging, whereas certain murderers were allowed out to run errands—and sometimes absconded while doing so. The fact was, the jail administration in New Orleans was as corrupt as the rest of the city's system of justice. Silvio hoped to be able to take advantage of that.

He rattled on the bars of the gate to the corridor. Eventually a female guard appeared. She was fat with a very white skin. Rivulets of sweat ran down her face. "Yessuh?"

"I want to see one of your inmates, a quadroon named Madeleine."

The guard grinned, showing an alarming lack of teeth. "The whore? Who are you?"

"I'm a relative." He held out a dollar bill.

"Are you? Are you indeed? You better come in, then." She took the proffered bill.

She fetched some keys and opened the door, then led him down the corridor, past cells crowded with white women, most of them skimpily dressed. "Show us your dick, big boy," someone shouted, and several of the women cackled. "Hi, handsome, a dollar says you can come in my mouth," shouted someone else. For the first time in his life Silvio did not find such talk erotic. In one cell an old woman was on her own. She was urinating on the floor, standing up. As Silvio went by she lifted up her dress.

"That's Edith," said the guard out of the side of her mouth. "Don't take it personal. She does it all the time. Tha's why no one will share a cell with huh. . . . This is where the black prisoners are kept."

They had reached the far end of the corridor, where, on either side, there were two cells packed with black women, and a few quadroons.

Silvio looked, but at first could not see Madeleine. Then he noticed her, sitting on a bench, her legs drawn up to her chin.

"How 'bout some black pussy, white boy?" said one of the women nearer the bars. "Two dollars, honey," said someone else. "And yo' can stick it *anywhere*."

Silvio stood to one side so that Madeleine could see him. At first she didn't recognize him. Then suddenly she looked up. Was it really him? he could see her asking herself. He beckoned to her.

Tentatively, she stood up, rearranged her dress, and patted her hair. She walked forward.

Silvio turned to the guard. He pressed another dollar bill into her hand. "Is there someplace we can talk?"

She quickly pocketed the bill. "Sho' thing, honey. In mah office." She went to the door of the cell. "Stan' back, girls, stan' back. Let Miss Madeleine out. Huh rich sug' daddy done come fer huh." She opened the gate and Madeleine stepped into the corridor.

"What yo' wan' wit' her, han'some? She done suck the governor's dick all las' ni'. Make sho' she wash her mouth out." They all cackled.

The guard led Madeleine and Silvio back down the corridor and showed them into a small room, with a desk and window. The guard's cell was hardly better than the prisoners'. But they were alone.

"Fer a dollar, I can give yo' ten minutes. If yo' wanna come twice, the price goes up to three dollars."

With a start, Silvio realized that the guard thought he had come to make love to Madeleine, and was offering him the opportunity.

"We just want to talk."

The guard grinned. "Sho', honey."

Silvio led Madeleine into the office and closed the door behind them.

She stared at him like a frightened water rat, trapped in a gulley, and didn't move until he stepped forward to embrace her. As he enfolded her in his arms she began to sob.

"What happened, Maddie?" he said softly. "I was told you stole a watch."

Between sobs, she nodded her head. "We was thrown out of Madge Leigh's without no warning. I never told you, but . . . but I gotta son. He ain't well, and I needed to pay the doctor. If . . . I'd still been at Madge Leigh's, I could've borrowed the money, but . . . at Carrie's, I was new. No one would've lent me nothing. I was desperate . . . and I was found out."

The sobbing had not subsided. Silvio hugged Madeleine closer to him and then lifted her face to his. He kissed her. He was hardly the sentimental type, but he could believe her story all too well.

"Do you know the name of the man whose watch you stole?"

Still crying slightly, she nodded. "I think he's known as Cooney . . . James Cooney."

"Any idea where he lives?"

This time she shook her head. "All I know is, he's a tailor, makes religious clothes, fer priests an' choirboys. Why you wanna know all this?"

He ignored the question. "Where's your baby now?"

"Wit' . . . wit' Stella . . . *She* weren't fired. Anna-Maria knew Nino was sweet on her."

"Anna-Maria?"

Madeleine looked frightened all over again. She knew that Silvio slept with Anna-Maria. "She was there that day, when we was all . . . made to go."

This only confirmed what Silvio already knew, but it still made him angry. He lowered his voice and spoke more gently. "I need to know how much time I have, Maddie. When do you stand trial?"

"Monday, I been told. Why? Why, Silvio?"

"I'm going to find this Cooney. To get him to withdraw his charges."

"Oh, Silvio! D'you think you can do that?" Her body sagged against his, and for a moment he thought about the guard's invitation. But no, screwing in the jail was too sordid.

He disengaged himself from her embrace. "I have to go. But I'll be back, with good news, I hope."

She put her finger to his lips. "I'll be stronger now. Thank you."

Silvio opened the door and watched as the guard took Maddie back to her cell. He heard the other women call out. "My, that was quick." "How much did he pay yo', girl?" "Where yo' hidden the money?" The cackling started all over again.

Once outside, Silvio made for St. Louis's Cathedral, on Chartres, between St. Peter's and St. Ann. He was to meet Anna-Maria and the Archbishop of New Orleans, to discuss the wedding. At first, he had refused to believe what Angelo Priola was saying. Marry Anna-Maria? It seemed incredible. Yes, the old man had a temper, and it had exploded that night in Madge Leigh's, *un impieta di collera,* as they say in Sicily. But he had assumed Angelo would get over it. It had taken him a day or so to grasp the underlying truth—that Anna-Maria *herself* had told her father that she and Silvio had slept together. She had done it because, Silvio realized, she really did want to marry him. She had threatened to fight dirty and this was about as dirty as you could get.

After Angelo had stormed home, Nino had quieted Silvio down. Priola had been genuinely mad that night, Nino said, but only because he had hopes of Anna-Maria marrying into one of the grand old American families, the heir to a cotton plantation, say, or the son of a Civil War general. But that was cock's blood. No more likely than that Sicilians should love Rome. None of the grand families would want an alliance with a dago fruit importer. At the same time Nino pointed out that Angelo secretly had a soft spot for Silvio. Listen to an older man, he had said. "Angelo has no sons of his own. Think how powerful you will be as his son-in-law. If he gets his man in at the next election, the sky's the limit, and you'll be next in line to take over."

"But—"

Nino saw Silvio's objection a mile off. "Fuck her for six months. Give her a kid. Ain't hard. You don't have to pull out every time, once you're married. That will give her something to do, think about. Then go back to Madge Leigh's, like you always did. The main thing is to become part of Angelo's family. That's where the money is."

When Silvio eventually calmed down, he began to see that Nino spoke sense. For one thing, Angelo had promised to get proper immigration papers for Silvio and Nino once the wedding took place. For another, Silvio and Anna-Maria would live with Angelo, to begin with, in his house. That meant servants. Silvio couldn't help but relish that possibility. And he would surely be given an even better job. His English was good enough now for him to try his hand at anything. He still wrote with difficulty but he *could* write, and reading was getting easier all the time. There was no end to the things he could do for Angelo. And if the news got back to Annunziata . . . so much the better.

Anna-Maria was more of a problem. It had not occurred to him before that she might actually love him; but he was coming around to that view. All that fuss over Madeleine marked real feeling on Anna-Maria's part.

He had to admit that it *would* be good to be part of the Priola family, to enjoy the respect that such a marriage would bring. Silvio also observed that Angelo Priola himself paid little attention to his wife. He had all the women he wanted, as well as the comforts of a home life. After six months as the dutiful husband, Silvio could do the same.

Therefore, as he walked to the cathedral, he did not think it at all odd that he had just been to jail to see Madeleine. He wasn't giving up that life, just interrupting it for a few months. There was no need to tell Madeleine he was getting married: she would understand.

St. Louis's was a squat building for a cathedral, certainly by Sicilian standards. It was made of a creamy stone and was wide rather than high, with three black slate spires, narrow, again on the short side. Anna-Maria was already there. She was talking with the archbishop and a young priest about where the flowers would go. She kissed Silvio on both cheeks and called him "darling," as if they were married already. Silvio was bored by the talk of which hymns would be sung, of how strong the choir would be, and what sort of address the archbishop would make. But he suddenly paid attention when the archbishop said that, in honor of the occasion, and since Anna-Maria's father was such a prominent citizen, with many city notables attending the wedding, he was having a new surplice crafted.

"Oh yes?" said Silvio. "In that case, do you know someone called James Cooney?"

"Of course. I've known him for years."

"Where's he working these days?"

"At Brodick's. In Perdido Street, where he's always worked."

Silvio lost interest in the rest of the conversation, registering only that they were all to meet again on the day before the wedding, for a rehearsal. Then Anna-Maria and he walked out into the square in front of the cathedral.

"All that talk of weddings has made me feel sexy, Silvio. Take me back to the lugger and fuck me."

Sono schiavo? Silvio thought. Am I a slave? He shook his head. "I'm not interested, now that it's legal, Anna-Maria. I've got some business to attend to."

As she went to protest he interrupted her. "Look, you got me to marry you. Be satisfied with that. Haven't you got a lover for the afternoons? You're going to need one." And he was gone.

He stopped by Madge Leigh's, to pick up Nino. In readiness for taking on Vito Liotta, they had placed an order for some new hardware. Big Smith & Wessons, which made a lot of noise and frightened bystanders. The weapons had been brought secretly to the city, by boat, across Lake Pontchartrain, then down the canal to the Basin. Nino and he were due to go to see them.

But when he walked into Madge Leigh's it was as though Mount Etna had erupted. He knew immediately what was happening. Nino and Stella were having one of their periodic—and increasingly violent—fights. Silvio didn't know what got into them both, why these fights broke out, but once they started, they sure went at it. *Una zuffa zaffe.*

A bottle was actually in the air as Silvio entered the bar, on its way to Nino's head. He ducked, and it exploded on the wall behind him.

"You dago bandit!" screamed Stella. "All I ask is one lousy gift, something because it's my goddamn *birthday!*"

"I'm sorry," shouted Nino, ducking behind the bar. "I forgot."

"Forgot? *Forgot?* How could you forget? I told you last week, and again on Sunday." Now she threw a plant pot at him. "Find someone else to play your pipe, you wop, dago, vermin bandit. Don't come near me." Then she started to cry.

The danger was over. The barman, a man called Villardi, started to clean up. The other people in the bar stopped hiding, and Nino made promptly for the door, where Silvio was standing. They went out together.

The two men walked up CustomHouse Street to Basin Street.

"Some fight," said Silvio.

"My fault this time—no mistake." Nino slapped his forehead. "How could I forget her goddamn birthday. *Stupid!*"

Silvio stopped in the street. He turned to the other man. "She called you a bandit, Nino. How much does she know?"

Nino shrugged. "After-sex talk, nephew. Don't worry. She won't say anything, she's terrified of me." He grinned. "Can you say that of your new wife?"

He dodged as Silvio attempted to swipe him, but he turned back and grabbed the younger man's arm. "Listen! *Listen!* Cut it out. I got something to tell you." His tone immediately had Silvio's attention.

"Yeah, what is it?"

"Liotta wants a meeting."

"What?"

"Straight up. Got word to Angelo this morning."

"Why? And where?"

"To discuss business, he says. Our mutual interests. Where? Get this: at Toussaint House. A private room."

Silvio whistled. Toussaint House was a big old plantation on the river, some distance north of New Orleans. It was now a hotel with a restaurant, and boasted a fine garden with an alley of enormous oak trees. A meeting there would cost Liotta plenty.

"Is Toussaint safe?"

Nino shrugged. "Ain't no Buscettas here, like in Sicily. We'll use hostages."

Silvio nodded. "You met Liotta before, Nino?"

"Not this one, no. I met the father once. Mean bastard. They're a mean bunch all around, Silvio. Listen to an older man. I tell you, the only safe Liotta is a dead one."

Silvio found Perdido Street easily enough, and Brodick's, which was up one flight of stairs, above a shop selling boots. James Cooney turned out to be a small, wiry man, with cunning eyes and black hair swept straight back. He was making lace.

Silvio introduced himself and asked Cooney if they might have a word in private.

"What about?" said Cooney aggressively.

"A girl named Madeleine."

"I don't know anyone of that name."

"She stole your watch."

Cooney sneered. "I know who you mean. The whore. So?"

"I want you to drop charges."

Cooney sneered again. "Not a chance. She was—"

"Are you married?"

The tailor was surprised by the question. "Yes."

"Children?"

"Ye-e-s. Two. Boy and a girl."

Silvio spoke in a matter-of-fact voice. "Now, listen to me. If you don't drop charges, and drop them by the end of the day, I shall break all your fingers, one by one, so you can never make lace again. If Madeleine gets six months in jail—and she will if the charges aren't dropped—you better start counting your children every day."

Cooney looked at him in horror. The fact that these threats were delivered without shouting, without emphasis, made them all the more menacing.

The tailor tried to bluster. He couldn't believe this was happening to him. "Who do you think you are? You scum! You can't just come in here and—"

"Mr. Cooney, you can call me all the names you like. I don't mind. But if Madeleine is not released from prison by the end of today, I'll come back tomorrow and begin to do what I told you. The archbishop will have to go elsewhere for his lace. He gave me your address, by the way."

It was dawning on Cooney that Silvio's threats were not idle bravado. "Who *are* you?" he asked. "How does scum like you know the archbishop?"

Silvio smiled. "He's going to marry me."

At that moment Cooney understood who he was dealing with. "You're marrying the Priola woman?"

Silvio nodded.

Cooney suddenly stood up. "You oughta have said that before." He put down his lace and his needles. "I'll go to the jail right now. Don't worry, I'll see to it." And he ran out.

Silvio picked up the strip of lace. He had a feeling he'd be seeing it again soon.

"Silvio? *Silvio!* Sorry to wake you, but there's someone to see you." Stella had stuck her head around the door and was whispering.

Silvio, in his back office at Madge Leigh's, often tried to doze in the afternoons, since most nights he was out late. He opened one eye and said, "Who is it?"

"A nigger woman."

He frowned. This was unusual. "Check her for weapons and show her in." He swung his legs over the edge of the bed and shuffled on his shoes.

A minute later the woman came through the door. She was very

black, about fifty he judged, and wore a dark coat over a purple
dress and a matching hat. She seemed vaguely familiar.

"Don't you recognize me?" she said.

He stared at her.

Suddenly she changed her voice and said, "Yo' wanna
gris-gris?"

"Widow Milan!"

Without her voodoo outfit she was certainly very different.

"Come in," he said. "Sit down."

She did as she was told, unbuttoning her coat.

"Drink?"

She shook her head. "You said to come if I had an idea. Well, I
got me one."

"Okay. Try me."

"Man comes to me, says he wants to put the curse on a big
gambler, man called Ezra Bell. My man says Bell cheats at cards.
My man is nigger leader in railroad construction. Well known and
powerful. I figure if you can do somethin' about Bell, somethin'
public and real nasty, word will get 'round. That's mah idea."

"And who is Bell?"

"I understand he's a captain of one of them steamboats."

"And where does he play?"

"All along CustomHouse Street. But mainly, I hear, in the back
room at Bryce's, for the mixed-race game, and Mattie Marshall's,
for the white game."

Silvio smiled. "Mattie's? Ah well. Widow Milan . . . how much
you charge for *gris-gris*?"

"Fifty cents. A dollar maybe."

"I think the price just went up."

Silvio had never seen the lugger made ready for the river before.
He thought of her as a shore craft; but to his untutored eye she
seemed shipshape enough. She was to be captained by Cesare
Cagliari, one of the head roustabouts on Picayune Pier, and had a
crew of four, each of whom was an experienced sailor. Silvio's job
was to make sure they were ready for ten A.M. He had his own
pocket watch now, and it showed nine-fifty. All five of them were
standing on the levee by the gangplank that led to the lugger,
waiting for Angelo to bring the Liotta hostage.

It was the day of the meeting with Vito Liotta. In Sicily, when a meeting had to be arranged between two Mafia Dons, the Buscetta family was called upon. They were an extremely tough Caltanisetta outfit who specialized in security, for which they charged a hefty fee. During high-level meetings, each side would take one member of the Buscettas as hostage. He remained a hostage until both sides returned safely. If anything went wrong, two things happened. First, the Buscettas let it be known that such and such a family was not honorable. Second, they were free to seek revenge. But no one wanted a vendetta with the Buscettas. So usually, little went wrong.

In New Orleans, however, there was no Buscetta family. So, for their meeting, the Priolas and the Liottas had agreed to provide their own hostages. Each hostage would be kept in a secret hideaway—on the lugger in the case of the Priolas. Angelo had agreed that Nino would be the hostage held by the Liotta/Cataldo group. Vincenzo Liotta, Vito's twenty-one-year-old nephew, who had come to America with him, was to be turned over to Angelo. They were waiting for him now.

The exchange should have taken place at nine-thirty, outside the cathedral. Vincenzo was being brought to the lugger in a curtained carriage driven by Angelo's driver while Nino was taken to wherever the Liottas had decided to hide him. This was new territory and it was nerve-racking.

Silvio looked at his watch. Nine-fifty-five. They were running late.

Then, suddenly, three men appeared at the top of the levee—Angelo, his driver, and a thin, sallow-skinned man with a purple birthmark on his face. This must be Vincenzo Liotta.

The three men scrambled down the levee. Silvio and Vincenzo exchanged nods, but that was all. Angelo, his driver, and Silvio together looked on in silence as the other men boarded the lugger, and Vincenzo was led inside and locked in the saloon with two bodyguards. Soon the lugger was moving slowly out into the middle of the river. She would sail up and down the Mississippi all day until her crew was given the signal to return. The sign was when the Italian tricolor was raised above the American flag on Picayune Pier.

Angelo and Silvio went back to the carriage. It took them just over an hour to reach Toussaint House, traveling alongside the Carrollton railroad, and via the Pontchartrain Causeway and the

Great River Road. Here the levee ran the entire length of the Mississippi to their left, obscuring their view of the river. They saw fields planted with sugar, cotton, tobacco, indigo, sorghum, and hemp, and punctuated with shacks belonging to newly freed black slaves, as well as a few small, rickety, wooden chapels. It reminded Silvio of the poorer areas of Uditore, on the outskirts of Palermo.

At a quarter after eleven they turned off the Great River Road into the avenue of oak trees that led to a large, two-story house with a row of white columns along its façade. Angelo looked out between the curtains of the carriage. "This is Toussaint," he growled.

As the carriage approached the house an Italian-looking man stepped forward and held up his hand for them to stop, then opened the curtains of the carriage and peered inside. He appeared satisfied. "Mr. Liotta's in the *gar . . . garçonnière*," he stammered.

Angelo grinned grimly and turned to Silvio. "That's the side house. Before the Civil War, when the house belonged to one family, if they had guests all the single men stayed in the side house. Good idea, if you ask me. Out of harm's way. *Garçon* is French for young man."

"Sono ragazzo?" Silvio said under his breath. "Am I a child?" A fucking French lesson, at a time like this?

They rode round to the side of the house. Next to a small building stood another carriage. They all got down. "Wait here," Angelo said to his driver. He led Silvio inside.

The door opened onto a hall, with a polished wooden floor and lush plants growing in pots. Long lace curtains covered the windows and fell in swathes to the ground. Off the hall was a large room, the door to which was open. Angelo went in and Silvio followed. The room inside was long and low, with a large fireplace at one end. Leaning against the fireplace and smoking were two men. As they saw Angelo and Silvio they straightened up, threw their cigarettes into the fireplace, and came forward.

There were no handshakes.

"I'm Vittorio Liotta," said the smaller of the two men. He was very thin, with fine bones, like a bird, the skin stretched tightly over his skull and jaw, shiny and sleek looking. He had gray eyes set close together, thin eyebrows, thin lips, gray hair. His jaw jutted out slightly. Silvio thought he looked like a cardinal. Vito

Liotta's clothes fitted beautifully, like his skin. Silvio guessed he was about fifty.

"This is Natale Pianello." The other man was taller, fatter, darker-haired, but with a pale skin, unusual in a Sicilian. He didn't look nearly as fit, physically or mentally, as Liotta, but his eyes were brown, like the Mississippi, and just as deep. He had a gold ring on the little finger of his left hand. He nodded his head in acknowledgment.

"You know who I am," said Angelo. "This is Silvio Razzini."

"Hello, Silvio." Liotta smiled slightly. The change of surname didn't fool him.

Liotta pointed past them. They turned. There was a table with four chairs, a jug of water, some fruit. "Shall we?"

They walked down the room and sat at the table.

Liotta poured water, offered fruit. No one drank or ate anything.

"Angie," Liotta began, after this ritual had been completed. "The way I see it, this town can go two ways. We can fight, in which case you might win, I might win, but either way there'll be blood, bad blood. And the law will be involved. Or we can coop-erate, work together, divide up the place, keep to our own, relax, enjoy our grandchildren. Me? I go for that. There's enough for both of us in this town. Plenty."

Angelo sipped his water. "Vito, let me ask you something. Say I was new in this town and you had been here fifteen years. Say you had built up the wharves, like I have, and then someone like me, just off the boat, comes to you and says what you just said. Eh? What would you say, Vito? What would you say?"

Liotta shrugged. "I'd react like a businessman, Angie. I'd say to myself, I've had fifteen, sixteen good years with no real competi-tion, with everything my own way. Now the picture's changing, the world's turning. Popes come and go. Etna erupts—suddenly you get new rivers where there weren't any before. It happens. Nobody can keep a whole city to himself, I'd say. It don't happen in Sicily, it can't happen here. I'd be realistic. I'd tell myself that I have to give a piece away. If I don't want a war."

"You say you're a businessman, Vito. In business you have to earn things. You don't get given them on a plate."

"There ain't no rules, Angie. You know that." Liotta paused, and bit into an apple. "Yes, I'm new in town. But that ain't the point. Point is, I'm here now and I ain't going away. If it wasn't me, it'd be someone else. The reason you're here today, Angie, is you know this town is too big for one Don. The docks are huge. The bars, the gambling, the whores . . . it's some town, Angie, but it don't *belong* to you. I'm here now and you gotta deal with me. Either we talk or we fight."

Angelo sipped some water. "Vito, you know what happened to Giancarlo Cataldo. And Alfredo. I don't fight so bad."

Vito nodded. "Giancarlo and Alfredo were Cataldos, not blood Liottas. You think I'm gonna be a *vittima facile* in a war, Angie? A pushover? You think I'm easy, like they was?" He smiled grimly. "I don't believe you think that, Angie. Oh no."

He shifted in his seat. He wanted to change the mood. "Listen. I got something for you." He stood up and turned. "Gianni!" he yelled. "Gianni! Now!"

There was a pause. What was happening? Was this a trick? Silvio was uneasy and looked at Angelo. He was nervous, too.

At the far end of the room, two men appeared. As they approached the table Silvio and Angelo could see that one of the men, presumably Gianni, was clearly Italian. The other clearly wasn't—he was black. The black man was tall and strapping, but hung back.

Vito had remained standing. Now he said, "Angie, you gotta know two things. Most important, I ain't Giancarlo or Alfredo. I ain't a Cataldo. No way. Second, as I say, I'm a businessman. Sometimes, as a businessman, you gotta share. I'm asking you to share with me, but first I'm gonna share something with you." He pointed to the black man. "This is Nelson St. Joseph. He's the boilerman on the *Memphis* steamboat."

Angelo looked up sharply and Liotta chuckled. "I see you heard about the race."

As Silvio well knew, everyone was talking about next week's steamboat race, run from Natchez to New Orleans, between the *Memphis* and the *T. P. Leathers*. Bets were being placed on the result all over town.

Liotta stepped across and put his arm around the black man's shoulder. "Angie, Nelson here is gonna arrange it so the boiler of the *Memphis* blows during the race. You can make as big a bet as you like on the *Leathers*. You'll win a fortune. It's a gift, from me to you." He nodded to Gianni, who led the black man away.

Liotta sat down again, picked up the remains of his apple. He chewed for a while. Then: "I ain't asking for your blessing, Angie. This ain't no beauty contest. I'm talking to you as one businessman to another. And as a Sicilian. *Da uomo a uomo*. Man-to-man."

Angelo remained silent.

"You can see I've got power." Liotta waved in the direction of where the black man had been taken. "You can see I've got . . . well, let's call it imagination. Like Silvio here." He tapped his temple. "I'm here now, Angie. I want a piece." He finished his apple and threw the core out of the window.

There was a long pause. Silvio watched Angelo think. At length his future father-in-law said, "Vito, Silvio and me, we're gonna take a walk."

"Please," said Liotta, standing up again. "The gardens here are beautiful. They remind me of Aquasanto."

Liotta and Natale Pianello watched as Angelo and Silvio headed off down the alley of oak trees. The branches of the trees met overhead, and there was plenty of shade as the two men strolled away from the house toward the river, speaking quietly, their heads bent together.

They reached the end of the alley and stood, still talking. Each was animated. Then, after a few minutes, they began to retrace their steps. Every so often they stopped and talked some more. When they were about a hundred yards from the house, the talking stopped and they walked the rest of the way without speaking. They reentered the room and sat in the same seats they had vacated.

Liotta, who had been smoking by the window, sat down also.

Angelo refilled his water glass but didn't drink from it. "Vito," he said at length. "We are both Sicilians, so there is no need for me to say much. I prefer now, as always, to let my deeds, my actions, speak for me. I therefore tell you this and you can make of it what you will. You have made me a gift. You have said that the *T. P. Leathers* will win the steamboat race and that I can make a fortune by betting on her."

He raised his eyes and looked squarely at Liotta. "I refuse your gift."

Liotta drew his thin lips together as Angelo went on. "I further say that the *Memphis* boiler will *not* blow, and that she will win the race. If you have already placed your bets, I advise you to lay them off." He stood up. "We'll go now."

David Martell walked into the telegraph room at police head-quarters and smiled at the woman seated behind the desk. "Good morning, Sheila."

"Good morning, Mr. Martell. Something I can do for you?"

"Yes and no. I have a telegram to send, but it's confidential. I need to send it myself. I hope you don't mind."

Sheila did mind. What if everyone did this? She'd soon be out of a job. But Martell was the chief of detectives.

"It's time for my lunch, anyhow, Mr. Martell. Shall I just leave you to it? You know how everything works."

"Indeed I do. Thank you."

She went out, closing the door behind her.

Martell sat at the telegraph desk and took out a piece of paper from his pocket. He spread it on top of the desk and began to operate the transmitter. His message was short.

TO: PINKERTON CHICAGO PLEASE SEND LIVESEY PORTRAIT URGENT MARTELL NEW ORLEANS END

* * *

Angelo Priola puffed on his cigar and said gruffly, "Two cards, please."

He was handed two cards. It was some time since he had played at Mattie's, but he was here today under instructions from Silvio, who was nowhere to be seen. Next to him was Mattie herself, then came Arthur Cody, one of the nimble pickpockets on the payroll, then Vincent Mistretta, also on the books and no mean poker player, then—between Angelo and Vincent—came Ezra Bell. He took a card.

Arthur took three and Mattie, who had dealt, gave herself two.

Angelo looked at his cards. He had a pair of kings, nothing. He threw his hand in.

Bell said, "A hundred."

"And fifty," said Mistretta.

"I'm out," from Arthur.

"Me, too," said Mattie.

That left Bell and Vincent.

"Two hundred," said Bell.

"And fifty," Vincent immediately countered.

"Three hundred."

"Out," said Vincent, and the hand finished without any cards being shown.

Mattie dealt again.

As he gathered his cards up Angelo grumbled, "This cigar stinks. Can you get me another, Mattie?"

Mattie gestured to the waiter, who went out. It was the signal.

"One card," said Angelo.

"Two," said Bell.

"Three," said Vincent.

"Three for me," said Arthur.

"I'll take one," said Mattie.

"One hundred dollars," said Angelo after a pause.

"Two," replied Bell.

"Out," said Vincent.

"Too rich for me," Arthur added, laying his cards on the table.

Mattie just shook her head.

The waiter returned with a fresh cigar, which he handed to Angelo.

"Three hundred," said Angelo, holding a match to the end.

"Okay."

"Four."

"Okay."

"Five."

Bell paused. "Okay."

"I'll raise you to five and see you."

Bell laid down his cards. "Full house, kings and jacks."

"Well, I'll be—" Angelo laid down a full house as well, but with three eights and two jacks. "You lucky—"

"Hold on," said Vincent. "Look at this." He turned over his cards, to reveal two sevens, a five, an ace—and a jack.

"*Five* jacks," whispered Angelo.

"No," said Arthur. He turned over his cards. "Six."

All eyes turned to Bell.

"Don't look at me," he growled. "I play straight."

"Why would we cheat, to *lose* a hand? Don't make sense."

"I do *not* cheat!"

Angelo turned to Mattie. "This is your house, Mattie. It's up to you."

Mattie turned back to the waiter. "Fetch the law."

"Now hold on!" shouted Bell, getting to his feet.

Mistretta was too quick for him. "Sit down," he hissed, taking his gun out of his pocket. "Wait."

Bell stared at him, or rather at the gun. Slowly, he sat down again.

"Everybody leave their cards where they are," said Angelo, puffing cigar smoke into the room. "The cards is evidence."

13

Dick Saltram's enthusiasm was contagious. The ice factory had been his idea, he said. It had taken more than a year to build, but now people were beginning to sit up and take notice. He was leading Silvio, Nino, and Angelo Priola through the factory, showing them every room. They had already seen where the ammonia was condensed. They had seen the water purifier. This was essential, he had explained, because not only did it make the water easier to freeze, but it ensured that if the ice was mixed with food, and later melted, the food was not contaminated. Now they were in the big room on the ground floor where the ice was formed.

"Of course we can produce ice in any shape, and we do. But in general we find this is the most popular form." He led them to a row of boxes. "These are easy to lift, and the way we freeze them, they last for twelve to eighteen hours, depending on weather conditions. Here," he said. "Look at this." He raised one box. Inside the ice, they could see, were three roses.

"What on earth did you do that for?" Priola asked.

"I can answer that," Silvio said. "This is what gave me the idea in the first place, when I saw it at Donovan's Garden."

"Yes, we supply them," added Saltram. "These blocks are used as decoration for society dinner parties. In this weather, and with all the candles the nobs burn at their dinners, the room gets very hot. So they order a couple of these, to put on the table, to cool the room. To make them look nicer we put flowers in them." He smiled.

Priola turned to Silvio. "Run through your plan for Saltram. He may be able to spot any snags."

Silvio faced Saltram. "About three percent of the fruit that arrives at our wharves is already rotten. That's not a problem for us—we don't have to pay for it, just throw it away. But depending on the fruit—where it comes from, and the season—as much as another ten percent goes rotten on our wharves, or before it reaches where it's going. Most of the fruit is shipped out three days after landing, but a lot goes upriver, and those journeys can take two, three weeks. My idea is to have warehouses on the wharf which are refrigerated and to gradually fit our steamboats with refrigerated holds."

"My point is this, Mr. Saltram: How can you do that if the ice blocks only last for eighteen hours?" Priola looked puzzled. "That wouldn't make much difference to a two-week voyage."

Saltram was ahead of him. "No, I can see what Silvio's getting at—that's the life of a single block. If you build a small room of blocks, with the walls two or three blocks thick, and if the room's not too large, the outer blocks preserve the inner blocks. With a two-block wall, say, you get a life of nearly double the eighteen hours you get for a single block—maybe thirty hours. With a three-block wall you might get as much as forty hours."

"But that's still peanuts on a two-week voyage."

Silvio interjected, "So we build refrigerator stations along the river, and restock the holds at every stopover."

"But think what that would cost. Thousands of dollars!"

"Which is what we are losing anyway."

Priola shook his head. The idea was too new for him.

Saltram knew that Silvio was convinced but saw the business slipping away because Priola, the boss, couldn't bring himself to face the issue.

"Mr. Priola, if you don't make this innovation, someone else will. But I'd prefer not to argue with you. Instead, may I propose an experiment?"

"What sort of experiment?" Priola sounded belligerent, but he couldn't hide his interest.

"I'll build one of these rooms here in the factory. A small ice room with two-block walls. Then you can leave one set of fruit inside, and one outside—see what happens. After that, you can make up your mind."

"Yeah! Okay, I like that."

Mostly, Silvio knew, Priola liked the fact that this solution postponed a decision. But it was all they could do, for now.

"When would you like the experiment to begin?"

Priola looked at Silvio. "When's the wedding?"

"Sunday. Four days from now."

"And how soon can you have the ice ready?"

"That amount? Tomorrow."

"Fine. Go ahead then. We'll come back on Saturday. I'll pay you whatever it costs."

They made their farewells, shook hands, filed out, and got into Angelo's carriage. He seemed lost in thought, but after they had ridden a couple of blocks Silvio could keep silent no longer. "Well?" he said. "What did you think?"

"I think you're a very smart young man, Silvio, real foxy, and we should pay attention to this experiment. Incidentally, what kind of name is Saltram? It's not Italian?"

"No, but Saltram is. He's from Reggio di Calabria. His real name is Scalice, but he anglicized it, to make it sound more American."

Priola frowned. "Is he ashamed of Italy?" Then he smiled at Silvio. "It's a good scheme, and one day it will work. But not now. Not for us."

Silvio grew irritated. "Why not? I've done the arithmetic— you've seen the figures. It makes financial sense."

"In normal times, yes. But these ain't normal times, or they won't be soon."

"What do you mean? You talk like a Milanese. Talk Sicilian."

"You're smart, Silvio. I'm more than happy to have you as a son-in-law. But you're not yet wise. We're going to need a lot of extra money in the weeks ahead. It's not the time to start any fancy undertakings."

"It ain't fancy."

"All right, it ain't fancy. It's a good scheme, okay? But we gotta watch our strength."

"For the fight against Liotta, you mean?"

"Yeah, for the war. The steamboat race is just round one. If our boat wins, we keep the black businesses and Vito Liotta has to think again. But if he wins, the black outfits swing to him and the war starts sooner rather than later. If he wins he turns his attention straight to us. If he wins the race, we ain't got long before the fighting starts."

* * *

From the *Times Picayune*:

FUNERAL OF STEAMBOAT CAPTAIN

The funeral of Ezra Bell, captain of the Mississippi steamboat *Baton Rouge*, was held yesterday at Metairie Cemetery. Captain Bell, who was fifty-nine, died in a drowning accident after being charged with cheating in a poker game two weeks ago at Mattie Marshall's club on CustomHouse Street. Suicide had been suspected, but over the weekend the coroner reported an open verdict, saying there was insufficient evidence for the direct cause of death to be established. Captain Bell's body washed ashore below the Tobacco Press. It was badly mutilated and may have been attacked by eels.

The funeral was attended by Captain Bell's widow, Mabel, and his two children, plus a small gathering of friends. The Reverend O'Hagan officiated.

* * *

"Ersters, suh? Muffuletta?" The waiter squeezed by, carrying the tray high above his shoulder. There wasn't much room on deck, not with this party in full swing.

Silvio had never adjusted to oysters, fresh or cooked, but muffuletta was different, and he took one. It was, after all, an Italian dish, a sandwich with meat and cheese, all swimming in olive oil. He sank his teeth into the bun and looked out at the riverbank.

The party had been Angelo's idea, but Silvio was nervous. The whole river was having a party today, in honor of the steamboat race that was due to finish there at Picayune Pier in an hour or so. Hundreds of boats, big and small, lined the wharves, many of them decked out with flags. The wharves themselves were thronged with all manner of people, from clowns to melon sellers, magicians, professional gamblers in their white suits, Negro bands, peddlers hawking nuts, banjo players in bow ties, men selling cheroots, women singing arias from the great Italian operas. Some were even wearing tame snakes or carrying baby alligators in jars.

A lot was riding on the steamboat race, and not just money. Silvio sometimes wondered if he had too many ideas for his own good, and that certainly applied to today's events. At the meeting

in Toussaint House, Angelo and he had taken a walk to discuss
their response to Liotta. Inside, Angelo had been livid with Vito,
but he hadn't let it show. All that talk of being a businessman.
Bullshit, as Anna-Maria would say. *Concime!* How dare he come
to New Orleans and demand that Angelo give up a piece of his
business because he had stepped off the boat. A real *squalo*, a
shark.

So, on their walk down the oak alley, Angelo had been keen to
teach Liotta a lesson, and it was Silvio who had come up with the
answer. Liotta himself had provoked it, by producing the boilerman, Nelson St. Joseph. Vito clearly thought he had the result of
the race in the palm of his hand, and was showing off. But the
boilerman was black and therefore totally at the mercy of Widow
Milan.

The widow was doing well since the death of the steamboat
captain. Word had gone around town that her *gris-gris* on Ezra
Bell had worked in no time, and her custom had more than
doubled. Therefore, she had been anxious to repeat her success
and was more than ready to approach Nelson St. Joseph the next
Sunday in Congo Square and warn him that if the *Memphis* lost
the steamboat race, his own run of bad luck would be equally
disastrous.

In this way, the race had become a trial of strength between Vito
and Angelo. The widow had reported back that Nelson St. Joseph
had appeared frightened when she delivered her threat, but Silvio
had since heard that Vito had also threatened the man's life if he
failed to blow the boiler. Who was the nigger afraid of most?

They were an hour from knowing, maybe less. Upriver, the
Mississippi curled out of sight beyond the Jackson Avenue
ferry, in the area of town known as the Irish Channel, maybe three
miles away. That's where they would first glimpse the winning
steamboat.

Silvio finished his muffuletta and went in search of a drink.
Angelo had really gone to town for this party. The best food,
expensive wines, a lot of his political cronies, a couple of judges
even. And they had all come.

Anna-Maria was there, of course. People kept congratulat-
ing her and Silvio on their engagement. The wedding gifts were
going to be something. Inside him, secretly, Silvio still couldn't
get used to the idea that Annunziata was married, but people

already treated him with more deference as Angelo's son-in-law, his *genero*, and he found he liked that. *Genero* sounded like "general."

He reached the bar and took a bourbon, nodding to Madge Leigh. Carrie Freemantle was here, too, as was Stella, who, like others, carried a small telescope so she could better see upriver. Stella was more awkward than some of the other girls, but Silvio had found he had a soft spot for her, particularly since he had been told she had looked after Madeleine's son while Maddie had been in prison. That problem, thank God, had been solved satisfactorily and he had set her up in a room of her own. He suspected that Anna-Maria knew everything but had decided to accept it. After all, she now had what she wanted. Or soon would have.

While he was talking to Stella, Silvio saw Nino edging toward him through the crowd. Nino jerked his head to one side, mouthed "Saloon," and retreated. Silvio excused himself, threw a last glance upriver—nothing—and made his way aft. When he opened the saloon door, Angelo and Nino were both there, seated and nursing drinks.

"Close the door," growled Angelo.

Silvio did as he was told, then sat down.

"If Vito wins today," Angelo said with a sigh, "he'll make sure everyone knows. That means, to start with, we lose the nigger business. In no time he'll have a piece of the nigger wharves, whorehouses, the best bands. The Sicilians in town will be watching him, and watching us. If he wins they'll be expecting a war."

"And if *we* win?" Nino stubbed out his cheroot.

"We buy time. But that ain't the point."

"What do you mean?" Silvio spoke more roughly than he intended and Angelo looked at him sharply.

"Think," said Angelo. "Think how foxy Liotta's been. When we met him at Toussaint House he offered us the black boilerman as a gift. We could have bet on the *Leathers* and won a fortune."

"But," exclaimed Silvio, "if we'd accepted his gift, we'd have had to go along with him in other ways as well. Like sharing the docks. You want that? You know what they say in Sicily: the fox doesn't sleep with the chickens."

"I agree," replied Angelo calmly. "And we couldn't do that. But even so we've gone head-to-head with him. It was a good idea of

yours, Silvio, to take him on with Widow Milan, and an even
better one to have her on the ship today, to keep up the pressure.
But we've played into his hands. Even if he loses today he's won
something. We've had to deal with him, see him off. Everyone
knows that. They know this race is a tussle between us." Angelo
looked at Silvio. "Vito may even have known we had Widow
Milan on the payroll."

Silvio was shocked. "You mean he set us up?"

"I ain't sure. I'm just saying he's a foxy fucker."

Silvio was dazed. He had never been outthought like this
before. *If* he had been outthought. "Then we kill him," he said at
length.

"Except he ain't gonna sit around and wait for us to do it, like
the Cataldos did. Anyone who dreamed up this little trap is gonna
watch his back even in his sleep. And Liotta don't sleep much."

Silvio couldn't believe it. He had been so pleased with his plan
to have Widow Milan countermand Liotta's orders to the boilerman. This couldn't be a trap, it *couldn't*.

A shout went up from outside. Silvio and the others scrambled
for the door. Everyone was craning their necks upriver. Silvio saw
Stella with her telescope to her eye. "What is it?" he gasped.
"What is it?"

"A steamboat," she said.

"One or two?" If it was two, the *Memphis* was still in the race.

"One."

"Which one?"

"I can't see yet. It's too far away."

For three more minutes Silvio waited in agony as Stella
strained her eyes, searching for the name of the winning steamboat. His heart turned over in his rib cage. He simply refused to
believe that Liotta had outthought him. Silvio's plan to enlist the
widow's aid had been clever—fucking brilliant. But, he realized,
cleverness wasn't everything. Brains weren't everything; you
needed balls and had to be prepared to shed blood. That's where
Liotta had the edge this time—maybe. Silvio had been too busy
making up for that slip after he'd thought too slowly to prevent his
parents' death. Angelo had paid too much attention to Silvio's
schemes, perhaps, and not enough to Nino's undoubted ability to
scare people. That was one reason why Angelo had cooled on the
ice deal with Saltram.

Silvio saw it now. At the very point when he was to join Angelo's family, his influence had ceased to grow.

"Nearly there!" shouted Stella. "I can see the writing between the smokestacks. I can't read the letters yet . . . yes, yes, I can. . . . It's . . . *T. P. Leathers*—yes! The *Leathers*."

Silvio went cold. The *Memphis* had yet to appear. Her boiler must have blown. Liotta had won.

"I have to repay you, Silvio. I owe mah freedom to you. You can have anything you want."

Silvio and Madeleine were back in their regular room in Madge Leigh's. Madge Leigh had been only too happy to take her back: she was delighted that Silvio should think enough of Maddie to rescue her from jail. But it was all done very discreetly. Anna-Maria was not to know.

"You please me just the way you are, Madeleine. I don't want you to change."

Madeleine took off her slip so that Silvio could see her body, touch it all over. He was embarrassed by her gratitude and embraced her to avoid showing it. There was something he had to tell her.

"Madeleine . . ." He faltered.

"What is it?" She looked up at him.

"I . . . there's . . ." He faltered again. *Sono maiale?* Am I a pig?

"I know about the wedding," she said softly.

"You do? How?"

"What d'you think us girls talk about all day? It was the first thing I heard when I got out of jail. Them other girls couldn't wait to tell me."

"I'm sorry—but I want to go on seeing you. I really do."

She looked at him. "Men don't marry whores, Silvio. I always known you liked me, but I ain't never expected marriage, not wit' you, anyways—"

"I'll make it up to you, I promise. You'll see. A couple months of marriage with Anna-Maria, I'll get her pregnant, we can go back to the way we always were, in the evenings, afternoons—"

She put her hand on his mouth to shut him up. "Stop that, Silvio! I'll be here whenever you want me. I already told you that."

He embraced her again. After a moment she pushed him away, gently.

"There's one thing you might do for me, though."

He propped himself up on one elbow. "There *is*? What?"

"You know how this city works. You got power. I gotta think about my little boy. I need a man."

Silvio looked at her, puzzled.

"Don't be selfish, Silvio. You got Anna-Maria, soon have a family. I need a man. I need to get into them quadroon balls."

Suddenly Silvio saw what she was getting at. The quadroon balls were famous in New Orleans and unique to the city. They were a special way for beautiful but poor quadroon girls to meet rich men. The girls were taken to the balls by their mothers. There they were introduced to wealthy men who were as often as not married but were looking for young mistresses. All negotiations went on between the men and the mothers, who sold their daughters into a gentle sort of sexual slavery, which was nevertheless well paid and relatively comfortable. The mistresses were invariably set up with rooms of their own and provided for. Many men in New Orleans maintained two households—one white, one quadroon—for most of their lives.

Silvio smiled and nodded. "You're so beautiful, Madeleine, you'd have no problem finding a man at one of the balls. But I have to find you a mother, to introduce you." He nodded. "I'll see what I can do."

Later, after they had made love, Madeleine fetched some wine from downstairs. When she returned she poured two glasses and got back into bed with Silvio. "Guess who's at the bar."

Silvio, taking the wine, shook his head.

"David Martell, the chief of detectives."

"So?"

She shrugged. "When I was in jail, I heard some of the other girls talking. They was saying Martell's not as straight as he makes out. That he knows Vito Liotta, an' they each own a piece of the Red Lantern, on Rampart."

Silvio buried his nose in his drink, thinking. He didn't want Madeleine to see the surprise on his face, betraying his ignorance. Liotta and Martell! This Liotta was moving fast. This Liotta was smart as well as ballsy, very smart. Foxy, as Priola would say.

Silvio drained his glass. Soon as this wedding was over, there was going to be one helluva war.

"The trousers look just fine, sir. Now try the jacket." Silvio had never been called "sir" before, or if he had, he couldn't remember the occasion. This new suit, by Chivasso of course, was part of Priola's wedding gift. It was light gray worsted, from England, and highlighted his swarthy complexion, making him more dashing than ever.

The suit was the only wedding chore he had to go through with, unless you counted the rehearsal, later today. He had at one stage been bothered about choosing the right gift for Anna-Maria, but her mother, a small shrew of a woman who drank all day long, had come to the rescue for once. She had pointed out that there was an antique writing bureau in a shop on Magazine Street that Anna-Maria had fallen for. She would be able to take it on their honeymoon to New York, and use it to write home. It had cost him thirty-five dollars—a small fortune—but the problem had been solved.

He was looking forward to New York. It was, he was told, the only town in America that could rival New Orleans. There were fewer brothels but more theaters. He had never been to a real theater. They would be staying in hotels, another new experience, except it was probably like being on board ship, in first class of course. He had also been told there was a sizable Italian population in New York, and he wanted to see that, too.

For the time being, of course, Anna-Maria and he were going to live in New Orleans. But that might not always be the case.

"I'll wrap the suit, Mr. Silvio. Will you take it with you, or shall I send it?"

"Send it, please."

"My pleasure."

Silvio went out. He looked at his watch: eleven-thirty. There was time for him to walk to Dick Saltram's ice factory and still be there by noon, when he was supposed to meet Angelo and Nino, to judge the experiment. Angelo was only coming under protest, saying it was a waste of time, since he had already made up his mind. But Silvio wasn't giving up so easily.

He walked west down Basin Street and turned into Commerce Street. That took him to New Levee Street and the West Cotton

Press. He turned from New Levee into Race Street and then onto
Religion Street, which brought him near to the orange market. If
he looked north from here, he could see City Hall, where the
police headquarters were. He hadn't yet mentioned to Angelo
what Madeleine had told him, that Martell and Liotta were in business together. Angie was burdened by this wedding business just
as he himself was. It would have to wait.

Silvio stayed on Religion until he reached Felicity, where the
factory was. From here he could see across the river to the New
Orleans and Apelouses Railroad. A long line of brown-and-cream
railroad cars stretched west.

As he reached the factory on foot Angelo's carriage was just
arriving, so they all went in together. Saltram was sent for, and
when he appeared he led them into the big ice room.

"The experiment is at the far end. This way, please."

By the back wall Dick Saltram had built a small cold room,
about the height of a man. "I laid the ice in the boxes because,
obviously, when it melts it turns into water and you wouldn't want
the holds of the ship sloshing about with water, saturating the fruit.
The boxes are designed to hold the water for a few hours until you
can throw it away. They have handles, to make it easier to carry
the ice, which can be quite heavy.

"Now, I put a crate of peaches, a crate of melons, and some
oranges inside this cold room. And there you can see an identical
range of fruit just lying here, in the open room. Let's look at that
first."

He picked up some oranges. One or two seemed fine, but they
were very soft. Others, however, were disfigured with patches of
a whitish blue. *"Necrotic coryneum,"* he said. "Mold."

The peaches were worse. The skins had wrinkled and some had
turned brown. When they were handled, they felt squishy and the
skins broke. Inside, there were brown patches on the yellow flesh.

The melons seemed least affected. But then Saltram said,
"Watch this," and he cut one of the melons in half. Although its
flesh was a deep pink, it was bone-dry.

"Now let's look at the refrigerated fruit." He stooped into the
little room and reemerged a moment later with some oranges and
melons, which he handed to Silvio. Then he went back for the
peaches.

All the fruit had a fine coating of dew, tiny drops of water, but the fruit itself was firm, too firm to eat in fact. None of the oranges showed the slightest trace of mold, the skins on the peaches were smooth and fresh-looking, and when Saltram cut into a melon, its flesh was succulent and juicy.

The others all stood waiting for Angelo to speak.

"Mr. Saltram, I understand you are Italian but have changed your name. Why? Are you ashamed of being Italian?"

This was not at all the kind of response Silvio was expecting. He went to interject but Saltram cut him off.

"No, no. It's okay." He held out his arm, to stop Silvio. "Mr. Priola, I am interested in science and technology. That's where the future is. Occasionally I need credit, from the banks. *They* are prejudiced against Italians. I was getting turned down for loans, I never even got interviews—because of my name, Scalice. So I learned English and changed the name of the company. That's all. I'm still a Catholic, we speak Italian at home, my mother's fettuccine is as wonderful as ever, and my younger brother will soon be joining the choir of St. Louis's. I'm not ashamed of being Italian, but I'm not a fool either, and I don't want to be poor."

Priola nodded. He appeared to sympathize. "I'm impressed by your experiment, Mr. Saltram. I cannot deny that. You have the brains of a bishop, as we say in Sicily. But I have a number of problems at the moment that are no concern of yours, except insofar as they affect my decision to make new investments."

"Angelo?"

They all turned to Silvio. "Instead of sending Anna-Maria and me on an expensive honeymoon in New York, Angie, why not spend the money on fitting out one ship—just one—and let it sail between New Orleans and Natchez? Those boats bring cotton downstream, and that doesn't need to be refrigerated. So we don't need any refrigeration plant in Natchez."

Angelo seemed to be listening hard, so Silvio hurried on. "See what effect the freezing has on business in, say, six months. I know what you're worried about"—he wouldn't mention Liotta in front of Saltram—"but I think we should get into refrigeration before anyone else does. If it works as well as I think it's going to, Angie, it will be great publicity, and bring us a lot of trade. If we don't do it, and others do, we may lose trade."

Angelo eyed him. "You'd give up New York for that?"

"I'm not giving it up. This thing will be a success. I'm just delaying it for a few months."

"What about Anna-Maria?"

"She'll do what you tell her."

Angelo could at least agree to that.

He stood for a moment, thinking. Then he looked from Silvio to Saltram. "All right, sir, you got yourself a deal. Real foxy. We choose a ship and you can fit her out, and supply the ice." He looked at his watch. "Now you'll have to forgive us. We can do my daughter out of her honeymoon but we can't delay her rehearsal."

St. Louis's Cathedral had been built facing the river and the French Market. The square in front of it was partly paved with stone and partly planted with trees and grass. Pigeons and seagulls strutted there in equal numbers.

When Silvio and the others arrived, Anna-Maria and her mother were already in the nave, as was the archbishop. They were standing at the top of the main aisle, where the actual ceremony would take place.

"You stand there," the archbishop said, addressing Silvio. "That's exactly where you will stand tomorrow, with your best man on your right." Nino, grinning sheepishly, stood where he was shown, near the pulpit.

The archbishop then ran them through the ceremony, including the signing of the register and the music.

"I understand there will be several civic dignitaries, Mr. Priola. Where would you like them to sit?"

"As near to the front as possible, but there's no need to keep them all on the bride's side. Silvio hasn't got any of his family in America, so we're going to have to help him out." He smiled fondly at Silvio. It seemed that the experiment had impressed him, as well as his future son-in-law's readiness to put business before pleasure. Presuming marriage to be a pleasure.

The archbishop spoke again. "Let me just check the routine things. The ring?"

Everyone looked at Nino.

He reached inside his collar and pulled out a piece of string, on which was threaded a thin gold band. Silvio suddenly thought: Where have I put Annunziata's ring?

"I must say that's an original way to make sure you don't forget it," said the archbishop, smiling. "Now, flowers?"

"All organized," said Mrs. Priola. "Patrick Donovan will be here at nine tomorrow morning. And so will I."

The archbishop nodded. "That just leaves the various fees. . . ." He trailed off, looking at Priola.

"Yes," Angelo replied. "I'll see to that now. Shall we go into your office?"

The archbishop led him out of the nave. Anna-Maria and her mother followed.

As he went Priola turned and called to Silvio. "Why not get some ice for the wedding breakfast? You know, those blocks with flowers in them. Since we're going into refrigeration, we may as well start in style."

Smiling, Nino and Silvio strolled down the aisle toward the main door of the cathedral. "I was never married," said Nino. "I cared for Annunziata's mother, though, and I suppose we might have married if she hadn't died." This was as near intimate as Nino ever got. He stopped just before they reached the door. "I'll make sure Annunziata knows about the wedding." When Silvio said nothing but merely looked at him, he added, "It's best this way, Silvio. Believe me. Listen to an older man. Learn from his mistakes. I can send for her now. Now that it's safe. She has a family, a boy, named after me." He didn't mention his grandson's second name.

Silvio didn't know what to think. Part of him was touched by Nino's intimacy, but part of him was repelled by the calculation that lay behind what he had said.

They went on through the door of the cathedral, into the square outside. Two covered carriages stood alongside the trees. One was Priola's.

Silvio reflected that Nino need not have told him he intended to send for Annunziata, and presumably Gino. He could just have gone ahead and done it. Silvio would have understood and it would have been kinder. Nino really did have a cruel streak. Mostly it was Stella who bore the brunt of it, but not always. Not for the first time, Silvio wondered if after his marriage to Anna-Maria the link to Nino might be broken. It wasn't such a bad idea. There would always be a use for a violent man like Nino, but Silvio believed that he was cleverer, and that was what counted. If he got away from Nino he would also be getting away from Annunziata, if she was brought to America. He had been too young and too slow thinking to prevent the death of his parents, but now, now his wits were beginning to—

"Excuse me?"

Silvio was jolted out of his reverie.

Two men stood in front of them.

"What? What is it?" Nino was already very nervous.

"Are you Antonino Greco?" The taller of the two men was speaking. He had a mustache and wore a fedora hat.

"No, I'm not," said Nino, and made to walk past the men.

"Just a minute," said the other man, barring his way. "I think you *are* Greco, and that you are wanted in Italy, for murder."

Silvio's heart seemed to do a somersault. This wasn't happening, please God. Instinctively he reached for his gun, as did Nino, but the other men were too quick for them. They already had their guns out.

"Don't move," said the one with the mustache. "I am a policeman and I have authority to shoot you if you resist arrest. Now raise your arms and turn around. Put your hands against the wall of the cathedral."

Silvio obeyed immediately. He was sweating in fear. Nino took his time, but eventually followed suit. He uttered one word: *"Merda!"*

Quickly, expertly, their weapons were taken from them, and their clothing searched.

One of the men—Silvio couldn't see which—pulled his arms behind him and in no time had fixed handcuffs to his wrists. Already terrified, he now felt he would die of shame. Thank God the square was temporarily deserted and there was no one to witness his humiliation.

Nino, too, was handcuffed and the pair were swiftly led across the square to the second curtained carriage. So that's where the police had been hiding.

They were helped into the carriage and it immediately set off at a fast clip. The curtains were closed, so they couldn't see where they were going, but Silvio reckoned they were heading west and north, out of the French Quarter and in the direction of City Hall. During the journey the policemen didn't speak, but just sat there holding their guns.

Silvio was desperately trying to think. Every so often, the carriage rolled, and the policemen's guns swayed. But they never quite pointed away for long enough. Any lunge at the policemen would have been fatal.

Then the carriage slowed, almost to a halt. Silvio guessed they were turning into Canal Street and waiting for a break in the traffic. Suddenly Nino let out a great bellow and threw himself headfirst through the open window of the carriage. However, the man with the mustache himself lunged forward and grabbed Nino's arms, which were handcuffed behind his back. The second policeman, with exemplary training, ignored what was happening and kept his gun trained on Silvio's heart.

"Don't *dare* move," he hissed. "I promise I'll shoot you dead."

Nino exerted his colossal strength, as if determined to turn the carriage over, but the handcuffs held him back. It wasn't long before he was subdued and pulled back inside. "Try that again," said the man with the mustache, "and I'll simply shoot you. It's all the same to me."

Nino sat back in the carriage as best he could, breathing heavily. Within five minutes they heard the wheels of the carriage rattle over cobblestones and Silvio assumed they had entered the police yard. After the carriage stopped, they were forced to wait. Silvio heard the gates to the police yard being banged shut. At this point he grew even more worried. Not only were they being arrested; they were being kept away from public view. This was unusual for the New Orleans police, who liked to boast about even their smallest successes in the fight against crime.

Eventually the two men were taken down from the carriage and led into a building. Inside, the building had a smell that Silvio recalled. It didn't come to him immediately, but when it did he almost gagged. It was the smell of the disinfectant used in the Parish Prison. Was that where they were being taken?

It didn't seem so. For the time being at least, they were led down into a small cell in the basement of the police station. The cell door was locked and a guard posted outside.

Nino spoke at last. "I want to see a lawyer."

"All in good time. Then you can see your lawyer, your doctor, your tailor, and your undertaker." The guard cackled.

"Shithead!" spat Nino. "This man here is getting married tomorrow."

Now the guard cackled even louder. "I hope the bride ain't knocked up. If she is, the little bastard's going to grow up an orphan." He laughed loudly at his own joke.

Then they all lapsed into silence.

After five minutes the two men who had arrested them came back again. "Stand up and come over here," said the one with the mustache.

Nino didn't budge.

"Look at this," said the policeman, and threw a piece of paper into the cell.

Still Nino didn't budge.

Silvio, however, not knowing what on earth was going on, was not so sullen. He went and stood over the piece of paper. After a moment, realizing what it was, he gasped and choked out, in Italian, "You'd better look at this. It's serious."

Nino glared at him, but did move at last, and stood next to Silvio, following his gaze.

He, too, gasped, though he did his best to hide the fact.

The object on the floor was a photograph of a drawing. *The drawing Nino had sent to London with the priest's scalp!* The drawing of himself.

"That's you all right, Greco. It's a good likeness, even though you shaved off your beard. We were tipped off about you. We've been following you and your pal here for some time. We received this photograph in the mail just yesterday. Our little abduction didn't take long to work out and it went very smoothly."

"I want a lawyer."

"You'll get a lawyer, all in good time. When we're ready for you to have one. The English priest didn't have a lawyer. You can wait."

He turned to go, but spoke on his way out to the guard. "See that they get some food. We'll be back at nine."

"Very good, Mr. Martell," replied the guard.

Silvio caught his breath. They had been arrested by David Martell, the chief of detectives himself. Silvio's mind went back to what Madeleine had said, to a link between Martell and Liotta. Did Liotta have a hand in this arrest? Should he have mentioned this to Angelo? Would it have made any difference? He kept his thoughts to himself. It was too late now.

And why were Martell and his sidekick coming back at nine

o'clock? That was an odd time for police work. The courts would be closed. The Parish Prison would be closed. It would be dark. Silvio's sense of foreboding grew. As they said in Sicily, the fox was born at night.

But there was nothing they could do. They were given food, as Martell had instructed—some all but inedible gristle—and were forced to sit tight until nine. It was impossible for them to get word out and by now people must be wondering where they were. Somebody would ask questions soon. Tonight there was to have been a boozy party for Silvio at Madge Leigh's.

Nine o'clock came and went. Ten o'clock. Eleven. At half-past eleven there was a commotion in the corridor and Martell and the other man reappeared.

"Get up," Martell commanded. This time their ankles were tied and they were blindfolded.

"Now, you're going to be taken somewhere. Policemen are going to carry you. I remind you that I have authority to shoot you, and if you struggle, or try to call out, I *will* shoot you without any warning at all. Is that clear? Don't speak, just nod your heads if you understand and agree."

Silvio nodded. He couldn't see if Nino did the same.

"Now lie on the ground."

Silvio lay on the hard floor and after only a few moments he felt himself being lifted by three or four men, who grunted and gasped their way out of the cell, down the corridor, and out into the yard. He was bundled onto a wooden surface, which suddenly moved and which he realized was a wagon, the kind that had been used to carry Giancarlo Cataldo's remains at his funeral. Where *were* they being taken?

But he didn't dare ask. He lay still as the wagon rumbled forward, out of the yard and into the street.

After about half an hour the horse began to pull up a sharp incline. The only high hill in New Orleans led to Metairie Ridge. Metairie Ridge? *They had been taken to the cemetery!* The police were going to kill them and bury them right away, without any record, any witnesses. By this time it should have been Silvio's wedding day; instead it was the day he would die and be buried.

The driver made the horse steady. Silvio was manhandled off the wagon. He felt himself being taken down a slope—into the cemetery proper?—but then passed from one set of hands to another. Now, as he was shuffled forward, he heard the footsteps of those carrying him. They rang out, as if they were walking on something hollow.

All at once he realized where he was. That ridge had not been Metairie. It had been the levee, and he was now aboard ship. He was relieved and apprehensive at the same time. It didn't look as though he was going to be killed immediately—but where were they taking him? Italy—to stand trial? South America? Or was he going to be dumped at sea, as he and Nino had dumped the Orestanos? Again he wondered whether this was all Vito Liotta's doing. Being kidnapped and abandoned at sea had a terrifying symmetry with what he and Nino had done to the Orestanos. But Vito Liotta would never have contacted the police, would he? That was something no real Sicilian would have done.

A rumble from below told Silvio that the ship's engines had started. They would be putting out to sea soon, or heading upriver. Nino and he had been spirited out of New Orleans as quietly and as cleanly as they had entered two years ago.

Sono cadavere? he wondered. Am I a living corpse?

For a while the ship's engines built up steam, the rumble gradually getting louder, the juddering more insistent. Obviously it was not a steamboat but an oceangoing vessel. Then, when it must have been close to two o'clock, Silvio heard the slapping of water on the hull and he realized the ship was under way. Despite his fear, his exhaustion overcame him and he fell asleep.

14

Courtroom number six was high and circular, with brown marble columns to match the wood of the court furniture. The public was so close you could reach out and touch them. All the benches were packed. This trial was attracting a lot of attention. Every time he turned to look at the crowd, a score of heads craned toward him. Silvio was now a celebrity.

It was ironic, he thought. New York was to have been the place where he honeymooned with Anna-Maria. They had planned to see the hotels, the theaters, the shops, the areas where the Italians lived. Instead, all he had seen were the insides of the Bowery Jail, and courtrooms. His only glimpse of real New York was that small area of Manhattan outside the courtroom: Foley Square.

It wouldn't be much longer now. The trial was nearly over and they should have a verdict by the end of the week. Martell and his men had been very clever—to begin with. Nino and Silvio had been spirited aboard ship without anyone knowing. Technically this was illegal, but no one was about to argue Nino's case, that he wasn't Antonino Greco, the Quarryman. However, in sending Nino and Silvio to New York, Martell had made a mistake. If the two men had been put on board an Italian ship and dumped in Palermo or Naples two weeks later, then that would have been that and no amount of legal niceties would have rescued them. But Martell had chosen the first ship to leave, the *City of New Orleans*, a coaster bound for New York, stopping off at various Atlantic ports on the way. This had provided time and opportunity for Nino's cunning. The moment they had been released from their ropes and blindfolds, once they were out to sea, Nino had begun to proclaim loudly that he was not Antonino Greco but Domenico Grado, and that he had always been Grado. He was so convincing, he persuaded two seamen to send messages for him, to Angelo, from Fort Pierce and Newport News. They were assured that they would be handsomely repaid later for their cooperation.

As a result, by the time the *City of New Orleans* reached New York, a week after it had left the Mississippi, a campaign had been begun in New Orleans to get Nino and Silvio released on the grounds that they had been abducted by mistake. Angelo Priola, using all the influence at his disposal, managed to round up more than twenty witnesses, each of whom traveled to New York at his expense, to testify that Nino and Silvio were who they said they were. Angelo had already been organizing passports for them, as he had promised when Silvio agreed to marry Anna-Maria. This process was presented as evidence in the extradition hearings.

Some of the witnesses had been very effective indeed. There had even been a written affidavit, sworn by the Archbishop of New Orleans and submitted to the court, that Sylvano Razzini had been due to be married the day after his abduction. That had been extremely dramatic.

While they were cooped up in the Bowery Jail, they had been able to receive visitors and were provided with decent food. Vincent Mistretta had visited once. He had been sent on ahead by Angelo and he brought clothes, and money. The cell Silvio shared with Nino was tiny, about the size of the cabin they had occupied on the *Syracusa* but without natural light. The walls were similar to the yellowy green he had seen in the Parish Prison in New Orleans when he had visited Madeleine—but the smell was far worse.

"Vinnie," Silvio had hissed, after the guard had left and the money had been handed over, "what about Liotta? He went outside the code, told Martell. He don't get no respect for that."

Mistretta shook his head. "Ain't what I hear. Liotta owns Martell. The Cataldos did business with Milton, the mayor. Milton owned Martell. Liotta takes over the Cataldos, he takes over Martell. All that happened, as I hear it, Martell had someone—a cop—working undercover in Madge Leigh's. He heard Nino fighting with Stella, and she called him a bandit—"

Silvio looked at Nino and groaned.

"Anyways, the cop tells Martell. Martell, I hear, had some picture sent from Chicago, from some detective agency, but that weren't enough. Nino's shaved his beard, after all. So Martell weren't sure and asks around. Of course, it ain't long before Liotta hears. The whole thing plays into his hands. But he says he ain't gone outside the code and most people are too scared to disagree with him."

"Bullshit!" Silvio shouted. "*Concime!* I don't buy that. Nobody could buy that. Liotta can't bend the rules. People got to know, Vinnie, you got to make sure people know. We get out of this—Vito's dead. *Omertà?*" He spat.

But Silvio now understood the full picture, the terrible beauty of Liotta's plan. In making the arrests on the eve of the wedding, the police not only hit Nino and Silvio; they hit at Anna-Maria and her father as well, humiliating them in public. Liotta considered this an apt revenge for the Priola family's ruthlessness toward the Cataldos. Third, and perhaps more important in the long run, David Martell's sensational arrests had been flashed around the country and on the strength of this, the mayor had promoted Martell from chief of detectives to chief of police. This was an extremely popular move in New Orleans, a maneuver that had proved decisive when the election took place. While Nino and Silvio were in prison, awaiting trial, Milton had been reelected.

All of this infuriated Silvio. Yet again he had been outthought by Vito Liotta. Just as in the episode with the steamboat race. Liotta's success was more than galling. It was demeaning. Worse, it brought back those terrible moments when his parents had been killed. His life seemed to be cursed by the slowness of his brain. *Sono buve?* he asked himself repeatedly. Am I a dumb ox?

So he had been sullen the day Angelo and Anna-Maria arrived at the Bowery Jail to see him. They had come by train—more than a week's journey—and were staying in New York in the very hotel where Anna-Maria and Silvio were to have spent their honeymoon.

Anna-Maria had brought Silvio the latest Mark Twain. She sympathized with Silvio's position, but she was angry, too. She had predicted that sooner or later Silvio's association with Nino would backfire on him. Now it had.

After a while Angelo and Nino had been allowed to walk in the prison yard and Silvio and Anna-Maria were left alone together. Anna-Maria suddenly looked nervous. For a moment Silvio thought she might want to do it, right there in his cell, but then he saw that she was too upset for that.

"Silvio," she had said. "Silvio, I've got something to tell you."

The tone of her voice was strange. Silvio was puzzled. "Well?" he said, more aggressively than he intended. "What is it?"

She looked hard at him, leaned forward, and took his hand. She was wearing a blue dress that hid her figure and almost no make-up. "Madeleine's been killed."

He jerked his hand away. "No! What do you mean, killed? Murdered?"

She nodded, distraught that he should still care so much. "I'm sorry, Silvio. I'm really very sorry."

He glared at her. He couldn't forget what Anna-Maria had done to Madeleine, but here in this cell she did seem genuinely upset.

He felt like crying, but couldn't. Too much was still happening too quickly. "Tell me," he said quietly. "Tell me. How?"

Anna-Maria spoke in scarcely more than a whisper. "She went to a quadroon ball—"

Silvio groaned. He had arranged that.

"She was a great success, Silvio. Scores of men asked her to dance. She was invited onto the terrace by several men, and accepted. One time while she was outside she was stabbed. Her body was found the next morning."

Silvio had begun to sweat. "Why? *Why?* Some sex maniac?"

Anna-Maria shook her head. "Apparently not. And Father doesn't believe so, either. He . . . he knew about you and Madeleine. . . ." It clearly pained Anna-Maria to say this. "He looked into Madeleine's death. It seems two other girls were killed around that time, too. Two other"—she said the next word softly—"whores."

She paused, to let Silvio take in what she was saying. "Father thinks that Madeleine was killed for what she knew. The other girls were friends of David Martell." Anna-Maria was trying to be gentle but looked hard at Silvio. "Did Madeleine ever say anything to you, Silvio, about Martell and Liotta? Father told me to ask you."

Instinctively Silvio shook his head. He couldn't admit now what he had not admitted before. But he saw it all quite clearly. Liotta had suddenly discovered—from one of the other girls?— that there was a chance Madeleine knew that Liotta had set up Nino and Silvio with Martell, that a Sicilian had gone outside *omertà*, and as such would forfeit all respect throughout the New Orleans *malavita*. So he'd had to kill the evidence.

Slumped in his cell, Silvio felt his anger boil up again. Liotta would be made to pay, once this trial was out of the way. But in front of Anna-Maria he forced himself to be calm.

"What about Madeleine's son?" he asked. "Who's looking after him?"

"Stella. Don't worry, she's a good mother."

Anna-Maria and he had parted tenderly after that. She had handled herself well in giving him the news, and he had responded. If the trial went well and he was not extradited, he told her, he would be home in no time and they could be married just as soon as it could be rearranged. He kissed her on the cheek.

It took him days to adjust to the news about Madeleine. When he was allowed outside into the exercise yard, he would hurl stones violently at the wall. As time went by, however, he found himself more obsessed with Vito Liotta. Vito had to be dealt with. This fox had to be killed.

Silvio turned his attention back to the court. Today was the first day of the closing speeches. The prosecution would sum up its case today, the defense tomorrow. The judge would add his concluding remarks the day after. Silvio was looking forward to it. He believed they had a good chance of winning their fight to remain in America.

The clerk of the court appeared. "All rise," he said. "Judge Proctor presiding."

The judge, a tall, lean, spare man, strode swiftly to his seat and sat down. He nodded to the prosecuting attorney. "Mr. Routledge."

Routledge stood up. With his bull neck he looked more like a docker than a lawyer, but Silvio knew he had an able mind.

"Your Honor, something most unusual has occurred and I crave the court's indulgence. It *is* very important and I think I can convince you why a short alteration in procedure would be in order. May I approach the bench?"

Proctor nodded, and also beckoned forward the defense attorney, Frank Weston, the lawyer Angelo had found. For a few moments there was a whispered conversation between the three of them, which grew heated as the minutes passed. Then Proctor raised his hand. "No, that's enough, Mr. Weston. I'll allow it."

Routledge returned to his seat smiling. Weston came back to his scowling.

"What is it?" whispered Nino, but Weston motioned for him to be quiet.

Routledge stood. "Before my concluding remarks for the state, let the record show that I call one extra witness, according to the procedural alteration His Honor has just allowed." He hesitated, for effect. "The state calls Henry Livesey."

Silvio wasn't sure at first who this Henry Livesey was—until he noticed Nino go white with horror and mutter through clenched teeth, "The priest! The English priest!"

Of course! The man Nino had scalped. Silvio felt sick.

There was a rustle of noise as the public strained to see the new witness.

A tall, thin man in a priest's black cassock entered the court. There was a brief flash of white at his throat—his dog collar.

A priest giving evidence. This was bad. The court would have to believe him. But it had been more than two years since the episode in Sicily. Would he still remember Nino?

Livesey took the stand and read the oath.

Then Routledge said, "The court is grateful to you for coming all this way, Father Livesey."

The priest nodded. "I would have been here earlier, but the ship I was traveling on encountered bad weather and lost one of her engines."

"No matter. You are here now. Will you please tell the court about certain events which took place, in Sicily, in 1879?"

And for fifteen minutes Livesey gave what was obviously a well-rehearsed account of his kidnapping by Nino. Everyone was fascinated. When he described how his scalp had been sliced off and mailed to London, there was utter silence in the court.

"I apologize for doing this, Father Livesey, but so that everyone can judge for himself the barbarity of the crime that was perpetrated on you, could you please bow your head so that we may all see your scalp—or what is left of it."

Livesey leaned forward in the chair so that the top of his head could be seen by every member of the jury. Hair was growing again but haphazardly and thinly. The flat top to his skull could be plainly seen, like a slice taken out of an apple.

After a moment, a long moment in which all eyes were on

Livesey and his disfigurement, Routledge said, "And now, Father Livesey, let us come to the reason we have brought you all this way, three thousand five hundred miles from London. Can you please tell the court if the man who performed this barbarous operation on you is in this room today? If he is, can you please point to him?"

This was the test. If Livesey fingered Nino, they were done for. The flat skull, the priest's outfit, the three and a half thousand miles traveled to give evidence: it was a powerful combination that no amount of false witness, however convincing, could overcome.

Livesey looked across to the table where Nino and Silvio were seated. His eyes fastened onto Nino's. They narrowed in hatred and contempt. "That's him," he said, pointing. "That's Nino Greco, the Quarryman."

PART THREE

—✦—

Sottocapo

15

"You have a visitor, Randazzo. Come on, get up!" The guard opened the door to Silvio's cell and pulled him roughly off his bunk.

Reluctantly, he allowed himself to be led outside. Ucciardone Prison, on the edge of Palermo, was every bit as bad as the Parish Prison in New Orleans, maybe worse. Silvio was required to work eight backbreaking hours a day quarrying fine marble. When he returned to his cell he was allowed half an hour's rest before the evening shower and the filth they called dinner. Now some stupid visitor had disturbed his thirty minutes of peace.

He would soon have spent four years in this one cell. Four years with just a bed, a crucifix, and Mark Twain for company. The regime at Ucciardone was hard, and so were the other men, prisoners, and guards. There were no friendships in this jail; instead, there was brutality everywhere. The guards had whips and enforced their authority with a lashing at the slightest provocation. Prisoners would betray each other for the smallest reason, the most meager privileges handed out by the governor.

Silvio, it was true, had been left pretty much to himself, on account of his links to Nino. After four years even that was beginning to fade.

Once the English priest had given evidence against them in the New York court, Nino and Silvio had lost their fight to stay in America and had been put aboard an Italian naval frigate in New York Harbor, which had left American waters even before an appeal against extradition could be lodged. They were manacled for the whole voyage, kept in the bowels of the ship, and hadn't been allowed to see daylight even once. They had been unloaded at Palermo and removed to the Girganti Prison in the center of town, to await trial on charges brought by the Italian authorities. That had taken place late in 1882. Nino had been found guilty of thirteen murders—two in the Palermo docks in 1866, eleven in the Dragonaro quarry in 1879—and of the kidnapping and assault of Father Henry Livesey, who had proved himself an indefatigable traveler and witness, arriving in Palermo to give evidence, just as he had in New York. Nino had received twenty years for the murders, ten for the mutilation of Livesey, and five for the kidnapping, the sentences to run consecutively, thirty-five years in total. He would be seventy-five before he came out. If he lived.

For his part in the kidnapping, Silvio, as a minor, was sentenced to two years. For his part in the massacre of the Lazio Brigade soldiers, he, too, received twenty years' hard labor. As with Nino, the sentences were to run consecutively. He would be forty-three, an old man, before he was released. Liotta's plan had worked. He had gotten rid of Nino and Silvio in one bold stroke.

Silvio hadn't seen Nino since the Palermo trial. Because the Quarryman was such a notorious figure in Sicily, still something of a symbol for many people, the authorities in Rome had judged that attempts might be made to free him. They therefore removed him to the north of Italy, to a prison near Bologna, where, they felt, he was far more secure and where his fame, or notoriety, counted for much less.

Silvio had been allowed to stay in Sicily, on the humanitarian grounds that he was only a young man and should be near his family. His only family, of course, was Bastiano and Smeralda. Smeralda came occasionally, but Bastiano had been part of the attack on the Lazio Brigade, was now the Don of Bivona and himself much sought after by the authorities. So he could hardly walk into a prison of his own free will. Smeralda usually came on Sundays, but today was Friday. Why the change in routine?

Not that Silvio cared especially. When he had first entered prison he had been angry, angry at the Americans for arresting him and smuggling him aboard the *City of New Orleans*, angry at himself for allowing it to happen, angry at his friends in America for not having prevented the English priest from giving evidence, angry at Nino for his explosive nature that had helped land him where he was. He was also angry with Anna-Maria—for being right. He *should* have separated himself from Nino while he had the chance. Most of all, he was angry with Vito Liotta, for making all this happen, and for being so *fucking* clever.

There had been no word from Anna-Maria, but he had heard that she had waited until he was sentenced—and then married Dick Saltram, the ice maker. Silvio couldn't blame her. She wasn't about to wait for twenty-two years to marry him.

Angelo, of course, had gotten word through, bless him. If Silvio had had dependents, Priola would have looked after them, but not even Angie could spirit Silvio out of Ucciardone Prison from four thousand miles away. Angelo would come to terms with Liotta, of course; he had to. Probably he already had. He wouldn't necessarily take revenge, not if he judged that a lasting peace was now possible—with two Dons in New Orleans. No one could make war all the time.

It had taken months for Silvio's anger to work itself through. Then he had become depressed. When he wasn't laboring in the quarry, his thoughts alternated between dreams of freedom—the bars and brothels and gambling joints of New Orleans, the busy, bustling life on the Mississippi, the vast open skies of Louisiana— and the reality that he would be in prison, between these four walls, with no Madeleine, no bourbon, no absinthe, no blocks of ice with flowers in them, for the next God knew how many years. *Sono cadavere,* he repeated to himself time and again. I'm a corpse, a living corpse. His time in Ucciardone stretched ahead of him as far as his own life stretched back, all the way until he was a baby. He had no mother, no father, no wife, no children. He had no one to blame but himself, his own stupidity. He felt very sorry for himself, became listless, would sometimes weep silently at night, when there was no one else to see. The guards had looked upon his listlessness with contempt, and vowed to whip him out of it.

Then he met Carmelo Giaccone, the prison doctor, who had stopped by Silvio's cell one evening and dropped off a book. He must have noticed the Mark Twain, Anna-Maria's gift that Silvio kept with him, to read and reread. Few prisoners were literate. "Read that," Giaccone had said. "It might help." He was a tall man with long fingers, surgeon's hands. He smoked small cigars.

Silvio had said nothing at the time, just lain on his bed as usual. But he wasn't indifferent to the doctor or his gesture. Whether it was because Giaccone was an educated man, or because his gift was the first time anyone in years had done anything for Silvio, he picked up the book.

It was an Italian translation of a Russian book, a story about a man who had committed several crimes and gotten away with them, but was then accused of something he hadn't done and imprisoned for it. Silvio wasn't a fast reader. He had not been able to read at all before he went to America, and there he had read more in English than in Italian. So it took him two weeks to finish the book. Next time the doctor came, he said, "I finished the book. How was it supposed to help?"

Dr. Giaccone looked at him. "You finished it. That's the first positive thing you've done in months. While you were reading it you weren't feeling sorry for yourself."

"Is that important?"

"Look, I know prison's not New Orleans, or the Via Scina, or the almond orchards of Indisi, but you're still a young man, Randazzo, and smart. The way you've been going, you won't see thirty. Believe me, I know."

"And one book changes all that?"

"Not one book, no. But it's a start. I gave you that book, not because it has any great message, or because it's beautifully written, but because it was about prison, about someone who felt as angry as you. So I knew you'd read it, and finish it."

"So. I finished it."

"Want another?"

To his surprise, Silvio realized he did want to read another book. Giaccone brought him an American story by someone called Edgar Allan Poe, about a man who was cast adrift on a becalmed sea—and this time Silvio read it in less than a week. The doctor brought other books, and gradually Silvio found he looked forward to the evenings when he got back from the quarry and could lie on his bed and escape into a world beyond the prison bars. The books weren't always stories. Sometimes they were about history, painting, voyages, science. They brought back those afternoons on the lugger with Anna-Maria.

Sometimes the doctor came in on Sundays and they would discuss what they had both been reading. Silvio came to enjoy these discussions almost as much as he enjoyed the books themselves. Often the doctor saw things in the books that Silvio had missed entirely. As the saying went, some people's taste was for olives, others' for almonds.

One Sunday, when Silvio had been in jail nearly three years, the doctor had said, "How would you like to help me in the surgery?"

At first Silvio was alarmed. He was reminded all too forcefully of Dr. Tolmezzo on the *Syracusa*.

"You were sentenced to hard labor," said Giaccone. "I can't change that. But on Sunday mornings, when you don't go to the quarry, I perform minor operations on prisoners who are ill or have been injured. I need an assistant, and the man who's been helping me has just been released."

"If I help you, it means giving up my free time."

"Yes."

Silvio said yes anyway. He realized he'd been maneuvered into this position, outthought yet again. But he liked the doctor and the way Giaccone forced him to think. From then on he spent his Sunday mornings in the prison hospital learning some of the skills that Tolmezzo might have taught him had the Orestanos not interfered. He learned how to dress wounds, stitch cuts, manipulate bones that were dislocated, apply plaster of paris, and much else. This produced an unexpected dividend one day at the quarry when an explosion had gone wrong and some stones had fallen on a guard, breaking his leg. Silvio had been able to manipulate the guard's bones back into their original positions, thus easing the pain the man suffered, and minimizing blood loss, very possibly saving the man's life in the process—at least, that was what Giaccone said later. There was now no talk among the guards of whipping Silvio into shape. In fact, a flask of wine had found its way into his cell that night.

Some other prisoners, intrigued and not a little suspicious of his relationship with the doctor, had questioned him about the books he was lent. Since none of these men could read, Silvio petitioned the prison governor to be allowed on certain evenings to read aloud to other interested prisoners. Once everyone got over the novelty of this, it proved very popular.

It took Silvio months before he noticed he was beginning to feel less sorry for himself. The doctor was clever, like Vito Liotta, but in a very different way. He, too, had the brains of a bishop.

Silvio had reached the end of the corridor.

Although he was free of the black depression of the early

months, he was still a prisoner. The four years he had so far spent in Ucciardone had been a waste; he could never have those years back.

At the end of the corridor there was an iron grille. He waited while it was unlocked. Now he and the guard descended a metal staircase to the level below. It reminded him faintly of the staircase on the *Syracusa*, which led from one immigrant deck to another. That happened often nowadays: bits of his narrow, constricted life in prison evoked some part of his past. That's all he had—a past.

They reached the floor below and another iron grille. This, too, was unlocked. He was led across the main reception hall to a metal door.

"Stand there," said the guard, indicating a spot some distance away.

Silvio obeyed.

The guard then approached the door and lifted a small flap over a spy hole. He appeared satisfied by what he saw inside, for he unlocked the door and held it open. He nodded Silvio through. "Half an hour, no more."

Silvio walked through the doorway, which was then locked behind him. He had been in this room before, several times, and knew it contained one window, barred of course, a table and two chairs, a tin ashtray, and nothing else. It was painted green and smelled of cigarettes. Visitors were told they must take away the remains of any cigarettes that were smoked during the interview.

The opportunity to smoke was one of the best things about these interviews, and for that reason alone, Silvio was looking forward to meeting Smeralda. It went some way toward making up for having his peace disturbed.

But his visitor wasn't Smeralda. It was Annunziata.

For a moment he was speechless. There had been no word from her while he had been in jail—and he couldn't blame her. She was married, with a child. He had nearly been married. Like the roads at Bivio Indisi, their lives had gone separate ways.

Annunziata looked pale, drawn, but still very, very beautiful, her blond hair pulled straight back in a way that emphasized the spectacular bone structure of her face.

He was nervous, not knowing how to greet her, but she came

toward him and held her face up for him to kiss her cheek. Her skin was as soft as ever.

They sat down. She fumbled in a bag and took out some cigarettes. "Here."

He held them and lit one, never taking his eyes off her. She had filled out, had bigger hips, woman's hips. But it was her face that was most changed, her eyes especially. He couldn't make out whether they were harder or more fearful.

"You're in black," he said, noticing her clothes for the first time.

Her eyes filled with tears. "Gino took little Nino to Palermo, to show his family. There was a cholera outbreak. . . ."

Silvio was shocked. "Both of them?" he said softly.

She shook her head. "No, only little Nino caught the cholera. But . . . but, after he died, Gino went crazy. He blamed himself. He cried, he drank." She sighed. "And he got careless. There was a robbery, near Caltanissetta. Gino lost his temper, gave away his position. He was shot." Through her tears she looked at Silvio. "I think Gino wanted to die. Oh, Toto! He loved his son more than he loved me." She held her hand to her eyes, to stem the tears.

"Zata, I'm sorry. What can I say?" No wonder she looked drawn.

He had to help her. He had never seen her cry like this. It was terrible, worse than being in pain himself. "Zata . . . I never stopped . . . you know . . . it was just—"

"No!" Annunziata held out her hand for him to stop. Her other hand still covered her face to hide her tears. "Toto," she managed softly, between tears. "No, please. I'm here for a reason. We don't have much time."

He said nothing, allowing her to try to compose herself. She wiped her eyes with the back of her hand, and then dried her hands on her skirt. When, finally, she looked at him, he thought he had never seen anyone so sad.

When at last she spoke, her voice was uncertain. "Last . . . last week . . . my father was shot in Bologna Jail—"

"No! *No!*" Silvio stood up, sending his chair clattering across the floor. "Zata! Zata!" He went to her, but again she held out her arm, to stop him.

"Toto, listen, please. It's important." Insistently, she pushed him away from her. "Listen to what I have to say. Please."

For a moment he stood over her. But her tears had dried now.

Her weak moment was over. "Sit down, Toto." She was gentle but she meant it.

He picked up the chair and sat down.

She waited for him to be seated, then took a deep breath. "He's still alive, just. I went to see him. He was too weak to say anything, but I know he recognized me. No one has been arrested, but we understand that a few days ago a man called Concetto Pianello was transferred from Bologna Prison to Padua. Now, Pianello's brother, Natale—"

"Is Liotta's *consigliere*. I know. Jesus! Liotta is responsible for this attack. Why?"

"I'm telling you what Bastiano says, and Father Ignazio. Vito Liotta believes in making unexpected moves. No one thought he would touch my father in prison, so that made him an easy target. It was a way of putting pressure on Angelo—showing that no one in the Priola family is safe. He's showing how wide his powers are now, what a long reach he has. Also, there was always the chance that my father would escape, and return to America, for vengeance."

Silvio was stupefied. He was also close to tears himself. Nino near death! He couldn't take it in. Liotta must be sick. Except that he wasn't sick, he was evil. More than a fox, *un squalo*. A shark. What was Angelo thinking now? Was he safe?

"How about Angie?" he said softly. "Any news?"

"So far as we know, Angelo is fine." For a moment Annunziata fell silent. There was only the sound of Silvio breathing cigarette smoke into the room. Then she spoke again. "Toto, I was sent this time because they felt it was safer, but also because ... well, because Bastiano wanted to shock you."

Silvio stopped smoking.

"After the attack on my father, we believe your life may be in danger, too. You and my father killed three Orestanos in the Atlantic Ocean, and two Cataldos in New Orleans. Neither of these families will be happy until you are both dead. Liotta may be clever enough to get to you in jail."

Sono bersaglio, he thought. I'm a target. Silvio had reached this conclusion himself only moments before Annunziata had said it.

"Toto, we can't let you be killed. I can't lose another man." She tried to smile, a feeble smile. "I have a message for you, from Father Ignazio. He has a plan to help you escape."

* * *

The quarry was less than two miles from Ucciardone, half an hour's walk in the early morning and a bit longer in the evening, after a hard day. Cloudy or chilly days were always preferable to sun, and rain was best of all, because then the quarrying was canceled and the prisoners got to lie in bed all day.

But today, *the* day, the sun was shining remorselessly and the reflected heat, from the rough stone walls of the quarry itself, only made matters worse. It was barely eleven-thirty but Silvio was already drenched with sweat.

The hard-labor gangs were divided into groups of ten, each with two guards, each guard having a pistol and a whip to enforce his authority. Today there were four gangs scattered about the quarry, two of them hacking at the walls, dislodging the rocks, one gang inspecting them and sorting them according to color— brown, gray, or white—and a fourth gang loading them onto carts. A five-minute break was allowed every hour.

Silvio knew what was coming and the knowledge made him sweat even more. Annunziata had visited him again twice since their first meeting. Each time she had more specific information about the plan, which had been conceived by the abbot and Silvio's uncle, Bastiano. The problem with the plan was that it was extraordinarily risky, and if it failed, Silvio would surely be made to suffer. He would undoubtedly be moved to the mainland, but before that the prison guards would certainly beat him, maybe even kill him.

In their subsequent meetings Annunziata had looked less strained than on the first occasion—animated even. Silvio wondered whether this was because she still cared for him. He found he was recovering his old feelings for her. There were still thorns on the gorse bush, as they said in the hills. Annunziata's skin was still the color of almonds, and although she had been married, she had not lost that virginal quality that had first drawn him to her. Then he checked himself. He had cheated on Annunziata, deceived and misled her. Was she now getting her own back? Was there really a plan to help him escape, or was she making it all up, to build up his hopes and then dash them? At the end of their last meeting he had put the question to her. As a reply, she merely stood up, leaned forward, and kissed him on the lips.

He was just twenty minutes from knowing what the truth was, one way or the other.

Everything depended on whether the guards acted true to form. Normally, at noon, the gangs stopped, ate their lunch where they were working, but were allowed to sit down. The guards, however, liked to eat all together. In practice, this meant that seven guards sat down with one another, while one of them, the unlucky one, patrolled the four gangs. From the point of view of the guards, this wasn't much of a risk. There was only one way out of the quarry, and that led past where they were having lunch.

But—and this was the important part—they usually had lunch at the same place, where the stones had been arranged in such a way that they could sit around a large rock that served as a table.

Twelve o'clock arrived. There were hardly any shadows now and everyone was feeling the heat. The senior guard blew his whistle and all the prisoners stopped work. Each man carried his own piece of bread and cheese, and flask of water. They all found stones to sit on and began to eat quickly. The food was hardly appetizing, but as soon as it was finished they could stretch out on any flat ground and snatch twenty minutes' rest.

But Silvio only nibbled his bread. He had in the preceding days established a routine of eating more slowly than everyone else. If he finished his food and didn't lie down, it would seem odd. But the last thing he wanted right now was to be flat on the ground.

Out of the corner of his eye he looked at the guards. Were they going to their usual spot to eat? They hadn't moved yet. Three or four of them were standing arguing about something. Two others were also talking together, at some distance from their colleagues. Why didn't they go to their normal spot?

But then the larger group started to walk toward their "table," still arguing as they went. The others followed, leaving one guard, a small, swarthy man, to oversee the gangs. He was a long way from Silvio. That made it more risky.

Silvio started on his cheese. His hands were clammy with sweat.

The guards were sitting down. One, two, three, four. Three of them were still arguing, still standing. The ones who were seated took out their food, which was much the same as what the prisoners had but with fresh tomatoes added and a little wine. The wine was against regulations, but this was Sicily and who was to know?

Finally, the three other guards all sat down together. The seven were in place. Silvio, nibbling his cheese, now transferred his attention to the small guard overseeing the gangs. He was coming toward Silvio, but slowly, and was a good thirty yards away. That was a lot of ground to cover, when the time came.

Silvio alone knew, or thought he knew, that only feet away from the guards were seven sticks of dynamite. The fuse was buried under more rocks, which were strewn apparently haphazardly across the ground but in fact had been arranged by Bastiano and his men to conceal the wire. Somewhere, out of sight above the lip of the quarry, Bastiano and the others were waiting for the right moment.

Except that now was the right moment and nothing had happened.

Had Annunziata misled him? Was this all a cruel joke?

Or were they waiting for the small guard to move closer to Silvio, making his job easier? But the guard wasn't moving and time was passing. Worse, he could now see that one of the men at the "table" was getting up. That would—

A wave of warm air swept across his face—blast. Milliseconds later he heard the explosion, which was amplified as it reverberated around the walls of the quarry. Immediately, a huge cloud of dust filled the area. Stones and even boulders were lifted into the air, and were now falling all around. Silvio was on his feet and running toward the small guard. He had to cover the thirty yards before the other man recovered from the shock and drew his gun.

Silvio was halfway toward him before the guard adjusted to the fact that all his colleagues were badly injured or dead. Then he saw Silvio heading his way, realized what was happening, threw down his whip, and reached for his gun.

Ten yards to go. The guard's hand was on the butt of the pistol.

Five yards. He was raising the barrel.

At three yards Silvio jumped. The man's arm was lifted, the barrel pointing at Silvio's chest. Silvio was too late.

He jerked himself to one side, but even as he did so the bullet slammed into his shoulder. His body swiveled in midair from the impact. A hot tide of pain flooded his entire arm. Even so, he landed on the guard, sending him crashing to the floor. The pain made Silvio cry out. Tears filled his eyes and made his cheeks sticky as they mingled with the dust on his face.

But he forced himself to his feet. He couldn't get caught now. After what had happened, life in Ucciardone wouldn't be worth living.

The small guard wasn't moving. There was blood by one of his ears. He had hit his head when he had fallen and was unconscious.

Silvio looked about him. The smoke from the explosion was beginning to clear and he could see his fellow prisoners standing up, dazed, but rapidly taking in the fact that they were unguarded. The guards at the "table" were all slumped over. One, or maybe two, moved, but only barely.

Silvio was breathing in short bursts. The pain in his shoulder made him start to groan.

Then, through the clearing smoke and dust, he saw a figure on horseback. He began to move toward it, trying to raise his good arm, to show where he was, who he was.

The figure came toward him. The pain in his body was growing worse. He was losing a lot of blood. For a delirious moment he thought that the figure on horseback was Nino. Then it looked like the priest, Father Livesey. No! Finally he saw that it was his uncle, Bastiano, smiling. Then he fainted.

"Careful. *Careful!* Pull the bandage back slowly. I've been bleeding, and it will have stuck to my flesh."

"I've tended wounds before, you know." Annunziata looked down at Silvio, lying on the bed, and smiled.

He smiled back, but briefly. He was sweating with pain. He had lost a lot of blood in the quarry, and a two-day journey on horseback hadn't helped. They had traveled to the *bivio* via Sambuca, moving at night. They were now waiting for the doctor to arrive, from Bivona.

"Who . . . whose bed is this?"

"Mine."

"There'll be blood on the sheets."

"It will wash out."

"Where . . . where will you sleep?"

"Don't worry about me. Here, drink this."

"What is it?"

"Warm brandy."

"I haven't had brandy for four years."

"Then it might help knock you out."

He took the glass, sipped the brandy, and then downed the rest in one gulp. He looked up at Annunziata, the flesh on his face glistening with sweat. "It's good to be here. I wasn't . . . I wasn't sure the plan was real. . . ."

"Why not, Toto? Why wouldn't it be real?"

He lay back on the bed and closed his eyes. He opened them again. "I thought it might be a trick, that you were . . ."

He fell asleep.

When he awoke—how many days later he didn't know—the light told him it was very early morning or the hour before dark. But the deep silence everywhere meant it could only be morning. The doctor had arrived at some point—that he remembered—and fixed his shoulder, stopping the bleeding and strapping the bones tightly so that they would knit together. Silvio was now more comfortable and the sweating was subsiding. But he still grew very tired. Being hit at close range by a bullet had taken a lot out of him.

Even so, he felt different this morning. For a start, he felt hungry, which hadn't happened before. Some line had been crossed.

The light was improving. For the first time he took in the room where he lay—Annunziata's room. There were lots of flowers, a religious painting on the wall, a hairbrush, what looked like a couple of glass jars containing—what, makeup? There was a very old picture magazine and a candle stuck in a bottle. The windows—oh, how he loved windows—had curtains, sewn, he was sure, by Annunziata herself. The contents of this room were far poorer and more pathetic than the contents of Anna-Maria's cabin on the *Syracusa*, but the *feel* was much the same. This was a woman's room.

Some things that he didn't at first recognize caught his eye. What looked like a long piece of wood with some string hanging from it. A jumble of short leather straps. A tiny book with a white cover. With a start he realized what he was looking at. The wood and string had once been a bow, the straps had once been a bridle for a donkey, and the book was a Bible, a child's Bible. These things had once belonged to little Nino, Annunziata's dead son, gifts he had never grown old enough to use. Silvio turned his gaze away and looked out the window. He felt like he was intruding.

"You're awake."

He turned. Annunziata stood in the doorway.

"What happened to your black dress?"

"I've been in mourning long enough."

Instinctively he looked at her son's effects.

She followed his gaze but all she said was, "Are you hungry?"

"Starving."

"I'll be back soon."

She went out but quickly came back with a jug of coffee, some warm bread, and fig jam.

Silvio sat up on the edge of the bed, holding his shoulder to prevent unnecessary movement. He held the coffee jug under his nose. It had been four years since he had drunk or eaten anything fresh. He put the bread to his nose, then the fig jam, groaning in pleasure.

Annunziata spread some jam on the bread and handed it to him.

He munched and chewed and swallowed. He took some coffee. Draining his cup, he refilled it from the jug, using his good arm. He poured coffee into Annunziata's cup.

"It's good to have you back, Toto. We need you here."

He looked at her sharply. "What do you mean?"

"You'll see. It's better if you learn it for yourself."

He looked at her intently. "Bastiano isn't Nino. I always knew that."

But she wouldn't be drawn.

Starting his third cup of coffee, he said, "What news from Palermo, then? What happened that day, when I was rescued?"

"About thirty prisoners escaped. Three guards were killed in the explosion, two lost limbs, all the others suffered injuries. You're famous all over again, Toto."

He grunted. "And . . . what news of Nino?" He said it softly.

She nodded. "He's better. Out of danger." Her eyes filled with tears, but she held them back.

She got up and went to the window. "People want to see you, Toto. Would you like to go for a walk? Are you strong enough?"

"Well, I'm not going to stay in bed all day, like I was in prison. Let me just finish this coffee . . . it's *so* good."

Outside, the sunshine glared and bounced off the walls of the

buildings. Young children he had never met immediately came
running up to him. He was a hero they had been told about.
Hearing the commotion, adults came to look—Bastiano, Smeralda, Alessandro Alcamo, Ruggiero, who had been Nino's servant and had such a good singing voice, Laura and Elisavetta,
the cooks, Paolo and Gaspare, whom he'd last known as children, now verging on manhood. With all of them he shook hands
and embraced them—but carefully, avoiding use of his injured
shoulder.

"You look pale, Silvio," Bastiano said. "Like the underside of a
leaf. Take your time, get your strength back, then we can talk.
You're safe here: use the sunshine, the breeze from the mountains,
the cold of the streams to get the stench of Ucciardone out of your
system. We have fresh almonds, figs, olives, fish, fruit, and wine.
Tonight, in your honor, Elisavetta is roasting a lamb."

Silvio and Annunziata walked on then, past the buildings and
down to the river. They crossed the shingle to the thin stream,
so unlike the Mississippi, so meager and so clear. Silvio bent,
dipped his hand in the cold water, and splashed it over his
face. "Better even than coffee," he said, smiling. "You can't drink
the Mississippi."

He looked about him, up toward the Indisi Mountains where an
eagle soared, for a moment blocking out the sun. "God, how I
missed this."

Annunziata was dipping her hand in the stream, too. She put
her wet fingers to her mouth and moistened her lips. "Why did you
go, Toto?"

He looked at her sharply. "What do you mean? You know why
I went—I was made to."

She picked up a small stone and threw it into the stream. "But
you wanted to go."

"I did *not*! I hated the idea. You were the one who turned off,
like a tap. I didn't open your parcel till I was on the liner. I thought
it was food and I was so sick traveling. . . ." He trailed off. "Why
do you say I wanted to go? What put that into your head?"

She didn't answer right away but threw more stones into the
stream. "I went to see Father Serravalle. I had a message for
him—Bastiano wanted a meeting—but I asked him to hear my
confession—"

"And you told him about us!"

Still staring at the water, she nodded.

"And he told you I *wanted* to go to America—yes?"

She nodded again.

"Don't you see, Zata, he said that on purpose, to drive a wedge between us, to make you think I had no . . . feelings for you."

Neither spoke for a while. A goat slithered on the far side of the stream.

"So you got married thinking I didn't . . . thinking I'd gone off to America and forgotten you?"

She nodded.

"But didn't you get my letter?"

She turned sharply. "What letter?"

He shook his head. "It was a long time ago. I had someone write a letter for me."

"What did it say?"

He shook his head. "Not now, Zata." He picked up some stones and hurled them into the water. On the opposite bank, the goat looked startled. "I can't believe Father Serravalle told a lie, such a . . . blatant, awful untruth."

"I never imagined, not for a moment, that it wasn't . . . I never doubted what he said."

Silvio moved closer to Annunziata. "He has to pay for this, you know."

She looked up at him. "Don't forget it was his plan that rescued you from prison."

"I don't care. I can't do anything with my arm like this, but I can think. And . . . just as soon as I get my strength back, I'll have a little surprise for Father Serravalle." And he kicked at the shingle, sending it spraying across the water.

On the far bank, the goat ran off.

"How is the lamb, Silvio?"

He looked across the table at Elisavetta and grinned. As he was able to eat only with one hand, his fingers as well as his mouth were smeared with gravy. "Better than I've ever known, *carissima*." He waved around the table. "Lamb, olives, wine, fruit to come, cheese . . . I never thought I'd see this for more than twenty years." He raised his glass. "Let's not forget Nino."

All the others at the table raised their glasses. "Nino!" they cried together.

The diners began conversing among themselves and Silvio turned to Bastiano, who was seated next to him. "Tell me about Zata's dead child. How did it happen?"

"It's not a good story," replied Bastiano, lowering his voice to a whisper. "Gino took the boy to Palermo—"

"Yes, she told me. What I mean is, how come Gino didn't know the city was affected?"

Bastiano looked at him out of the corner of his eye. "The boy wasn't baptized until he was nearly a year old. You know how it is here . . . there were things happening, Zata wanted Serravalle to make the service, he was busy and then ill . . . it all took time. Anyway, Ruggiero Priola came to the celebration and *he* told Serravalle what was happening in Palermo. But Serravalle wouldn't let him tell anyone else—he didn't want anything to spoil the baptism. You know he has a soft spot for Zata. So when Gino decided on the spur of the moment to take little Nino to see his relatives in Palermo, no one here knew anything about the cholera outbreak. Gino didn't find out until he arrived—and then it was too late."

"So Serravalle killed little Nino—"

"Silvio! You can't say that."

"Why not? It's true. Does Zata know that Serravalle kept the news from her?"

"No—and don't you tell her. It took her long enough to get over the child. Don't reopen the wound, Silvio, please."

Silvio looked down the table at Annunziata. She was sitting with some of the older children, laughing and trying to persuade them to eat more lamb. Sensing Silvio's eyes on her, she turned her gaze on him.

She was still wearing the white dress she had worn during the day, but she had put some sort of flower in it. She looked very beautiful.

Silvio turned back to Bastiano. "She ought to have another child, don't you think?"

As the days went by, Silvio's strength returned. He walked every day by the stream, and gradually he began to do little chores, like fetching water or watching the loaves in the bakery. The doctor came, reported that he was making good progress, but did not take the strapping off his shoulder—these things could not be rushed, he said.

As a semi-invalid, Silvio had plenty of opportunity to observe life in the *bivio* and he noticed that some things were the same as always and some things had changed. The band was smaller now, sixty or seventy rather than a hundred strong. And although Bastiano was in charge, as Don, he did not play the dominant role that Nino once had. Rather, he was the first among equals, with three or four other men in practice having just as much say, including his *consigliere*, Alessandro Alcamo, the brother of Annunziata's dead husband. Another change, which surprised Silvio, was the authority Annunziata herself possessed. Before, no woman had ever had any kind of influence in the *bivio*. Silvio learned that Gino had been a creative force before his terrible death, and that he had always listened to his wife, who had shown herself to be a highly intelligent strategist and planner of robberies. She had the brains of a bishop, they said. After Gino's death, Annunziata had retained her authority as well as her beauty. It didn't take a genius to see that Alessandro was as fond of Zata as his dead brother had been.

Most mornings, Silvio and Annunziata walked by the river. Most evenings, after dinner, she went back to the room with him. His shoulder was still strapped up and he found it difficult to take off his shirt or sharpen his razor with one hand. Sometimes they smoked a last cigarette together, before turning in.

Annunziata wanted to know all about life in America. "I'm a widow, Toto, so I want the real truth," she said. They had days—nights—at their disposal, so Silvio described exactly what life had been like in New Orleans. Annunziata was both fascinated and horrified by his descriptions of the brothels and gambling joints. She listened, rapt, in the dark, as he talked of Negroes, quadroons, the music of New Orleans, the carnival, life on the river. Each night he talked of some new aspect of America or he read to her from the book he had, by Mark Twain. Sometimes they both fell asleep in midsentence.

Silvio had been sprung from prison in mid-October, and within several weeks of his return to the *bivio*, the nights began to turn cold. There was always a risk in lighting fires. Heat for cooking was one thing, but the smoke from fires could be seen and even smelled for miles around and thus betray their whereabouts. Fires were frowned upon and kept to a minimum.

One night, as Silvio lay on the bed explaining exactly what absinthe was, Annunziata had interrupted him. "Toto," she whispered, "I'm cold." In an instant he had his arms around her, the blanket pulled over both of them, and they were kissing passionately. His injured shoulder still restricted his movements, so Annunziata rolled over and sat astride him. She was still wearing the white dress he associated with his return—she slept in it—but Silvio was faintly surprised to discover that she was naked underneath. He gasped as she lowered herself slowly onto him, then paused for a moment. He had wanted this for so long, ever since he ceased to be a child, and he searched the gloom for the expression on Annunziata's face. She had her eyes closed.

With one hand he undid the buttons on her dress, reached inside, and freed one of her breasts. He lifted his head and kissed her nipple.

"Bite me," she whispered urgently. "Please."

All at once that morning in the *giardino segreto* came flooding back, when she had spoken the same words—the morning that had ended in disaster.

But that wasn't going to happen now.

That night he made love to Annunziata with all the skill, all the care, all the knowledge he had acquired from the other women he had slept with. They were by turns gentle and violent. He found that although Annunziata had only ever been to bed with one man before, she was an instinctive lover, responsive, adventurous, and, ultimately, uncontrolled.

It was a still night and sounds traveled. They could hear people coughing in their sleep in the other rooms of the *bivio*. They could hear the mutter and murmur of the mules and horses tethered on the hill, the bleating and rustling of the goats. None of it made any difference. As Annunziata reached the pinnacle of her excitement she cried out. It was a short cry, stifled the moment it was uttered, and she realized what she had done. But it gave way to a clutch of sobs almost as loud and infinitely more passionate.

Silvio, whose own pleasure had reached its climax at the same moment, held her afterward. They rested together in the gloom, their breathing gradually returning to normal. As he lay there Silvio realized that so far as the others in the band were concerned, there could now be no disguising their relationship.

* * *

As his strength returned, and the strapping on his shoulder was removed, Silvio began to play more of a part in his uncle's "family." He wasn't yet able to scramble over the hills, or ride a mule, or aim a *lupara*, but he was brighter, and younger, than Bastiano.

It was also true that Bastiano Randazzo did not have the fundamental understanding of violence that Silvio had learned from Nino. Until Silvio's rescue, Bastiano had made most of his money through a protection racket involving the olive oil produced between Filaga and Cammarata. All the farmers and landowners paid Bastiano fifteen percent of their produce, in return for which Bastiano made it known that he was their protector. If anyone else attempted to muscle in on the area, it was Bastiano and his band who saw them off. Since Nino and Silvio had left for America, Bastiano's men had been responsible for seven deaths, one a year. It wasn't sensational but it had been enough.

It was a good living but scarcely exciting. Nino had been a better strategist than Bastiano in that he had occasionally mounted a more spectacular robbery, and then distributed some of the proceeds to the local people. This had achieved several goals at once. In the first place, the quasipolitical nature of Nino's crimes had drawn many followers. Thus his "family" had been considerably bigger than Bastiano's and this was useful in fending off rivals. In addition, the wider distribution of the proceeds of the more spectacular robberies had not only made Nino a popular figure but ensured that his security was better—the local people, who were bound to know where the band lived, were much less likely to betray them. Bastiano, on the other hand, hardly felt safe enough even to visit Bivona, to be seen as the Don.

But it was the lack of numbers that really counted. As soon as he was able to, Silvio brought this matter up with Bastiano.

"I went for a walk yesterday evening," he told his uncle, one day in early December. "I counted fifty-nine men. It's not enough."

Bastiano knew that what Silvio said was true but he didn't want to admit it in front of the others. "Come," he said, and led his adopted son into his own rooms. He had a bottle of grappa, and uncorked it, offering it to Silvio.

Silvio shook his head.

"The olive-oil business suits us fine, Silvio. It's easy, safe, predictable. What more could you want?"

Silvio knew he must press his case. "Bastiano, look at what you just said. If the business is easy, someone else is going to want to get his hands on it. Same thing with security. Someone's going to move in on you sooner or later. It's not as simple as you think."

"This isn't New Orleans, you know. Sicily isn't sophisticated."

"Sicily is no different from New Orleans, or anywhere else. What counts, anywhere, is strength, *muscolo*. Sooner or later, as I keep saying, it's going to be very easy for someone else to get together a band of seventy men, or a hundred even. Then they'll come for you. They may not even have to. If they get word out that they are stronger than you, some of your people are going to leave, slink away, join the stronger side while they can, before the fighting starts. If enough people go, fighting would be suicidal."

Bastiano took a swig of grappa. "*We* rescued *you*. What do you know? Life has changed since you were a boy."

"No, it hasn't. Bastiano, you know I'm right. The way Nino operated is the only way it can work, out here in the mountains. It's the same in the towns, too. You've got to have an eye-catching job every so often, and you've got to do something with what you take to keep the people on your side. And you've got to take the fight to the other side, keep moving, keep thinking. Like a fox. Like Liotta. Otherwise, sooner or later, you'll shrink so small, that some other family will take you out."

Bastiano said nothing. But he continued drinking.

"Answer me one question."

Bastiano glared at him.

"I want an honest answer. How many men have you lost in the last three months?"

Bastiano didn't answer immediately.

"Come on. How many?"

"Six."

"Six*teen*! I already asked around." Now Silvio seized the bottle from him and took a swig. This was going to require some tact. "What sort of Capo can you be, Bastiano, once you start lying to yourself? You know, deep down, that what I say is right. Instead of resisting me, why don't you hear what I have to say. I have a plan, a plan which could bring us a lot of money *and* attract attention. If you like it, you can tell the others it's your idea—I don't mind."

Bastiano still said nothing.

"The olive-oil business is okay as far as it goes. But the men get lazy, doing the same thing all the time, dealing with the same people. Like donkeys grazing in a field. Ultimately, they grow careless. Something new can help sharpen them up." He handed back the bottle.

Bastiano swallowed more grappa. "Okay. Tell me your plan."

Silvio plunged in. "You know Caltabellotta?"

"The village just beyond Burgio?"

Silvio nodded. "And the home of Frederico di Biondi."

"Yes, I know that. So what?"

Silvio tapped his temple. "Think. There are two very important facts about di Biondi that can work to our advantage. In the first place, he's one of the cruelest landlords in Sicily. He pays the people who work for him less than half what they earn anywhere else. So he's very unpopular—"

"But he gets away with it! And that's because he's protected by the Carcilupo family. We can't go head-to-head with them."

"I'm not suggesting that. But hear me out. Di Biondi also has a collection of very rare, and valuable, paintings—Tintoretto, the Carracci, Luca Giordano." Before he'd read the doctor's books in Ucciardone Prison, Silvio would not have had the faintest idea what these names meant.

Bastiano was silent now.

"Say we were to steal those paintings—"

"How on earth . . . ?"

"Listen! I'll come to that. Say we were to steal those paintings. Say we were then to get word to di Biondi that he would only have his paintings returned if he paid his farmworkers a proper wage. Say we gave him a deadline, and if he didn't play ball, we returned one picture to him, but torn into strips. I've thought a lot about this and Nino's kidnap of that English priest was the biggest mistake he made. *Ottuso.* But kidnapping paintings—things—is different. No one's going to send any troops anywhere to recover paintings. Paintings won't cause a diplomatic incident. The paintings only mean something to di Biondi. We give him a deadline. If he still doesn't improve the workers' wages, we send him another picture, a Tintoretto perhaps, but this time just the ashes.

"And, of course, we let the farmworkers know what's happening. Word will spread all over Sicily. The newspapers will write about us, about you, Bastiano. You'll be a hero."

"Maybe, but what's in it for us? I don't care about the farmworkers of Caltabellotta."

"Then you are wrong, Bastiano. That's what Nino taught me—that how other people *see* what we do is as important as *what* we do. When you rescued me from that quarry, it was a spectacular coup. It made the authorities respect and fear you, but it did nothing for us, in the sense that no one earned any money for it. Now, let the profit be me, or at least my ideas. And hear me out on di Biondi."

Bastiano didn't move or say anything.

"He has about eighty-six paintings in all. So I was told by Father Ignazio when he was here the other day. He knows a local priest who has seen them. Di Biondi won't miss two or three. We'll ask him what his least favorite pictures are—and we'll hang on to those. There are dealers in Palermo or Messina who will pay us for them. They'll take them to Paris or London or New York and make a fine profit, but that's their affair. So long as they give us a good price, we shall be happy.

"But the most important thing, Bastiano, is that we make a splash. If this works—and it *will* work—we shall become more famous, and more popular. More people will join us, and it will get easier for the family to hold on to the olive oil. You know I'm right."

Bastiano looked quizzical, but his eyes shone. He was more excited by Silvio's plan than he had let on. "How did you find out about di Biondi?"

"Annunziata told me. Gino's relatives came from Caltabellotta. Some of them still work for di Biondi."

"I never knew you were an expert on art."

"I'm not an expert. I just read some books in prison."

"You like reading?"

"It has its place."

"How will we get in? To di Biondi's castle, I mean."

"I don't know yet, but some of us need to visit Caltabellotta and talk to Annunziata's in-laws. They'll be able to help."

"Do you feel fit enough to go?"

"I don't see why I shouldn't try it. I don't have much pain from my shoulder these days. But in any case I could see the doctor in Bivona. It's on the way."

"Okay. We'll do as you suggest. Only one thing. I'm not passing off this plan of yours as mine. It's your idea and your show. And you're the man with a reward on his head. If you're right, and we need to make a splash, it will be much bigger if the whole thing is masterminded by the man who made such a spectacular escape from Ucciardone."

16

As Silvio's shoulder improved, he ventured further afield in his morning walks with Annunziata. Eventually, he said one day, "Follow me." He set off not along the river but through the olive groves. After a little while, however, she skipped ahead of him. "I know where you're going," she called back.

Forty minutes later they scrambled onto the mossy ledge they had called, as children, their *giardino segreto*. Silvio, tired from the hike through the trees, lay on his back and looked at the sky. "I haven't been here since—"

"Neither have I," Annunziata replied softly. "It was your birthday."

"And I never received the gift you planned." He grinned and pulled her to him. They kissed and then she moved back and began to unbutton her dress. She stepped out of it exactly as she had done on that morning all those years ago.

He feasted his eyes on her body—the blond down on her thighs that caught the sunlight, the mound of hair below her flat brown belly, the soft patches around her nipples that were the color of almond shells. He took off his own clothes and stretched them on the moss for her to lie on. He maneuvered himself alongside her.

He kissed her and placed the palm of his hand on her stomach. He began to speak. "Close your eyes." She did so. "Now think forward to a year from now. We are married and on our honeymoon in America." Gently, he massaged her stomach. "We are taking a steamboat up the Mississippi from New Orleans to Memphis. You can hear the slapping of the water against the bottom of the boat. Occasionally the boat rocks as we sail through the wake of other boats going in the opposite direction." He moved his hand down her thigh. "It is evening, the daylight is beginning to fade and the lights of the boat are being lit. Long shadows are cast down the deck. In the distance the band strikes up." Silvio's hand settled over the mound of hair beneath her belly. She opened her legs and his fingers probed farther. "Tonight we are having dinner with the captain. There will be wine, ice cream, chocolate, dancing." He kissed Zata's ear as his fingers moved deep inside her. "You will be wearing a long dress, which shows your shoulders and the tops of your breasts. There may be singing. After dinner the captain, who will have fallen for you just as I fell for you all those years ago, will take us onto the bridge. Ahead of us is the huge river, black in the night." Silvio's fingers moved gently up and down as she moved her hips against his hand and a tiny moan gurgled in her throat. "From the bridge you can see other steamboats coming toward you, their lights sparkling like stars, reflected in the river. On the banks, wooden churches—black as coal—slip by, silent, guarding their secrets. The rumble of the engines of the steamboat shudders through the whole structure, sending waves that collide with the bank of the Mississippi."

Annunziata bit her lip and he stopped. He knew her well enough now to realize she was not far away. Her hand clenched and closed over some moss. Her moans grew louder, more frequent. His hand moved more swiftly up and down, pressed against her more firmly.

She opened her eyes and looked at him. Her lips parted. Then her eyes closed again, she called out, and her back arched. She screamed as she could never scream in the *bivio*, again and again and again, subsiding into a series of choking sobs. There was a fine line of sweat on her upper lip.

They lay, motionless, for several minutes.

At length she murmured, "If we'd done this all those years ago, when we were children, would it have been as good?"

"It would have been different."

"Do you make love outside, in America?"

"There's nowhere like this, Zata. I met no one like you."

She sat up and kissed him. "When can we go?"

"Not yet, maybe not ever."

"But I'd like to. These stories you tell me . . . When you read, from that man—Mark Twain? It's a lovely way to learn." She took his hand from between her legs and kissed his fingers. "Sicily's so *small*!"

"It's big enough, Zata." He lay down on the moss. "This is good enough for me."

"That's because you've seen America."

"I didn't see Sicily, until I came back from America. The figs, the rivers, all these hills I know so well. So few people. Those eagles up there—" He pointed. "I'd be worried that in America . . . you'd change. I don't want you to change."

Now he kissed her.

"Why should I change?" she murmured. She lay back down on the moss and pulled him to her. "You haven't."

Silvio's plan to steal the paintings proved popular when it was first outlined to the other men. Several had already realized that if they didn't represent a threat to their rivals, their rivals would come after them. Two men with relatives in Caltabellotta—Giacomo and Benedetto—accompanied Silvio, to observe discreetly the routine of di Biondi's household, to obtain any other information regarding the strength of the local *sbirri*, and to try to pinpoint the exact whereabouts of the paintings within the household.

After a day or two in the village, Silvio left Giacomo and Benedetto behind to make a more detailed reconnaissance. They had been specifically asked to reconnoiter the castle and the bars, picking up gossip, and they came back to report that in two weeks' time di Biondi was leaving for Rome. He would be gone for a month, and the castle would be closed, with just a skeleton staff in occupation. At the same time they had discovered that part of the castle was connected by a door to a small church in the village. If they could get the key to the church and let themselves in at night, they could use the hours of darkness to break down the door that led from the church to the castle.

"Okay," Silvio said. "But what about the pictures themselves? Do we know where they are?"

Benedetto, who was the brighter of the two men, replied, "Di Biondi has a *galleria*, a room on the second floor that overlooks the valley. His most important pictures are there. Others are in his study, which leads off the *galleria*, and in the dining hall, which leads off the *galleria* at the other end. He must have one or two in his bedroom, and other places around the castle. But the main paintings are in those three rooms—the *galleria*, the dining hall, and the study."

"How reliable is your information?"

Benedetto nodded toward the other man. "Giacomo has a nephew who used to work in the castle, but was fired a month ago—for breaking a valuable glass pitcher. I think he'd be willing to act as our guide."

"Any ideas how we get into the church?"

No one spoke for a moment. Then Annunziata said, "What about Father Ignazio?"

"I don't follow you," said Silvio.

"He could pay the priest of Caltabellotta a visit. Stay with him. With luck he could take an impression of the key to the church and we could get old Cavero to make us a new one."

Silvio smiled. "Good idea." Cavero had been assisted by Nino in the past. He could be trusted to help. "Well done, Zata," he said.

The evening after Silvio returned from Caltabellotta, he was lying in bed with Annunziata when she said, "Alesso Alcamo attacked me today."

"What do you mean 'attacked'?"

"Just that. I was down by the river, washing clothes. He came up to me and called me a whore. He said I was dishonoring his brother's memory, sharing a bed with my cousin."

Silvio, remaining calm, blew smoke into the room. "He did, did he? What did you say?"

"I slapped his face."

"Good. He's just jealous."

"He said something else before he left. He said all the women in the *bivio*—Smeralda especially—think that what we are doing is wrong. They're too frightened to say anything but . . . they say we're . . . unnatural."

Silvio continued smoking.

"Can't you do something to stop them talking, Silvio? I don't like it. Smeralda's your mother, or as good as. You've got brains—everyone says so. Think of something."

Again, Silvio pulled on his cigarette and they lay in silence for a while. Then he said, "Zata, there's something I've never told you." He recounted the incident when his parents had been killed. "Ever since then I've been worried about not thinking quickly enough. But I realized in prison—after what happened to me in

New Orleans—that what matters is not speed, or not only speed, but doing the right thing, making the move that is appropriate to the situation." He put his arm round her. "I had a lot of women in America and with none of them did it feel the way it feels with you. I'm not giving that up. And I'm not saying anything to the women. They can stew. They may feel differently after this Caltabellotta business, when they see how successful it is, what a difference it makes."

"Am I really different than all those women in America, Toto?"

He tightened his arm around her and kissed her hair.

She was silent for a moment. "I've only been with you and Gino and . . . Gino was . . . selfish. I never wanted sex with him like I want it with you."

She reached across his body, took his hand, and placed it between her legs.

It took a day to alert the abbot about the Caltabellotta plan. It took another day for him to send word to the priest in the town that he was planning a visit, and two more days before he arrived. He stayed three days with the priest, and it was two days before he learned which key to copy. On the fifth day, the impression reached Cavero and it was two more days before the new key reached Silvio. Nine days in all.

Silvio then waited another five days before making his move. He sent one man ahead to Caltabellotta to follow di Biondi on his journey. The landlord was going to Rome via Palermo, where he would put to sea directly for Ostia, the port of Rome. The man who was following di Biondi would shadow him until he set sail. If, at any point before Palermo, di Biondi changed his mind and turned back, Silvio's man would know it, and hurry back ahead of the landlord, to raise the alarm. If the shadow hadn't returned within forty-eight hours, they would know di Biondi was at sea and could not return with any speed.

The shadow did not return.

Silvio set out with twelve men. This was a difficult calculation. The number of paintings they planned to take was bulky, and they needed enough muscle to cope with any resistance. At the same time they didn't want to draw attention to themselves, alert the Carcilupos, or put at risk more people than necessary. The twelve would be supplemented by one or two from within Caltabellotta—including Giacomo's nephew, Primo, who was to act as their guide inside the castle. But that was enough.

As usual they rode at night. Silvio's shoulder gave little trouble now and he managed easily enough. Their first stop left them overlooking the tiny hamlet of Cannalicchio and on the second night they reached Il Pavone, the mountain overlooking Caltabellotta itself. During the day, while everyone else rested, Bastiano went on to the village on foot, to ensure that all was as it should be. He came back to report that everything appeared normal. "As quiet as a fox's smile" was how he put it. Even the bar was empty.

At dusk they began to move out, in ones and twos, leaving the mules with a guard. It took them two hours to skirt the mountain and reach the outskirts of the village, by which time it was nearly eight o'clock. They waited for another two hours in the tiny valley carved by the river Bellapietra. Most of the villagers would be asleep by eleven and Bastiano's men would have all night.

At ten-thirty they set off, one at a time, with instructions to rendezvous at the church. Silvio went last.

Caltabellotta consisted of three streets shaped like a capital "A," and there were just two churches. The village lay on the side of a hill overlooking the road from Burgio to Sciacca, on the south coast. As Silvio made his way up the hill he could see that the village was completely dead. There were dim candles in one or two of the houses, but otherwise the only signs of life came from the occasional bleatings of the sheep, or a mule sneezing.

The first church he came to stood by itself on a rocky promontory, overlooking the road he had just left. But ahead was the castle and, adjoining it, the other church.

Silvio kept to the shadows and stood still for a while. There was always the possibility of ambush. He waited for ten minutes. There was no movement in any part of the square in front of the church. At ten past eleven he walked round the edge of the square and approached the church. He took the key from his pocket, inserted it in the hole, and turned. It grated in the lock and sent a screech skidding across the square.

Silvio froze.

But the sound died in the night. Silvio quickly gripped the handle and turned. Another grating sound shot across the square. Again he froze. Someone must surely have heard this time.

A minute passed. Two. Five. Then he pushed at the door and he was inside. He found the pew nearest to the door that led to the castle and sat down. He had left the door to the church open, but only by the amount that would allow a man to squeeze through.

After a few moments someone else sat down on the pew beside him. Then another, then another. No one spoke. They had all been watching Silvio from the shadows. Bastiano came and stood in front of Silvio. He was to be the last man into the church. "The door is locked again," he whispered.

Silvio had thought hard about how to crack the door to the castle. At first he had envisaged using a mule to pull it off its hinges, but taking a mule through the streets of the village late at night was tricky. Explosives were obviously no good on this occasion. They had to get through the door without waking either the entire village or the skeleton staff in the castle itself.

But the door was wooden, not sturdy—and there was a small gap between it and the floor. Silvio had had a very thin saw made up, with a blade small enough to fit between the door and the floor. His men now took turns to saw up one edge of the door, then across, then down the other side. It was noisy, but according to Primo, who was to be their guide inside the castle, none of di Biondi's staff slept anywhere near the door to the church.

It took half an hour before there was a hole big enough for a man to crawl through. Then the men began to disappear through it one by one. On the other side there was a small hall that led to a stone spiral staircase. Their first task was to find the castle staff and round them up.

Primo led the way. There were eight staff in all, he had said, in five bedrooms. Silvio's approach was simple. They were all locked in their rooms save for one, whom Primo identified as di Biondi's butler. Silvio told the others that if they made any attempt to escape, to shout or scream or to cry for help, then the one servant he took with him would be garroted.

Two men were left to guard the servants' quarters. Then Primo led the way to the *galleria*.

Even in the moonlight, it was a magnificent room. There were four large windows down one side, and painted wooden beams on the ceiling. The floor was marble, patterned in black and white, and the walls were lined in pale oak paneling to about the height of a man. Silvio reflected that despite its many attractions, the new world held nothing to equal the best of the old world.

They set to work, taking down the paintings and cutting them from their frames. Silvio had decided it would be easier to transport them, and get them under the hole in the door to the church, if the paintings were removed from their frames and rolled up. He ordered the cutting to be done carefully so as to spoil the paintings as little as possible. He had no idea which one was the Tintoretto, or the Carracci, but he instructed his men to treat all the paintings as if they were immensely valuable.

It was a time-consuming business. They needed a flat piece of floor to be able to cut the canvases. Then the frames had to be stowed away—otherwise they would get in the way of the work. Every so often a number of rolls were taken out of the gallery and back downstairs to the church. The rolls gradually began to accumulate in the nave.

Midnight came and went.

They were done around five. Sixty-two canvases were piled up in rolls in the nave of the church. They withdrew quietly from the castle, leaving the castle staff locked inside the bedrooms not knowing whether Silvio and his men were still in the building or not.

One by one they climbed under the door linking castle and church. One by one they left the church in the manner in which they had arrived, each of them carrying about half a dozen rolls of canvas, depending on size. Bastiano went first, Silvio last, locking the church door behind him, for effect as much as anything. He knew that the more mystery attaching to this crime the better.

Leaving Caltabellotta, Silvio kept to the shadows and made it to the upper reaches of Il Pavone just as dawn was breaking. They took turns sleeping and keeping guard all that day, then rode back at night to Casteluzzo, where they spent another day. In the small hours, two nights after they had left Caltabellotta, Silvio climbed into bed alongside Annunziata. He was exhausted and wanted to sleep; but she didn't.

When news of the Caltabellotta theft was made public, it caused a sensation. All the Sicilian and most of the Roman and Neapolitan newspapers carried the story. The chief of police in Palermo was quoted as saying that every Sicilian port would be closely monitored so there was no chance the paintings would leave the island. The Archbishop of Palermo condemned the desecration of church property in the break-in. Di Biondi, when he was contacted, promised a reward for information leading to the recovery of the paintings and the arrest of the culprits. He had cut short his time on the mainland and was returning immediately to Caltabellotta, he said.

Silvio's first move was to send one of the younger mafiosi to Messina, where they had a contact who was an art dealer. He was brought back—blindfolded, for security's sake—to inspect the paintings and advise. Silvio then sent an anonymous note to the editors of the Palermo and Messina newspapers. His letter drew attention to the wages of the farm laborers in Caltabellotta and compared them unfavorably with those in nearby Menfi and Chiusa, where the workers received twice as much for the same work. Silvio made it clear that the paintings would be returned as soon as di Biondi agreed to pay his workers the same as people were paid elsewhere.

The newspapers loved this. A MASTERPIECE OF CRIME, said the *Corriere di Palermo*. OILS CREATE TROUBLED WATERS wrote *Il Mattino di Messina*. The reports also demonstrated that Silvio had judged right, in that ordinary people interviewed by the newspapers agreed with the robbers that di Biondi should increase the wages he paid to his workers. Everyone seemed to believe that Silvio would keep his word.

Meanwhile, the art dealer from Messina arrived at Bivio Indisi. Fabio Ganzirri was a small, sweaty man but he knew his trade. Silvio explained that if events went according to plan he would be sending back all but two or three of the paintings now unrolled in front of Ganzirri. He then asked the man to place the paintings in order of value. Ganzirri was delighted to oblige. He began with the Carracci, saying their work would fetch high prices in Britain. Then came the Tintoretto, the Luca Giordano, two Canalettos, a Bellotto, a Palma Giovane, and so on and so on. Ganzirri then attached approximate values to the twenty-five most valuable paintings.

Silvio sent Ganzirri back to Messina, blindfolded until he was well away from the *bivio*, but told him they would be in touch shortly. He then contacted the newspapers again. Since di Biondi had not responded to his earlier request, he said, he was giving notice that, unless the wages of the workers at Caltabellotta were increased by the weekend, the painting by Palma Giovane would be returned to di Biondi, torn into strips.

When the newspapers contacted di Biondi, to pass on this information, he told the reporters that he thought Silvio was bluffing. He pointed out that Silvio had once been close to the Quarryman and knew that kidnapping was a crime abhorred by everyone and often backfired.

Silvio was ready. The correct tactic, he knew, was to raise the stakes. That weekend he sent not one but *two* paintings to the editor of the *Corriere di Palermo*. Both paintings were torn into shreds. With them was a note saying that two more pictures would be returned in the same state the next week, if di Biondi made no attempt to negotiate. At this rate they could be returning paintings for thirty weeks.

On the following Friday, faced with the inability of the police to do anything about the robbery, and with the newspapers following the dispute daily, di Biondi caved in. He announced that he was henceforth increasing the wages he paid to his farmworkers to bring them in line with other workers doing similar jobs in nearby villages. BANDITS BEAT DI BIONDI trumpeted the headline in the *Corriere di Palermo*.

Silvio's next move was to announce that once the people of Caltabellotta had been receiving their new wages for a month, he would return the pictures. He was as good as his word, leaving them in a cave near Sicula, then once more contacting the Palermo newspaper. What he didn't tell the *Corriere* was that he had retained two, a Tiepolo and a Guido Reni, which were quietly sent to Messina. He was quite sure that Ganzirri cheated him, but even so the price was good, easily doubling the band's income for that year.

With Annunziata the sex was better than ever.

Within a month of di Biondi's capitulation, five of the sixteen men who had left Bastiano's "family" asked to come back. Bastiano would have turned them down out of pique but Silvio reminded him that these men knew where they lived and, for a reward, could always lead the police or the army in a surprise attack. There was no point in alienating good men for a silly reason. Bastiano allowed himself to be overruled.

Over the next three months, aided by several simple robberies of olive-oil shipments, the band's reputation grew. More men joined, swelling their numbers to nearly a hundred. Nighttime deliveries of olive oil to needy families were partly responsible. So, too, was an incident in Palermo, when a precious gold cross was stolen from a convent in the Aquasanta area. A little pressure judiciously applied in the right quarters and Silvio was able to send another note to the editor of the *Corriere di Palermo*, telling him where his reporters could find the cross. The paper returned the cross to the convent, boosting its own role in the affair but not neglecting Silvio's. Then, with the strength of Bastiano's band still increasing, the neighboring families took fright. The next-door band, led by the Imbriaci family, which controlled the olive oil in the Cangioloso area, proposed an alliance. Bastiano and Silvio accepted.

This brought their strength to more than one hundred and fifty men. The area they controlled had doubled, and they were now one of the biggest outfits in Sicily.

The merger with the Imbriaci, however, did pose one unusual problem. Cesare Imbriaci naturally did not expect to be Capo of the new family. He had proposed the merger from a position of weakness, and therefore sacrificed the overall leadership. He was also prepared to accept that Bastiano would keep his own *consigliere*—Alesso. But he did expect that he would be *sotto-capo*, the operational head of the various regimes, and Alesso agreed. He thought it showed the proper respect for Imbriaci. Unfortunately, neither Bastiano nor Silvio saw it that way. Both felt strongly that the leaders—*Capo, consigliere, sottocapo*—should be members of Bastiano's family. Accordingly, Imbriaci became merely a *caporegime*, in effect head of his own family, as he had always been, but now merely one part of a bigger outfit. Bastiano, as *Capo*, made Silvio his *sottocapo*.

Imbriaci was irate, but since he had been the supplicant, he had to accept the situation. Alesso, however, was annoyed that Bastiano had neglected his advice. His jealousy of Silvio, and Silvio's relationship with Annunziata, accounted for part of his reaction, but there was more to it than that. Alesso had always assumed that when Bastiano went, he would take over as Capo. Now he could see Silvio coming up behind him. "Jealousy is like a tooth-ache," according to the Sicilian proverb. "It spoils the taste of everything."

* * *

About three months after the di Biondi affair, Father Ignazio sent
word that he wished to see Silvio. Silvio's shoulder was completely healed by this point and he rode all the way from Bivio
Indisi to Quisquina. For security he took two men with him.

The abbot received him courteously. Silvio was given dinner,
allowed a bath, and spent a comfortable night in the monastery's
best guest room. After breakfast the next day Father Ignazio asked
Silvio to walk with him in the monastery's olive and almond
groves. This, Silvio hoped, was when the business the abbot
wanted to discuss would be broached. Was it a new venture? Or
did the abbot need his advice on something? Was it news of
Angelo Priola, or Nino?

They had reached a place in the terraces where a large tree
below the high stone wall provided deep shade, and it was cooler
than anywhere else. Here the abbot stopped.

"Silvio, I wish to speak to you about Annunziata."

Silvio was astonished. What business of the abbot's was
Annunziata?

"There is a great deal of feeling, mainly among the women
in—"

"I don't care. People shouldn't interfere."

"Silvio, it is not a matter of interference. What you are doing
with Annunziata is wrong."

Silvio thought of his nights with Annunziata. He said, more
gently, "How can it be wrong, Father? It is so comfortable."

Father Ignazio modified his voice to match Silvio's. "Come,
my son, you know in your heart that what is happening is
wrong. You and Annunziata are cousins. Such a liaison is against
nature, against God. You and she are mocking him."

Silvio was quiet for a moment, thinking. *Sono peccatore?* Am I
a sinner? he asked himself. No. The abbot had clearly been influ-
enced by the women in the *bivio*. They had never liked Annunziata and him being together, but they had never had the guts to do
anything—until now. That made him angry—but only with the
women. He didn't dare get angry with the abbot. Father Ignazio
was too powerful and too useful to antagonize.

He tried a different tack. He had to be soft on the outside while
remaining hard within, as Nino had always said. "Father, let me
talk to you as a man." He stood directly in front of the abbot. "I

cannot give up Annunziata. My need is physical. She has an effect on me quite unlike any other woman I have known. I know every part of her body, every part of her soul. I won't give her up. I can't."

"Silvio! You are an intelligent man. You have the brains of a bishop, but on this matter you are not facing facts. You and Annunziata are cousins. The church says that you may never be married. Which means that any child you may have will be a bastard. Is that what you want? Is that what Annunziata wants? Don't be a fool. You cannot go against nature."

Silvio was miserable. Until now he had been perfectly happy with Annunziata. They were so strong together that the glowerings from the women in the band could be ignored. But Father Ignazio was a more formidable force than all the women put together, so far as Silvio was concerned. Even so, he was not about to abandon Zata.

"Father, you appeal to my head but you ignore my heart. I've seen the world—can you say the same? My heart tells me Annunziata is the woman for me. Doesn't that mean anything in the church? Surely the church is more interested in a man's heart, and the happiness he can bring to a woman."

"Of course the church is interested in the heart, Silvio, but in the true workings of the heart. You, I fear, have been misled by yours. Annunziata can never be yours entirely and there is no point in pretending she can. You must give her up, Silvio, and you must do so now."

The abbot was as implacable as Silvio himself. He stared at the older man, suddenly angry. "What do you know, Father? You've never been with a woman, have you? How can you know what's in my heart? How can you know the joy, the love, the *goodness* that Annunziata brings out in me? How can you understand the joy I bring to *her* heart? Lovemaking is . . . unlike anything else and . . . if you have never experienced it, then you don't . . . you can't judge others." His anger was dissipating as he realized what he was saying, and to a priest. He found he was close to tears.

He sat down, under the tree. He shook his head. "I love Annunziata. I won't give her up."

Father Ignazio did not sit down but instead turned away from Silvio and stood for a long while looking down the valley, toward

Catera. Eventually the abbot turned back. Birds rode the thermal current, high in the air.

Silvio looked up.

"My son, I understand more than you think. I'm a great deal older than you and this is not the first time that I've seen men—good men—led astray by their hearts. So don't lecture me. And don't take it out on me either. The problem is yours and I'm trying to help. From what you say, you face a desperate situation. Annunziata and you may never be married—*never!* Get that simple fact into your head—into your *heart*. I will not let you ignore me on this matter, Silvio." He gestured to the almond trees. "We prune plants that go rotten. I'm doing the same with you. To make you strong again, inside. And you have to face what's happening to you now, before it gets worse, as it certainly will. What you are doing is a mortal sin."

He paused, selecting his words. "My first duty is to God—"

"Bah!" shouted Silvio. "Is it your duty to God that enables you to help us? Is it because you do God's work that you harbor *intusi* and *mezzatacce* and *malandrini* in your abbey? Is it part of the Almighty's grand design that you help us break into churches so we can steal great works of art, many of them religious works? You are the man who kept secret the news about the cholera outbreak in Palermo—which killed Annunziata's son! Were you doing your sacred duty then, *Father!*" He spat out the last word.

The abbot waited for Silvio to finish and then breathed out loudly. "Would you say I'm a bad man, Silvio?"

Silvio shook his head.

"We live in an imperfect world. One has to meet life as one finds it, and there are so many injustices around us that there are very few clear-cut issues of right and wrong. One has to construct one's own morality as one goes along, guided by God. I say this not to excuse myself but to explain. I must say, however, that of the very few clear-cut moral situations there are in the world, the one you face is perhaps clearest of all. I repeat: what you are doing with Annunziata is wrong. It is against nature and must be brought to an end. Now."

Silvio could think of nothing to say. Neither of them would give way.

"I am not prepared to compromise on this, Silvio. Unless you do as I say, I shall be forced to approach the archbishop."

Silvio glanced sharply at the abbot. "What do you me~
can you do?"

"I can do more than you think, my son. The teachings of the
church are quite clear on this. I shall ask the archbishop to have
both Annunziata and you excommunicated."

Silvio stared hard at the priest. This was catastrophic. He was
not an especially religious man, but for him, like all Sicilians, like
all Italians, the church was part of his life, a form of solace, comfort, companionship. Hated and loved in equal measure. There
was more, of course. The minute Father Ignazio applied to the
archbishop, the whole world would know. Even before the inquiry
into his misdemeanors took place, Silvio would be condemned as
godless, a misfortune in most people's eyes that was far worse
than anything a mafioso could do. Support for him, for Bastiano's
family, would collapse. The authorities would know, roughly,
where he was.

Silvio realized he was holding his breath. "If you do this," he
said, thinking as he went along, "the income for Quisquina will
fall. We shall no longer send you oil, oranges, wine, cash."

"There are others to take care of us, Silvio. You get as much out
of our partnership as we do."

It was true.

Silvio continued to sit for minutes. He could think of nothing to
say, no fresh arguments to use. He couldn't even think of any new
insults to heap on the abbot.

He knew only one thing. That he would prefer excommunica-
tion to a life without Annunziata.

Silvio returned to the *bivio* in subdued spirits. As he rode through
the countryside, the rocky gully of the Magazzolo River, he
couldn't help but think of what the abbot had said. But Silvio didn't dwell directly on Father Ignazio's words. Instead he
thought about Annunziata and himself and marriage and children.
Both Annunziata and he were solitary individuals, in effect with
no parents or brothers or sisters or children. Until prison, he had
rarely thought of family. But in Ucciardone the doctor had talked
about his family, talked about it with such an ordinary, unaffected
joy that Silvio had been envious in a way that he had rarely—if
ever—been envious before. Afterward he had begun to notice that

even the most vicious criminals in Ucciardone had families, who visited them, cared about them, despite their obvious faults.

On the ride back from Quisquina, he thought hard for the first time about Annunziata and their future together. Yes, he told himself, he did want to marry her, he did want a son. But he recognized that it was a problem, at least in Sicily. However much he loved this island, he needed to take Annunziata to America. In America, behavior that was forbidden in Sicily was accepted.

When he reached the *bivio*, Annunziata wanted to know what Father Ignazio had said but he pretended they had discussed various other picture collections that might be treated like di Biondi's.

No sooner had he returned, however, than Silvio and Bastiano received a visitor. This was none other than Ruggiero Priola, from Palermo. He had plenty of news, and a new project.

Ruggiero's news from Palermo was that Nino was truly on the mend. He would live. More, the Quarryman was learning to read and write. And he wanted to see Annunziata.

Ruggiero's news from America was that Anna-Maria now had two children, two boys. And Angelo, surprisingly, was doing better than ever. There had been a tricky patch for some time, but an accommodation had been worked out with Liotta, who now owned half the docks. However, thanks mainly to Angelo's new refrigerated ships and warehouses, scattered along the Mississippi, his business had continued to prosper. In fact, it had prospered to the point where, in the 1886 election, his candidate for mayor had won and he now had the police on his side. It was now Angelo who was putting pressure on Vito.

Silvio listened to Ruggiero's stories with the occasional pang of nostalgia. From time to time he missed New Orleans, missed the bustle, the laughter, the smells, the sheer busy-ness of the city. Since the abbot's threats, he was convinced he must take Annunziata there. As Ruggiero spoke, Silvio began thinking over what had happened in New Orleans. It was ironic: Angelo had not been in favor of refrigeration when Silvio had first mentioned it. Now it had turned around the Priola fortunes.

But Ruggiero also had a project. His family had learned, he said, that poppies were being grown in the Tavolacci area of Sicily, and a small factory had been established, at Bagheria, for refining opium. The opium bags were shipped by the Liotta family every month to Palermo, where they were loaded onto ships bound for Marseilles, the biggest market. Each load was worth a fortune. Bagheria was only a couple of miles from the coast at Porticello. Ruggiero proposed that Silvio, Bastiano, and the others hijack one of these loads and immediately transfer it to Porticello, where a ship from the Priola line would be waiting to set sail right away.

Silvio liked the plan, or most of it. He didn't like drugs—he had seen what absinthe could do to people—but it was the timing of the raid, and the opportunity for revenge, that appealed to him. The raid could take place soon, almost certainly before Father Ignazio could get to Palermo and approach the archbishop. Silvio reckoned that if he could somehow convert this robbery into a political spectacular, which benefited a lot of other people, he could become so popular in the public's eye that no action by the abbot or the archbishop could reverse it. Also, there was so much money in this deal that afterward maybe he and Zata could finally make the break and take off to America together. All that talk about New Orleans had rekindled the old fire.

But how could this straightforward robbery be converted into something more . . . political?

The answer came to him one night while he lay with Annunziata after they had made love. Sex was still *so* good between them, so beautiful, that every night underlined for him the importance of their relationship. They fitted together so naturally, like an almond in its shell.

His plan was cunning rather than clever—foxy, as Angie would have said. But it should work.

They would hijack the opium—but then blow up the factory at the same time. This would accomplish two things. They would have one load of opium, which was worth a small fortune. But—and this was the cunning part—they could present the explosion as a civic duty. They were against drugs and this was the way to deal with drug factories. Some of the proceeds from the sale of the opium could also go into the Bagheria area afterward. That would help, too, and damage the Liottas. That was the sweetest reason of all—to outwit them.

17

Silvio got down from his horse and stretched his back. After two days' riding from Bagheria, he was sore, stiff, and in dire need of a drink. But the trip had been worthwhile. He had met with Ruggiero Priola in Bagheria and, discreetly, they had reconnoitered the opium factory. Silvio was forced to admit that the Liotta family had been clever. The factory was right in the middle of town, but on a side street. Its buildings formed part of a complex that included a stables and an orphanage. No one would ever think of looking there for such an enterprise. Plus, there was always so much bustle and business that visitors from out of town did not attract attention.

The orphanage was the only problem, as far as Silvio could see. However, when he compared notes with Priola, he discovered that the next load of opium would be in the factory during the time of the Feast of St. Joseph, the local patron saint. From nine-thirty in the morning until well into the afternoon, the orphans would be at the cathedral, then at the festivities celebrating this annual event. It meant that the factory had to be blown during the day rather than at night.

Now that he was back from Bagheria, his enthusiasm for the new plan lifted his spirits. They could finally outfox the Liottas.

As he approached their rooms he was thus disconcerted to find Annunziata a changed woman. Normally, she would throw her arms about him, hug him, and offer to fetch him a glass of wine. This time she watched him walk up to her without smiling. As he went to kiss her she stood unflinching and did not part her lips.

"Zata? What's the matter?"

For a moment they just stood staring at each other, at arm's length. Then he said, more gently, "Annunziata, tell me. What is the matter?"

For reply she suddenly raised her fists and began to flail at him, bouncing blows off his chest and shoulders. He resisted her easily, and hugged her to him. He was surprised to see that she was crying.

"Zata! Zata! Please. What is it? Why are you crying?"

She stopped trying to fight, and sagged in his arms. But still she sobbed. "You lied to me. You lied about what Father Ignazio said. I know everything. I know that you argued, I know that you didn't discuss what you said you discussed—and I know about his threat to excommunicate us. Oh, Silvio! Can he do it? Can he? Can he?"

So that was it. *Velono!* The abbot had been spreading his poison. Silvio held Zata to him and kissed her hair. Then he led her into the room, where he made her sit down. He poured them both some wine. It was dusk. Quietly he explained about the opium factory, his plan to blow it up and then to announce what he had done. He explained that the publicity, and the popularity that would result from such an act, could put him, and Annunziata, beyond the reach of either the abbot or the archbishop.

He could see from her eyes that she wanted to believe him. "But what about Smeralda, and the other women? They are never going to forgive us."

"They never mattered before."

"I thought it would pass. I thought that they would eventually drop their opposition. Nighttime always passes. But these last months have only hardened them. If the abbot and the archbishop side with them, if we are excommunicated ... I'd die. What would Father say?"

Silvio held Annunziata close. "Zata, I told the abbot I wouldn't leave you. We spoke as men and I told him I have a physical need for you. We fit together like trees by a river. I make you this promise. If my plan here in Sicily works, we shall go to America. The church doesn't matter in America. No one need know you are my cousin. I promise. I'll be able to wear the ring you gave me, and I'll buy a ring for you."

She smiled then, and nodded her head.

But that night, after they had made love, he found that she was crying again.

* * *

The most dangerous time for the mafiosi was weddings. The presence of a large group of men and women at a church was clearly risky. Silvio was therefore uneasy when, two days before the Bagheria project, the wedding of Domenico Garisi and Maria Cattarelli took place in the church of the Madonna dell'Olio.

There was another reason for Silvio to dread the wedding: Father Ignazio was officiating.

However, as he had agreed to be best man, there was no getting out of it. He had been surprised by Domenico's invitation. The groom had always been close to Alesso Alcamo, but recently, since the success of Silvio's plans as *sottocapo*, they had grown less intimate.

It was very hot as the procession trooped up the track to the chapel. Armed men stood on the ridges at either side, ready to give the alarm and to fire the first shots if they were needed.

The abbot was already in the chapel when the procession came to a halt in front of the wooden door, which had a statue of the Madonna above it. The guards on the ridges remained where they were, and another group of obviously armed men stood nearer the church. No chances were being taken.

Father Ignazio made a fuss of Domenico and Maria and then, swinging the incense burner, led the way into the church. There was no music but there were many flowers. As best man, Silvio followed Domenico. Maria had four bridesmaids, but Annunziata—very pointedly—had not been asked. Silvio knew that had hurt her.

She sat now, on the groom's side rather than the bride's, and well to the rear of the nave, next to one of the stone columns that supported the roof, under the gallery. It would have looked bad if she hadn't come, but now that she had, she kept her distance.

Though there was no musical accompaniment, hymns were sung and everyone joined in lustily. The abbot had a fine speaking voice, which lent confidence to Domenico and Maria in their responses. In no time they were husband and wife.

Then, as usual, the abbot asked everyone to be seated for the wedding address. Silvio found two chairs for the bride and groom so they could sit in the place of honor, in the middle of the aisle. He himself sat in the front pew.

"Friends," boomed the abbot, looking around the church. "What a glorious day. What wonderful sunshine, what a heavenly breeze on the hillside today, what perfect conditions for this, the most agreeable and mysterious sacrament known to man. What a gift from God to Maria and Domenico, who can now start their life together without any shadow over them, literally or metaphorically.

"Like many of you, I have known Domenico since he was a little boy and was frightened of men who wore black robes and had beards. Monks can be pretty terrifying, I know."

Everyone smiled.

"Maria I have known less long, only since she was a pretty twelve-year-old who sang beautifully at birthday parties. She is still as pretty, but, like all women, has given up birthdays."

Laughter.

"I am thus as overjoyed as any of you by these events today, and absolutely delighted that I have been able to play a small part in helping these two achieve happiness on this earth. I also bring a blessing from someone you all know and miss as much as I do— Nino Greco."

A buzz went around the church. Most of them had never known a leader like Nino. He was obviously in better health, and that cheered them.

The abbot went on.

"I cannot, however, let this opportunity—this wedding—slip by without addressing more serious matters. Marriage is a serious business. It is also a sacrament. That is to say, it is holy, sanctioned by God Himself. It is not for us, mortals on this earth for but a limited time, to question the sacraments. We should accept them, respect them, enjoy them, and not rebel against them."

Silvio was beginning to feel uncomfortable. *Sono ribelle?* he asked himself. Am I the rebel? He hadn't expected this. Was the abbot about to take their quarrel public, albeit in an indirect way?

"None of us is perfect. All of us go to confession, admit that we have done wrong, and ask for forgiveness. Now, forgiveness is a marvelous human quality, itself a form of love. God is merciful, just as Jesus was merciful. It is one of the qualities that separates us from the animals. But when we ask forgiveness, and receive it, it is not one-sided. It is a form of contract, for we are expected to change our behavior.

"In our lifetimes, we all make mistakes, and we all have to change. Some changes are more painful than others. But change is the essence of life, change within the framework provided by God and by nature. None of us can break that contract with the Lord, the contract which says that we are better than the animals, that we can forgive errors in others and be forgiven errors we ourselves make provided, provided always that we abide by the rules of nature.

"And the rules of nature? What are they? Well, first and foremost they are the Ten Commandments. Thou shalt not steal, thou shalt not covet thy neighbor's wife . . . you all know them as well as I do. Better. But the rules of nature do not stop there. They govern much else in our everyday life. Fields must be left fallow every few years, or they tire and cannot produce the goodness we need to live on. Parents look after their children, partly in order that children, later in life, can look after their parents. Relations between animals and human beings are an abomination, and against the rules of nature. And so are relations between members of the same family."

There, he had said it. The atmosphere was very tense now. No one moved, or said a word. Silvio didn't dare look to right or left, nor could he bring himself to look at the abbot. He was livid. The abbot would be made to pay for this breach of confidence, for attacking his conduct in so public and dramatic a way.

But the abbot hadn't finished. "This is in some ways the most pathetic aberration of all. It is pathetic because—"

Suddenly there was a commotion in the church. A noise came from the back, someone muttering and others answering back. Silvio heard the sounds of feet shuffling, and a Bible or a hymn-book falling to the floor. He sensed others turning round and plucked up the courage to do so himself.

He was just in time to see Annunziata marching back down the aisle to the main door. Everyone watched her go, including the abbot, who trailed off in midsentence. Annunziata reached the back of the church, pulled open the door, and slammed it shut behind her.

She wasn't in the room. Or anywhere in the *bivio*. Or by the river. That left the *giardino segreto*.

By the time he reached it, he was sweating and out of breath. It was a hot day and he had scratched himself on the branches of the olive trees as he had hurried up the hill. He flopped onto the cool shaded moss to regain his breath. Annunziata sat with her legs drawn up to her chin, which rested on her knees. Her arms hugged her shins. She had been crying.

Silvio let some time elapse before he spoke. An eagle soared overhead, riding the currents of air. Goats bleated on the far side of the valley, on the slopes of the Indisi mountain. He licked the blood from one of the scratches on his wrist.

"Zata," he finally said, speaking softly. "That was horrible, I know. I didn't see it coming, and I blame myself. I should protect you from harm. But think of this. I have never known such happiness as these past weeks, with you. You are the only person I have ever loved, Zata. I loved my parents, but as a boy, a child. That was very different. I am fond of Smeralda and Bastiano, but . . . it doesn't compare."

A breeze disturbed Annunziata's hair and she pushed back a wisp that had fallen over her face.

"We're different, you and me, Zata. Different from the others—"

"Are we?" Suddenly she turned toward him and spoke vehemently. "You are, maybe. You've been to America. You were born strong, or learned to become strong, after your parents were killed." Zata's mouth was turned down and her bottom lip was quivering. She was close to tears again. "What about me? I'm not strong. I know you think I'm strong, Toto, and I'm strong when I'm with you, but . . ." She trailed off.

"You *are* strong, Zata. I've seen the way the others look at you, listen to you. There's never been a woman here like you."

"Anyone can think things, Toto, even women." She wiped her eyes. "Look at the way we all live." She shook her sad head. "I've always wanted to break away, but I was never strong enough. When Gino took little Nino to Palermo, we said it was to show him off to the relatives—but there was another reason. I wanted Gino to get a job there. I wanted to live in Palermo, to send Nino to school maybe. Maybe Gino would sail on a boat to America, see what it was like." Her shoulders sagged. "Look what happened. If I hadn't wanted what I wanted . . . little Nino would still be alive." The tears were pouring down her cheeks now, but she smiled. "Gino would be alive, of course, and I wouldn't have known lovemaking with you."

Another silence.

Then Silvio went on, gently. "Zata, we're not old. We've had twists in our lives, bad things, that's all. America *is* different. People like the abbot, like Smeralda—they're old, old-fashioned, old bones. In New Orleans there's an area called the *vieux carré*, that's French for the 'old quarter,' but it's where all the new things happen. The new dress shops, the flower shops, bookshops with Mark Twain and other writers, shops selling French pastry, satin shoes, whole shops selling just toys."

He lowered his voice to a whisper. "Zata, it doesn't matter whether you're strong. *I'm* strong. Let me be strong for both of us. In a few days there will be the raid on Bagheria. The abbot and Smeralda won't matter after that—"

Annunziata went to say something but he hurried on.

"—but even if they do, we can go to America. We can get married there, have children. The schools are even better in New Orleans than in Palermo. When I was in prison I thought a lot about children—"

"Stop!" she cried. But it was a whisper all the same. "Toto, I want to come to America, I want to be with you. My body never needed a man before you, but now . . . now you know how I need you." She put her fingers to her temple. "But in here, I'm not you. In here, the abbot matters, Smeralda matters. I wish they didn't, but they do." Again, she wiped her eyes with the ball of her hand. "I'm crying not because we're cousins, Toto. I want you to make love to me right here, right now. That's how much I want you. I'm crying because I don't know what to do. My head and my body want to come to America, but my soul, my conscience, tells me that somehow that would be running away." She shook her head, the tears flowing again. "I don't know. I don't know."

Silvio moved forward over the moss and put his arms around her. He kissed her wet, warm, salty face. Her lips parted and she pressed her body hard against his.

Silvio sat on the hill of Solunto and enjoyed the first fingers of dawn. It was shortly after five. He had chosen this spot because from here he could see both Bagheria and Porticello. For days now, members of the band had been watching the Liottas deliver cartloads of poppies, one cart at a time and always at night. Earlier that day, the Priola-line steamship, the *Ustica*, had put into Porticello and unloaded some crates of her own. Silvio had no idea if the crates were genuine or empty and he didn't care. All he cared about was that this project was going according to plan.

The plan for blowing up the factory was simplicity itself. Alesso Alcamo, who had grudgingly approved Silvio's scheme, would wait for the orphans to leave for the service and festivities, around nine-thirty in the morning, and then slip into the orphanage and climb the stairs to the top floor. Reconnaissance had shown that all the buildings in that complex had skylights. Alesso would climb up through one of the skylights in the orphanage, cross to the factory, and drop the explosives through the skylight in the appropriate part of the roof. He would escape the way he had come.

According to Ruggiero's information, the cartload of opium would leave the factory at about eight A.M. for the ride to Palermo. At about ten-thirty, it would cross a railway bridge in an out-of-the-way spot. As the road approaching the bridge was very steep, the cart would slow down drastically. Silvio and his men, having watched the cart leave the factory from their hilltop at Solunto, would stage their ambush as the cart slowed, on the rise of the railway bridge. From the bridge there was a fast road to Porticello.

The morning was sunny, hardly a cloud in the sky. Eight o'clock came. Right on schedule, the cart emerged from the factory gate and pulled away. There were just over four miles between Bagheria and the railway bridge; it would take the cart about an hour and a half to get there. Say nine-thirty, the same time that Alesso was to enter the orphanage to blow the factory. After Silvio had delivered the opium to the *Ustica*, the men would split up and make their own way back to Bivio Indisi.

Solunto was three miles from the railway bridge. Now that Silvio knew the cart was on its way, it was time for him to make a move. He first of all dispatched one man to Porticello, to alert the captain of the *Ustica* that the operation was under way and that he should begin to get up steam. If all went well, the opium should be delivered on board ship between eleven and twelve that morning.

Then he himself set off, with ten others. The cart, he had been told, had a driver and two guards. Eleven men should be plenty.

The road from Solunto was overshadowed at first by Mount Catalfano but then moved closer to the sea, giving the most wonderful views of the glittering blue water in the distance. For a time the road ran alongside the railway, then left it. Just before they reached the bridge, the line came into view again.

The bridge itself was deserted. It was a new construction and was perfectly sited for their purposes. At this point the railway line was cut into the rock as the land rose to form cliffs at the sea's edge. The road therefore rose also, in a continuous gradient, from the south side of the railway to the north, where it then divided, one fork going to Palermo, the other to Solunto and Porticello. Silvio had examined the railway timetable and no trains were due until just after ten, by which time they should be well clear.

Two men were stationed to the north of the bridge, high up, hidden among trees. Two more were positioned to the south of the bridge, one hidden in a gulley, the other in the ruins of a cottage. That left seven to huddle under the railway bridge itself. It was five past nine.

To the west, the railway line ran straight for a long way, certainly as far as Ficarizzi. To the east, it began to curve as soon as it passed under the bridge and so could not be followed by the eye for more than two or three hundred yards, when it entered a cutting.

Silvio lit a cigarette, to help calm his nerves. He missed American cigarettes; indeed, at times he simply missed America. America didn't have the lethargy of Sicily, or its obsession with tradition. The church took a backseat in America, thank God. People like Father Ignazio did not have the power, the overwhelming power, that they had in Sicily. Silvio and Annunziata had been on edge with one another since the episode after the wedding in the *giardino segreto*. They still made love, but even then Annunziata was locked up inside herself, going through the motions because she needed the physical release, as he did, but otherwise not letting him near her emotionally. Some mornings she just got up, left the room, and didn't come back. He longed to take Annunziata to America, away from the crabby women and away from the abbot.

The people in Sicily, he had decided, could be as arid and harsh as the landscape.

Father Ignazio had caught up with Silvio during the wedding and told him he would be seeing the archbishop at the very festivities that were being celebrated in Bagheria later this day. The timing was tight, but perfect if all went well. Silvio ought be so popular after today's exploit that nothing the archbishop said could detract from it. Annunziata's attitude would change afterward, too. Silvio needed her more than ever. He thought about children more and more these days, and he couldn't bear to start all over again with another woman. It had to be Annunziata.

Nine-thirty arrived. No cart. Silvio lit a fresh cigarette.

Five minutes later a low two-tone whistle from the man hiding in the ruin told them that the cart was within sight.

Silvio peered around the edge of the bridge and after a few seconds saw the cart. It was bigger than it had looked when seen from that hilltop in Solunto, a four-wheeler, drawn by a big brown horse. One guard sat with the driver; the other was pretending to sleep on top of the load. Boxes of oranges lay on top, presumably to hide the bags of opium. The cart looked like hundreds of others on its way to market, or to the docks in Palermo.

As it mounted the hill the cart slowed. Silvio motioned his men to wait. Let the others struggle up the hill, do their work for them. Let the horse tire itself out. Down the line a locomotive hooter sounded. Odd. Nothing was due for nearly half an hour. But the line was clear in both directions.

Once again, Silvio had worked out a simple plan. At the top of the hill there was a water trough, placed there by a religious order that looked after animals. The order had calculated that horses pulling heavy loads would be tired at that point and in need of refreshment. They were right. Silvio was relying on the near certainty that the driver of the opium cart would stop and allow his horse to drink from the trough. Silvio would ambush them there.

Sure enough, as the cart approached the top of the hill, the driver pulled over and steered the horse to the watering trough. The cart stopped and the horse began to drink greedily. It was barely a quarter to ten but the day was already hot.

Silvio was just about to give the signal when the air around them shifted—and in the distance an explosion was heard. Alesso had hit the factory right on schedule. Alesso might still be sulking, so far as Silvio was concerned, but when he put his mind to it, he was highly professional. Instinctively Silvio looked back toward Bagheria. He couldn't see anything from here of course, but what he could see, now that he looked, was a train, steaming slowly toward him, around the bend, from the direction of Bagheria. He was confused. It shouldn't be there, not according to the timetable. Then it dawned on him: it was a freight train, two wagons only. He had only inspected the passenger timetable. There wasn't time to wait for it to pass. In a moment the horse at the trough would have drunk its fill and the cart would have moved on, away from the hill.

"Now!" he hissed to his men. "Let's move."

They clambered up onto the road. The guard who lay on the oranges looked as though he was really asleep, not pretending. The driver was relieving himself, facing away from Silvio and his men. The second guard was polishing his gun.

Quickly, silently, Silvio and his group ran up behind the cart. Seeing this, one of the other men, hidden in the trees beyond the bridge, quietly emerged from his cover and approached the driver. The second lookout, in the trees on the far side of the road, did the same. Within moments the cart was surrounded.

Silvio fired into the air, to frighten the man on the oranges and to waken him. This guard nearly jumped out of his skin, but the one who was polishing his gun turned quickly in his seat and might have fired if Silvio had not screamed, "Drop it! *Drop it!* If you don't want to die, drop it."

The man quickly saw he was outnumbered and threw his weapon to the ground.

Silvio turned to one of his men. "Tie them both to those trees—"

He said no more, for a shot rang out behind him. He turned, to see one of his own men, who had been on the south side of the bridge, firing *at the train.* To his horror, he realized that the train had stopped, almost under the bridge, that the doors on the wagons were opening, and that men, men in uniforms, were streaming out.

It was a trap! There had been a leak within the band, the militia had known they were coming, and the opium was simply a lure, the bait in the trap. For a moment Silvio stared in disbelief as more and more men jumped down from the train.

He stared for only a moment. "Disappear," he hissed to his men. "We've been betrayed. Vanish. *Sparite!* You know what to do, where to go."

He himself was already running. He couldn't go south—that was where the train had halted. He couldn't go west. If he could reach Palermo, he could get lost in the maze of streets. But he didn't know the ground between here and Palermo and the men in uniforms might know it much better. He couldn't go north, not far anyway, for that way lay the sea. That left east, back toward Bagheria. There was a festival, and today masses of people would be milling around. That was his best bet, his only chance.

Sporadic shooting could be heard behind him, but he didn't look around. So long as the militia were pinned down, shooting, they couldn't come after him. He was not being a coward. He was acting prudently. He left the road as soon as he could, keeping to trees and gulleys as he put more and more distance between himself and the militia.

Although he had regained his fitness, he had to stop twice to catch his breath. So far as he could tell, he wasn't being followed, but once the militia had the situation under control at the bridge, they could easily ride the train back to Bagheria and overtake him. That was not the same as catching him, but it did mean he had to keep moving. If he could get beyond Bagheria, he would be safer.

He reached the outskirts of the town just after eleven. To begin with, he found a small courtyard that appeared to be empty and there he lay down, to recover. Not only was he tired, after running a few miles, he was sweating profusely. If he walked through the town in that state, he would only draw attention to himself.

Just after eleven-thirty he moved on. Now he kept to the busy streets, ambling along like anyone else, enjoying the festivities, laughing at the acrobats, inspecting the fruit on the stalls, stopping to watch the conjurors. His gun was well hidden.

Slowly he worked his way through the town. He came to the railway station. There were militia everywhere, but he followed a water seller as he crossed the square in front of the station and managed to keep himself hidden from view. He passed the cathedral, where the morning service had just ended and groups of people were standing on the steps, taking the sun.

Past the cathedral, he suddenly came across a street packed with people, who were not moving. Instead, they were craning their necks forward, looking at or for something. He tried to push through but found it difficult.

A man was coming the other way, out of the crush. Silvio stopped him. "What *is* all this? Why the crowd?"

"There's been an explosion at the orphanage."

The orphanage? What about the factory? But he couldn't ask that.

"What happened?"

The man shook his head. "Who would do such a thing? A bomb went off in the sanatorium."

"What! And—?"

"Three children—two girls and a boy. And a nurse. All dead. The animals who did this are going to pay. It makes you sick." The man moved away.

Silvio was dazed. The man was right. It *was* sick. Alesso had made a mistake, a terrible mistake. He had dropped the explosives through the wrong skylight—with disastrous results. As the man had said: How could he have done such a thing?

Then the truth struck Silvio. *Sono scemo!* I'm a fool! *There had been no mistake!* It had been deliberate. It was part of a plan, a joint plan by Alesso and the Imbriaci family, with the militia. Maybe even the Liotta family had been involved. Alesso and the Imbriacis had taken revenge on Silvio because he had been made Bastiano's *sottocapo*. The militia had scored a considerable coup in recapturing a much-wanted criminal. Except that Silvio hadn't been caught—not yet. The more he thought about it, the more Silvio realized he was right. The whole plan was a setup. Not by Ruggiero Priola, of course; the opium factory had been genuine enough. But after Silvio had worked out his plan, Alesso, still jealous about Annunziata, still worrying that he had a rival to become the next Capo, had seen a way to adapt the Bagheria business to his own ends. Silvio had intended the ambush of the opium and the blowing of the factory to produce cash *and* good publicity. Alesso had simply rearranged things so that Silvio and the others would be caught when they tried to steal the opium, and he had deliberately killed those children so that Silvio's name would be vilified all over Sicily and beyond. Silvio remembered now: Alesso had actually volunteered to handle the explosives.

People swirled around Silvio. The killings in the orphanage changed everything. If Alesso was collaborating with the militia, or the Liottas, to that extent, he must surely have given them the exact whereabouts of Bastiano's camp. It was the end for Bastiano's family. Alesso had clearly decided that if he couldn't be Capo, nobody else could. Another batch of militia was probably already ensconced at Bivio Indisi, waiting for men to arrive back exhausted, when they could be picked up with no trouble at all.

Where was Annunziata? She had been one cause of the rivalry between Silvio and Alesso. Did Alesso want her, too?

Still the people swirled around Silvio. What should he do now? He couldn't go back to Bivio Indisi, that was certain. He couldn't go to the abbey at Quisquina either. When word got out that he had led the group that had killed three orphans, very few places would be safe for him. No one would have any compunction about turning him in. He would be viewed as a child killer, a murderer of orphans. If he was caught, he would surely be lynched.

Orphans. He had been orphaned yet again. Cut off from his loved ones. The pattern of his life.

His thoughts kept returning to Annunziata. Where was she? What would she think? Would she believe him, or would she, too, believe he had killed those children?

Suddenly, surrounded by all those other people, he felt very lonely. There was nowhere he could go. In time, of course, they would all regroup. In time, Alesso would be dealt with. In time, normal life would reassert itself.

But the more he thought about that, the more he began to realize that it wasn't necessarily true. Earthquakes weren't unknown in Sicily and they changed the landscape permanently. An earthquake had helped create the *bivio*; now a different sort of earthquake looked as though it had destroyed that way of life. It was by no means certain that Silvio's relationship with Annunziata would ever recover its earlier intensity and passion. He realized now—he could admit it to himself—that she had been permanently damaged by the attack on her by Smeralda and the other women. And Father Ignazio's outburst in the church had been devastating.

Silvio spied a small courtyard just off the road. He slipped in there and took out his cigarettes. He lit one and pulled on it, again wishing he had an American cigarette right now.

America: he could go there. He dismissed the idea as soon as he thought of it. *Sono pazzo?* Am I crazy? That meant smuggling himself on board a ship, sailing the Atlantic, and smuggling himself ashore as an illegal immigrant again. There was the mainland of Italy, but that meant risking the docks at Messina, where there would surely be a lookout for him.

He couldn't stay in Sicily, though: that much was certain. There was no one he could trust to hide him even for one night. The more he thought about it, the more he understood that he had no alternative but America. Then he reminded himself he couldn't leave Annunziata. As he had told the abbot, he had a physical need for her. He had left Annunziata before, but it had been different then. Before, they had not been lovers. As he pulled on his cigarette, he thought back to some of their evenings in the darkened room. Would he ever again enjoy that rapture?

Not in Sicily. But in America it would be different. Old Angelo, after all, owed him a thing or two. Once he settled in, Silvio could send for Annunziata. They could start fresh. As man and wife. Have children.

It wouldn't be easy to get there, of course. His first task was to reach Palermo. Ruggiero Priola surely owed him something after the fiasco of the last few hours. The opium job had been his idea.

All at once Silvio saw the way out of his predicament. Why had he been so slow? Salvation was only a few miles away, moored in the harbor at Porticello. The *Ustica* was preparing to leave for Marseilles, her captain and crew unaware of what had happened in Bagheria. All Silvio needed was a package that *looked* as though it contained opium. He could take it on board and insist he stay with it until they arrived in Marseilles. Then he could work out a deal to get him ashore.

Marseilles wasn't America, but it was a long way from Sicily. In Marseilles he would have time to plan his second emigration. Ruggiero would help.

At least he was thinking again. He had put the awful events of the past few hours behind him, at least for the time being. He felt better already, now that he had an immediate aim and a long-term goal.

He threw down the remains of his cigarette and went back out into the street. He turned away from the orphanage and walked back to the cathedral square. He even had the nerve to approach a militiaman. "Excuse me," he said. "Can you tell me, which is the road for Porticello?"

PART FOUR

—✦—

Consigliere

18

Silvio stood at the corner of Canal Street and Chartres and pulled his oilskin coat more tightly about him. He pulled down his wide-brimmed hat, not to hide his face but to keep the rain out. New Orleans hadn't changed much in seven years, he thought. The streets still turned to quagmires when it rained, the horses pulling the streetcars still slithered all over the place. You could still hear loud music at all hours of the day, no matter what the weather.

He walked along Chartres, keeping to the sidewalk. As he passed CustomHouse Street he noted the signs. Madge Leigh's was still there, so was Mary O'Brien's. Mamie Christine's—that looked new. He reached Bienville Street, then Conti. There were more balconies now, and more streetlights, by the look of it. Who operated the rackets around here? he wondered. Priola or Liotta?

He walked into St. Louis Square. He felt ... curious. It was more than half a decade since he had been here, that day when Nino and he had left the cathedral after the wedding rehearsal. He rarely thought of Nino now. Had he learned to read and write yet?

He didn't linger in the square. The rain was still fierce, driving in from the west, and in any case he had an appointment, of sorts. He walked straight into the cathedral. It was not quite two o'clock. Inside, it was dark. He could hear the rain outside and see it slapping against the lunette windows that lined the dome, where the nave crossed the transept. The cathedral was virtually empty. Two or three people sat near each other, but not together, on one side of the nave, about halfway down. They were waiting their turn for confession.

Silvio took a seat, in the rearmost pew, next to the main aisle. He waited.

The cathedral had changed hardly at all since the last time he was here, all those years ago. The pulpit looked as though it had been cleaned, and some of the pews were new; but that was all. The smallest sound still echoed around the entire building.

He heard footsteps behind him, firm, substantial. A figure went by him without stopping. Silvio followed the figure with his eyes. Yes, that was Angelo Priola. He must be in his late sixties by now, but as Silvio had guessed, he still came for confession every Tuesday. Angelo stooped a bit now, and was definitely grayer— there were snail's trails everywhere—but he still carried his hat in his hand, still knelt in the pew in the same way and crossed himself. His was not a bad memory, Silvio told himself. All those years and he still remembered that Angelo took confession on Tuesdays.

Silvio had quite a wait. The confessors went in one by one and were there for anywhere between three and ten minutes. The rain still slashed against the lunette windows high above. An occasional hoot from the steamboats on the river could be heard.

It had taken Silvio more than two months to reach America, and another four to make it to New Orleans. The *Ustica* had dropped him in Marseilles just three days after leaving Porticello. Organizing a deal to get himself smuggled ashore was no problem, except that it involved rendering various services to the captain of the *Ustica*, who had business associates in Marseilles. Silvio spent a month working for nothing as an enforcer in a protection racket by the docks. He worked for a second month at the same racket to earn enough to pay for his passage, steerage, on a ship bound for New York. On arrival in New York, he had again been smuggled ashore, in New Jersey, again on condition that he allow himself to be sold by colleagues of the ship's captain to the highest bidder. An Italian clothier who specialized in uniforms had won the auction. For four months Silvio pretended that he couldn't speak English, and gradually convinced his bosses that he could never survive in America all by himself. As a result, over that time, they gradually relaxed their supervision of him. He was in no hurry anyway. He wanted to see New York, the bits of it outside the courthouse and the jails, and he guessed that after he had escaped from Sicily, the authorities in New Orleans would have been alerted to be on the lookout for him. He didn't want to go back too soon.

After more than three months in the uniform factory, however, he had sufficient money in his pocket for what he planned, and judged that enough time had elapsed. One evening after work, he went to a local bar, leaving his few meager belongings by his bed, and never came back. Later that night he took a train to Pittsburgh and the next day boarded a steamboat down the Ohio River, bound for Cairo, where the Mississippi was reached. At Cairo he changed to a bigger boat, and sailed for 1,200 miles down the Mississippi, past Memphis, Vicksburg, and Natchez, arriving at New Orleans nearly three weeks after he had left New Jersey. He bought fresh clothes along the way.

He had not contacted Angelo immediately. He had been away from New Orleans for nine years and he had to be certain of his facts before he broke cover. For all he knew, there was a warrant out for his arrest.

He did not think it prudent to get a job on the docks. Someone might recognize him. He knew the clothing trade a little by now, so he finagled something at a workshop that specialized in making fancy costumes for Mardi Gras. The work was seasonal and he would be fired as soon as the carnival had come and gone, but that suited him. By then he would be ready to move on.

He had found a room on North Rampart Street and started to drink and screw systematically in the bars and brothels on Bourbon and Burgundy streets. Whores had always been the best-informed gossips.

Angelo, he found, had reached a most interesting accommodation with Vito Liotta. Angelo had the raw muscle still, but Vito had brains, and Angelo recognized that. There were now two Dons in New Orleans, pretty evenly matched save in one respect: refrigeration. Angelo's partnership with Dick Saltram, now his son-in-law, his *genero*, had been an enormous success, and the shipping business had gone from strength to strength. The Priolas still had the lion's share of the river, whereas Liotta took most from the rackets in the Quarter. Both Dons were doing well, and for the moment at least, Liotta seemed to have lost his vindictive streak. He must be feeling sure of himself. Good.

A turning point had been reached, however, in the election of 1886, where Priola's candidate, Harrison Parker, had beaten Liotta's Milton. Martell had promptly changed sides—and succeeded in having himself reappointed chief of police. Angelo's business interests were able to run uninterrupted until the next election.

Martell's defection, though good for Angelo in the short run, was not beneficial in the longer term. Martell, being of Irish stock, could not be expected to think like a Sicilian. However, Silvio could see, as surely as Angelo must, that Vito Liotta would now need to act. Martell was in a position to lean on Liotta's gambling interests and on his girls. Martell's defection had disturbed the status quo and a new Mafia war now seemed likely, especially as fresh elections were due at the end of 1890. It was time for Silvio to move.

Silvio watched as Angelo rose from his pew and entered the confessional. As he gazed around the cathedral he thought of Anna-Maria. Whore gossip had told him she was pregnant; already a mother of two and in her mid-thirties, she was becoming plump and matronly. Dick Saltram was a faithful husband and generally given credit for having the refrigeration idea in the first place. Silvio would remember that. His thoughts drifted from Anna-Maria to Annunziata. Christ, he missed her! This last six months he had lost count of the times his body had ached for hers. Most of all he missed their nights together in the *bivio*. Sex, talk, Sicilian wine, a cigarette, more talk, more sex, more wine, sleep, sex, talk, breakfast. The sound of goats and sheep on the hillside nearby, the sweet smell of olives and figs.

He missed it—he longed for it—but he had done nothing about contacting Annunziata. *Non sono matto!* He wasn't stupid, for God's sake, and she would be guarded, by Alesso Alcamo and by Father Ignazio, if not by the police. No one knew where Silvio was and it had to stay that way, at least for the time being. Annunziata had been so odd the last few days before he had been forced to leave Sicily that he couldn't in any case be certain how she would respond to overtures on his part. In a year, when he was more settled, and if he could be certain of the intermediary, then he would get word to her. Then he would convince her to come to him. Meanwhile there were always whores to satisfy his physical needs. The other ache he would just have to get used to.

Eventually Angelo was done. He left the confessional, walked across the nave to the main aisle, turned to face the altar, dipped his head, and crossed himself. Then he turned and marched back down the aisle toward the exit, looking straight ahead.

Silvio waited until he was level with his pew. "Hello, Angie."

Angelo stopped, turned, and looked down. His mind was miles away and he didn't recognize Silvio.

Then, slowly, it registered. "Silvio!" he breathed after a minute. He sat down on the pew, side by side. "I thought you'd come. Maybe sooner, maybe later."

"I've been here awhile. Watching."

"That figures. You always were foxy." He started to offer Silvio a cigar, then remembered where he was. "You got a place to stay? You need money? That was some dumb job you pulled in . . . where was it? Bagheria?"

"I was set up, Angie. Alesso Alcamo. It was a plan to force me out."

"That was dumb, too, then. Allowing yourself to be forced out."

Silvio sniffed. "That's three times, Angie. First the steamboat race. Then outside this very cathedral. Then Alcamo. Three times I've been tricked. I would never have hurt kids in an orphanage, Angie. Tell me you believe that. I'm an orphan myself, for God's sake." He put his hand on the older man's arm. "Tell me!"

"Sure. Sure, I believe you. But the point is, you're here now. And you've got to figure out what you're gonna do. Things have changed since you went away, Silvio. The city's bigger, the river's busier 'n ever. There's more graft, more kickbacks, more people to pay. The politicians have moved in. We gotta real good scam now. The lottery. We're skimming more than twenty percent off that. Fourteen grand a month. But we got people to pay. The lottery license has to be renewed. That takes tact and graft. We gotta spread it about, make friends.

"New people all round, Silvio. Nogare's out. He caught the clap and his brain's gone. There's Saltram, of course, the *genero*. He don't have your balls or your brains but he's nice enough to Anna-Maria." He held out his middle finger and forefinger. "Two kids now, you know, two boys." He shook his head. "And another kid on the way. That lovely daughter of mine's gonna be like her mother in five years. Maybe it wasn't so bad you got arrested." He was going to smile until he saw the look on Silvio's face.

Silvio shifted in his seat. "What do you think I've been watching these past weeks? Who do you think I've been listening to— the alligators? Things *have* changed, Angie, but maybe not as much as you think. People still get frightened, don't they?"

Angelo's eyes narrowed. "What does that mean?"

"It means that's why I've come to you now. You have to move on Liotta. The election is months away, and between now and then there's going to be a war. Am I right?"

Angelo looked at the younger man curiously. "It's started. The refrigeration factory was blown this morning."

Silvio tried not to show his surprise. Instead he nodded his head, as if to say "I told you so." As if to say he still understood New Orleans. "Liotta's going to war because Martell changed sides. He got greedy. You had the river sewn up, the fruit and the cotton, you had your rackets in the Quarter, but he had more, thanks to Martell."

Angelo sighed, and nodded. "I should never have let Martell come across."

"Which means Liotta has to either take on Martell in the Quarter, or you on the wharves. Yes?"

This time Angelo didn't even reply. He just let Silvio continue.

"You're easier. He takes you on, he beats you, Martell comes back across anyhow. Martell's clever—he always goes with the winner. No one is going to hit the chief, huh? This hit this morning, it proves my point."

Silvio rubbed his face with his hand. Someone else was going by and he didn't want to be recognized. "You need a plan, Angie. A Sicilian plan."

"And you got one, I suppose."

"*Sono volpone?* Am I a fox? I wouldn't come here empty-handed, after all this time. Nogare's out, you say. You're going to need a good *consigliere*. You know that. This is going to be a war and you need a general."

For the next half an hour Silvio outlined for Angie's benefit what became notorious later as the Cathedral Plan, the chapter of terrifying events that was to shape New Orleans life for generations to come.

Silvio left only one detail unexplained—his real reason for conceiving the plan in the first place.

Silvio stood on the promenade of the St. Charles Theatre and looked around him. The stalls were thronged with people, as were the boxes above the stalls. A band played in the pit. It was the evening of the lottery draw, and if he hadn't seen it for himself, he would never have believed the number of lottery addicts in New Orleans. Angelo had said the lottery was a new scam, and Christ, was he right. As the night for the draw approached, the entire city seemed to come to a standstill; everyone devoted time, thought, and energy to selecting their numbers. The behavior was weird, *fatidico*. Silvio had seen grown adults stop children in the street and demand to know their ages. The newspapers printed local superstitions about certain numbers. A stray dog, it was said, signified a six; a drunk man counted fourteen; a dead woman fifty-nine; if a woman exposed too much leg, eleven; to dream of a fish or water, thirteen. Silvio thought about the lottery much as he thought about voodoo, and like voodoo, he couldn't deny its power over people.

Nor could he deny that it made money hand over fist. The company controlling the lottery was Angelo's, although he shared it with Harrison Parker, the mayor of New Orleans, and Thomas Whitgift, another friend. The company was allowed by law to hold back thirty-seven percent of its take. Expenses had to come out of that share, but Angelo had, of course, found a way to skim even more money from the scheme. The winning tickets were selected by numbered balls rotated in a wheel. These balls were picked out—theoretically, at random—by two blindfolded boys taken from a local orphanage. Angelo had succeeded in tampering with the blindfolds, and since each ball was a different color, according to its number, the boys could be trained to select the right colors, even if they couldn't read the actual numbers. As a result, as often as not, the winning numbers belonged to men within the Priola organization, who were paid handsomely for their trouble—but the bulk of the winnings went right back to Angelo, Parker, and Whitgift.

Silvio was watching carefully tonight, partly to see exactly how the lottery business worked and partly to see if he could think of a way to ensure that when the license came up for renewal, next month, the Priola organization would be awarded a new five-year contract. Liotta wanted a piece of this action, too, of course, but Angelo was determined to hold on to it. *"Sono scoiatolo,"* he was given to saying. "I'm a squirrel." And as they said in Sicily, "A squirrel doesn't share its nuts."

Outside the theater it was raining. It was raining and had been raining for nearly a week; the levees were threatened in several places. Silvio had forgotten about Louisiana's problems with the levees, but the lottery people were more than familiar with it, because they had their own steamboat, which stopped off at all the main landing points, selling tickets. The hot, bony hills of Sicily were a long way away.

The band in the pit was building up to a crescendo as the moment for the draw approached. On stage, a local actor had appeared, with the two orphans. Two sexy women brought on the wheel. They were followed by David Martell, the chief of police. He was there to see that everything played out fairly.

Applause broke out in the auditorium.

The music finished, the orphans were blindfolded. There was a drumroll as the first orphan was placed next to the wheel. Silvio could see Angelo, Parker, and Whitgift watching from a box in the second tier.

Another drumroll and the wheel stopped. The orphan leaned forward and selected a greenish ball. The actor took it and called out, "Seventeen!"

Applause and cheers.

The second orphan was led to the wheel. It was spun a second time and stopped. The orphan took a reddish ball.

"Number nine!"

Seven times this was repeated, and seven times the applause filled the auditorium. People lived in hope that someone right there in the theater would one day be the winner of the jackpot, but Silvio knew that wouldn't happen tonight. Tonight it had been predetermined that the winner lived in Shreveport. That was hundreds of miles upriver, too far from New Orleans for anyone to suspect that a scam was operating.

The evening wound down. The actor and orphans left the stage, the band went home, and the audience gradually thinned out. Not one of them appeared to know the whole business was fixed. No wonder Liotta wanted a piece of it.

It was a license to steal.

19

It was early evening. Silvio lay in bed at Mamie Christine's reading the *Picayune*. He had never been one to read the newspapers, but now, with an election only months away, and with the Cathedral Plan about to go into effect, he needed to stay on top of things. Usually he had sex with Virginia, a blond American whore. No whore could take the place of Annunziata, and no sex could be like the sex he'd had with Anna-Maria, but Virginia was fine. She had good skin, she liked fucking, and she was genuinely pleased with the gifts he gave her. She loved gadgets as much as Silvio did and had been delighted when he had given her a newfangled camera device. She didn't ask questions. Yes, she was fine.

After sex she would go downstairs in her dressing gown, fetch a couple of drinks and the paper, then come back and doze while he read. He liked to feel a woman's body close to him while he was reading. It was as close as he could get to those times with Annunziata in the *bivio*.

After his reunion with Angelo, things had worked out well. So far. The old man—Silvio thought of him as an old man now—had been very fair. He had given Silvio a share of the take on the wharves and, for old times' sake, had given over his share in Mamie Christine's. Just as he had been forced to change his name years before, so Silvio had to change it again. He was now Sylvano Priola, a relative of Angelo's, newly arrived from New York, and publicly referred to by Angie as Vanni. He combed his hair differently and wore spectacles. It wasn't much of a disguise but he was nine years older, a bit heavier, and because of prison his skin was rougher. It was enough. In the family, of course, he was still Silvio.

He took off his glasses to read the paper. He was looking for

anything on the election and anything on the Mafia war. Today
both had made it to the front page of the *Picayune*.

WATERFRONT WAR CLAIMS 24TH VICTIM ran the headline.
Silvio read the article underneath.

> The body of a Sicilian roustabout was pulled out of the river
> early today. It was discovered between the Cotton Press and
> Quarantine. His throat had been cut by a wire, according to a
> spokesman for the city police department. The victim was
> later named as Giuseppe Figline, age thirty-two. He lived at
> 59 Esplanade Street and was a legal immigrant.
>
> The murder of Figline brings to twenty-four the number of
> killings that have taken place on the Mississippi waterfront this
> year. To begin with, this newspaper sympathized with the views
> of the police chief, the redoubtable David Martell, that so long
> as the brutality was confined to gangland murders, he proposed
> to do nothing about them. And it is certainly true that all the vic-
> tims so far have been Italians—and Sicilians at that. Slightly
> under half of them have been illegal immigrants, and those who
> haven't been garroted have been stabbed, which, we under-
> stand, is another traditional Sicilian method of murder.
>
> So it is easy to sympathize with Mr. Martell's views, that
> there is a gangland war going on at the waterfront and that the
> rest of us should leave well enough alone.
>
> But is that really so smart? Do we want this fine city of ours
> to become a violent cesspool, with murder as common here as
> it is in New York or Sicily itself? While this war continues to
> rage there is always the threat that it will spill over into the rest
> of the city and that innocent people will be hurt, or worse.
>
> Twenty-four dead bodies is an awful lot of mayhem. It is
> surely time that Mr. Martell showed us who is chief of police in
> New Orleans. We can't have one law for Sicilians and one for
> everyone else.

Silvio smiled to himself. He had been waiting for this, or something very like it. Phase one of the Cathedral Plan was working.

Now he turned to the other article he had been looking out for.
It was lower down the page and was headlined: MILTON TO RUN
ON LAW-AND-ORDER TICKET. It read:

Mr. James Milton, the former mayor, who is expected to be the main challenger to the incumbent, Harrison Parker, in the November election, last night announced that he will make a cleanup of the city law-enforcement agencies his number-one priority if elected.

Addressing the Women's Association of Metairie Suburb, at a fund-raising dinner ($10 a plate), Mr. Milton pledged to put more policemen on the streets, to pass stiffer penalties for convicted criminals, and to strengthen the customs and immigration department so that far fewer immigrants enter the country illegally and settle in New Orleans.

In part, Mr. Milton said: "This once-fine city is in danger of becoming a second New York, where the gangster has a free run, where the ordinary, law-abiding citizen is afraid to leave his house, and where, even if he stays at home, he is apt to be burgled. I aim to put a stop to that. When I was mayor we captured people like Nino Greco, notorious villains who were also illegal immigrants, and we sent them back to Europe, where they belong. Elect me and we'll do the same again."

Silvio lay back on the bed and let the newspaper slide out of his fingers to the floor. He reached for his cigarettes and lit one. Beside him, Virginia stirred slightly. He blew smoke into the room, a half smile on his face. It was time for phase two.

"We got a problem with the lottery." Angelo looked old today, Silvio thought. His skin was pale and it didn't look as though he had shaved properly, as though he couldn't be bothered. They had taken to meeting in the back room at Mamie Christine's. It was private.

Silvio put down the paper he was reading. The weeklong rain showed no signs of abating and the Mississippi had burst its banks at Doheny's Plantation, an hour upriver. Two people had been drowned.

"Yellow fever's broken out at Shreveport. The whole area's quarantined."

"Why is that a problem?"

"No one can get in or out. Nineteen people have died. They're burning tar in the streets to fumigate the place, and they've let the gas out of the street lamps. Bodies are being burned on the sidewalk, right where they fall. Nine people from a traveling Mexican circus have died—so they may have brought the fever with them. People are fleeing in droves, those who're outside the cordon."

Silvio thought of Annunziata, losing her child in the cholera outbreak. Sicily, they used to say, was a long way from God. So, it seemed, was Shreveport.

"Our man, the winner, hasn't been in touch. He may be dead; he may have fled."

"I still don't see why you're so worried."

Angelo groaned. "A winner's good publicity. People grow suspicious if there are no winners. They want to know where the money goes. Even if the winner's a patsy, we gotta have one."

"Can't you have someone go look?"

"I asked Mistretta and Cuono. Refused. They ain't stupid."

Vincent Mistretta and Luca Cuono, he remembered, were two of Angelo's *caporegimes*.

"So there'll be a delay."

"It don't work like that. The new license comes up next week. We know that the commission that awards the lottery franchise is split, almost fifty-fifty. If we can't administer it right, can't even come up with a winner, it'll count against us. We could lose the vote. What's more, Liotta will get it—and with the money he'll make he could overtake me." Angelo shook his head. "We gotta think of something."

Bourbon was brought in. In Sicily, Silvio had missed the bourbon. Now he missed the red wine from the hills of Montemaggiore. That was life for you.

The bourbon didn't help. An hour later they still hadn't solved their problem. Their muscle and money didn't matter. Yellow fever was yellow fever and no one would risk his life, no matter what threats or promises were made.

Two hours passed. Another bottle of bourbon was carried in, and the afternoon paper. The incessant rain had created a disaster at Doheny's Plantation. The levee had flooded and the death toll now stood at four.

"Jesus!" Angelo whistled, looking at the front page of the *Delta*. "I don't know which is the worse way to go, flood or fever."

"What did you say?" Silvio played with his eyeglasses.

Angelo pointed to the paper. "I said I didn't know which is worse, to die of a disease, or be drowned. Why?"

Silvio's eyes were shining. "Which is more important to you? To find a winner this week, or get a new license?"

Angelo stared at him, uncomprehending. "To get a new license. But we can't get one without the other. I don't see—"

"The man in Shreveport, the patsy who won the scam, he's on the payroll, right?"

"If he's alive, sure. But—"

"And he'll do as he's told?"

"Of course. What *is* this?"

"Announce that he's dead. Announce that under the circumstances—yellow fever in Shreveport and a burst levee at Doheny's Plantation—a prize this week is inappropriate anyway. Announce that you're donating the winnings to establish a relief fund for the victims of the Shreveport disaster and the Doheny Plantation rescue. You could even send the lottery steamboat to help."

Silvio smiled grimly at the other man. "It's a lot of money, Angie, and you're going to give it all away. But believe me, it will get you that new license. Who could resist you after such a gesture?"

Angelo grinned, and let out a soft whoop. "Real foxy, Silvio. I've been wondering whether you still had it in you. Now I know. You're my *consigliere* from now on. I don't know if Vito knows you're back yet, but he won't be in doubt for much longer, that's for sure."

Silvio could never approach St. Louis's Cathedral without trepidation. However, on this day at least, he knew where Martell was and it was nowhere near Chartres and St. Peter's streets.

He entered by the main door, accompanied by two or three other people, the women in hats. Silvio didn't know why women always wore hats to baptisms, but in America they did. He walked down the main aisle and turned off toward a group of people gathered near the font. He looked at his watch: ten minutes to noon.

Angelo saw him and halted his conversation with the man he was talking to. He shook hands with Silvio, then turned to the other man. "Judge, this is a relative of mine from New York. Thomas McCrystal . . . Vanni Priola. Vanni Priola . . . Judge McCrystal."

The two men shook hands.

"Excuse us, judge," said Angelo, leading Silvio away from the crowd. The judge nodded and turned back to the baptism.

"I didn't tell Anna-Maria you're coming," Angelo whispered. "Don't worry, she's family. Even if she recognizes you, she won't show it. She's a good girl."

Silvio nodded. "And Saltram?"

"He knows. I've already told him. I had to."

They moved toward the font, the service about to begin. Silvio kept out of the way, though. He had his own reasons for being here and they did not include being a godfather to Anna-Maria's first daughter.

At one point in the ceremony Anna-Maria did look his way. Their eyes met, she looked away—then suddenly looked back again. Silvio took off his spectacles, smiled, and almost imperceptibly, nodded. Then he put his glasses on again. For a moment Anna-Maria looked shocked and may even have swayed slightly on her feet. But then she recovered and turned back to the service.

Silvio transferred his attention to the judge. He had recognized his face but had not known his name. He had seen him in Mamie Christine's. Here was a judge who liked whores. That was New Orleans for you.

As soon as the baptism was over, Anna-Maria gave the baby to her mother to hold and came up to Silvio. "I gather you are new here, Mr. Priola," she said loudly.

"Yes."

She hooked her arm in his and they strolled down the aisle together. "This is what we missed, Silvio," she whispered.

"It's Vanni in public," he whispered back. Then: "I haven't forgotten—or forgiven."

She hugged his arm. "It's good to have you back. Father's missed you." She hesitated. "I missed you."

He looked down at her. "How is it with Saltram?"

"He's a good man. Safe. A good father. Not the lover that you were—I never had sex like I had with you. We were like rabbits—huh? But . . . it was lucky for me we didn't get married—" She felt him stiffen and hugged his arm again. "No, Vanni, it was hard on you, I know. But you would never have wanted to be the father

Dick has turned out to be. I miss the sex but I like being a mother. That's growing up, I suppose."

He stopped and looked down at her. "We all grow up, Anna-Maria."

They walked on. "Saltram knows I'm back. Angie told him."

She nodded. "He's as safe as I am. Don't worry."

They had reached the main door of the cathedral. People were standing outside in the sunshine, talking. There was to be a reception at Angie's, but no one seemed in a hurry to move. Anna-Maria leaned forward to kiss Silvio. "It's good to see you," she whispered. "Come and have dinner. We can talk." As she said "talk" she pressed his hand.

She left him and went back to her mother, to take the newly baptized baby.

Just then Silvio noticed a young man run into the square in front of the cathedral. He stiffened, but the man slowed, and approached Angelo. The two men conferred, then Angie looked across at Silvio. He beckoned him over. As Silvio approached, Angie said to the younger man, "Tell Mr. Priola here what you just told me."

The young man was still breathless from running. "Some of our men were ambushed this morning. Corner of Esplanade and North Claiborne."

Silvio's face betrayed no emotion. "And?"

"Enzo Fiorano was killed. Gorlasco was hit in the leg, someone else in the eye. It's bad, but that ain't all."

"What do you mean?" Angie was belligerent now.

"It was broad daylight. There was a buncha people around. Ordinary citizens. Some saw the attack, one got hit."

"Bad?" Angelo again.

"I ain't sure. But not dead."

Angelo looked at Silvio. "This will change things."

Silvio nodded. "Now Martell's got to move."

Angelo spoke to the man who had brought the message. "You did good. You can go home now."

"Thank you, Don Angelo." He went.

Angelo and Silvio walked across the square together, out of earshot of anyone else. They stopped.

"We ain't never tried anything like this before, Silvio."

"No. Phase one worked. Looks like phase two is on course as well."

Martell did move swiftly. One of the bystanders had heard one of the gunmen shout something like "This is for Carona." The remark was taken to mean that the ambush was a retaliation for the killing of Orazio Carona, one of Liotta's *caporegimes*. As a result, now that the gangland violence had spilled over to the general public, Martell made fourteen arrests, all of them known associates of Vittorio Liotta. One, Girolamo Regalmici, habitually wore a yellow oilskin rain cloak. Three witnesses said one of the attackers wore a yellow oilskin. Liotta himself was not arrested, since on the morning in question he was attending a funeral in Metairie suburb.

The speed of Martell's actions, and the fact that all those arrested were well-known gangland members, pleased the papers. "Who knows?" said *The Mascot*. "Perhaps these villains have been involved in some of the waterfront killings these past few months. Let them all hang." Reporters were allowed into the Parish Prison, where they found that, to a man, the accused protested their innocence. Some even had convincing alibis. However—and this was what clinched the argument against them for many people—three out of the fourteen were illegal immigrants.

A week later Harrison Parker was reelected mayor of New Orleans.

Silvio stopped at the top of the gangway and looked up. The liner towering over him had a familiar outline and he allowed himself a half smile.

"Welcome aboard the *Ustica*," said the officer before him, dressed in an all-white uniform. "The bridge is this way."

Silvio followed the man forward. The last time he had been aboard this ship had been in very different circumstances, when he had been fleeing Sicily. Now, as Angelo Priola's *consigliere*, he was treated with more respect.

The officer reached the steps to the bridge and began to ascend. Silvio followed. As he rose he looked out over the levee to the roofs and balconies of the city. Then across the river to Algiers. Would Annunziata ever see this? What would she think of it if she did? Mostly he tried not to think of her—it hurt too much—but today was different.

He reached the top of the outside staircase and saw that the door to the main bridge was open. He went in.

The captain came toward him, his hand out. "Happier times than our last meeting," he said.

Silvio nodded, accepting the handshake. "When do you leave?"

"In time to meet the tide in the Gulf. An hour from now. Mr. Priola said you wished to send someone a message."

"Yes." Silvio held up a package. "Give this to Ruggiero Priola in Palermo. He will know what to do with it."

"And in case customs should ask, may I know what is in the package? It's not opium this time, I hope."

Silvio smiled. "It's a book."

He had given a lot of thought as to how he should contact Annunziata when the time came. Now that the Cathedral Plan appeared to be working, he judged that the time was right. But he couldn't send a letter—he didn't want to put anything in writing about his whereabouts, and in any case Zata couldn't read. If she had someone read the letter to her, everyone would know in next to no time what he had said. But the book—Mark Twain's *Life on the Mississippi*—was different. Ruggiero Priola could give it to her secretly, and tell her the title. That would convince her that Silvio had sent it, and reveal where he was, that he wanted her to come to him. Ruggiero would do the rest. And it wouldn't give away anything to anyone else.

"Mr. Priola will be meeting the ship, as usual. I will give him the package as soon as we dock."

"Thank you."

Silvio shook hands again with the captain and went back down the steps off the bridge. He was half tempted to sail with the *Ustica* himself. How he would love to lie in the Sicilian country-side again, reading to Zata. It was extraordinary: she responded to his stories, first intellectually, then erotically. The rain, the mud in the streets, the smells of the cooking, the details of the women's clothes, his descriptions of the new music . . . it was, he supposed, a form of sensuality, of immersing herself in fresh, strange details, of escape, just as sex, sometimes, could be an escape. God, he missed her, just as he missed the eagles, the goats, the silver undersides of the leaves on the olive trees, the way the light caught the stonework of the *bivio*. New Orleans wasn't the same the second time around.

But he knew that was unrealistic. When he reached the levee he turned and looked up at the bridge. The captain, who had watched him leave the ship, saluted and closed the bridge door.

Silvio sat in the curtained carriage and looked across the square to the main entrance of St. Louis's Cathedral. It was nearly eleven A.M. He had been sitting here for half an hour, watching. And waiting. A quarter of an hour before, Natale Pianello had entered the building. Vito Liotta's *consigliere* had noticeably aged since Silvio had last seen him at Toussaint House. Then Angelo had arrived, with Vincent Mistretta and Luca Cuono, two of his *capo-regimes*. Then Pino Spatole, Angelo's *sottocapo*, had appeared moments before Vito Liotta himself, accompanied by his *capo-regimes*, Vanni Brancaccio and Biagio Gela. Carmen Sinagra, Liotta's *sottocapo*, had been the last to enter.

Silvio was surprised at the scope of this meeting. Gatherings between Dons sometimes took place in Sicily, but as he now understood things, Angelo and Vito held a top-level conference every year. They aired their grievances, discussed new business projects, settled disputes. Five attended from each side, he had been told, and the meetings were held in the vestry of the cathedral. This was a clever choice of venue: since no mafioso would violate the precincts of a cathedral, there was no need for hostages. Everyone felt safe.

Angelo had instructed Silvio to arrive last. It was still not certain that Vito knew Silvio was back in New Orleans and he wanted to surprise the other Don. The fox goes last, until the kill, as they said in Sicily. The meeting was set for eleven. Everyone else had arrived.

As the cathedral bell began to chime the hour, Silvio got down from the carriage. He entered the cathedral and strode down the nave. The vestry, he had been told, was at the far end of the building, past the altar and to the right. It was, he reminded himself grimly, a part of the cathedral he had never seen.

He found the room and entered without knocking.

Everyone was seated at a huge table covered by a green baize cloth. Angelo and his men sat down one side of the table, Liotta and his down the other.

Liotta fought hard to hide his shock at seeing Silvio, but he failed. His eyes widened, his tight mouth sagged open, he swallowed hard. Vito, Silvio was pleased to note, had not aged well. The sockets of his eyes had darkened, his hair had receded, and a vein in his temple stood out, meandering over his skull like a miniature Mississippi. The flesh on his hands and jaw had grown less tight and shiny—looking more like paper or parchment.

Silvio sat in the empty seat next to Angelo. The old man was savoring the effect Silvio's entrance had had on the other side. "Vito," he growled, "this is my new *consigliere*, a nephew of mine, Vanni Priola." He paused. "If anything should happen to him, an accident maybe . . . I'd take it personal, real personal. I, like you, rely on *omertà*."

He had said it. The reference to *omertà* drew attention to allegations, seven years ago, that Liotta was not a man of honor, that he had betrayed the Sicilian code of silence in telling Martell that Nino and Silvio were in New Orleans.

Vito placed both hands on the table, palms up. "Why are you saying this to me, Angie? I would have thought Silvio had grief enough, now that Alesso is marrying Annunziata."

Had Silvio been standing, he would have needed to sit down. *What was this?* He knew nothing about Annunziata marrying Alesso—Alesso! And Liotta realized that, of course. This information had to be very fresh. It was a typical Liotta barb, one that he had used to regain the ground he had just lost.

Silvio's mind reeled. Was this information even true? Liotta was quite capable of making it up, simply to disorient Silvio. He fought not to show his feelings, determined not to give Vito the satisfaction of seeing how dismayed he was. But he was sure that he had failed. His package wouldn't have gotten to her yet. Now it might be too late.

Vito never took his eyes off Silvio as he continued speaking. "What's got into Martell?" he growled. "All these arrests of my men! You really think we ambushed you, Angie? Days before this meeting? That ain't exactly smart now, is it?"

"Someone shot up Enzo Fiorano, made Maria a widow. Someone smashed Gorlasco's leg. He's still on the payroll but can't work, so it's costing me, same as the widow is. These things happened, Vito. You saying you weren't involved? What am I supposed to think? Who else gets to benefit?"

"It wasn't me, Angie. I swear."

"Maybe you got some freelances, Vito. Maybe you ain't pulling rank enough."

Angelo played his part well, Silvio thought. He wasn't overdoing it. Vito was genuinely puzzled and didn't as yet suspect a thing. Silvio fought to keep his mind off Annunziata. He had to concentrate on the business.

Angelo held up the palm of his hand. "Vito, we got other things to talk about. I just say this, then we can move on. Maria Fiorano is going to want revenge—or maybe you want to pay her?" It was a rhetorical question and he smiled grimly. "That's all I'm saying, Vito. There's a score to settle. Now let's move on. You got anything new?"

Liotta conferred briefly with Natale Pianello. He nodded and said, "We got one deal for you. Funeral parlors. There are seven companies doing funerals in the central part of the city. None of them does well. Why? Because their chief business comes from the hospitals and there are only three hospitals, two in my area, one in yours. They compete for the business, keeping their costs low. Result—seven outfits, each one making nigger profits. My idea is we can lean on the funeral parlors so that only one outfit services each hospital, gets all the business. Then we gradually put up prices. The three parlors start to make money, we take fifteen, twenty percent."

Angelo didn't confer with Silvio but replied immediately. "I congratulate you, Vito. A tidy idea. A little unexciting maybe, a bit—how can I put it?—*cipolla rossa,* but discreet, good business. The funeral parlors can be sewn up without anybody noticing. I like it. I accept."

Now it was Angelo's turn. He helped himself to water from a jug on the table. "Fire fighting is done in this city on a voluntary basis. Volunteers attach themselves to one of ten fire teams and are paid by the city according to whichever gets to a fire first. The most successful teams make a lot of money, hundreds of thousands of dollars a year. Since 1860 the alarms have worked by means of the Gamewell telegraph system: whoever sees a fire presses a button at one of the alarm posts situated around the city, and thirty seconds later the telegraph delivers the alarm simultaneously in the ten firehouses.

"Vanni here has made a map of the alarm posts. Twenty-three are in your area, Vito, twenty-eight in mine. From the alarm posts we have traced the wires and have found a way of intercepting the alarms before they reach the firehouses. This means we can arrange it that some firehouses receive the alarm thirty seconds or more before the others. We can therefore predetermine which firehouse team gets to a fire first, at least in the great majority of cases over any one year. These, of course, are the teams that will make most money.

"Now, we know there's fierce rivalry between the teams. On average, it takes them anywhere from five to eight minutes to reach a fire, and you've probably heard the stories of firemen reaching a fire before the rest of the team and hiding the fire hydrant under a barrel so that rival teams couldn't start fighting a fire, and claiming the award, before their own team arrived.

"We believe the teams will pay handsomely for the privilege of having this secret advantage so they have the odds permanently stacked in their favor. We have six teams in our area of town, you have four. It will be more effective if we operate together. We think you should pay us a small part of your earnings since we'll have to fix the wiring all over town, even in your areas, and that will cost us."

Liotta was conferring with Pianello. He looked up. "How much?"

"Ten percent of what you make."

"More than three would be an insult."

"I am willing to consider eight."

"Four."

"Seven and a half."

"Five."

"Six."

"Five, Angie. You can't do it at all without our help. Don't be greedy."

Angelo paused. "Five it is. Choose your teams and we'll arrange to fix the alarms as soon as you're ready."

The meeting broke up.

They left the cathedral one at a time so as not to attract attention, but Angelo and Silvio rendezvoused immediately afterward, at Mamie Christine's.

"You think he suspects anything?" asked Silvio. He wouldn't mention Annunziata. He didn't want the old man to see how raw he felt.

Angelo was on his first bourbon of the day. He shook his head. "Not yet, no."

"This fire fighting business. How long before it brings in any dough?"

Angelo shrugged. "Who knows? All that was just to keep him sweet. So he thinks it's business as usual. Only you and I know . . . that ain't true."

"Virginia, how well do you know Judge McCrystal?"

"Who?"

"You know, he's here from time to time, the oldish man who appears so fond of Kitty. He's got red hair and coughs a lot."

"Oh, you mean Professor Perran."

So that's what he called himself.

"Okay. How well do you know Professor Perran?"

"Why are you asking?"

"Ginnie!"

"Well . . . it's awkward."

"Why?"

She hesitated. "Mostly he likes Kitty but . . . sometimes . . . he pays for both of us."

Silvio pursed his lips. *Perfetto.* "You haven't forgotten how to use that camera I gave you?"

"Of course not. You've seen me work it lots of times. Why? . . . No, Silvio, no!"

He looked at her and smiled.

"Silvio, I won't." Then: "Please don't make me."

Silvio eased himself up on one elbow and held Virginia's chin in one hand. These sessions with her reminded him of Madeleine and helped him take his mind off Annunziata. "Ginnie, Ginnie. *Sono pugilato?* Am I a boxer? I thought you'd learned by now. This is a rough town. You've got to make the most of whatever hand you're dealt." He patted her shoulder. "I'm not asking you to get something too dirty . . . just something I can use to, well, call the shots if I need to."

"Such as?"

"A picture of him with you or Kitty. Just enough so he won't want his wife to know. Or anyone else."

"But how am I going to do that?"

"Does he drink?"

"Silvio, what's in that devious mind of yours?"

"Get him drunk. *Sborniato.* He doesn't have to be conscious when you take the picture. If he's passed out, it will be easier for you. Just make sure he's recognizable and in some sort of . . . disarray."

"What are you going to do with the photograph?"

"Bank it. I'll only use it if I need to. But I can't let this chance slip by. A fox who isn't hungry isn't a fox. There are only four judges in this town. If I could control one . . . well, that would be something. It would be like being *camerlengo* when they elect a Pope."

There was a silence in the room. Virginia was thinking. Then she said, "And if I do it, what will you do for me?"

He eyed her. "How would you like to go to the carnival ball?"

"Oh, Silvio! You mean it?"

"Of course I mean it."

"I'd love it. Lordy, all the other girls will be green as melons." She sat up. "Why didn't you say so before, you silly man." She gave Silvio a big kiss, on the lips.

20

Standing on the corner of Canal Street and Decatur, Silvio watched the pickpocket go to work. The man—whom Silvio knew to be a small, nimble Negro—was working the streetcar stops. He was dressed in a crimson velvet robe and an elaborate mask that gave him a long pointed nose and a permanent grin. It was the garb of a Venetian courtier.

He didn't stand out, though. On the contrary, this was the middle of Mardi Gras and a parade was due here at any moment. The street was thronged with clowns, kings and queens, devils and Chinese, sham soldiers, monkeys, Romeos, Hamlets, pages, people selling hot nuts, huge cigars, cotton candy, and rice cakes.

Strictly speaking, Silvio was too senior to be patrolling the streets, making collections from pickpockets. But the Mardi Gras was a busy time and manpower was stretched. It was the first carnival season since Silvio had been back in New Orleans and he had heard that the festivities had changed quite a bit. Originally held to celebrate Shrove Tuesday and the period of fasting known as Lent, the carnival season now started on Twelfth Night, January 6, and lasted virtually nonstop until the middle of February. There was a parade most afternoons and evenings, followed by balls in the French Opera House, the Grand Opera House, or the Washington Artillery Hall. Visitors flocked to the city, either down the Mississippi on a steamboat, or on the new railroads. Private railroad cars painted fancy colors stood in profusion in the Carrollton Railroad Station. The visitors brought cash with them—which was what attracted the pickpockets and made their trade a particularly lucrative one during Mardi Gras.

Pickpocketing had long been a protection racket in the quarter. Angelo had the area bounded by Canal Street, Royal Street,

Esplanade, and the river. Liotta had the streets in the Quarter to the north of that. The pickpockets paid twenty dollars a day for the privilege of being allowed to work their particular patch, except at carnival time, when the rate went up to thirty a day. Angelo's outfit was taking 120 dollars a day out of Canal Street alone.

Silvio watched as the "Venetian courtier" stood back from the crowd at the streetcar stop. Sooner or later, someone would pat their pocket where they kept their wallet, to check that it was still there. That would mark him as the courtier's victim. Then, when the streetcar arrived, the courtier would join the throng as it pushed to board. At the last moment he would "allow" himself to be elbowed out of the way—and make his escape.

Silvio observed, amused, as the streetcar arrived and the scene was played out to perfection. He then ambled after the courtier, who walked north a couple of blocks until he came to a small thoroughfare known as Exchange Place. He ducked in there. Dusk was fast approaching and he could go through the wallet in relative peace.

"Hello, Arthur," Silvio said.

The masked head turned swiftly toward him. The grin was obscene.

"Jesus, Mr. Priola. Ah thought yo' was the po-lice."

"Just enjoying the carnival, and making the collection."

"Who are your fancy friends?"

Silvio was mystified by this remark, until he noticed that Arthur's masked face was looking over his shoulder.

Silvio turned—and went cold.

Three figures stood behind him. A clown, a devil, and a Chinese. They must have followed him into the alley as nimbly as he had followed Arthur.

"Get lost, nigger," said the devil, in English.

Arthur ran.

Outside, in Canal Street, the parade was beginning to pass by. The theme was "Light" and many of the floats were lit—for the first time ever—with electric lightbulbs. That's what Silvio had particularly wanted to see. He thought Mamie Christine's ought to be one of the first outfits to have the new lighting.

Crowds lining Canal Street were cheering and clapping.

"Now, you *mezzatacca*," said the devil. He unwrapped something from around his waist. A garrote.

They closed in on Silvio.

His mind was racing. They were Liotta's men, of course, despite the fact that Vito had agreed at the meeting in the vestry that no harm should come to Silvio. The Cathedral Plan was working its way through, but it now looked as if Silvio would not live to see its end.

The others inched closer, trying to back Silvio against the wall of the alley. If he allowed that to happen—*finito*.

Suddenly the Chinese lunged at him. Silvio aimed a punch to fend him off, but as he did so the clown threw himself forward and grabbed his other arm. In an instant the two men were trying to drag him to the ground. After a brief tussle he felt his legs being kicked from under him. His back hit the cold and dirty cobbles in the alleyway. The two men were on him and he sensed the third man, the devil, moving behind his head.

Outside the alley, in Canal Street, the parade was passing. The dusk was turning to dark and in any case all eyes were fixed elsewhere.

The clown moved, shifting his weight across Silvio's body. The Chinese man was at his feet—and Silvio, realizing what was happening, immediately kicked and kicked and kicked. The clown was trying to remove his boots. Silvio knew why. The streets were muddy, scattered with stones, broken glass, broken shells, and splinters of wood. Even if he broke free, he wouldn't be able to run very fast without his boots.

The Chinese man sat on his feet. Despite Silvio's kicking, the clown managed to prize the boot off his right foot. Then he set about the left one.

Silvio gave a heave and kicked at the same time. The Chinese man clung on, but the clown was dislodged. This was the only chance Silvio would have. He slipped his left foot out of his boot and broke free. The devil, with both hands on the garrote, was slow to intervene but shouted, "Stop him!"

Too late. Silvio was on his feet and running. He couldn't go west, toward the parade, because the devil blocked his way. So he went east. Exchange Place gave onto Iberville Street, which ran north–south. It was deserted; everyone was watching the parade. South of where Exchange Place joined Iberville, Exchange Alley ran off, going east. Silvio dashed in there.

Just as he reached Iberville, however, his right foot struck a nail in a horseshoe that must have fallen off a mule. He gasped in pain and had to stop to pull the nail clear of his flesh.

The others reached the end of Exchange Place. Silvio ran, limping now, down Exchange Alley, his mind still spinning. He couldn't keep running indefinitely, not in his stockinged feet in these streets, not with his right foot bleeding. He had to find a sanctuary, had to find help. He was approaching Bienville Street when the idea came to him.

At the corner of Exchange Alley and Bienville Street there was a bar and restaurant. Outside were crates of garbage—bottles, old food that had been scattered about by scavenging dogs and rats. He ignored it. The others were too close. If he was right, if his memory hadn't failed him, what he wanted was a block away, on the corner of Bienville and Royal.

He turned left as he reached the end of Exchange Alley. Or he would have if he hadn't slipped on some of the garbage in the alleyway. His feet went from under him and he threw out an arm to break his fall. Straight onto some shards of broken plates. The ball of his left hand was sliced, and for the second time he yelped in pain. His spectacles fell off.

But he could now see what he wanted, and he forced himself to his feet. Bienville Street was as deserted as Iberville had been. The new electric lights on the parade floats were as popular as the new street lighting on Canal Street itself.

The others were close behind but Silvio forced himself forward. There was only a block to go. Twice on the way his foot struck something—tiles fallen from roofs? more horseshoes?—but he willed himself to ignore the pain.

Then he was there. At the meeting with Liotta, Angelo had mentioned the plan to infiltrate the fire teams. As part of his research for this, Silvio had compiled a map of firebox alarms in the city. And he had remembered correctly: there was one at the corner of Bienville and Royal. He ran up to the box and punched the button. He punched it again, and again, and again, then sagged, exhausted and in pain, against the post supporting the firebox alarm. Now he was in the hands of the fire teams. Normally, he knew, they took five to eight minutes to reach a fire. He had to hold out that long.

The devil and his two cronies knew that, too, however, and they were now upon him, circling him, moving in. The clown threw

himself at Silvio, and when he tried to punch him away the man
hung on to Silvio's wrist. The Chinese followed up and grabbed
Silvio around the waist. This time the devil joined in, too. Their
immediate aim was obvious—to drag Silvio off the street to a
small alley near a boarded-up cobbler's shop.

Silvio kicked out to stop them, tried to hook his leg around part
of the firebox alarm, as a delaying device. But the clown grabbed
his foot and twisted it free. Silvio was hauled away from the post.
He judged that a minute had elapsed since he had pressed the
alarm.

As the Chinese man and the clown dragged him along the sidewalk, the devil aimed a kick at Silvio. The pain was exhausting,
rendering him less able to struggle. His face and hair were now
matted with dirt and grit.

Two minutes had surely elapsed.

Once they had Silvio in the alley, the Chinese man held him
down while the other two men began to rain kicks on him. They
kicked his face and neck, they attacked his kidneys and aimed at
his groin. He felt his lip punctured and one of his eyes began to
swell. At one point, however, he managed to grab the devil's ankle
as his foot came toward him. Silvio pulled and twisted the ankle at
the same time. The devil, upended, squealed in pain as he fell,
striking his head on the wooden shack that formed one side of the
alley.

That bought time for Silvio, but the devil was now fuming with
rage. He brandished the garrote. "Okay, hold him," he growled.
"Let's do this thing."

The clown now added his weight to that of the Chinese man
and Silvio's body was pressed hard to the ground. Silvio struggled
but the kicking had achieved its intended effect; he was much
weaker now. Surely four minutes must have elapsed?

Silvio felt the devil behind him. He struggled to free his arms,
but the clown held on to one of them and the other was pinned by
the weight of his body. Silvio pulled and pulled. One arm came
free, just as he felt the garrote going around his neck. He grabbed
the rope just under his ear and wedged his fingers between it and
his flesh.

"His hand!" hissed the devil. "Grab his fingers."

But it wasn't easy to unravel Silvio's fingers, and after a
moment he felt the weight on his body slacken. The clown had

moved. Silvio heaved himself upward, but he was too weak now for it to mean anything.

Then Silvio smelled burning. What was happening? He saw the clown putting a cigarette to his mouth and, moments before it happened, realized what they were going to do. The clown held the burning end of the cigarette to Silvio's hand.

Jesus! The pain was scalding. But he still didn't let go of the garrote—he didn't dare. Within seconds of doing that he would be dead. He'd never get a second chance, not once that rope started to bury itself in his neck.

But the pain from the cigarette was getting worse. He could smell burning skin and his whole hand seemed to be swelling. He had to stop it—he couldn't endure it any longer.

And then he heard the bell of the fire team. It sounded about four blocks away.

But the devil had heard the bell, too, and had tightened his grip on the garrote. Could he strangle Silvio even with his fingers inside the rope? He was certainly trying to. The cigarette still ravaged his skin. Drying tears caked the corners of Silvio's eyes.

The sound of the fire bell was getting closer. He had to hang on, maybe another thirty seconds. The pain in his hand, though, was beginning to outweigh his fear of the garrote. Was the rope beginning to starve his brain of blood, making him light-headed? He wanted it all to stop; he wanted to sleep. Please God . . . !

Silvio heard voices. Firemen sometimes ran ahead of the engines. Were those firemen's voices that he could hear? He tried to shout for help but was too weak.

Suddenly the burning at his hand stopped and the weight was lifted from his body. The rope around his throat went slack. The three men in costumes got up. Two gave him a final kick and then, casually, so as not to draw attention to themselves, they sauntered away. The devil, Silvio noticed, was limping.

From the *Times-Democrat*:

AMBUSH CASE PUT BACK FOR THIRD TIME

The trial of the fourteen Sicilians arrested in the wake of the shooting at Claiborne and Esplanade streets in May last year, when one faction of roustabouts was ambushed by another, with guns, and when an innocent bystander lost an eye, has been delayed for a third time. The trial was originally scheduled to take place last September; it was then put back a month, then to January, and will not now take place until the second half of February, according to sources inside the district attorney's office.

The reason for the delay, according to the source, is that a number of witnesses have changed their stories and two of the defendants are too young to appear in court.

The defendants have now been held in prison, without trial, for eight months. Their defense attorney, Mr. James Falmouth, described this chain of events as "a disgrace. My clients are innocent and should either be brought into court, to rebut the charges against them, or released. If the trial does not take place in February, as now scheduled, I intend to petition the governor to have all charges dropped."

It is understood that some of the witnesses who changed their story now claim that in the wake of the ambush they were pressured by the police, who were anxious to make rapid arrests to satisfy public opinion. Many citizens were outraged by the attack, made in broad daylight, and which seemed to indicate that a waterfront gang war had spilled over to the rest of the city.

Several witnesses, the *Times-Democrat* has been told, are now less confident of the identifications they made at police request either on the day of the attack or the following day.

Whatever the outcome, it is noticeable that since the arrests, criminal activity on the waterfront has fallen remarkably. All concerned citizens will be thankful for that.

"You're late!"

"I'm sorry, Mr. Priola," said the doctor, letting himself into the back room of Mamie Christine's. "But it's my day at the orphanage and we never know how many patients there will be." He lifted Silvio's foot and carefully unwrapped the bandage. It was nearly forty-eight hours since he had trodden on the nail while being chased in Iberville Street.

"Orphanage?"

"Yes. All the doctors from the Charity Hospital help out there. Free of charge, of course."

Silvio watched as the doctor went to work on his foot.
Orphans—and orphanages—had played a big part in his life, he
reflected. He winced as the doctor applied some iodine to his
wound. The attack on him by Liotta's men had shaken him, but
not in the way that he expected. Silvio wasn't a coward, he wasn't
stupid, and he wasn't old. He still loved the whores and the music
of CustomHouse Street—he would never get tired of that. He
loved having fancy clothes and people to do things for him. But
he had never been the same since he had been forced to return to Sicily, and had been rescued—if that was the word—by
Annunziata.

"You work free?"

"Sure. Who's going to pay us—the orphans?" The doctor
smiled.

"Where is this orphanage?"

"Top end of Esplanade."

"How many?"

"Hundred and twenty, hundred and thirty maybe."

"What sort of treatment do you give?"

"It varies. Today I had to stitch a scalp. Someone had their hair
pulled out in a fight."

Silvio winced again.

The doctor was rebandaging his foot. "You'll live. The wound's
quite clean."

"What else? What other treatment, I mean?"

"Well, the big thing right now is to get them some fresh lemons,
oranges, fruit."

"That's a treatment?"

"Sure. You see it a lot in poor people—scurvy, it's called.
Bleeding gums, pains in the arms and legs, anemia. It's obviously
caused by a deficiency in the diet. We don't know what, but lemon
juice, fresh oranges, grapefruit clear it up in no time. I take what I
can, and so do the other doctors, but there's never enough."

Silvio's thoughts went right back to his first lesson with Nino,
that day in Bivona, when—who was it?—yes, Frederico Imbaccari had been made to send half his orange crop to the orphanage
at Santo Stefano.

"There," said the doctor. "You can put your shoe back on again
now. I'll come again in a couple of days, to take the bandage off
and check. But I don't expect any problems."

"I want you here tomorrow—"

"It's too soon. You're fine until—"

"No. Come tomorrow. At this time. I'll take you down to the docks, to the Priola wharves. You can have all the lemons and oranges you want."

From an editorial in the *Times-Democrat*:

SICILIANS MAY BE RELEASED TODAY

Is the peace that New Orleans has known these past months about to be shattered? The rumors coming from judicial circles that the fourteen Sicilians held after the shooting at Claiborne and Esplanade streets in May last year are about to be released, for lack of evidence, will be a cause of concern for all right-thinking people in this city.

The law is a fine thing, and must be upheld. But who can have failed to note that while these men have been in Parish Prison, violence on our streets—and on our wharves in particular—has all but disappeared? This, surely, is evidence itself, a silence far more eloquent than any words we could offer.

The law must be followed. But the citizens of New Orleans will be watching events from here on, and paying particular attention to what happens on the wharves. If a return to violence should now occur, on anything like the scale that took place before, we will know who to hold responsible: those who are about to be released—and those who release them.

Silvio gazed down at the carnival ball. It was three days since the attack on him and he had recovered most of his strength and composure. This evening the French Opera House was rendered as ancient Egypt, and the carnivalgoers were all decked out as Egyptian gods and goddesses. The band of the 71st Regiment was playing "If I Ever Cease to Love." Many of the women at the ball, on Shrove Tuesday itself, were debutantes, being presented to society by their parents for the first time, and they wore white ball gowns.

In Silvio's box were Angelo's wife, Anna-Maria, and Dick Saltram. Silvio had not forgotten his promise to Virginia, and she accompanied his party. The older women were dressed in long

ball gowns, in any color but white. Silvio had bought Virginia a
new gown for the evening and she was happier than he had ever
seen her. Vincent Mistretta and Luca Cuono, Priola *caporegimes*,
stood nearby, acting as bodyguards for the evening. Angelo had
not yet arrived. His health had not been good lately—liver
trouble—and he had a doctor's appointment. Another tradition of
the carnival ball was that once you had left it you were not allowed
to reenter.

The band changed to a slower tune, a waltz, and Anna-Maria
stood up and approached Silvio. "Dance?" she said.

On the dance floor, Silvio whispered, "We haven't done this
since the *Syracusa*. At least I don't throw up anymore."

She smiled. "At one point, back then, I thought it was the idea
of sex that made you feel ill."

He smiled back. "I was really naive, huh?"

"There was a certain charm about it." She pressed her groin
to his.

He was surprised, but immediately aroused. She had always
been able to do that to him.

"Don't worry," she said, "it's crowded here. No one can see."
She moved against him. "Have you not noticed I've been getting
slimmer?"

"*Sono cieco?* Am I blind? Of course I have."

"I've rented a small house, Silvio. On Esplanade, out of the
way. We could go there, on Tuesdays. Like in the lugger.
Remember? Remember what I used to do to you?"

Silvio did indeed remember.

"I'll do it to you again. I'll bet no one does that like I do."

It was true. God, it was true. There'd been Annunziata in the
meantime, of course. But he didn't want to think of her. Just then
he saw a woman staring at him. He stared back. There was something familiar about her, but he couldn't quite figure out what.
Then he had it. He looked down at Anna-Maria. "Will you excuse
me? I've just seen an old friend."

"I'll excuse you only if you agree to come to my place on
Esplanade on Tuesdays."

He gave her a kiss on the cheek. "Tell me how to find it, and I'll
be there." Then he was gone.

He reached the edge of the dance floor. The woman saw him
coming. She turned toward him but made no move forward.

"Stella," he whispered. "Is it you?"

She knew she knew him. That's why she had been staring. But she hadn't recognized him yet.

"It's Silvio," he said gently. "Remember?"

Her hand went to her mouth. But then she smiled, almost sheepishly. "Oh, my! You're back."

He nodded. "Same me, but a new name. Vanni Priola. You can guess why."

He guided her to a table, taking two glasses of champagne from a passing waiter. They sat down and toasted one another.

"You know Nino's in jail?" he said softly.

She nodded. "Don't worry. I'm okay. I found a man, a good man. He ain't here tonight; he's a captain of a steamboat and he's working. I'm doing fine." She sipped her champagne. "I'm sorry about Madeleine."

"Yes. Vito Liotta had her killed. That's one reason I'm back. He's got to pay."

There was another pause. Then, still in a whisper, he said, "Stella, what happened to Madeleine . . . to her body . . . do you know?"

She nodded again. "She's buried in the cemetery by the Ursuline Convent on Chartres. After the way she got killed, they took pity on her, gave her a decent funeral."

"And her child?"

"Edward? He lives with me. I adopted him."

"How old is he now?"

"Twelve."

"And . . . does he know?"

"Oh yes. I ain't hid nothing."

"Does he look like her?"

She nodded.

He looked across to his own table. Angelo had just arrived. "I'd better be getting back. Where do you live, Stella? I'd like . . . I'd like to see Edward. Would that be okay by you?"

She smiled. "Sure, Silvio—I mean Vanni. I'm at 421 Dauphine. Come and eat lunch. You know I was always a good cook."

"I will. Soon." He rose, kissed her, and moved back across the dance floor. As he went he noticed Carmen Sinagra, Liotta's *sottocapo*. He was limping. That answered one question at least. Now he knew who the devil had been.

When he arrived back at the table, Angelo was seated next to Silvio's place. He didn't look good, but now was not the time to discuss health. As Silvio sat down, the Capo leaned across and whispered, "Liotta's men were released today. The doctor told me. He's physician at the Parish Prison."

"What reason?"

"Insufficient evidence, according to the DA. Two were too young to stand trial, three illegal immigrants have been repatriated to Sicily. The eyewitnesses have changed their tune. They're no longer sure they were fired on by the people they first identified. It's a mess."

"How's Martell taking it?"

"Hard. He's angry, feels he's failed."

"Does he suspect anything?"

Angelo shook his head. "We were lucky with those illegals. That made it real."

"And Liotta?"

"Mad as hell. Bewildered as a wasp that's hit the windowpane. What would you expect? He knows something funny is happening, but he ain't sure what. He must be working on his revenge right now."

Silvio shook his head. "Not if he's smart. If he's smart he'll stay cool, allow the heat to go out of the situation. If he acts too soon he's the obvious suspect. So, for once, he won't act too quick—and that gives us time, and the initiative. He'll plan something careful, something spectacular to show he hasn't lost his touch. But it has to be safe from his point of view. That will take a while. For once, we're ahead of him. Phase two worked perfectly."

"Which means . . . phase three can begin?"

"Today is February eleventh. We need to move fast for some of the same reasons Liotta won't. Say three weeks from now. Make sure it's a dark, rainy night. And that Liotta's in town."

"See, you turn this key here, put the engine on the track, release the lever—and watch!"

Silvio took off his glasses and watched as the miniature railroad engine ran along the tracks, going 'round and 'round in a circle. He was enchanted, both by the machine—one of the new clockwork models from Germany—and by the boy. Edward was dark, like Madeleine. He had Madeleine's brown eyes, her voice, her

skin, the same pucker to his lips when he laughed. And he laughed
a lot. Stella had done a good job, Silvio thought, and so had her
husband, who was with his steamboat today. Apparently he loved
gadgets and machines, and had treated his adopted son to this
magnificent toy.

So far the lunch was turning out to be a great success. It had
begun awkwardly, but that had been Silvio's fault. Though he told
himself that in theory he liked children, he was in practice rather
nervous around them; they were so adult one minute and so
childish the next. Then Edward had come up to him and asked
point-blank, "Are you my real father?"

"No," said Silvio sadly. "I wish I was. But I knew your mother
well. You can be proud. She was a fine person." The boy was just
like him, an orphan.

"That's what Stella says. I can't remember her really, except her
smell. I was two when she caught the fever."

Stella had looked at Silvio, her eyes imploring him to keep up
the pretense. She had said that she hid nothing from the boy, but
clearly that didn't extend to the cause of Madeleine's death.

"Do you visit your mother's grave?" Silvio asked.

"Sometimes. We take flowers."

"Would you take me? I don't know where it is."

Edward looked at Stella.

She nodded. "Come back afterward. I'll have coffee ready."

The boy led Silvio along St. Philip's Street and then onto
Chartres. Silvio double-checked that his bodyguard was nearby.
There was no need for the child to know, but he wasn't taking any
chances.

At the convent, Edward rang the bell. After a moment the gate
was opened by a nun.

"I've come to visit my mother's grave," said Edward seriously.
"This is an old friend of hers."

The nun smiled and let them in. "You know where to go?"

Edward nodded. "Thank you, Sister Bridget."

Inside, he led Silvio across a cloister and through an arch.
Something about the convent—the smell perhaps, or the peace—
reminded Silvio of Quisquina.

Through the arch was a green patch of ground with trees and
carved headstones. Edward walked straight across to a headstone

beneath a tree. "Here," he said. "Look, it says, 'Madeleine Du-
pont, fallen angel.' I can read."

Tears were forced into Silvio's eyes, but he held them back. Be
hard on the inside, he told himself. He had known Madeleine was
dead, of course he had. But seeing her grave like this, he felt her
loss all over again. And seeing her grave, with her child playing
and skipping by the headstone, set his mind in a whirl.

Madeleine was dead but she lived on in Edward. The similarity
was uncanny. His thoughts tumbled over themselves. Nino would
live on in Annunziata, as Angelo would in Anna-Maria. Even
Anna-Maria had children. He, Silvio, was the odd one out—
orfano, no parents, no children, no bloodline to continue after
him.

He placed the flowers he had brought on the grave and stood up
again. Silvio suddenly felt very lonely. He had brains, and had
used them to fashion a niche here in New Orleans. Yet, he now
understood, that wasn't enough. He had become too obsessed by
Liotta. Settling his scores was important, but it shouldn't be the
whole of his life. The other half was Annunziata. Madeleine had
been taken from him but Annunziata hadn't, not yet. There was
still time to do something about that. It would complicate matters,
might even fuck up the Cathedral Plan completely, but it was
possible.

He looked down at Madeleine's headstone a final time. He was
glad he had come. She had helped him see what he must do.

21

David Martell was not a tall man. His chief characteristics were a bushy, drooping mustache and a floppy fedora, which he always wore when he was outside. Of Irish extraction, his father had been a detective in New Orleans, and his brother was a detective in Memphis. He was unmarried and lived with his mother on Franklin Street. He was, in fact, married to his job and worked in his office most evenings until eight or nine. No matter how late he worked, he always made an early start the next day.

On Tuesday, March 23, 1891, he worked late at City Hall as usual. He finally took his fedora from the hat stand just inside his office door at 8:40 P.M. and went out. A light rain was falling. His first stop was Dominick Virgut's oyster restaurant on Rampart and Poydras streets. After policing, Martell's only other passion was oysters, and Virgut's had the best.

The chief was in the restaurant for over an hour, chatting and eating oysters and drinking milk—he never drank alcohol. He left Virgut's about ten-twenty-five. It was still raining, and he rolled up his trousers to keep them clear of the mud.

To reach home he had to walk west on Rampart, before turning north on Girod. It was dark that night, and not only because it was raining. The new electric streetlights were temperamental, dimming and brightening every so often for no apparent reason.

As he reached the corner of Girod and Basin streets, Martell was passed by a boy of twelve or thirteen, going in the opposite direction. As the boy went past he looked up at Martell, his eyes searching the chief's face. Martell walked on. A few moments later the boy whistled. This whistle would later be recalled. It was a low-pitched, two-tone whistle, and carried in the evening air.

Martell turned left on Basin Street and approached Franklin.

About halfway along this block there was a small shack, a break in the tall houses but with a covered porch in front that extended over the sidewalk. When he reached the porch, Martell stopped to light a cigar. As he fumbled for the matches in his pocket, a shot rang out in the dark from across the street. Martell was hit in the shoulder and his body was thrown back against the shack. Dropping his cigar, he reached for his own gun, but more shots resounded in the night and he was hit again, in the stomach and legs. Nevertheless, Martell's fingers found his gun and dragged it from its holster. He stumbled into the street. Before he could pull the trigger, however, more shots came out of the darkness, spattering his chest and arms.

Still Martell came forward. He got off one or two shots into the night, but they coincided with a fourth fusillade from across the street. This time he was jerked one way and another, the gun fell from his hand, he sank to his knees, and pitched facedown into the mud.

The sound of the last fusillade died on the night, leaving just the hiss of the rain. For a brief time Martell's body lay in the street, being rained on, with no other sound. Then a few voices could be heard in the distance, wondering where exactly the shooting was coming from.

In the immediate vicinity all was quiet. No one moved or stirred. No one wanted to be next.

Then a clatter of footsteps reverberated on the wooden sidewalk. Running away.

Silvio watched as Anna-Maria's eldest child, a boy called Angelo Junior, wriggled on his grandfather's lap, reached up, and pulled old Angie's whiskers. At times like this, Silvio could get moody. He was still a young man, still enjoyed his afternoons and evenings at Mamie Christine's but, more and more, he liked coming to these meetings at Angie's. Part of him liked domesticity.

Anna-Maria appeared in the room, with a coffee jug, smiling. She really was looking trim these days. She took her son from his grandfather's lap.

"Coffee?" said Angelo.

"Sure." Silvio waited for Anna-Maria to take her son from the room. "Okay, tell me what you hear." He took off his spectacles.

"Parker moved swiftly. He ordered his deputy chief of police to pick up as many of Liotta's men as he could lay his hands on—including Vito himself. Last I heard, there were seventeen in the Parish Prison. The yellow oilskin was real foxy. At least three people spotted it, and of course remembered it from the ambush case. In fact, everything's happening just as you said it would, that day in the cathedral. There's only one problem."

Silvio looked sharply at Angelo. "Which is?"

"Martell's not dead."

"What!"

Angelo nodded. "It's true. He was hit eleven times—and still he lives. He's bad, of course, very bad. But he might just recover."

"Where was he hit?"

"Everywhere but in the head and heart."

Silvio frowned. "How could someone be hit eleven times and live?"

"It happens. It's happened."

Silvio scratched his chin. This might sink his whole plan. "Is there—?"

"No," said Angelo firmly. "We couldn't even get into the hospital, let alone the room he's in."

"Is he talking?"

"I can't say. Naturally we're getting our information from the policemen on the payroll. And from Parker, of course. I'll stay in touch, but we can't make ourselves too obvious."

Anna-Maria stuck her head back around the door. "You want the papers?"

She answered her own question and carried them into the room. She had the *Mascot*, the *Picayune*, the *Times-Democrat*, and the *Delta*. The shooting obviously occupied the front pages of each of them. POLICE CHIEF GUNNED DOWN said the *Mascot*. MARTELL HIT 11 TIMES IN SICILIAN ATTACK ran the *Delta*. But it was the *Picayune* that pleased Silvio the most. Its headline was just one word: VENDETTA! And below: "Sicilian racketeer and sixteen others held after police chief is gunned down. Attack believed to be revenge for arrests in the North Claiborne Street ambush case." The main article read:

Mr. David Martell, the New Orleans chief of police, was shot several times last night by a number of assailants who attacked him on Girod Street between Basin and Franklin streets. Mr.

Martell, who was on his way home after dinner and a long day at the office, attempted to return the fire, but it is not known whether he injured any of his attackers. He was rushed to Charity Hospital, where his condition was described as "critical."

Police responded quickly to the attack and by two o'clock this morning, when the *Picayune* went to press, some seventeen men, all Sicilians, had been arrested and incarcerated in the Parish Prison. Among them is Vittorio Liotta, a fruit importer, who many police suspect is head of one of two Sicilian families in New Orleans who are contesting control of the fruit wharves on the Mississippi.

The attack on Mr. Martell is believed in some quarters to be a revenge assault brought about by his arrest of a number of men last year who were alleged to have taken part in an ambush of roustabouts working for the rival Priola family, which also controls part of the fruit wharves. Following that ambush, in which one man was killed and several people were injured, including innocent bystanders, Mr. Martell arrested fourteen men belonging to the Liotta faction, though not including Mr. Liotta himself. However, charges were later dropped against these fourteen, eleven of whom were subsequently released (the other three, illegal immigrants, were returned to Sicily).

Besides arresting these suspects, the police also spent the latter part of yesterday evening finding witnesses to this cowardly attack. Among the evidence known to have been collected so far are certain witnesses who saw one of the assailants wearing a yellow oilskin rain cloak. More than one policeman has remarked to the *Picayune* that a yellow oilskin rain cloak was worn by one of the defendants in the earlier ambush incident.

The mayor of New Orleans, Mr. Harrison Parker, has promised that "no effort will be spared in this case to search out and prosecute all felons who were responsible for this dastardly crime." Meanwhile, the *Picayune* will keep readers informed of Mr. Martell's well-being.

When he finished reading, Silvio handed the paper across to Angelo and sat thinking as the other man cast his eyes down the columns.

At length Angelo looked up.

"If Martell lives," said Silvio softly, "he might just identify his attackers."

"He's on the payroll."

"Angie! Don't be naive. That won't make any difference this time. It won't matter whose payroll he's on. If he saw who shot him, he'll finger them. Wouldn't you?"

There was silence between them.

Then Silvio said, "The *Picayune* article says exactly what we want said. Phase three is working like I promised it would. We can't lose our nerve now." He looked hard at Angelo. "There must be someone at the hospital, someone who owes us a lot. The article says Martell's condition is weak. It won't take much. There must be something we can do."

Angelo was shaking his head. "I don't like it. It's too risky. We could jeopardize our whole plan—"

"There'll *be* no plan if Martell lives. Don't you see, Angie, if Martell comes out of this, if he fingers his attackers, if the world then finds out what you and I already know, we're in trouble, *bad* trouble. So don't tell me you don't like it. Just get one of our payroll people to repay his debts. I don't care how it's done. Just make sure it happens, and happens soon."

The New Orleans Charity Hospital was located on Gironde and Cannon streets, near the gasworks. It was a three-story building made up of six wings leading off a long central corridor. Ironically, it was funded by the tax levied on immigrants landing at New Orleans.

Throughout the night the mayor had led the vigil at Martell's bedside. There were doctors, nurses, police, reporters, his widowed mother. Dominick Virgut, who owned the oyster restaurant, was there some of the time, as were various city officials.

Martell himself drifted in and out of consciousness. Around eleven the next morning, the doctors ordered everyone out of the room.

"But what about security?" complained Parker. "These people tried to kill him. They might come again."

"Very well," said the doctor. "One guard. But one only."

Parker looked at the four police in attendance. His eyes settled on Frank Cassidy. "Okay, Frank," he said. "You're the biggest. You stay."

Cassidy returned Parker's stare. "Yessir!"

The rest trooped out.

Cassidy stood by the bed. He listened as the group slowly drifted down the corridor outside. He waited a few moments for the sound to disappear, then opened the door a fraction. Yes, they had all gone. There was no one within thirty yards of him.

Quickly he closed the door again and went back to the bed. He didn't dare dwell too much on what he was about to do. But he had been receiving payoffs from the Priolas for three years now and had always known that someday he would be called on to return the service.

He eased one of the pillows from under Martell's head. The chief stirred and appeared to wake. He opened his eyes and Cassidy froze. Then Martell's eyes closed again and he lay still.

Without waiting any longer, Cassidy gripped the pillow in two hands and laid it across Martell's face. Later he recalled how weak the chief had been, how frighteningly easy his debt to the Priolas had been repaid. Martell had hardly struggled at all.

From the *Times-Democrat*:

MARTELL DEAD; LIOTTA GANG CHARGED WITH MURDER

The New Orleans chief of police, Mr. David Martell, died today, shortly before noon. Dr. Robert Coe, physician-in-chief at Charity Hospital, who certified the chief as dead, at 11:48 A.M., said that Mr. Martell died in his sleep, from complications arising from bullet and shotgun wounds sustained when he was attacked last evening.

Police Sergeant Frank Cassidy, from Metairie, was with Martell at the last. In an interview he said that the chief opened his eyes and groaned. "I went to stand next to the bed," said Cassidy. "The chief looked up at me and then his eyes closed. He tried to say something but I couldn't hear. I leaned down and held my head next to his mouth. Then I could hear him quite distinctly. He said, 'The dagos did it.' I didn't know if he had died then but I thought he had. I went to fetch Dr. Coe and he certified that the chief was dead."

Following the chief's death, the District Attorney for New

Orleans district, Mr. Clarence Foley, announced that he was charging five of the arrested Sicilians in the Parish Prison with murder, and another eight, including Vittorio Liotta, with conspiracy to murder. All thirteen have been remanded in custody until the trial, which is expected to take place in about three months.

* * *

Anna-Maria lit a cigarette and offered one to Silvio. "That was good, very good. You haven't lost your touch."

Silvio lit his cigarette and blew smoke into the room. "You don't behave much like a mother."

She laughed. "Mothers get horny, you know. God, how I get horny sometimes." She kissed him.

"What did you tell Saltram?"

"I didn't tell him anything. He's not a bad lover, Silvio. He just doesn't make me horny like you do. I have lunches with girlfriends, I go shopping, I have dress fittings, I go to the library. He won't get suspicious so long as I'm home by five."

This was the second time—since Silvio's return to New Orleans—that he and Anna-Maria had slept together in the middle of the day. The small house on Esplanade Street she had rented had been chosen partly because it also had some old slave quarters at the foot of the garden with a separate entrance on Barracks Street. As a result, Anna-Maria could enter the building on one street, Silvio on the other.

Silvio would never have admitted it to Anna-Maria but she was better in bed than ever. She had lost none of her adventurousness and he found the idea that she had sought him out after all the years both flattering and erotic.

Virginia wasn't pleased. He hadn't told her what was happening, but he couldn't spend his entire days in bed with women, so had been forced to cut down on his sessions with her.

He liked the fact that he could relax totally with Anna-Maria. Normally Sicilian men never talked business with their women; but this was America, and Anna-Maria was American almost as much as she was Sicilian, maybe more so. Also, her father confided in her.

"Any news about Liotta?" Anna-Maria said. "The press is full of little else."

Silvio blew out more smoke. "He's got a good lawyer, James

Falmouth. We're expecting him to try and reach the witnesses. He won't make any headway with ours, but he might frighten some of the independents. He'll almost certainly have a go at the jury once it's selected."

"Are you worried?"

"*Sono rinoceronte?* Am I a rhinoceros? How thick is my skin? Sure, I'm worried. Liotta's been set up. By us, by me. Liotta knows it but can't do much about it from Parish Prison. He also knows that I used Martell to get at him, just as he used Martell to get at Nino and me, all those years ago. *Siamo pari.* We're equal. That must be as hard for him as it's sweet for me."

He drew hard on his cigarette. "The weakness in my plan is that the prosecution has to give the names of their witnesses to the court in advance, whereas the defense doesn't. Which means that Liotta can intimidate the hell out of our people but we can't do the same to him."

"You're certain he'll try something like that?"

"He has to. It's the only hope he's got. Frank Cassidy's brainstorm, to say that Martell told him the Sicilians did it, will be the clincher for most juries."

"But why didn't Cassidy make Martell say Liotta himself had done it? Wouldn't that have been more convincing?"

Silvio shook his head. "That might have looked too pat, too obvious. Put Cassidy himself under too much pressure. No, Cassidy's behavior was perfect. He'll be getting paid for that. But it does mean Liotta has to fix the witnesses and the jury."

"So what are you going to do?"

"I'm not sure yet. We've got to come up with something special, something that will surprise Liotta and put him at a disadvantage. I have to hit him when he's least expecting it."

For a moment they both smoked in silence. There was a bottle of champagne by the bed and Silvio refilled their two glasses. He handed one to Anna-Maria. "I want to ask you a question, and I want you to promise not to get angry."

"Is it about Annunziata?"

"How did you guess?" He was surprised.

"I've been watching you. I've been watching you watch my children. Silvio, I always know what's going on inside you." She took a sip of champagne. "What do you want to know?"

"I want to know what you hear. At our meeting in the cathedral with Liotta, he said something about Annunziata and Alesso Alcamo. Is it true, or was he winding me up?"

She eyed him over the rim of the champagne glass. "If I tell you, will you promise not to get angry?"

He gave her a thin smile. "I'll try."

"Alesso is the Don in Alia. Bastiano's in jail, as perhaps you know. They caught him after the orphanage. People were so incensed, they betrayed him. And there was a reward, of course. Imbriaci is Alesso's *consigliere*. They still have the orchard rackets around Bivio Indisi, but they also have the lands around Valledolmo and Fontane Murata."

Silvio nodded grimly. "And Annunziata? What about her?"

Anna-Maria paused. "She's going to marry him."

So it was true. Silvio said nothing. Then, after another long pause: "When?"

"No one knows. At least I don't. The story is that Annunziata wants to be married by the abbot of some local monastery and he's very ill at the moment, too ill to perform the ceremony."

"Are they living together, as man and wife?"

"I don't know."

"Anna-Maria!"

"You said you wouldn't get angry."

"Anna-Maria . . . *please*."

She nodded. "That's what I hear."

Again Silvio said nothing for a while. Then: "Who told you all this?"

"Father still keeps in touch with his Priola cousins. They're in business together, after all. Like always."

"So Angelo knows what you've just told me?"

She didn't say anything. The answer was obvious.

There was another long silence. At length it was Anna-Maria who broke it. "I'm sorry, Silvio," she said in a whisper. "I'm really sorry."

22

William Pinkerton was a tall man, ferocious looking at times, ramrod straight, with a walrus mustache and a balding head. His office, on East Van Buren Street and South Michigan Avenue in Chicago, was no less imposing, paneled in Canadian maple, decorated with oil portraits of the detective's Scottish ancestors. At precisely ten-thirty that morning his secretary showed into his office a much smaller, swarthier man, of stocky build and as southern European in outlook as Pinkerton was a highlander. It was April 1891.

Pinkerton and Guido di Passo may have been totally different in physical appearance, but they were very alike in other ways. William Pinkerton had made his father's agency the greatest detective bureau there was, sought after by law-enforcement agencies all over the world. He himself entertained, and was entertained by, the greatest names in America. But he never forgot who he was, how the family made their money.

Di Passo was, without question, his best agent. Born in Genoa, he spoke his native Italian, French, and Portuguese as well as English. It was di Passo who laid the groundwork for the location, and killing, of Butch Cassidy and the Sundance Kid. It was di Passo who solved the Philadelphia insurance fraud and the Cincinnati lottery scandal. When William asked him to his private office, it was usually for an important job.

Di Passo was faintly surprised on this occasion to see that there were two other people with Pinkerton.

"Guido," the boss said, "I'd like to introduce Harrison Parker, the mayor of New Orleans. He's the reason I've asked you in here today, when I know you should be on vacation. And this," he said, turning to the other man, "is Angelo Priola, the chairman of the

Concerned Citizens of New Orleans, a committee that supports the mayor. They have asked for our best man and I've told them you're it."

They all shook hands. Parker, di Passo could see, was a stocky creature with a thick neck, a bulbous nose, not much hair, reddish what there was of it, and, he noticed, very thick fingers, like carrots. Priola was elderly, gray-haired, obviously Italian.

The older men had stood up when di Passo had been shown in. Now they all sat down again. Coffee was brought and then Pinkerton got down to business.

"Guido, Mr. Parker has a problem, a difficult problem, but he believes he may also have the solution, which is where you come in. I have to tell you that the solution is very dangerous. I'll let him give you the background and then we can all discuss the feasibility of his solution."

Di Passo nodded and sipped his coffee.

Parker cleared his throat. "Mr. di Passo, a couple of months back we had a very bad crime in New Orleans. Our chief of police was murdered." Parker had a deep but not unpleasant voice. A smoker's voice. "He was shot in the street on his way home from dinner, and he died the next day. We are pretty certain that we know who did it—in fact, a number of arrests were made within a few hours of the killing. Unfortunately, the evidence against them is collapsing. We had a number of witnesses who claimed to have seen the shooting. In the last few weeks, however, several have changed their minds and now say they don't think they would be able to identify the people who fired on the chief. Two have simply disappeared.

"We still have a few witnesses who are willing to testify, but it begins to look as if these mafiosi, or people on their behalf, have been intimidating witnesses. Now, our fear of course is that once the trial starts, they will try the same tactics with the jury, all of which makes our job harder, much harder.

"Therefore, Mr. Pinkerton and I have worked out a plan. What we need is someone on the inside, someone who is not afraid of these men, who is tough and does not live among them, who can obtain an unequivocal confession out of one of them, a confession that will put their guilt beyond any doubt and that it would be impossible for a jury to ignore or go against."

Pinkerton himself took up the story. "Guido, the plan is as

simple as it is risky. We have prepared an alias for you. You will become a north Italian counterfeiter named Fabio Verro. There is such a person, currently doing time in Holland for counterfeiting, put away by one of our men. We're going to send you to Amite, a small town in upstate Louisiana. There you'll live in a small hotel, as if you were on the run and in hiding. You'll have with you a bag of counterfeit money. One of Mr. Parker's most trusted policemen will 'recognize' you there one day and 'arrest' you. He'll make a fuss about it so that your arrest will be in all the papers. You will then be taken to New Orleans, where you will be put in the Parish Prison awaiting extradition to New York.

"The prison governor will be aware of our little . . . deception and he will put you in a cell with some of the criminals on trial for the murder of Chief Martell. After that it's up to you.

"Only five people, apart from you and I, will know about this plan. Mr. Parker here, Mr. Priola, the arresting officer, the prison governor, and the attorney appointed to represent you. He will come to see you every few days, as an attorney would, apparently to discuss your case. Of course, the real reason he'll be there is for you to describe any progress you're making in the investigation. He can pull you out as soon as you're ready.

"This is a very risky venture, Guido. I can't force you to do it against your will. If your heart's not in this one, don't do it. If you get found out once you're inside the prison, you'll be killed, no doubt about it. What I can say is that Mr. Parker has offered a fairly hefty fee for doing the job—so I can offer you twice your normal rate of pay. If we get going right away, we should be able to have you arrested in two weeks' time. The trial is about three months away, so that gives you . . . let's say two months, to get the job done. Now think about it very carefully, and let me know your decision. These gentlemen and I will stroll around Grant Park and the lakeshore for half an hour. When we come back, I'd like you to give us your decision."

Pinkerton stood up, and Parker and Priola did likewise. They took their hats from the hat stand.

"Any questions before we go?" Pinkerton looked at di Passo.

The detective shook his head. "Nothing that can't wait."

They went out.

At first di Passo sipped what remained of his coffee. Then he got up and inspected the portraits of William Pinkerton's ancestors. Then he went to the window and watched his boss and the men from New Orleans emerge from the building and stroll over to Grant Park, across the street. Lake Michigan lay beyond, gray and uninviting. His emotions were mixed. This job could not have come at a worse time. Di Passo had been married six months earlier and his wife was already irritated that, in his job, he spent so much time away from home. Her feelings had been compounded by the fact that just three weeks ago she found out that she was pregnant.

This job would take him well away from home for two months. Perhaps more. Worse, it was in the nature of the job that he would not be able to contact her, and she would not be able to contact him.

On the other hand, the extra money would come in very handy. With Maria pregnant, there would soon be another mouth to feed. With a child in the offing, it would soon become harder for him to get away at all, and he liked traveling. And, when he was honest with himself, he liked the sound of this job. As a northern Italian himself, he knew that these southern men, these Sicilians, could be very slippery and tough, real tough. He relished the chance to test himself against them. This was in some ways the ultimate challenge of his career, to see how he would fare in direct combat with the Mafia.

He was still standing at the window and saw Pinkerton and the other men coming back across the park. He liked William. They went back a long way. It was just like the old man not to pressure him on this one. He had that particularly Scottish attitude to morality: a man must make up his own mind without distractions.

Well, he had made up his mind on this one. Maria wouldn't like it, but the money would help give their son a better start. Di Passo didn't doubt for a moment that his firstborn would be a boy.

"How nice to see you again, Silvio. This *is* a surprise. I'm afraid Edward's not here. He's with his father—I mean my husband. They've gone to Honey Island, to look at the albino alligators."

Silvio smiled at Stella. "Don't worry," he said. "I've come to see you. Can I come in?"

Stella's small parlor was immaculate, save for the toy railroad train in the corner. When they were seated, she said, "What can you possibly want with me?"

"I want to help with the boy's education."

Stella, in the process of fixing a bracelet on her arm, stopped what she was doing.

Silvio removed his spectacles. "I'm serious. I've got money—you know I've got the money. I want the boy to get a good start." He paused. "Don't be offended, please. I know what steamboat captains earn—a good wage, though the river isn't want it was, with all these railroads springing up everywhere. But let me help. The boy doesn't ever have to know. I'm doing this for Madeleine. And for me."

Stella smiled and placed her palms facedown on her knees. For a former whore and bar girl, she looked quite prim. "Silvio," she said softly, "you ought to put Maddie behind you. Stop harking back. What's done is done. Edward's a happy boy. He don't remember his mother like you or I do and we don't often talk about her. It wouldn't be fair. Sure, you can help with his education, if you really want to. But Edward ain't your family, Silvio. Ain't you got no family of your own? Ain't that the way to go? You're softer than you was. Women gonna find you more attractive. It ain't my place to offer advice, but that's what I think. You need your own kids."

Silvio looked at Stella. He thought back to the fights she used to have with Nino, the screams and the tears when he forgot her birthday. Now she was so calm. And *wise*.

People changed. And she was right. It was time to recognize the change in him.

"Tell me, Mr. Russo, how long have you lived in America? And have you always lived in the South?"

"This is my first visit to the South. I'm a New Yorker most of the time."

"And what is your business?"

God, they were pushy, these Southerners. Guido di Passo had been in Amite for three days now and he was beginning to think that Pinkerton and Parker had made a mistake in having him stay at such a small hotel, the Astoria. It wasn't even a proper hotel, with people coming and going. Instead, some people lived at the Astoria all the time. It was the sort of place where old people retired to. The elderly woman addressing him now, for instance, over dinner—which all the guests took at the same table—was a widow, and lonely. At any rate, she loved to talk. But di Passo wasn't sure how long he could keep it up. He hoped he would be arrested soon, before he made some major error.

"I'm in the money business. I'm down here looking at likely investments."

"Oh, my! And do you have anything special in mind?"

He shook his head. Would she never give up?

Amite was a pleasant town. In order to pretend that he was out working every day, di Passo had taken long walks around the financial district, the river, the shopping area. He knew where all the funeral parlors were, and the fire station, and the schools. After dinner he strolled down to the stretch of river near the hotel. He loved the levees and walked along them for about an hour every evening, looking down at the river on one side and the land on the other. There he could smoke in peace.

That night, after dinner, he took his walk as usual, and sat on the levee while he smoked a cigarette. Oceangoing vessels came up the river this far and he watched one marked ROTTERDAM on its stern. Curious. A link between him and the real Fabio Verro.

He finished his cigarette and made for the hotel. He usually turned in early. Parker's man wouldn't jump him at night—it was too risky. So there was nothing to wait up for. And he couldn't write letters. Maria hadn't liked that. In fact, she hadn't liked any part of the plan and they had parted with the strain between them showing. But she would get over it. He hoped.

He slept well. He always slept well. No dreams. Next morning he awoke early, as he usually did. Breakfast was from seven to ten and he was always the first down. He liked to have a smoke before eating, so he went to sit on the porch, in a rocking chair. He took out a cigarette. In truth, this was the best time of the day in Louisiana, or so it seemed to him. The air was still, cool, and what dew was left at this hour brought out the smells of the exotic plants. He lit his cigarette, drew on it, and leaned back.

"Freeze, mister."

At last.

Slowly, di Passo raised his arms and turned his body. A man in a dark blue uniform had emerged from behind a huge pillar that supported the balcony above the porch. He held a gun.

"Jerry!" yelled the policeman. "You can come out now!"

A younger policeman appeared from behind a bush opposite the Astoria. He, too, was armed.

There was movement inside the hotel. The policeman had awakened people. That was all part of the plan. Two early risers appeared on the porch.

"Get back, ma'am. Get back, sir. This man is a wanted criminal. Jerry, put the cuffs on him. Quickly now."

The senior policeman stood in front of di Passo as the younger man grabbed hold of his arms, pulled them behind his back, and handcuffed them together. There were now four or five people just inside the hotel lobby, looking out onto the porch.

"Vincent Russo, I am arresting you in the belief that you are in reality Fabio Verro, a counterfeiter, wanted in the city of New York. I am also arresting you for the circulation of counterfeit U.S. Treasury bills in several denominations, in several states. You will be put aboard a railroad train later today and taken to New Orleans, where you will await extradition.

"Jerry, now that he's cuffed, I can manage him. Run on ahead and tell the stationmaster to hold the New Orleans train."

He turned to the spectators in the lobby of the hotel. There were about ten of them. "Okay, folks, you can go back to your breakfast now. The drama is over. Mr. Russo, you come with me."

But Guido knew that the spectators in the Astoria would not go back to their breakfasts just yet. The sight of him being led away in handcuffs was too much. It would be the subject of their conversation for days, for weeks to come. Their gossip would fuel the local newspapers, and the local papers would tantalize the New Orleans editors. Nothing could better advertise Fabio Verro's criminal nature than if he should arrive in the Parish Prison already a star of the newspapers.

So Guido judged that a little more was called for. To allow himself to be led away, plain and simple, was just too straightforward for those who were watching.

As the two men crossed the road in front of the Astoria, a cart rumbled by. The policeman's attention was distracted for a moment, and di Passo suddenly made a run for it. People would be watching, he knew, and it would provide more fuel for gossip if he should try to escape. It would also make him much more credible as a criminal. The policeman wouldn't shoot, of course, being in

on the plot. In any case, after a short "attempt" at escape, di Passo
would allow himself to be recaptured.

He ran after the cart, and heard the policeman start to give
chase, shouting. Guido thought he would run as far as the levee
and then, out of sight of the spectators at the Astoria, give himself up.

Suddenly a shot rang in his ears. The back of his neck was
immediately wet with sweat. Was the policeman shooting? Surely
not. Was he really in on the plot after all, as he was supposed to
be? A horrible thought struck di Passo—that Pinkerton and Parker
had changed the plan without telling him. No, Pinkerton would
never do that. But Parker might, without telling Pinkerton.

A second shot rang out, and now di Passo stopped. This wasn't
funny.

The policeman caught up with him and grabbed him. "Jesus!"
he breathed. "Someone's shooting from the goddamn hotel!" He
turned and shouted. "Stop your shooting! Hold it!"

Di Passo stared at the policeman. It was true. His gun was in its
holster.

The policeman, still holding di Passo's arm, pulled him back
the way they had been going. "That's enough realism for one
day," he hissed between his teeth. "You nearly got yourself killed.
Some guy in the Astoria must keep a shotgun under his bed. I'll
deal with him later. Come on."

"Do you still read like you used to?"

Anna-Maria pulled the bedclothes over them. These days, she
reflected, she and Silvio talked almost as much as they made love.
"No. The children take up a lot of time. But most nights I read in
bed for about half an hour. You?"

Silvio shook his head. "I read when I was in prison. It kept me
going. I even read to the other men. Can you imagine? Me. But
here in the Quarter, so much is happening. And with Liotta after
my skin all the time, it's hard to concentrate."

"Where's your bodyguard when you're with me?"

"Outside. Don't worry, he won't talk."

"Are you sure? Dick's been acting funny lately."

"How do you mean?"

"Nothing I can put my finger on. Maybe I'm making it up."

"You two still do it?"

"Why? You jealous?"

He smiled at her, and kissed her. "You hear any more from Sicily?"

"You mean about Annunziata?"

"*You* jealous?" He tried to grin, but his sadness didn't quite allow it.

"Yes, I heard something."

"*Sono vulcano?*" He looked at her levelly. "Tell me."

She stared back. "They set a date for the wedding."

"When?"

"August sixteenth. Three months from now."

Di Passo—or rather Fabio Verro—did indeed arrive in New Orleans as a celebrity. The press had done their work well. Several residents of the Astoria had contacted the *Amite Gazette*, and the editor of that organ, mindful that Verro's journey to New Orleans would take him overnight, had telegraphed the New Orleans *Picayune*, which had printed news of Verro's arrest, and the "shootout" at Amite, on its front page. Prominently displayed also was the fact that Verro was due to arrive in New Orleans on the Amite train later that day.

By the time he arrived, the afternoon papers had picked up on the story and there was a small welcoming party to see him descend, still handcuffed, from the railroad car. He was transferred—swiftly—to the Parish Prison, where the arresting officer was instructed to report immediately to the governor.

Governor James Tucker was a portly man, with a pale skin, a round face, and heavily oiled hair.

"Why have you brought this man to my prison?" he demanded of the Amite policeman.

"For speed, sir. He's a wanted man in New York. I propose to begin extradition proceedings today. Once the documentation comes through, he can be put aboard a coastal steamer, and be in New York in a matter of days."

The governor appeared to think this over. The chief warden was also in the room and Tucker wanted no suspicion to attach to himself. "How long will the extradition take?"

"A month, maybe two. Depends on his lawyer."

Tucker addressed di Passo. "You. Do you have a lawyer in New Orleans?"

"Why would I have a lawyer here? I ain't never been before."

Tucker regarded di Passo with a measure of distaste that was clearly not an act. "You are Italian, yes?"

Di Passo nodded sullenly.

Tucker addressed himself to the head warden. "Put Verro with the other dagos. Then send out for Ralph Freemantle. He'll do as a lawyer."

The policeman took back his handcuffs and went off to give interviews to the press about how he had caught the counterfeiter. Di Passo was led back down to the ground floor to the long-term wing. Here the cells were smaller, and mostly housed just two men. He was led along the corridor that linked all the cells until the head warden stopped at a cell occupied by just one person.

"Room in here for another, I think. Make way, you've got company. A celebrity, the man you all read about in this morning's *Picayune*, Vincent Russo, alias Fabio Verro. Another Eyetie." He clanged the door shut behind di Passo. "Watch your back, Verro. Your cellmate is one of Liotta's mob. Name of Gino Fazio. Here on a murder rap. Sweet dreams." He laughed and was gone.

"It's slow, real slow. But we're making some progress." Silvio, Angelo, and Harrison Parker were breakfasting in Parker's club, the Pickwick, which was located well away from the Quarter, in the Garden District. They were in a private room and could not be overheard. Parker was doing the talking.

"Di Passo has been put with Gino Fazio. There's no point in putting him in with Liotta himself. He'll never crack. But Fazio is unstable. Worse, or rather better, from our point of view, he's got dysentery. It's draining him and he's getting weaker. The only risk from our point of view is that di Passo himself might catch the disease. If he does we'll have to pull him out."

"And how is Liotta? Do we know?" Silvio was still certain Vito would try something.

"As you would expect. He's living well. He has all the best food and wine sent in. Even a few glasses of absinthe. But he works most of the day. People come and go all the time. He has his people in the jail, of course, and he's spending money like water. His tactic is obvious, but effective. He will intimidate or buy off as many of your witnesses as he can. He's already gotten to a few, and may get to more. He won't get to all of them, but maybe enough. Obviously, he doesn't know about di Passo.

"His other tactic is to 'find' new 'witnesses' of his own. They'll provide convincing alibis for himself and his people. In the end, all these witnesses may just cancel one another out. I suspect that it may come down to what di Passo finds out. If he finds out anything."

A week later they met again. Another breakfast in the Pickwick. This time Parker had more news. "Fazio is definitely cracking. His health is going with the dysentery, and di Passo has managed to convince him that the others are trying to poison him. That has turned Fazio against the rest."

By the next week the Pickwick breakfasts were becoming routine. Now Parker had even better news to report. "Fazio's mind has gone completely. He has begun to talk. He rambles, but di Passo is beginning to get some pure gold. For example, Fazio has told him about the initiation ceremonies of the Liotta family. How they have to prick their forefinger to draw blood, then hold it over a candle while someone reads from the Bible. Fazio also said that he helped torch Fanny Decker's whorehouse back in 'eighty-eight. And he helped plan some of the Liotta mayhem directed at the Priolas. He even told di Passo that he began in New Orleans by collecting protection money on Rampart Street."

"That's perfect for us," said Angelo. "Di Passo's real foxy. If the judge allows him to say all that, and he then goes on to describe how Fazio confessed to the murder, we're home free."

The next week Parker was less cocky. "Di Passo's still getting good stuff. Mainly Liotta's link to Deveraux, the former chief of police. That's good because it goes to motive, makes out that Liotta wanted Martell out of the way so he could replace him with Deveraux."

"So why are you worried?" Angelo, despite the early hour, was smoking a big cigar.

"Di Passo's got dysentery himself. He's growing weak. Yet he's getting such good stuff, he doesn't want to pull out. He's crazy. He could kill himself in there, or make himself so ill he can't give evidence. We've got enough now, don't you think? It's time to pull him out."

That proved easier said than done. Di Passo insisted on staying another week—by which time the trial was only two weeks away.

Then, when he was ready to be released, the prison governor, Tucker, was away on a training course that he couldn't avoid. His deputy was not part of the plan and so could not be asked to sanction di Passo's release. All of which meant that the Pinkerton man was not released from the Parish Prison until a week before the trial began, by which time he had lost thirty pounds and was extremely ill. When Parker first saw him after di Passo had been "extradited," he was shocked. In addition to the weight loss, his skin was pale and he was unable to stand. He was obviously too ill to give evidence.

"We're going to need him," Parker told the others at one of their now regular breakfasts. "Liotta's men have been working hard on the witnesses. Clarence Foley, the D.A., says that our original fourteen witnesses have now shrunk to eight. And that could shrink further." He turned to Silvio. "Isn't there something you can do?"

Silvio shrugged. "Maybe, maybe not. For sure, we can't do anything until the damn jury is selected. Do we have a judge yet?"

"I was coming to that," said Parker. "The answer is yes. Old Tom McCrystal."

Silvio looked at Angelo, who returned his gaze. They both smiled.

"Now that," said Silvio, "is what I call a break."

"Silvio, what you doin' here? You never go to confession."

It was Tuesday and Silvio was seated in the rearmost pew of St. Louis's, the very place where he had sat, months ago, when he had first arrived back from Sicily and outlined the Cathedral Plan to Angelo. He patted the pew beside him. "Sit down, Angie."

Angelo slumped onto the pew.

"I like it here, Angie. Reminds me of Sicily. That painting over the altar. There's one just like it in Palermo."

"You getting homesick? After all this time?"

"I've been doing a lot of thinking." He turned to the older man. "You knew things about Annunziata, about her and Alesso. But you didn't tell me."

Angelo's expression changed. "It was for the best, Silvio. What could you have done?"

Silvio looked away, back toward the altar and the picture above it. "*Sono ragazzo?* Am I a child? You should've told me, Angie. I had a right to know." He paused. "And I found out anyway."

"And what good's it gonna do you? It ain't as if you could go back to Sicily and stop it happening."

Silvio said nothing, but turned his gaze back to Angelo.

The older man was startled. "Is . . . is that what you're thinking of doing? You're crazy! You gotta stay here till the trial's over— and by then Annunziata will be married."

"Wrong. No one in Sicily will expect me to go back. They'll think like you, that I'd have to be crazy. Once the trial starts here, there isn't a lot we can do. Almost everything that can be done I've already thought of."

"But what are you gonna *do*, Silvio? Alesso will be protected. Soon as the *sbirri* find out you're back in Sicily, they'll be after you like a buncha weasels. Every policeman on the island will want the reward and glory of capturing the beast of Bagheria. Ordinary people will turn you in. You can't take on the whole island. That ain't foxy."

"*Don't* tell me what I can and can't do, Angie. I'm the one who's going to give you this city on a plate. I'm the guy who's outthinking Liotta—remember? So don't lecture me. *Don't!*" He paused, to calm himself. "I can go back as a deckhand on one of the fruit boats. I can go via North Africa. All I need from you is a boat and a set of false papers. Easy. Just make sure the boat leaves the day after the trial starts. I'll do the rest."

"Professor Perran?"

The judge looked up. He was sitting with Kitty, drinking bourbon and listening to the Tio brothers. "Yes?"

"I'm Vanni Priola. I own the place."

"Yes?"

"I wonder if I might talk to you for a moment."

"No, I'm busy. Go away."

Silvio stood without moving, looking down at the man.

"I said: Go away."

"Kitty works for me. She'll do as I say."

The judge clenched his fist. "I thought I—"

"It won't take long. Five minutes. Then I'll leave you in peace. It's important." He nodded to the back of the bar. "In my room."

"It's okay," Kitty said softly, playing her part. She stroked the back of the judge's hand. "I'll be here when you get back. Don't worry."

Silvio led the way as the judge rose to follow. When he reached the back room he held the door open as His Honor walked through. He closed the door behind him.

"Now, what *is* all this? I was just beginning to enjoy—"

"You don't remember where we met before, judge?"

"What do you mean? Where did we meet?"

"At a baptism, in the cathedral. Angelo Priola's daughter—and granddaughter, of course."

The light of recognition suddenly shone in McCrystal's eyes. He nodded. "I thought the name was familiar." But then he frowned. "So? I still don't see why—"

Silvio threw a photograph onto the table between them.

McCrystal looked down casually—then scrutinized it more closely. "What is this?"

"You, Your Honor. Drunk, *sborniato,* as we say where I come from. Dead to the world, and slumped across Kitty Clarke, half-naked."

"When . . . when was this taken?" The judge grabbed at the photograph, but Silvio was too quick for him.

"What does it matter when it was taken? What matters is what you are doing. What matters is what your wife will think of this, or the mayor."

"You're blackmailing me!"

Silvio paused before replying, "Yes. That's right."

McCrystal said nothing. He looked outraged, then sad, then angry all over again. Finally he sat down and rubbed his eyes. "What do you want?"

"Nothing. At least, not yet. There will come a time when I—or friends of mine—need a favor, maybe. But for now I just want you to know what I have. And don't worry. No one else, apart from Kitty, of course, and the person who took the photograph, will ever know what I know. Unless . . ." Silvio let the sentence trail off.

The judge glared at Silvio. It was half fury, but also half self-pity, and Silvio began to despise him. Why couldn't he take the consequences of his actions like a man? He watched as McCrystal rose, left the room, and wove his way back between the tables to where Kitty was sitting. He grabbed her arm and pulled her from her seat, toward the stairs. It was difficult to see if he was angry or excited by what had just happened.

Silvio smiled to himself. Another part of the Cathedral Plan had slipped into place.

On the Sunday of that weekend, Silvio was early for his time with Anna-Maria. For him, Sundays were no different from any other days; he worked and played as normal. He left Mamie Christine's at two-thirty. His bodyguard, Eduardo, fell in behind him. They walked down CustomHouse Street and turned onto Royal. It was then that Silvio suddenly spotted Dick Saltram coming out of a tobacco store, smoking a cigarette. Silvio was just about to shout to Saltram when a gesture by the other man caught his eye.

Saltram patted his breast pocket. Silvio himself often made the same gesture—when he was checking that his gun was in place. He was puzzled and alarmed. Saltram was not a violent man. Why did he have a gun, and where was he going? He watched as Saltram turned off Royal into Toulouse. Silvio became more alarmed when he observed Saltram turn off onto Chartres and walk purposefully in the direction of the house on Esplanade where Silvio and Anna-Maria were to meet.

Fully alert now, Silvio followed Saltram, at a distance. He had to be certain that Saltram was actually going where he thought he was going.

Saltram walked along Chartres, crossing St. Philip's and Ursulines streets. By now Silvio had no doubts as to the other man's destination. As Saltram came to Esplanade, Silvio slipped into an alleyway so that he could watch in relative safety. Eduardo stood across the street, some way behind.

Saltram stopped outside the house and looked up. It was two-fifty. Again he patted his breast pocket, then disappeared into the courtyard.

Saltram had used the entrance that Anna-Maria herself used, on Esplanade. Did that mean he had followed her? Did he know whom she met? It was possible he didn't. Was Saltram intending to shoot his wife, her lover, or both of them? What did it matter anyway? He, Silvio, had to get to Anna-Maria before she arrived. Even if he didn't turn up for their rendezvous, and she did, Saltram would assume the worst—and God knows what he might do. No man likes being a *cornuto*, a cuckold.

But how could Silvio stop Anna-Maria? He had never seen her arrive, had no idea which direction she came from. If he didn't get to her until her carriage stopped outside the house, it would be too late.

He had no choice but to gamble on the fact that he knew vaguely where she *ought* to be coming from. At least, if she was coming from home.

He turned back down Chartres and made a right on Nicholls. If her cab from the Garden District came down O'Keefe, it would probably cross Canal at University Place and proceed down Burgundy.

A carriage was coming toward him now. He cursed the fashion for curtained carriages: it was impossible to see inside. As the carriage went by he stood in the road and called out, "Anna-Maria! Anna-Maria!"

The carriage rattled on.

He lit a cigarette and looked at his watch. Three o'clock exactly. Anna-Maria was usually a little late, because she liked him to arrive first. But she was never *very* late. She had to get home afterward.

Another carriage appeared. That too was curtained. Again he called out as it went by. Again it rode on.

He began to sweat.

Saltram was emphatically not a violent man, but sexual jealousy, Silvio knew, could do funny things to people. Look at Alesso Alcamo; he had been driven to extremes. All of a sudden Silvio was thinking of Annunziata. Now that he had made the decision to go back to Sicily, he was calmer inside. His only worry was being caught by the police. There was no death penalty in Italy now, but he would surely be lynched.

That gave him an idea, but he didn't have time to dwell on it. There was another carriage coming toward him. It, too, was curtained.

As it rattled by he shouted out, "Anna-Maria! Anna-Maria!" If he shouted any louder even Saltram would hear him, three blocks away.

Suddenly the curtains were pulled back and a head came out. It was Anna-Maria. She saw Silvio standing in the road and immediately called out for the coachman to stop. It was obvious to her that something was wrong.

Silvio ran to catch up to the carriage. He opened the door.

"What's wrong?" she whispered.

"Your husband. He's found out."

Her hand went to her mouth.

"I spotted him by accident in the street. I followed him—he's at Esplanade now. . . . He's got a gun."

She nodded abstractedly. "I told you he's been acting odd lately. And it's been getting worse. Gruff, drinking. Out of character. Rough on the children, which is very unlike him. What are we going to do?"

"Get away from here for a start."

"But after that? I must see you, Silvio. You know how I need you."

"Anna-Maria! He's mad as hell, *strano,* crazy, not behaving right. And he's probably guessed it's me you're sleeping with. We're not exactly strangers."

"He'll calm down—"

"Will he? How do you know? He could explode at any moment."

"I know Dick. He's not like that."

"Anna-Maria! I *saw* him today. He was all keyed up. Smoking. God knows how many drinks he's had."

"But he's not a killer, Silv—"

"Sure he is! If he's mad enough. You never talked about how much he loved you. Everyone's a potential killer when their wife is cheating on them. Look, we can talk about this later. We've got to get away from here. You'd better—"

A wave of warm air swept over them just then. Before Silvio had time to take it in, a loud *boom!* rolled over the rooftops, billowing upward and outward, and dissipating toward the river. Silvio looked behind him, to see black smoke rising in the hazy afternoon light. The clatter of falling pieces of wood, shards of glass, and other debris could be heard above the shouting that had broken out. People were moaning, and a dog whined. A woman screamed, and screamed again.

"No!" cried Anna-Maria. "No! Dick, *no!*" She made to get down from the carriage.

"Stay!" whispered Silvio. "Anna-Maria, *please.* You don't want to see what's happened, believe me. And it's too late anyway."

She fought him, raining blows at him, determined to get down, to see for herself what had occurred.

Silvio resisted, holding her arms. Eventually, she collapsed in tears. He hugged her then, feeling her warm, sobbing body against his. "Stay here," he said more gently. "We both know it's not safe for either of us to go looking. We must get away. That was meant for me."

23

The day the trial opened, the courthouse was besieged by hundreds of spectators. At nine in the morning Vittorio Liotta and the other defendants were transferred from the Parish Prison to the courthouse by wagon. The courthouse, St. Patrick's Hall, was situated at the corner of St. Ann and Conde streets. It was a tall building, with huge windows on either side of the judge's bench, which had an imposing canopy above it. Outside it was raining.

Silvio stood at the window of the D.A.'s office and looked down into the yard of the courthouse. Clarence Foley had cooperated, allowing him to use his own room, but Silvio was taking a risk in coming here at all. Still, he couldn't help it. After yesterday's explosion, which had killed Dick Saltram, he had to see Vito Liotta one more time in the flesh. Not only had that bomb been meant for Silvio, it had been hidden under Anna-Maria's bed, exactly the same device that Nino and Silvio had used to kill Giancarlo Cataldo all those years before. Liotta might be behind bars but his mind was still active, still creative, still foxy enough to devise a timely, symmetrical revenge. And obviously he still had clout on the street, enough *forza* to find out where Silvio went in the afternoons.

Anna-Maria was still in a state of shock. She hadn't been allowed to see the remains of Saltram—they were too grisly. Her attitude to Silvio was mixed; although he had been the cause of her husband's death, he had also saved her own life. She was at home with Angelo and the children, the house guarded like a fortress.

As Silvio looked down from the D.A.'s office into the yard, the gates opened. Two wagons rolled in, and came to a stop. The doors were thrown open and the defendants began to get down.

They were all handcuffed to each other, except for one man. Liotta. He clearly had some extra sway with the guards, for he was left entirely alone. He was wearing a dark gray suit, a white shirt and cravat, and shiny brown shoes. He laughed and joked with the guards, as though he was without a care in the world.

Silvio stared down at him. After a moment Liotta must have felt the weight of his gaze, for he suddenly looked up, to the window where Silvio was standing. Their glances locked and the smile faded from Liotta's face. Both men knew it was now a fight to the death.

In the courtroom, the public benches were filled long before the trial opened at ten-thirty. One by one, the players in this particular drama began to arrive. The first to come was the press, representatives of the *Mascot*, the *Picayune*, the *Times-Democrat*, and the *Delta*, as well as René Lefevre, an artist sent by the *Delta* to sketch the proceedings.

The prosecuting attorney, Clarence Foley, arrived at about ten-ten. He was a tall, thin, stooped man, with a shock of iron-gray hair that seemed to sprout from his head. He unfolded his papers and sat calmly talking to an assistant. Next in were several police, security in case any of the prisoners tried to escape.

At about ten-twenty-five the defending attorney, James Falmouth, arrived with his aides. He nodded civilly to the D.A. and began setting out his papers on the table provided. Falmouth was a barrel-chested man with sandy hair and a freckled skin. He had big hands.

At ten-thirty-one Judge McCrystal was shown in. Everyone stood and watched as he took his seat.

Without any further ado, a side door in the court was opened and the defendants were shown in. Liotta did not come first. He didn't want anyone to think that he was in charge, so he came in second from the end. Immediately there was a buzz of conversation across the courthouse as people began to discuss the appearance of the defendants. Neither Silvio nor Angelo was in court, but Parker was.

The clerk of the court stood and began to read the indictment. One by one, in alphabetical order, they pleaded not guilty. Each time they did, a section in the public gallery applauded loudly. Liotta had a great deal of support.

* * *

That night Silvio and Angelo met at the Capo's house in the Garden District. Anna-Maria, wearing her black widow's garb, had prepared a light supper of spaghetti and tomato sauce. In honor of the occasion, they drank Sicilian wine. Silvio was leaving the next morning on the Priola fruit ship the *Ragusa*. It was the first time that Anna-Maria had agreed to meet him since the explosion. She looked ravaged around the eyes.

The talk was general until the pasta was finished. Then, when the salad was on the table and the second bottle of wine had been opened, Angelo said, "Jury selection started today. Foley calculates it might take four, five, or even six days. The trial proper won't start until next week."

Silvio nodded, helping himself to more wine. "I figured. I should be in Sicily by Wednesday of next week. Thursday at the latest."

"Then what?" Anna-Maria was belligerent. She repeated herself more softly. "Then what?"

Silvio shrugged. "We'll have to see."

"You sure you still wanna go?" Angelo stretched his hand across the table and took hold of Silvio's wrist. "There's something you don't know." Silvio could see the old man's forehead glistening with sweat. "My liver. It ain't what it was. In fact, my liver ain't much of a liver anymore." He gulped some wine and then pointed to the glass. "This don't help much, neither." He gripped Silvio's wrist more tightly. "I ain't got long, kid—sorry, I know you hate that word. I got a year, maybe more, maybe less."

He sighed. "I'm getting old, Silvio. Maybe I ain't as foxy as I was but . . . but I know why Dick was killed. You got to live with that—and so does Anna-Maria." He squeezed his daughter's arm.

"Another thing. I heard you been sending fruit to some orphanage. Without my permission." But Angelo was smiling. "This war's getting to all of us, you included. You maybe most of all. It's sad, but Dick's out of the way . . . you can have . . . that wedding you never had before. And, with Dick gone, you're the next Capo. You sure you wanna risk losing that, in Sicily?"

Silvio took Angelo's hand in both of his and kissed the other man's fingers. "Angie, I want it. You know I want it. I earned it. But Sicily comes first. Don't worry, I'll be back."

"They know you there!" Anna-Maria couldn't keep quiet any

longer. "They know what you look like, they'll know what you've come for!"

Silvio turned his head to look at her. "I'm going," he said. "You know why. There's no point in saying another word."

Angelo sighed and refilled all their glasses. "I can manage Parker, I can manage Foley, I can handle di Passo if need be. But that still leaves the judge. You've kept him to yourself so far, but if you're gonna be away, you better tell me how to play him."

Silvio nodded. "You've got to be foxy." He smiled. "You can only use the judge once. It's the last bit of the plan. So you have to pick your moment."

"How will I know when that moment comes? And what do I say?"

Silvio told him.

On the Tuesday of the second week of the trial, Clarence Foley stepped into the main area of the court. He was dressed in a dark gray frock coat with a white wing collar. He solemnly addressed the jury, which had finally been agreed upon the afternoon before. "Gentlemen, the prosecution's argument in this case is a simple one. It is simple because, although this cold-blooded and cowardly murder has received massive publicity, the facts of the matter are themselves very simple, and easily stated. On the night of March twenty-third David Martell, chief of police of New Orleans, a most wonderful man, was gunned down in Girod Street as he walked home. He had just eaten a late dinner at Virgut's oyster bar after a long and hard day's work running this city's superb police force.

"He was alone as he turned into Girod Street and walked toward the house he shared with his mother. He was alone as he passed the corner of Girod and Basin Street. And it was there that he was attacked, set upon by six or seven men who fired a number of gunshots at Chief Martell, in a most cowardly and despicable manner. The chief was hit several times and fell to the ground. He had drawn his own weapon but had time only to fire it into the ground as he fell. Seeing him fall, and believing him dead, the cowards ran off.

"But Chief Martell was not dead, not then, and people soon came to his aid. Other police were summoned and he was taken to Charity Hospital. Police inquiries into the shooting were begun there and then, and a number of arrests were quickly made, mainly because people had seen the gunmen running away from the scene of the crime and could therefore identify the assailants.

"It is these witnesses who will be called before you, gentlemen of the jury, so that you can judge for yourselves the merits of their evidence. At this stage, I need to add two other things. One is a sad reminder that although he didn't die on the sidewalk, as his assailants no doubt intended, Chief Martell did die, the next morning. Which is why this is a murder trial.

"The other matter concerns the appearance in the dock of that gentleman—" Foley pointed dramatically to Vittorio Liotta. "Vittorio Liotta was not present at the shooting and certainly did not himself fire a gun that night. Why, then, you may ask, is he in the dock with the others? I will tell you.

"He is in the dock because he is the leader of a Sicilian family—a gang—in New Orleans. The Liotta family. And they are one of two such families in this city whose bitter rivalry has created so much crime, and culminated in this dreadful murder. These gangs, these Mafia families, are mercifully new in America, but they are centuries old in their native Sicily. It is your opportunity, and also your duty, gentlemen of the jury, to help stamp out this scourge before it grows any stronger on this side of the Atlantic Ocean. Vittorio Liotta organized this crime. It was his idea and all the detailed planning was his, as I shall show you, down to the use of a young boy to give the signal that Martell was approaching. Vittorio Liotta may not have been in Girod Street on the night David Martell was shot, but he is every bit as guilty of murder as the other defendants.

"Now, you may ask *why* Mr. Liotta and his associates would wish to murder Mr. Martell. Again, the reason is horribly simple. Some months ago, as a result of an attack on one Sicilian gang in New Orleans by another Sicilian gang, an attack in which a member of the general public lost an eye, a number of Mr. Liotta's associates were arrested. This was not unreasonable, as the victims of the attack were all members of the Priola family, the Liottas' deadly rivals. Unfortunately, after a number of witnesses had either disappeared or changed their testimony, proceedings against these individuals had to be dropped, and they were released.

"Mr. Martell had made the arrests in the earlier case. Therefore, this second attack, on Girod Street, was a simple but deadly act of revenge against Chief Martell, which is why so many of these defendants are, in fact, here in court for the second time today.

"I trust that on this occasion, gentlemen of the jury, they will not be allowed to go free again. You can see what happened the last time they were let off the hook." Foley sat down.

James Falmouth, for the defense, was less flamboyant but no less impressive. Though he had large, ugly hands, he used them expressively, like an Italian. His father had been named Giacomo Falmozzo.

"Gentlemen, you have heard from the district attorney, who has promised to convince you that the men in the dock carried out this heinous crime. Well, for our part, on this side, we shall be agog to see what evidence he brings into court. But the fact of the matter is, your responsibility in this matter is far graver than even he suggested. For we stand here on the edge of the greatest miscarriage of justice that there has ever been in the United States. Quite simply, gentlemen, the defendants are totally innocent of the charges so maliciously brought against them.

"As I hope to show, all of them have alibis—and convincing alibis at that. Of course, it is clear that *someone* killed Chief Martell. As to who that someone might be . . . well, I believe that may emerge in the course of this trial. From that, I believe you will see clearly why Vittorio Liotta and his business associates have been arrested. This is a most despicable case, which lays bare all the rivalries and tensions that can exist between businessmen. But business rivalry is one thing, a healthy thing on which the prosperity of this fine country has been built. Crime is something else entirely. I say to you now, as I shall say to you later in this trial, that none of the men sitting in the dock today, *none of them*, is guilty of the offenses they are charged with." He sat down.

Foley's first witness was Joshua Hampson, a black cobbler who had himself been arrested running from the scene of the shooting. He denied taking part, however. Instead, he said he had seen four men standing under a balcony of the sidewalk on Girod Street. They had held guns and, when Martell approached, had started firing. He had run, he said, simply to get away from the shooting. He identified three of the four men as sitting in the dock of the court.

The second witness was Emma Foster. She lived near the scene of the crime, had heard the shooting and looked out of her window. She had seen one of the defendants, Ruggiero Solazzo, standing in the street. Under cross-examination she confessed that when she saw him, Solazzo had been unarmed and, in fact, partially undressed, but it was definitely him, she said.

The third witness was Zachary Peeler, who said he had been walking behind Martell on Girod Street when the shooting started. He identified three of the defendants and added that one of them, Ruggiero Solazzo, had been wearing a yellow oilskin rain cloak. The defense naturally made much of the fact that one witness said Solazzo was partially undressed and another said he was wearing a yellow oilskin.

Because Angelo was not anxious to visit the court during the trial, he had agreed to meet with Harrison Parker every morning for breakfast, at the Pickwick, to review progress on a day-to-day basis. That gave the mayor time to talk to Clarence Foley each evening, after that day's session in court, and gather the D.A.'s reactions. In these early days of the trial, Parker reported that Foley was pleased by the early witnesses, who had, he felt, made a good impression on the jury and survived their cross-examination reasonably well. There were discrepancies in their stories— like the yellow oilskin testimony—but he felt the jury would discount that. Shocking events had occurred in rapid succession and witnesses could be expected to be fuzzy about the details. But the overall picture was clear enough: the people they saw at the scene of the crime were now in the dock. Foley's plan, in fact, had been to present three "uncontaminated" witnesses at the beginning of the trial, and the other four at the end of the trial, with those who they suspected had been "got at" in the middle.

The only bad news at this early stage was that di Passo was still ill. His temperature was excessively high and he was unable to hold down any food.

"Quattro Strade! Quattro Strade! Change here for Rocalmuto and Camicetti." The stationmaster had a rasping voice, which immediately jerked Silvio out of his slumber.

He looked out of the train window. It was strange that this was the first time he had been on a train in Sicily, but thank God for the railroads. He remembered when travel across the island was arduous and prolonged. These days, Cammarata was only hours away.

His journey had been remarkably trouble-free. He had disembarked from the *Ragusa*, after an eight-day voyage, at Tunis and immediately boarded a French boat bound for Marseilles that called at Porto Empedocle, the port of Agrigento on Sicily's southern coast. Silvio had put ashore without attracting attention. Then he had caught a train that took him along the Aragona valley, north to Cammarata. Cammarata was about twenty miles from Bivio Indisi; but he was going there because it was where Smeralda now lived. After much thought he had decided that only Bastiano's wife, his aunt, who had acted as his own mother for many years, could be trusted with the knowledge that he was back in Sicily. And she would surely know all the information he needed.

Silvio studied the train station through the carriage window for the second time. All the railroad buildings were painted a dark blood red, to set them apart from others. He heard a whistle sound. There were three stations between Porto Empedocle and Quattro Strade, and he knew by now that the whistle preceded the departure of the train. As it moved forward, picked up speed, and began to rock from side to side, he tried to doze again. But he couldn't help wondering if the local Mafia had moved in on the railroads yet. They must provide fertile ground for some profitable rackets.

On the fourth day of the trial proper, the Wednesday of the second week, just as Clarence Foley was beginning his examination of Mary Wrighton, the fourth witness, one of the defendants stood up in the dock and shouted, "I want to confess! I confess everything!" He then climbed over the railing of the dock and made to leave the courtroom.

This was not quite as shocking as it sounded. For the fact was that, as the second week of the trial began, it had become increasingly clear that not all was well in the dock. One of the defendants was fidgety and prone to sobbing without warning. This was none other than Gino Fazio, the man di Passo had milked and reduced to a wreck. Fazio was still racked by the effects of dysentery, which weakened him further.

Following his outburst, he was gently but firmly restrained by the court police, who could see that he was still ranting. He was led away, still shouting and sobbing, to the cells underneath the court. Foley quickly suggested that a doctor be called; the judge immediately agreed. There was then a ten-minute recess. This

suited Foley. It gave the jury time to consider what Fazio had said.
Yes, he was clearly under immense mental strain, but that didn't
necessarily mean that what he had said was wrong.

After the court resumed, Foley made no reference to Fazio,
continuing as if nothing had happened. It would have been inappropriate to gloat. He returned to his examination of the latest witness, Mary Wrighton.

She was one of those who had seen a group of men running
from the scene of the crime. She was asked if she recognized any
of the men in court. She pointed to Girolamo Regalmici, sitting
next to Vito Liotta.

When Falmouth rose to cross-examine her he asked if she had
been asked to identify anyone on a previous occasion.

"Yes, in the Parish Prison. The day after the shooting."

"And?"

She lowered her eyes.

"Well?"

"I . . . I failed to identify anyone."

"Including Girolamo Regalmici?"

She looked down, and nodded.

Next came a black laborer, Joseph Lansing, who claimed that
he had been walking a little way behind Martell, on Girod Street,
when he saw four or five men fire on the chief. He identified Vincenzo Liotta and Antonio Siculo, in the dock, as among these men.

Falmouth began his cross-examination of Lansing by asking if
he had gone straight home from work that night.

"Yessir."

"But the shooting occurred at about ten twenty-five. Wasn't that
a little late for you to be working?"

"Well, maybe I did stop off on the way. I ain't sure."

"Could you have stopped off at McCleery's Bar, on Canal
Street?"

Lansing looked wary. "Yeah. Yeah. Could've been."

"How many drinks did you have?"

Pause. "One or two."

"Are you sure?"

"Sure, I'm sure."

"I'll repeat the question, Mr. Lansing. How many drinks did
you have that night? Think carefully before you answer."

"I . . . I don't need to think. A coupla drinks. Three. Four at the most. I swear."

Falmouth brandished a bunch of papers at the judge. "Your Honor, I have here five affidavits from customers of McCleery's Bar to the effect that on the night of the twenty-third of March, Joseph Lansing had been drinking in that bar since about five in the evening, when he actually finished work, and that when he left he was incoherently drunk."

The next witness was Raymond Hattersley, who testified that he had seen a group of men running down Girod Street, one of them wearing a yellow oilskin rain cloak. However, under cross-examination by Falmouth, Hattersley admitted that it was dark that night and that the oilskin could have been any pale color. He also admitted that the color yellow had been suggested to him by the policeman who had interviewed him. Again, Falmouth made much of the fact that *two* men now seemed to have worn a yellow oilskin.

That evening Harrison Parker called a special meeting at the Pickwick, with Angelo Priola and Clarence Foley.

"I've invited the D.A.," said Parker to Angelo, "because we are presented with a problem. Falmouth is making mincemeat of the witnesses who have been intimidated, and instructed to change or contradict their stories. We have reports that Liotta's men have abducted relatives of some witnesses and are holding them until that witness's testimony is over, and completed satisfactorily from their point of view.

"The question is this: Do we proceed with all our original list of witnesses, and hope that the drip-drip effect will work with the jury? Do we believe that the sheer number of witnesses is so great that the jury will decide that not all of them can be lying, and convict? Or do we cut out all those witnesses we think Liotta has got to, and proceed straight to the last four, who we can be certain of? That way we lose the drip-drip effect, but we also prevent Falmouth from casting doubt on our whole case. What do you think?"

Angelo spoke first. "Do we have any idea of the defense they're gonna mount?"

Foley shifted in his seat. "All I know, all I'm allowed to know, is that the defense expects their side of the proceedings to last about eight days. Which, going by other criminal trials, means that they'll have anything from eight to twenty witnesses, all of them—I'm willing to bet—giving Liotta and his people rock-solid alibis. He has two aides with him in court, who I'm sure relay all the testimony to the defense witnesses. Those boys are coming and going all the time."

"So their tactic has been to mount as many witnesses as we have, right?"

The district attorney nodded.

"And whereas we gotta provide a list of our witnesses in advance, they do not. Right?"

Again Foley nodded.

Angelo looked at Parker. The mayor stood and showed Foley to the door. "Thank you for coming, Clarence, thank you very much. I'll see you tomorrow at the courthouse." He closed the door and returned to his seat.

"The problem, as I see it," he began, "is that the way things are arranged, they can have prior knowledge of our case, but we can't have prior knowledge of theirs."

"But we can," said Angelo, suddenly excited. "I should've thought of this before. We couldn't get at them before the trial started because, obviously, Falmouth wouldn't go out to interview these people himself. He would send an aide, and we didn't know which aides he was using. But now we do. Foley told us: they sit by him in court all day long." Angelo nodded to Parker. "We need a coupla men in court tomorrow. I'll arrange it. Have someone point out these aides and we can have them followed. As more of the story given by our witnesses emerges, then the aides transmit that to their side so they can contradict it specifically. Once we know who's giving evidence, we can exert a little pressure of our own. Right?"

Parker smiled. "Right."

Angelo went on. "Let's make sure all the witnesses give evidence. Real foxy. That gives us more time to get to *their* people. I wanna know as soon as we find anyone. Okay?"

Over the next few days the trial dragged on, with witness after witness contradicting himself, or failing to live up to the high expectations the prosecution had for them when the trial had started. One witness described some of the guns used. Then changed his mind. One woman said she had seen men running down Girod Street on the night in question, then agreed with

Falmouth that she hadn't actually *heard* the gunfire and that the men she saw running were actually going *toward* the spot where Martell had been killed. A third witness also saw running men. This time they were definitely running *away* from the scene of the shooting and they shouted at her in Italian. Under cross-examination she admitted that she only *assumed* the language was Italian. She didn't speak it herself, so couldn't be certain. Asked to be specific about the time this episode took place, she said nine forty-five, *before* the shooting. Having started so well, the case against Liotta was beginning to collapse.

Cammarata hadn't changed. Silvio stood at the edge of the main square—if you could call it that—and looked at the church of San Giovanni. The fountain set into the façade still wasn't working. Dogs still slept in the shade of the porch. The bakery on the other side of the piazza still advertised its wares on the same blackboard. How far he was from New Orleans and the trial.

Silvio had decided to start with Smeralda, but all he knew was that she lived in Cammarata, nothing more exact. He was therefore gambling on the fact that she would be at Mass and hoped to intercept her or follow her when she came out of the church. He had walked from the station, about five miles away, and was a little tired. He was happy enough to wait for the service to end.

When it did end, not many people came out. Those who did were mainly old. But Smeralda was among them. She was gray now, her hair swept back in a bun, with a lined face that was surprisingly hard. Brown, with cracks running down it, like the crevices on the slopes of Mount Busambra. He didn't move. He couldn't show himself in public. He would follow her home.

She stood talking to two other women for a while, then moved off, heading west. Silvio followed her at a distance. She turned into a tiny street that was really the edge of the town, overlooked by the gray bulk of Mount Cammarata itself. Halfway along, she disappeared into a dark doorway. Silvio followed her straight in but then stood inside the doorway for a moment. He let his eyes adjust to the gloom and listened. The doorway was in fact a short passage that led to a courtyard. Across the courtyard was another door and a window. He could see Smeralda moving about.

He walked down the corridor and across the courtyard. He

didn't knock but just stood in the second doorway and said softly, "Smeralda."

She looked up, startled. Then her eyes widened. Finally, the lines around her mouth tightened. "How dare you come here, you brute. You should have stayed in America, or hell. *Vattene!* Get out!"

"Smeralda! I didn't do it! You can't believe that I did. I was tricked, set up. That's why I've come back. To settle things. *Sono orfano!*"

"Bah! You've come back for Annunziata. You can't fool me, even if you can fool yourself. Leave her alone, *bruto*. She's going to be married. Now, I say again. Go. *Via! Via!*"

"Smeralda, I swear I did not kill those children. Alesso did it and shifted the blame onto me. Why would I do such a thing?"

She raised her arm and pointed her finger at him. "Because you are bad, unnatural. *Disumano.* I don't know what streak of evil in you makes you prey on Annunziata. Your father was such a good man. But that streak of evil must also account for what you did in Bagheria. Bah!" And she waved him away, dismissing him.

Silvio was shocked. It had never occurred to him that people like Smeralda would link his "unnatural" love for Annunziata, as they put it, with the killings in Bagheria. But it was, he supposed, obvious enough in their old-fashioned, superstitious world.

He got a grip on himself. He had hardly made a good start on his return and he had to salvage some of the situation.

"Smeralda, listen to me for a moment. Please. You were my mother once; don't turn on me now."

She turned back to look at him, but her face hadn't softened.

"Tell me, first, what news of Bastiano?"

"He's in Ucciardone, where you should be."

"Is he well?"

"No, he is not well. They are breaking his spirit. He will not make old bones."

Silvio sighed. "Smeralda, after the orphanage business, I ran away. I had to. But now I've come to try and settle things. So that the truth will be known. I'm not a good man, but I'm not the bad man that you think. Please believe me."

The look on her face was quite clear. She did not believe him. He realized that now. He should not have come here.

"I ask you one thing only. If you won't help me, then at least tell no one I'm here. Please, Smeralda, do this one thing for me."

Her face didn't soften. She just stared at him until he turned and walked away.

After three days of following Falmouth's aides each time they left the court, Angelo's men finally got lucky. The aides visited three people on the same day, all of whom turned out to be defense witnesses. Angelo's men were able to discover through the New Orleans grapevine that they were Liotta's people.

This breakthrough was discussed at the next Pickwick breakfast. "Now," said Angelo, "we'll keep following the aides. We need to know the identities of *all* their witnesses if possible." He turned to Parker. "There's one other thing I need to know. How long will the case last from here on?"

Parker steepled his fingers. "I saw Foley again last night. We have four more regular witnesses—all strong, people who Liotta didn't get to. Say four days for them, with cross-examination. It doesn't look now as though di Passo can give evidence. He's still too weak, still running a fever. I'm sorry, but there it is. A disaster, an expensive disaster."

"So," said Angelo. "It's now Tuesday, which gives me four days to get things organized. That should be enough. I can't act too soon because if I do, that alerts Liotta to the fact that we know who his people are, and it allows him time to find fresh witnesses."

That night Angelo was late arriving home. After the trial, and despite his liver trouble, he needed to relax—at cards. So it was past midnight when he let himself into the house. He was surprised to see a light flickering in the living room, and even more surprised to see Anna-Maria still up. She looked tired, ravaged by her bereavement.

"Couldn't you sleep?" he asked her.

She shook her head. "But I wanted to wait up anyway. I have some news. Nino's escaped from jail."

Angelo stared at her. "How? When?"

"Frank Cassidy told me. It came through on the police wire. In case he comes here. He tricked his way out of the prison hospital."

Angelo sat down. "The old fox. D'you think that's what he'll do? Come here, I mean?"

"Maybe," said Anna-Maria. "But that's not my main worry."

He looked at her.

"He's more likely to go to Sicily. There'll be *sbirri* crawling all over the island. They'll be looking for Nino—but they might just stumble across Silvio."

"Have some salami. This is the best in all Sicily." Ruggiero Priola handed the plate to Silvio.

Taking it, Silvio said, "Angelo still remembers this restaurant. He often talks about it. There's nothing like it in New Orleans, that's for sure."

Silvio's reception by Ruggiero had at least been better than Smeralda's. He had walked back from Cammarata to the railroad station, waited a couple of hours, then caught the Terme Imerese train, which connected with one to Palermo. Between Terme Imerese and Palermo the train had traveled through Bagheria and the very cutting where Silvio had planned the ambush, and then been ambushed himself, months and months ago.

Just as he had known Smeralda would be at Mass, so he knew Ruggiero would be at Calogero's restaurant. The walls and the floor were lined with marble tiles. Noise echoed this way and that. He had sat down at the back, around seven-thirty, and ordered a plate of prosciutto and some red wine. Then he had waited.

Ruggiero had arrived an hour later and found his regular table. As soon as he had finished saying hello to others he knew in the restaurant, Silvio got up, crossed the room, and sat down next to Ruggiero, saying as he did so, "Try not to look surprised."

Ruggiero had handled it superbly. He had hardly paused, in the middle of dabbing his bread in some olive oil, but gone on eating as though Silvio dropped by every day. His first words were, "You hungry?"

Silvio nodded. "Especially for information."

"Let's move, nearer the back." Ruggiero got up, leading the way. Carrying his bread and wine, he wove a route through the tables to the back of the restaurant, shouting to the owner, whom he obviously knew very well, that tonight he wanted a bit of peace and quiet. He found a table and sat himself against a wall. "You sit with your back to the room," he said softly. "I think it's safer."

He ordered dinner by barking instructions across the tables at various waiters, who didn't seem to need to write down anything he said.

That done, he looked at Silvio. "You look good. You haven't come to kill me, I hope."

Silvio smiled and gripped Ruggiero's wrist. "No. But I'm here to settle things. You know why."

"I guessed you'd have to, sooner or later."

"Where is he? Alesso, I mean."

"I know who you mean, *irato*. But it's all changed up there now, Silvio. After Bastiano was busted, we cleared out from Bivio Indisi. It was too dangerous, and in any case Alesso had made a deal with the Imbriacis and the Liottas. After he set you up, the Liottas in Bagheria gave him a reward, one of their smaller livings around Alia—Valledolmo, Vallelunga, Marcato Bianco. Plenty of olives, almonds, a little wine, figs, some quarries. He pays tribute to them, of course, but he does very well. He lives in a house in Vallelunga and operates from there. He's the Don in Alia."

"And Annunziata? They're going to be married?"

"Yes. August the sixteenth."

"Where?"

"Where else? The Madonna dell'Olio. They're hoping to live in Fontana Murata, on an estate that's coming up for sale. Some Englishman is selling and there's an auction quite soon."

"Where is she?"

The other man lowered his eyes, and colored slightly.

"Come on, Ruggiero. Where is she? You owe me, damn you."

Ruggiero shrugged. "It's no secret. At Quisquina. She's helping look after Father Ignazio. He's dying."

Silvio relaxed then. At last. After he had seen Smeralda, in Cammarata, he had half feared that the island might be closed to him, that no one would tell him where Alesso and Annunziata were. Now he knew.

That's when the salami was served.

"What are you going to do, Silvio?" Ruggiero tackled what was uppermost in their minds.

"I don't know yet, but I've got a few days." He forked salami into his mouth and chewed for a moment. Then he said, "Tell me, Ruggiero, you have always known the truth of what happened in the orphanage in Bagheria. Why didn't you go for Alesso?"

Ruggiero nodded. "I thought you'd ask, but the answer's simple. *Affari*. Business. I wanted to kill Alesso but was overruled by the family. I can't blame them. After the explosion, and the deaths, the *sbirri* and the militia went mad and clamped down completely. Even the foxes stayed home. They closed warehouses, whorehouses, gambling joints, interfered in all the rackets, stopped all kickbacks, at least for a while. I tell you, everybody was hit in one way or another. It was so bad a top-level meeting of all the families was called, in Corleone. There it was agreed that it was too dangerous and too stupid to have more vendettas. Everyone wanted a quiet life, a return to making money. So an accommodation was reached. The Liottas had to give Alesso a living, and they were told they had to look after Bastiano's family. In exchange for that, there were to be no killings, nothing to keep the police and militia on our backs. It was a business solution."

The spaghetti had arrived. Silvio was thinking as he ate. What Ruggiero said had all the logic of the Sicilian Mafia, a cynical realism that he knew well. He looked into Ruggiero's eyes. "I am not part of that agreement."

"I know. And don't worry. I won't interfere. I owe you that."

Silvio gripped the other man's wrist again. "Thank you."

For a while they ate in silence. Then a thought struck Silvio. "Fontana Murata? Isn't that the estate that belonged to the English priest . . . Livesey . . . you know, the man Nino kidnapped?"

Ruggiero nodded. "You've got a good memory. Reminds me of something, too. Nino escaped the other day. Tricked his way out."

Silvio whistled. "Foxy! Still foxy after ten years in jail."

"Be careful. There's *sbirri* everywhere. They think he might come here."

Silvio shrugged. "Maybe. But America's safer." He drank some wine, thinking. Then he said, "Tell me more about Alesso and the deal at Fontana Murata."

Ruggiero looked uncomfortable. "I have to tell you, Silvio, that we—the Priola family, that is—are backing Alesso in this."

Silvio went to interrupt but Ruggiero waved him down. "Let me finish. You haven't heard what I've got to say." He wiped his lips with his napkin. "The government made some geological sweep through the entire island recently. We've got someone inside—like always. Seems that the sulfur mines are all played out now, but . . . *but*, there's coal under Fontana Murata, loads of it.

With these railroads expanding all the time, there's going to be a great demand for coal, and Fontana Murata is a mile or so from the Caltasinetta line at Valledolmo. It's perfect. What's more, no one else knows what we know."

He looked hard at Silvio. "I shouldn't be telling you this, but I do owe you. What it means, though, is that you'll get no Priola help—none at all. You're completely on your own. I'm sorry, but it's best that you know the truth."

Now it was Silvio's turn to stare down Ruggiero. "You mean that Alesso is going to figure in some major way in this deal, largely by accident, because he was put out to pasture at Alia, all as a result of what he did to me?"

Ruggiero sipped his wine, then nodded.

"Jesus!" hissed Silvio. He gulped at his glass. "The house and estate are being auctioned, right?"

"Right."

"Is it a real auction?"

"So far, yes. We're leaning on people, of course. A few big local landlords are interested—Tamburello, Mancuso, Librizzi. But they don't know what we know, so we can't lean too hard on anyone in case they get suspicious. There's so much at stake that, for once, we're leaving well enough alone. The house and estate are valued at two hundred million lire, so we've set aside three."

"Who'll be doing the bidding?"

"I will. It's my territory, always has been, since Nino's day. You know that. It's why I know so much."

Silvio refilled their wineglasses and drank more of the red Salaparuto. He was at last beginning to enjoy his dinner. For the first time since he had landed in Sicily, he thought he saw an opening for himself.

Clarence Foley's predictions about the duration of the trial were borne out by events. In the final days of the prosecution's case, their witnesses performed well on the stand, resisting Falmouth's attacks on their credibility. Each claimed to have seen one or more of the men in the dock near the scene of the shooting at the time that it took place. The newspapers loved all this and the trial remained the main item of front-page news day in, day out.

Toward the end of that second week, Gino Fazio was allowed back into court.

Foley finished his case for the prosecution at about 2:30 P.M. on the Friday of that second week. Judge McCrystal decided to adjourn until the following Monday.

Silvio sat on the Pratomeno mountain, among the olive trees, and gripped the telescope he had found in Palermo. Behind him the mule he had bought in Manchi grazed peacefully. The new railroads continued to be a boon, enabling him to cover large distances. Pratomeno, which overlooked Vallelunga, was over fifty miles from Palermo, two long, hard days at least on a mule. He had reached Manchi in five hours.

From there he needed to get off the beaten track, and so he had bought a mule. A mule and a telescope were all he needed for the moment.

Below him, Vallelunga was coming to life as the sun rose and the day began to warm up. Vallelunga had one main street, straight, with three side roads that led off it. At one point the main street widened to form a piazza of sorts. Here were the church, the café, and the baker's. And that was all.

Silvio wanted to get a sight of Alesso for two reasons. He needed first to know how many bodyguards he had. Was he guarded at all? How did he move around? Second, he wanted to see his face. He didn't know whether the telescope would be powerful enough for that—but he had to try. He had to read that face, to know if . . . how . . . Alesso had changed since Bagheria.

All day Silvio sat there in the shade of the olive and almond trees. Vallelunga was like any sleepy village in Sicily. Two dozen terra-cotta roofs, like a rash on the flanks of a mule. It was hardly New Orleans. He found that the telescope did enable him to study the faces of the people who passed to and fro. But there was no sign of Alesso Alcamo.

24

On Monday, July 24, 1891, the defense began its case. James Falmouth's first witness was Ugo Pagliari. He was a baker, and lived out at Metairie. According to his testimony, on the night in question he was with Solazzo and Vincenzo Liotta, two of the defendants, at his home, celebrating the birthday of a mutual friend. Later that day and on the following days, more and more witnesses provided exactly the same sort of testimony, alibis for one, or two, or in some cases three of the defendants. In some cases, the defendants had three or four alibi witnesses. Parker could sense that the jury was becoming confused by the weight of testimony. They couldn't *all* be lying, surely?

Clarence Foley appeared not to make much of these witnesses, not to begin with anyway. However, on the evening of the fourth day, a Thursday, the defense called a Mrs. Aquila. She said that she was a seamstress who made costumes for Mardi Gras and fancy-dress parties, and she testified that on the night Chief Martell was shot, she was with two of the defendants, Carmen Sinagra and Vanni Brancaccio, fitting them for costumes for a party, at her workshop on Carondelet Street. This was a good mile from the scene of the shooting, and she said the men were with her until ten-thirty at least, because they all drank a little absinthe together, after the fitting.

Then Clarence Foley rose to cross-examine Mrs. Aquila. He held some papers in his hand. "Mrs. Aquila," he began. "Are you absolutely sure that the night Mr. Sinagra and Mr. Brancaccio visited you was the night Chief Martell was shot?"

"Oh yes," she said. "I remember it very well. It was raining."

"And how much absinthe did you drink?"

"I'm not sure. Coupla glasses."

"So you remember very well that it was raining, but not how much you drank?"

"I guess so."

Foley paused. "Do you drink absinthe a lot, Mrs. Aquila?"

"Some."

"Come now, Mrs. Aquila, you don't do yourself justice. Isn't it true that you drink a lot of absinthe, a great deal indeed?"

"Objection, Your Honor!" Falmouth was on his feet. "Mrs. Aquila's drinking habits are not on trial here."

"Your Honor," said Foley smoothly. "I believe I can show that this witness was not in a position to provide an alibi for these two defendants, if the court will indulge me a few more moments."

The judge nodded. "You may continue, Mr. Foley."

Foley turned back to the witness. "Mrs. Aquila, in my hand I hold several sworn affidavits from people who know you." He inspected the papers he was holding. "I see the signatures of Charles Harrison, Edna Denegre, James Buhl. Each of them testifies that you are addicted to absinthe, that normally you are dead to the world by eight in the evening—"

"That isn't—"

"And that the reason you have your own workshop is that you were dismissed from King's Carnival Costumes, because of your drinking habits." He held one sheet aloft. "This is the affidavit of Mr. Thomas King, manager of that company. He confirms that version of events."

There was silence in the court. Foley stood over Mrs. Aquila, whose eyes were downcast. "How can you say that these two men, Carmen Sinagra and Vanni Brancaccio, were in your workshop at ten-thirty that night, when you had passed out two hours before? How could you have known it was raining when you were unconscious? How, with your condition, could you possibly give an alibi for *anyone*?"

Again there was silence in the court as people waited for Mrs. Aquila's answer.

But her eyes remained lowered. She said nothing.

Foley returned to his place and sat down.

He had chosen his target well. By casting serious doubt on one alibi witness, he cast doubt on all of them: perhaps these "witnesses" all belonged to Liotta's family.

* * *

Silvio was learning far more about life in Vallelunga than he needed to know. He knew that the priest, a small, thin, balding man, visited a certain home twice a day, once in the morning and again in the evening. Was someone dying there, or was he having an affair? He knew which women bought three loaves at the bakery, and which ones bought two. He knew which children belonged to which houses. But so far he had not caught sight of Alesso Alcamo.

Was he away? It was possible. Silvio couldn't wait on this vigil forever. There were things he had to do if his plan, conceived that night in the restaurant in Palermo, during his dinner with Ruggiero, was to be put into effect. But finding Alesso was important.

It was late morning. He watched half a dozen children leave a building near the church. That must be the school, and schools were rare in Sicily. A little later two old women carried buckets to the main square, filled them from the fountain, and waddled back the way they had come.

Suddenly Silvio grunted to himself, almost without realizing it. Three figures were coming toward him, down the main street, from the far end of town. He aimed his telescope at them, and refocused. They were men, that was for sure. Two appeared to be arguing, but he couldn't see their faces.

They came closer. They were wearing shirts and trousers, no jackets. Silvio felt a gnawing sensation in the pit of his stomach.

Yes! Alesso hadn't changed much. The same high forehead, the same rather bony nose, the same self-confident way of standing with his hands on his hips. He was one of those arguing, of course. Typical. He always did like laying down the law.

The three men stood for a moment in the main piazza. Then the man Alesso was arguing with went off in one direction, and Alesso and the third man continued walking down the main street. They reached a house on the outskirts of the village, right underneath where Silvio was hiding, and went through a gate that gave onto a courtyard. They crossed the courtyard and entered the main house.

Silvio kept his telescope trained on the house. No one came or went. No one was posted outside, in either the courtyard or the street. Alesso did not reappear for the rest of the day.

Had he just returned from a trip? It was impossible to be sure, but what did seem to be true was that he wasn't bothered by security. He had one bodyguard but no one else. Alesso, it seemed clear, felt reasonably safe. He was cocky as a bantam. One bodyguard could still be a problem, but the situation could have been worse. A lot worse.

At the start of the third week of the trial Parker and Angelo resumed their breakfasts in the private room at the Pickwick. "It's difficult to know where the balance lies," said Parker. "They sowed doubt with a lot of our witnesses, and now we have sowed some doubts with a lot of theirs."

"And?"

Parker shrugged. "Foley says that in a close decision, the defense will always have the advantage."

"You don't think Fazio's confession swayed the jury?"

"A little bit, maybe. The fact that Fazio is unstable doesn't change the fact that he is a hood, but juries don't like crazies. They may simply ignore Fazio. In any case, that's not our main problem."

"What is?"

"There's been a burglary at the court office. The list of jurors was stolen. It has to be Liotta."

"Can't we tell the judge?" cried Angelo. "Have the trial stopped?"

"If we do that," said Parker, "Falmouth will ask for his people to be released, pending a new trial. Do we want that?"

Angelo remained silent. Then he said, "Why can't we do the same? Get to the jury."

Parker shook his head. "No. A guilty verdict has to be unanimous. So the defense only has to get at one, two, or three people on the jury, induce or bribe them to disagree with all the others— and you have a mistrial. We'd have to get to all twelve. That would be costly, time-consuming—and risky. If it leaked out, Falmouth would go to the judge and claim a mistrial anyway, and again he'd ask that Liotta and the others be released, pending a new court hearing. Do you want to run that risk?"

Angelo shook his head.

Again there was silence around the table.

"All we can do," breathed Parker at length, "is hope and pray."

Angelo shook his head. "No, there's still one card we can play."

The other man looked at him.

"We wait for the defense to end their case. Then di Passo has to give evidence."

"The judge will never allow it," said Parker. "The prosecution has completed its case."

"But there's a precedent," said Angelo quietly.

"Oh yes? How do you know? You a legal expert?"

"No. But it was a trick used against us, way back. In New York. An English priest, who'd been scalped. He gave evidence for the prosecution after the defense had finished their case. It worked against us then. Maybe it'll go the other way now."

The Serra de Moneta was a far more difficult observation post then Pratomeno. Because the abbey of Quisquina was three thousand feet above sea level, Silvio had to be higher than that if he was to properly observe all its comings and goings. But at that height there were no trees and he was forced to hide behind rocks and boulders. That made his vigil uncomfortable.

Strictly speaking, he didn't have to do this, not yet. The plan he had formulated did not call for him to see Annunziata, but he couldn't help himself. He *had* to see her as soon as possible, even if it was only from a distance, when she couldn't see him. He had ridden over from Vallelunga the previous day, on a journey that had brought back memories, taking him closer to Bivio Indisi than he had ever been before. Before he had left Vallelunga, however, he had seen a good deal more of Alesso and was satisfied that he was not heavily guarded and that he followed a simple routine. Silvio had bought bread at a bakery on the way and helped himself to water from the fountain of a village he had passed through. He was as content as the circumstances would allow.

He focused his telescope on the abbey. Monks were still working in the almond groves as they always had. Once he fancied he saw Luigi Garofali, who had been there the night it was decided that Nino and Silvio should go to America, but he couldn't be sure. As yet there was no sign of Ignazio Serravalle or Annunziata.

Silvio didn't yet know how he was going to kill Alesso, but he wasn't worried. The wedding was still a few days away, and between now and then there were things to put in place. As far as he was concerned, it was a stroke of good fortune that the house auction came first. That fitted his plan perfectly.

He suddenly noticed a flash of color to the left of his field of vision. A woman's dress? He was right. A woman—or a girl—was approaching the main gate of the abbey, up the long incline that he knew so well.

But it wasn't Annunziata. The dress was blue and the woman's hair was jet-black, more like Silvio's own than Zata's. The woman stood at the main gate and pulled at the bell. After a short delay a monk appeared, talked to her for a few moments, then admitted her.

An hour passed. The high sun beat down on the rocks of the *serra*, making the mountains almost white with heat. Above him an eagle, wings outstretched, circled on a current of warm air, looking for prey. Silvio had visited the abbey often enough to know that the visitor would be there for at least three hours. She would be fed, offered water and wine, and rest. She would not leave until the day began to cool.

Around three-thirty she reappeared. She stepped through the gate, and a woman in a black dress came after her. Silvio knew from the way that this second woman moved that it was Annunziata, even before he refocused his binoculars. His heart beat faster. She was as blond as ever, her skin as clear. There were the same lines around her face. Yet there was a change that he could detect even at this distance. She was listless. It was as if a light inside her had been extinguished.

As Silvio watched, the two women embraced. Then the woman in the blue dress turned and began to descend the incline away from the abbey gate. Annunziata stood and watched her go. After about a hundred yards, the woman in blue turned and waved to Annunziata, who raised her arm, then stepped back inside the abbey, closing the door behind her.

He had seen her. Inside him, he now knew, the same fire still burned. It was right that he had come. He had never really doubted that it was, but it was good to have it confirmed all the same. He took out the ring he still carried with him, and kissed it.

Suddenly he was jolted out of his reverie. The woman in blue had nearly reached the foot of the long incline in front of the abbey and was a good deal closer to him than she had been before. He now recognized her face. He had seen her before—in Vallelunga. Had she brought Annunziata a message from Alesso? And, if so, what? Had Smeralda betrayed him?

* * *

On the Tuesday of the third week, the defense finished presenting its case. There had been thirteen witnesses for the prosecution but twenty-three for the defense, all alibi witnesses. Foley had been able to dent some of them, but none so convincingly as Mrs. Aquila. It was difficult to know what the drip-drip effect of so many witnesses was having on the jury.

So, after Falmouth sat down, Foley rose. "Your Honor, in the few days since the prosecution finished its case, a new witness has become available. I had known about him before but had assumed he wouldn't be giving evidence since he was too ill. Over the weekend, however, I have been informed that his recovery is now taking place and he is anxious to do his civic duty—"

"Objection, Your Honor!" Falmouth was on his feet. "The defense has had no notice of this witness. The whole idea is most irregular."

"I agree it is irregular, Mr.Falmouth. The question is: Is the new witness important? Mr. Foley?"

"I would be happy to explain in chambers, Your Honor."

"Yes, I think you should."

The two attorneys and the judge adjourned to the judge's room, off the court.

"Now, is this another eyewitness, Mr. Foley? You've had thirteen and I don't see how—"

"No, judge." Foley explained about di Passo, how he was a Pinkerton agent and had been infiltrated into the jail to eavesdrop on the defendants.

Falmouth became agitated as Foley began this story, and eventually very angry."Judge!" he screamed. "You can't allow this witness. The evidence was obtained illegally and by the most tawdry piece of deception. It is an outrage."

"Calm down, Mr. Falmouth. You are not in front of the jury now. Have you anything more to say, Mr. Foley?"

"Yes, Your Honor. This is an important witness because his evidence is so unlike that of the others. It tends to corroborate what the others had to say, yet adds a lot of detail about how the Mafia works in New Orleans. He could be a very important witness, not just for this case, but in regard to criminal activity on a wider scale. Also, he caught dysentery in the prison, which is why we didn't think he could give evidence. He risked his life for this case and wants his day in court."

"I'm not interested in his health, Mr. Foley, or in the light he may throw on wider criminal practices. I agree that he may provide new evidence, but I'm not sure I want to create a legal precedent with such a move. That could give grounds for appeal—"

"There *is* a precedent, judge. The People versus Greco and Randazzo, 1881. A priest who had come to New York to give evidence, but whose boat was delayed—"

"Yes, yes. I remember the case, Mr. Foley. Thank you." He turned to the other man. "I'll allow this testimony, Mr. Falmouth, and no more arguments, please. The trial has already gone on long enough." And with that, they returned to the courtroom.

The main house at Fontana Murata was handsome. There was no doubt about that. It was large, made of yellow Cammarata stone, had a wide terrace and a formal garden that sloped away from the front of the house. There were box hedges, alleys of cypress trees, an ornamental pond, dried up at the moment.

Silvio had followed Alesso here. At a distance, of course. He had watched, earlier in the day, as Alesso had saddled his mule, in the courtyard of his house, and ridden north out of Vallelunga with another man. They had headed west, toward La Catena, along the road that paralleled the new railway, past the road that joined from the north, from Valledolmo, until they reached the Regalmici crossroads, where they turned right onto the Fontana Murata track.

At first Silvio hadn't known where they were headed and hadn't cared. He just wanted to study Alesso, to get as close to him as he could, so that he knew his man when the time came. He watched now as Alesso dismounted in front of the main house. It was obviously deserted and closed up. Alesso strutted this way and that, as if he were inspecting the property, as if it were already his. He took a knife from his boot and played with it, throwing it expertly at a tree trunk.

As Silvio watched this performance he made himself a silent vow: Annunziata would never live in this house.

Guido di Passo appeared in the courtroom, pale and emaciated, his eyes like dark sockets, his neck scrawny. His voice was quiet. He took his place tentatively on the stand and read the oath. Falmouth glared from him to the dock, where, as soon as di Passo had appeared, Gino Fazio had begun to fidget.

Clarence Foley took the Pinkerton man through his story very slowly. He began with his training. He then moved on to his other cases, to demonstrate his credentials. Everyone had heard of Butch Cassidy and the Sundance Kid, and the court was utterly silent, spellbound, as he recounted his efforts to mastermind their capture. Even Fazio stopped fidgeting.

Then Foley brought di Passo back to the case in question. He described the meeting in Chicago, where he had been introduced to Parker and been offered the job by William Pinkerton. He did not mention Angelo Priola. He described his journey to Amite, and the Astoria Hotel. He described his arrest, how he had nearly been shot by a fellow resident when he pretended to make an escape, and how he had deliberately been infiltrated into the prison and put in a cell with Gino Fazio.

All through the story, the public galleries were enthralled and the press scribbled away in earnest. Foley led di Passo through Fazio's deteriorating behavior. The Pinkerton detective explained how Fazio began confessing his part in various crimes on Liotta's behalf. He had, for example, described his initiation into the Mafia.

"Please tell the court what he said," Foley asked.

"He said it took place outside the city, in the countryside. He said there was a ceremony. He had to hold a piece of paper on which was printed a holy image. Someone pricked blood from his finger, and he had to drip blood onto the image. He said the image represented the authority of the Mafia, which was as absolute as the church's. The blood showed he was joining a brotherhood. Then the image was set on fire and Fazio was forced to pass it from one hand to the other until it was all burned up—the singeing of the flesh symbolized the pain he would feel if ever he betrayed the brotherhood."

Next, di Passo told how Fazio had described their attack on the ice factory, and another incident, in which a steamboat captain who refused to accept bribes had been murdered.

Falmouth tried to interrupt several times. "Your Honor, I object wholeheartedly to this line of questioning. These events have nothing to do with this case. Mr. Foley is willfully misleading the court."

The judge looked at the prosecuting attorney. "Well?"

"Your Honor, I agree that so far all this witness has given us is background information. But I maintain it is important to show the court what sort of people the defendants are. And I shall shortly be addressing the main issue."

The judge nodded. "Very well. You may proceed, Mr. Foley, but please get to the main matter as quickly as possible."

Foley wouldn't be hurried, though. Di Passo was going down well, and he knew it. As the truth was revealed Gino Fazio was becoming more and more agitated in the dock, and the jury could not help but notice. In fact, by now Fazio was a good bit more than agitated. He would occasionally call out, shouting "Rubbish!" or "Not true!" when di Passo was speaking. Several times the judge ordered him to be quiet.

Finally, Foley brought di Passo around to the shooting of Martell.

"Did Gino Fazio ever discuss the shooting of David Martell with you?"

"Yes, he did."

Utter silence in the court. Even Fazio was still.

"What did he say?"

"He said he knew who had done it."

A buzz of noise went through the court. In the dock Fazio was not shouting anymore, but sat whimpering in his seat. "He's lying. It's a lie. He's lying."

"Did he mention any names?"

"No, but he said he knew not only who had pulled the trigger that night but who had organized it and *why* it had been done. I'm afraid that both he and I had dysentery very badly at that stage and we were both very weak."

"I understand, Mr. di Passo, and the court is grateful that you have been able to give this testimony, despite your illness. I won't keep you much longer, but please tell the court if Gino Fazio said anything else relevant to this case while you were in Parish Prison together."

Di Passo hesitated, for effect. "During our conversations, he said that, although he knew who killed Martell, he didn't know everything. He said there was only one man who knew everything. Then, one day as we were going to the washrooms, he pointed out this man who knew everything, in another cell."

"And can you see that other man, the man who knew everything, in the court today? Look very carefully and tell us if that man is here."

"Oh yes," said di Passo. "I've no doubt. That's him." And he pointed at Vito Liotta.

Alia was a big village, twice the size of Vallelunga and nearly as big as Cammarata. It was situated on the side of a hill, the Zappalanotte, and consisted of six streets, three of which came together to form a triangular-shaped piazza in front of the church. Here there was a café, a bank, and not much else.

Silvio was still following Alesso. The other man had continued on here after Fontana Murata, which now appeared to have been the secondary reason for the journey. Alesso had been in the café for more than two hours, and Silvio, watching from the ruins of a cottage beyond the far side of the square, had observed a regular stream of people visiting the café. As Don of Alia, Alesso appeared to be fulfilling his obligations. A single bodyguard sat outside. Silvio had no doubt that he was armed.

By now Silvio had a good picture of Alesso's routine. It was hardly exciting, scarcely matched the bustle of life in the French Quarter, but that was so much the better from Silvio's point of view. He still hadn't fathomed exactly how he was going to end Alesso's days, but it would come, it would come.

He thought about New Orleans from time to time, but he didn't want to dwell too much on the trial. If he did he would only worry that Liotta might have gotten off and he had to concentrate on the job at hand, if he wanted to achieve what he had come all this way to do. He had to rely on Angelo.

He wondered about Nino and his escape. The old fox had been so near death. Now this. Even if Liotta got off, he'd have to contend with Nino now, as well as Silvio himself.

He brought his mind back to Alia. Alesso was leaving. Silvio watched as the two men mounted their mules and rode off south, back toward Marcato Bianco and Vallelunga.

He let them go. It was time to make the next move.

* * *

Guido di Passo's evidence created a sensation. Foley's examination had finished at about half past three on that Monday, so the judge had adjourned the trial for the day. Tuesday's papers were dominated by the prosecution's revelations. LIOTTA FINGERED AS MAFIA CHIEF, said the *Times-Democrat*. DRAMATIC JAIL CONFESSION REVEALED said the *Picayune*.

Borgo Regalmici was about halfway between Cammarata and Vallelunga, a tiny hamlet on the slopes of Mount Perziata along the road that led to the Dominican convent at San Giovane Gemini. Silvio had never been there. All he knew was that this was where Luca Mancuso lived.

Silvio had shown no sign of recognition when Ruggiero mentioned that Mancuso was one of the Priola rivals, interested in buying Fontana Murata, but he hadn't let it pass him by.

He had never met Luca. He had seen him, across the square, that time when he had shot Gaetano in revenge for Nino's betrayal, but that was all. Of course, he could scarcely hope for a warm reception today, having killed Luca's son. But if the old man would hear him out, there ought to be a way forward.

He asked the first person he saw where the Mancuso house was, and was directed to a large farm to the south of the hamlet. He rode up the main track, past farm buildings and machinery, and left his mule tethered to one of three small oak trees that formed a copse. The farmhouse and outbuildings were arranged around three sides of a courtyard, rather as in Bivio Indisi, and he walked toward a large door set into the wall of the main house. Before he could reach it, however, a voice to his right said, "Yes?"

He stopped, and turned. Two men sat at a table under a porch. One was old, gray, and squat. The other was about Silvio's age, and just as thin and dark. He got to his feet.

"I am looking for Luca Mancuso," said Silvio quietly.

"Who wants him?" replied the older man.

Silvio, having stared into Gaetano Mancuso's eyes before he shot him, saw the family resemblance there and then, even though the shooting had been twelve years ago. Before replying, he put his hand in his pocket, where his gun was.

"Sylvano Randazzo."

Both of the other men grunted in amazement as he said this.

Their reaction might have been more violent but for the fact that Silvio had now taken out his gun.

"You are Luca Mancuso?" Silvio asked the older man.

The old man nodded.

"Mr. Mancuso, I have some information for you. Valuable information."

"Why would you bring me information? Information about what? Why should I trust you? You killed my son." He indicated the other man. "Primo's brother."

Silvio looked at Primo, then back to his father. "I've ridden a long way and I'm thirsty. Offer me some wine and I will tell you."

"No wine," growled Luca Mancuso. Then he gestured to a jug. "Water."

This wasn't going to be easy but Silvio had never thought it would be. Sicilians were like the church: they didn't change. He accepted the water jug which Primo held out, and drank directly from it. He put the jug down.

"You are interested in buying Fontana Murata—yes?"

For the first time the impression on Luca Mancuso's face altered. But all he said was: "Go on."

"I understand from Palermo that the government recently completed a geological sweep of Sicily. There is coal under Fontana Murata. The property is far more valuable than anyone thinks. I'm told the expected price is roughly two hundred million lire. I can tell you that the Priolas have set aside three hundred million, not expecting anyone to go that high. But the property is actually worth more, much more. If, at the auction, you outbid the Priolas, you will become one of the richest men in Sicily."

Luca Mancuso eyed Silvio warily. "Why are you telling this to me? To make amends for killing my son? You think you can buy his life back?"

Silvio brushed sweat from his forehead. "Mr. Mancuso, your son was killed because he betrayed the entire family at Bivio Indisi. Because of your son, Nino and I had to flee to America and many people died. Gaetano deserved to die, and if I hadn't killed him someone else would have." He paused. "You know in your heart that what I say is true. You have never sought revenge— because you know that would have been unjust."

He took a deep breath. "I'm doing this for my own reasons. I never planned to blow up the orphanage, to kill those children.

Alesso Alcamo did it to trap me—because he wanted to be Don, the Capo, and because he wanted Annunziata. I had to escape to America for a second time, and while I was away there was a deal made between the Priolas and the Liottas. Alesso is now Don in Alia and will live in Fontana Murata, with Annunziata, unless I stop it.

"It so happens that the estate is currently owned by the English priest who Nino kidnapped. Or rather by his sister, since his death. If you outbid the Priolas, and pay more than three hundred million lire for Fontana Murata, the priest's sister does well, you become rich—and Alesso loses. It's a happy fact, maybe, and given what's happened, that the Englishwoman and you should benefit from my plan. But believe me, my main aim is to ensure that Alesso loses. I want him to lose Fontana Murata and then I want him, the Priolas, and the Liottas to know that I outthought them all. Then I shall kill Alesso. *Sono sciocco?* Am I a fool?

"*That* is why I'm telling you all this. I ask nothing from you except silence—that you tell no one I'm here. So I can complete what I came to do."

He stood facing them, waiting for a response. Luca Mancuso was a shrewd man, a true Sicilian cynic. What Silvio had told him was all perfectly true, but Sicilians always looked for the twist in the story. "Never forget the fox has a tail" went the saying. This time there was no twist in the story, but Silvio could only hope that Luca Mancuso was astute enough to recognize that.

The three men stood, staring at each other for almost a minute. The Mancusos were in the shade but Silvio was in the full glare of the sun.

Luca Mancuso never took his eyes off Silvio, but he eventually spoke to his son. "Primo," he growled. "Pass him some wine."

On the Tuesday, Falmouth rose for the cross-examination of di Passo. "Mr. di Passo," he began. "Do you see Gino Fazio in the dock this morning?"

Di Passo looked across to the row of defendants. "No."

"The reason Mr. Fazio is not in the dock this morning, Mr. di Passo, is that last evening, after the trial proceedings concluded for the day, he suffered a severe nervous breakdown. This is the second time Mr. Fazio has been unable to attend court because of his health, but last night's breakdown was brought about by your behavior, Mr. di Passo. Are you proud of yourself?"

"Objection!" Foley was on his feet. "This aggressive line of questioning is irrelevant to the main issue, Your Honor."

"Overruled," said the judge.

Falmouth steamed ahead. "Does it give you pleasure to reduce someone who is clearly nervous by nature to a gibbering wreck? Is that why you became a private detective, to *victimize* suspects?"

Di Passo was clearly unnerved by this line of questioning. He hesitated before answering, tentatively, "No, it doesn't."

But Falmouth wasn't interested in his answer. He wanted to make an impression with the jury. "Who chose Gino Fazio as the man you were to share a cell with?"

"The governor of Parish Prison, I suppose."

"And the governor, naturally, knew who the most vulnerable man in the jail was. What an unholy conspiracy, to pick on this hapless creature who is clearly so unstable that almost nothing he says while he is under duress can be relied upon."

Foley was on his feet again. "Your Honor, we may all agree that Mr. Fazio is not well, today. But does that invalidate what he told Mr. di Passo in prison, a conversation that took place over a number of days, at all times of day and night, and when there was no pressure put on Mr. Fazio other than that he put on himself, by doing something that landed him in jail?"

"Thank you for your guidance, Mr. Foley. I am sure we shall all bear it in mind. Mr. Falmouth, you may proceed."

"Thank you, Your Honor. I'd now like to ask you, Mr. di Passo, whether at any time Mr. Fazio told you the name of the person or persons who had killed Chief Martell?"

"Not in so many words."

"I'm sorry, but what does that mean: 'not in so many words'?"

"No."

"So, when he said that he knew who had done this killing, he could have meant anybody, anybody at all."

"Yes, but—"

"Thank you, Mr. di Passo. For all you know, he could have meant that the murder was committed by someone not in jail at the time he made his statement to you."

"Yes, but—"

"Thank you, Mr. di Passo."

"Hold on a minute," said the judge. "What were you going to say, Mr. di Passo?"

Falmouth looked angrily at the judge, but di Passo said quickly, "I was just going to say that if he knew who killed Martell, and if that person wasn't in jail with him, why was he so frightened to tell me?"

Falmouth ignored him. "I come back to the point I was making: it is a fact, is it not, that you spent several weeks in close proximity to Mr. Fazio, during which time you say he told you all manner of things about this so-called Mafia underworld and yet he never— not once—gave you the name of the person who killed Martell? Isn't that true? Please answer yes or no."

"Yes," said di Passo. "It's true."

"Which leads me to this thought, Mr. di Passo. Or rather a thought which I will frame as a question. You have seen Mr. Fazio, as we all have. He is clearly unstable and unwell. People in that state sometimes like to impress others since they are so . . . well, lacking in self-confidence. Mr. Fazio may well be such a person. Therefore, I ask you this: Do you think that when Mr. Fazio told you he knew who had done this killing, do you think that in fact he was telling the truth? Did he actually know, or was he showing off?"

Foley was impressed. Falmouth was doing a good job of sowing the seeds of doubt in the jury's mind.

"I had no doubt at the time that what he told me was the truth."

"The truth as it was or the truth as he saw it?"

"I had no doubt that he knew who killed Martell."

"And now?"

"I . . . I have no doubts now either."

Foley rubbed his chin. Di Passo had done his best. He had said he had no doubts but . . . he had hesitated, showing the jury that he did have doubts but wasn't admitting them.

Falmouth recognized that he had gone as far as he could, and sat down.

Foley rose. "Your Honor, no more questions."

"Very well," said the judge, looking at the clock on the court-room wall. It was 11:40 A.M. "I think we will recess now for lunch. We shall reassemble at one-thirty instead of two, when I shall hear counsels' concluding remarks."

* * *

Silvio picked up an old shoe. This was the room in which Annunziata and he used to make love, so this shoe, a man's shoe, could
well be his own. He looked about the room again. He wasn't sure
why he had come back to the *bivio*. One reason was that he had to
kill time while he waited for the auction. But there were other reasons, of course. His life in Sicily had been cut short suddenly,
beyond his control. Life at the *bivio* had been cut off in much the
same way, as was evident from the remains he had found so far. To
judge from the rubble, the state of the cupboards and drawers, the
beds and the outside sheds, people had left in a hurry and hardly
anyone had returned.

It was depressing. Flies buzzed everywhere. He went down the
stairs and out the back. He looked down to the dried riverbed.
How unlike the Mississippi was this pathetic stream. It symbolized the difference between the size and strength of America and
the thin, arid presence of Sicily. He hadn't thought that when he
was last here; now he did.

He turned to go. It was a mistake to have come back.

"Gentlemen of the jury, this has been a long case but not, I think,
a complicated one. The facts of the matter are not in dispute." The
judge put on his spectacles and scrutinized a piece of paper in
front of him. "David Martell was chief of police of New Orleans
and, on the night of March the twenty-third, was shot, receiving
eleven wounds from which he died the next day. There is no doubt
that *someone*, or some people, murdered him. The question for
you is therefore as simple as it is awesome: were those killers the
same people as now sit before you in the dock of this court?

"Essentially, the evidence you have been asked to consider is
straightforward, too. The prosecution presented you with a long
line of witnesses who say they either saw the killing, or saw
people with guns running away from the killing, and then they
identified those people as one or other of the individuals in the
dock. It has to be said, I think, that the defense called attention to
several discrepancies in their accounts and it is for you to judge
what importance to attach to those discrepancies.

"The defense, for their part, presented an equally long line of
witnesses, all of whom provided alibis for one or more of the
defendants. Again, I should point out that the prosecution then
took issue with several of these alibi witnesses, presenting affi-

davits to the effect that these particular alibi witnesses had not been where they claimed to be.

"The evidence of Mr. Guido di Passo was quite different, as I am sure you appreciate. He is an employee of the Pinkerton's Detective Bureau, and on the initiative of Mr. Parker, the mayor of New Orleans, and with the cooperation of the prison authorities, Mr. di Passo was infiltrated into the prison, apparently as a common criminal himself, and once there he shared a cell with one of the defendants, Mr. Gino Fazio.

"Now, first let me address the morality of the situation whereby Mr. di Passo entered the prison. I, as the judge in the case, have allowed this testimony and it is not for you to decide whether I did right or wrong. I have decided that Mr. di Passo's evidence was admissible and that is the end to the matter. You must judge Mr. di Passo's evidence as you judge the evidence of all the other witnesses.

"What *is* a matter for you is the exact detail of what Mr. di Passo said to you. He outlined that Mr. Fazio told him a great deal about the underworld, but that when he came to discuss this case, what he actually said was that Mr. Fazio had indicated that he knew who had done it. You may feel that in the context of the other conversations which Mr. Fazio had with Mr. di Passo, the meaning was clear enough. Alternatively, you may feel that whereas Mr. Fazio was very explicit on other matters, he was vague—or rather ambiguous—on this one issue, and that the difference is important. That is a matter for you."

Judge McCrystal went on in this remarkably evenhanded way for several hours, reminding the jury of evidence they had first heard nearly three weeks before, and impressing on them that such evidence was every bit as important as evidence presented only a few days before. His summing-up lasted until the next morning, but at about eleven o'clock he was done and the jury was sent out.

The court officials moved onto other business, but the spectators, lawyers, and newspapermen involved in the case hung around the lobby of the courthouse, waiting.

An hour passed and lunch was sent in. Three o'clock came and went. At four-thirty, the jury asked for refreshments. At six, the judge sent word to ask if they were likely to reach a verdict that night. Came the reply: it was unlikely. And so at half past

seven, under the strictest security, the jury was transferred to the
St. Charles Hotel, where accommodations had been reserved
for them.

Angelo Priola, Harrison Parker, and Clarence Foley met that
evening at nine in the Pickwick Club.

"The longer the jury takes, the more likely they are to acquit—
isn't that the accepted wisdom?" Parker looked at Foley.

The attorney shrugged. "That's what the newspapers always
say. But I've known juries to convict after days in the jury room.
Don't forget there are thirteen defendants. They may be arguing
about which ones are guilty and which ones aren't."

"They will acquit," growled Angelo. "Get used to the idea.
What they are arguing about is whether to convict one or two of
the minor characters. In that jury room they all know that if they
convict Liotta, they will suffer. But nine out of the twelve jurors
are small businessmen. They know perfectly well that if they
acquit entirely, they are going to be the most unpopular men in
New Orleans—after Liotta and his men, that is. Their trade will
suffer, their children will be picked on, their clubs will kick them
out. Right now they are cursing the day they ever got involved in
this trial. They are also dragging it out so that they can all say to
their friends that they *tried* to argue for a conviction but were out-
voted. Each man will find some area of doubt to hinge his
acquittal on so he can tell himself he didn't compromise."

No one had anything to say as Angelo completed his bleak
analysis.

"The jury no longer matters," said Angelo after a while. His
chest heaved as he gave a big sigh. "Harrison, it's time I played
our last card. The foxy card. Silvio set it up, but it's up to me to
finesse it." He paused. "Let's hope that New Orleans is not so different from Sicily after all."

Silvio had never seen Alia so crowded. Carriages and wagons
were drawn up on all sides of the piazza. The tables outside the
café were full, children hung around in groups, watching everything. Of course, Fontana Murata was not the only property being
sold today, but it was the biggest, and would be sold last.

Silvio had been crouching in some ruins, the hiding place he
had used on his previous visit, and had been watching people
arrive for the sale. Luca Mancuso was there, in his best suit, with

his son, Primo, and another man who, Silvio guessed, was a banker. Luca had been civil enough after Silvio had outlined his plan, and had certainly turned up at today's sale as if he meant business. But Silvio would only be able to judge by results, maybe two hours from now. He was growing tired of watching events from the sidelines.

Alesso had arrived, too, looking cocky, dressed in a red shirt and black trousers, flanked by his bodyguard and Ruggiero Priola, who would, of course, be doing the actual bidding. They had walked up the steps of the town hall and disappeared inside with all the casual confidence of people who expected things to go their way. Like a couple of bantams.

Silvio had also noticed the arrival of a tall, gray-haired, formidable-looking woman with a large bosom and an elaborate hat. She, he understood, was the Livesey woman, the sister of the priest Nino had kidnapped and the current owner of Fontana Murata. She was accompanied by a man, smaller than her but wiry. She looked apprehensive.

Eleven o'clock had come and gone and the crowd on the piazza, he noticed, was thinning. The auction had begun. For over an hour a thin stream of people came and went to and from the town hall. Some were obviously clerks. Others were owners who, their property sold, hurried across the piazza and ordered a glass of wine or a beer at the café. Others were successful purchasers, who came out with either their families or their lawyers and stood on the steps of the town hall, discussing what they were to do next. A few came out looking worried; their properties had presumably failed to sell.

Another half hour passed. The heat grew more intense. Despite himself, Silvio found it hard not to think about New Orleans and the Liotta trial. Had a verdict been reached yet? Had he been proved right, and had Angelo been able to finesse the situation as Silvio had predicted? Ruggiero, inside the town hall, might know: Angelo could always telegraph Palermo. But Silvio couldn't show himself just yet. He would have to stay in ignorance for a while.

There was also something Smeralda had said, about his father. That had given him an idea he hadn't yet had a chance to follow up.

Suddenly the double doors of the town hall were thrown open and people spilled out onto the steps. All were chattering

excitedly, as if something noteworthy had just happened inside.
Then he saw the Livesey woman push her way through the
crowds and stride across to her carriage. Silvio might have been
mistaken but he thought he saw a smile on her face. From her
point of view, it seemed, the sale had gone well.

But who had the buyer been?

Luca Mancuso came out. He was talking to Primo, but they
both wore the traditional Sicilian poker face. You could not tell
whether, from their point of view, the result was good or bad. Then
two men approached Luca to shake his hand. Was that a sign he
had succeeded? Or were they old friends who hadn't seen him for
some time?

Before Silvio could reflect further, Alesso barged through the
crowd and ran down the steps in front of the town hall. He was followed by Ruggiero. Both men looked furious. At the foot of the
steps, they resumed an argument that must have started inside
the building. Their voices were raised and Silvio noticed Luca
Mancuso looking down at them. The smallest of smiles creased
his face.

Silvio had his answer. Now the final twist of his plan could go
into effect. There was just one item of personal business he had to
attend to first.

The day had started misty but promised to become sunny. Judge
Thomas McCrystal was an early riser and walked with his dog in
Library Park every day. Now that his children had left home,
indeed left the city, he found the dog companionable and these
early-morning jaunts helped clear his mind for the day ahead.

He turned off Tulane Avenue into the park.

"Good morning, Professor Perran."

The judge stopped.

Angelo got up from the bench where he had been sitting,
waiting.

McCrystal's eyes narrowed. "Who are you?"

"I'm Angelo Priola. I'm a relative of someone you know. Vanni
Priola."

The judge looked about him to see who was nearby. No one
was. "What are you doing here? You belong in the Quarter."

"I know. I'm trying to be discreet. Would you have preferred
me to come to your home?"

"I would prefer not to see you at all."

"We both know that's not realistic."

The judge stared at Angelo in distaste, restraining the dog, which was anxious to be on its way. "Walk with me, then. It's less suspicious."

Angelo fell in with the judge and his dog. "Think we'll get a verdict today?"

"I would have thought so, but juries are funny things. Unpredictable, especially in important trials like this one."

"What's your guess about the verdict?"

"You know better than to ask that."

"Do I?"

"Well, I'm not answering."

"They'll acquit. Liotta's interfered with the jury."

McCrystal looked genuinely shocked, as if the thought had never occurred to him. But it wasn't that. "You . . . you want me to declare a mistrial? I can't do that! Not unless someone comes to me with evidence. If I did that, Liotta would—"

"Relax, judge. We both know why I'm here, but I'm not asking you to risk your neck. Getting caught in a whorehouse is not a capital offense, not in my book. I know your power as judge is limited. But you *can* do certain things." He paused. "If they do acquit, and I'm as certain as can be that they will, all you have to do is give one specific little order. You'll be acting well within your rights and no one will suspect anything—not Liotta, for sure. If you do as I ask, you'll have the photograph—and the negative—tomorrow. I promise."

"A little thing, you say?"

"This is a foxy deal. No risk. I promise."

"I can't imagine what it could be."

Angelo told him.

Silvio got down from his mule and tethered the animal to the gate set into the wall of the cemetery. Just outside Castronuovo, the graveyard overlooked Lake Fanaco, which had the Serra di Leone on its western side. It sloped gently down to the water's edge and was a peaceful and colorful spot, with purple patches of bougainvillea festooning the walls in places, and a line of deep green cypress trees leading all the way to the black waters of the lake.

He picked his way among the gravestones. It was a long time

since he had been here, too long. Most of his life since his parents' death he hadn't been able to face the graveyard, preferring to turn his back on that whole part of his life. However, on the boat from New Orleans this time, he had found himself thinking of Castronuovo. Then Smeralda had mentioned his father and he had developed the urge to come. If he did succeed in killing Alesso, he would have to escape to America for the third time. After that, he would certainly never return to Sicily again. There had to be one last visit to his parents' grave.

He remembered, more or less, where the headstone was. The top left corner of the graveyard, near the line of cypresses on the far wall. The sun beat down on the back of his neck as he bent to read the inscriptions. He could be fairly certain that his parents' grave would be one of the least visited and therefore most over-grown, but that appeared to be true of not a few graves. Also, the carving of the names was not always clear, covered in places with yellow lichen. It all reminded him, faintly, of the graveyard in the Ursuline Convent in New Orleans. For a moment his thoughts went back across the Atlantic, to the trial. Was it over yet? The auction here had gone well, things were falling into place. Please God, let the same be true in New Orleans.

Cirami, Gristia, Cangioloso. He moved past the headstones one by one. Some of these families he knew, or had heard of. Pietroso, Velez, Randazzo—ah! It was a plain stone, yellowed like the others. Nettles grew everywhere, untidy, like a goat's beard. He looked down. The words were carved in plain lettering, not fancy and not deep. LORENZO RANDAZZO, 1834–1868 read one line. SYLVANA RANDAZZO, 1837–1868 read the other. Then, under-neath, TOGETHER IN LIFE, TOGETHER IN PEACE.

Tears pricked the corners of Silvio's eyes. It still made him angry that they had been taken from him, that he had been denied the chance to get to know them better. He knelt down and, with a twig, started to scrape away at the lettering, to make it easier to read. As he did so he searched his mind for memories. But all he could think of was that glint of gunmetal in the sunlight—the glint that should have warned him, that might have saved them. He looked at the wording one more time, pulled away the weeds and nettles that had grown up, and moved on. He lifted his gaze and looked across the lake. This was a beautiful spot, a type of beauty you never saw in Louisiana. Quisquina, he knew, was beyond the range of mountains to the south, but he couldn't see the monastery, not from here. Mentally, he said good-bye.

He retraced his steps, threading his way between the graves. He went out through the gate. Despite his anger, he was pleased he had come. He began to untether his mule.

"Visiting family?"

The voice came from behind him and he swiveled instantly.

Two policemen, two *sbirri*, lounged against the wall of the graveyard, smoking. That's why he hadn't seen them. *Merda!*

He tried hard to be nonchalant. "Just looking up old friends."

One of the policemen, dark-haired with a mustache, heaved himself away from the wall and came forward. "I don't recognize you," he said. "You're not local."

Silvio shook his head. "No, I'm from Palermo."

"What's your name?"

"Giuseppe Chiavelli," he said quickly, choosing a well-known suburb of the town.

"Why are you here?"

Jesus. "I came for the property auction in Alia. I was bidding for a friend in Palermo, who couldn't come himself."

"Who?"

"Does it matter?"

"Who?"

"Stefano Ciamba."

"Show me your papers."

"I don't have them with me." This, Silvio knew as soon as he said it, was unconvincing. If he had been bidding at an auction, his bids would not have been accepted without some identification. He had to rescue the situation.

"I left all my papers in Alia, when I came on here. I'm taking the train back to Palermo from there."

But the *sbirro* was suspicious. "What is the name of the friends you were visiting?"

Damn the *sbirro*! What *were* the names that he had read? Pietri? Girami?

"Girami."

"Who are they? Never heard of them around here."

Why was this man *so* suspicious? Did he want a bribe?

"The Girami were originally from Borgo Regalmici. They moved to Palermo, where I met some of them."

"And why should you visit the grave?"

"A debt of honor. You can understand that."

The policeman wiped his mustache with his hand. He turned to his subordinate. "Beppe. Our friend here was at the top of the graveyard, on the left. See if you can find the Girami headstone."

The other man did as he was told.

Silvio was thinking fast. He felt pretty sure he could overpower one *sbirro*, but was that wise? Any fight with the police would draw attention to him and that was the last thing he wanted. If he attacked a policeman, and word spread, as it would, Alesso might get to hear of it and go to ground. Silvio had to wait, and hope for the best.

The *sbirro* with the mustache lit a cigarette while he waited. "We are on an alert," he said. "There has been an escape from Bologna Prison. Antonino Greco, the Quarryman. He may come home."

So that accounted for their belligerence, and suspicions. Silvio cursed under his breath. Just his luck.

The second *sbirro* came back from the graveyard. He whispered to his superior. As he listened the other man looked up sharply, dropped his cigarette, and took out his gun. It all happened too fast for Silvio.

The *sbirro* took a step toward him. "There is no Girami gravestone. There *is* a Cirami stone—and a Randazzo. Where the weeds have been cleared away and the wording recently cleaned. So, you'll come back to Santo Stefano with us. I can't believe you're Sylvano Randazzo—you'd have to be crazy, *pazzo*, to set foot in Sicily—but we'll soon find out. If you are, Beppe here and I are rich men. Now, please, very carefully, drop your gun."

By the time that Liotta and the other defendants arrived at the courthouse from the Parish Prison that final morning, the public gallery of the court was filled to overflowing, and perhaps as many as two hundred people were gathered outside, milling on the steps. Several carried posters or placards. HANG 'EM HIGH read one. MAFIA = MURDERER said another. And a third: THE DAGOS DID IT! KILL!

The judge was a little late that morning, not arriving in court until ten forty-five, by which time the jury members were all seated in their places. He sent them out immediately and then he, the court officials, and counsel all disappeared. No one in the public gallery moved away. It was inconceivable that the jury would spend another night in a hotel and no one wanted to miss the final act in this long drama. David Martell's mother was there, allowed a seat in the front row. Harrison Parker was there, along with other civic dignitaries, in the same front row. Angelo had a man at Foley's desk, ready to rush the news to him as soon as it came.

Twelve o'clock arrived and went. Twelve-thirty. At a quarter to one the jury asked for lunch to be sent in. The empty plates and glasses were taken away at two. At two-thirty the unthinkable suddenly became thinkable. Court staff were instructed to book another night in the hotel.

At three-fifteen, the jury foreman told the clerk of the court that they were ready. The clerk informed the judge, who gave word that the attorneys and the press should be alerted. A buzz went around the public gallery as everyone suddenly realized that the moment they had been waiting for was at hand.

When the judge and attorneys were in place, the defendants were sent for and returned to their benches in the dock. Then the jury was brought in.

The foreman was a small, sandy-haired, wiry man who looked extremely nervous.

The clerk rose. "Mr. Foreman, will you stand, please."

The foreman stood.

"Have you reached a verdict?"

"Yessir, we have."

"And is that verdict unanimous in all cases?"

"Yessir, it is."

"Very well. We will take the defendants one at a time, starting with Vittorio Liotta. Do you find Vittorio Liotta guilty or not guilty of conspiracy to murder David Martell?"

The foreman had answered the other questions readily enough, but now he hesitated. He looked first at the judge, then at Foley, then at Falmouth, then at the ground.

"Not guilty."

The police station at Santo Stefano was new. Otherwise the town, what Silvio saw of it as he had arrived under police guard, hadn't changed much. Yellowed buildings that from a distance looked as though they were made of Parmesan cheese.

Fortunately there had been few people to see his arrival. On the road they had passed what looked like old Frederico Imbaccari, the banker who had visited Nino when he had been Don in Bivona, but that was all.

Silvio had been locked into a cell in the back of the building and the *sbirri* had gone off to telegraph police headquarters in Palermo for instructions.

Silvio was beside himself with anger and apprehension. How could he have allowed himself to be arrested, how *could* he? *Sono sciocco, sono sciocco,* I'm a fool, he kept repeating to himself. And it wasn't just getting caught. The wedding was approaching. He had to get to Alesso before that. *Why* had he visited his parents' grave? There had been no need, no need at all.

But Silvio was frightened as well as angry. If he went back to jail now, he would be lynched, he had no doubt. That made him think for a moment. Had Angelo needed to use their trump card? Was the New Orleans business a mess, like this fiasco in Sicily?

The judge banged his gavel hard on the desk before him. "Silence! Silence!" Again, he beat the desk. "Silence, I say."

It did no good, not then anyway. The minute the jury foreman had announced the not-guilty verdict, mayhem had erupted in the court-room. It had grown as other—similar—verdicts had been handed down. People were now standing and shouting, some pointing at the defendants, some at the jury. There were whistles, catcalls, whoop-ing, and groans of disbelief. "Lynch the eyeties!" someone had yelled. "And the jury," chorused others. "Justice!" cried another fac-tion. "We want justice!" Mrs. Martell was weeping, comforted by others near her. One or two people had tried to climb the barrier between the public gallery and the court proper but had been held back by the police. Even so, the judge was taking no chances and had sent for reinforcements.

He banged his gavel again. "Bailiff, I want you to eject anyone standing up or shouting. Do it now."

The police began to move among the public benches. They picked on two men, a woman and a boy, and began manhandling them to the door. At first, the shouting increased, but then, as people saw that the police meant business, more and more people sat down. The uproar began to subside.

The noise had not gone away completely but there came a point when the judge realized he could make himself heard. "Any more interruptions of that kind, and I'll have the courtroom cleared. Is that understood? The trial is not over. I will not say that again. If there are any more disturbances, the court will be cleared. Completely.

"Now, will everybody sit down, and calm themselves. Then we can proceed."

He allowed a moment for the court to become settled and for himself to gather his thoughts. This was obviously a tricky situation. He was mindful of a conversation he'd had earlier in the day.

The policemen who had ejected the members of the public came back into the room and positioned themselves where they could act swiftly in the event of another outbreak of trouble.

"I now address myself to the defendants." The judge looked across to the dock. "Gentlemen, you have been acquitted of the charges brought against you this day. However, I understand from the acting chief of police, and from Mr. Foley here, the prosecuting attorney, that several other charges against you are now pending. Also, because of the publicity this trial has received, and the way the trial itself has been conducted, and as you yourselves have just seen, there is a great deal of public feeling here in New Orleans, in regard to these events."

He adjusted his spectacles. "In the light of this, I do not feel it is right or proper to release you. There is also the matter of your personal safety to consider. If you were to be released, then in the first place and in view of the charges pending against you, some among you might choose to abscond, and that risk I cannot allow. I also feel that one or more of you might come to harm, given the manifestation of violent emotion we have just seen here in this court.

"Accordingly, I shall remand all of you in custody until such time as the acting chief of police deems that it is safe for you to be released. Bailiff, return the prisoners to the Parish Prison."

"You can't do this, judge!" Falmouth was on his feet and clearly very disturbed. "They've been acquitted, judge, acquitted fair and square. They should be released. This is an outrage!"

Liotta was also standing up in the dock. "We've been acquitted! We didn't do these things, judge! I demand to be released!"

But the bailiffs were already moving across the court. The noise was building up again. People were on their feet.

The judge beat his desk with his gavel, but to no effect.

Amid the noise and bustle, the defendants were led away—all except Liotta, who still stood and shouted: "We were acquitted! We should be free men. Judge? Can you hear me? Judge!" Then he, too, was manhandled along the defendants' bench and out through the door. His last words were: "Don't do this, judge! Don't do this!" Then he was gone.

The judge breathed a little more easily, now that the defendants were safe. It had been a sweat for a moment. But he had done it; he had kept his side of the bargain. The photograph was safe. He banged his gavel one more time and called out, "This court is now adjourned. Bailiff, clear the room!"

"Wake up, Randazzo, or whoever you are. Here's your dinner."

Silvio rolled off the bed. He looked at his watch. Seven o'clock.

The *sbirro* was at the door to his cell, unlocking it. There was another figure behind him, but in the gloom, Silvio couldn't see who it was.

Then the policeman stood to one side and a woman came forward. She looked at Silvio and smiled. He smiled back, involuntarily. He didn't recognize her. Or did he? She came forward with a tray. On it were a jug, a plate with food, and a chunk of bread.

She looked at Silvio a second time, smiled, and then said loudly, to the *sbirro*, "Ah! I've forgotten the glass for your wine. I'll bring it."

She laid the tray on Silvio's bunk and left the cell. The *sbirro* relocked the door and followed her back the way they had both come. Silvio was again alone.

But only for a moment. The woman was soon back, on her own this time. She had the glass with her. She held it through the bars. Silvio went to take it from her.

As he did so she gripped his hand and hissed. "Listen, quickly. There is a key at the bottom of the wine jug. Between nine and ten this evening the guard will eat his dinner. Open the door to your cell, leave, but lock the door again and *put the key back in the wine jug*. Do not drink all the wine. I shall then be able to put the key—which is a spare—back where it belongs, and I will not be blamed."

He went to interrupt but she motioned for him to be silent. "There's a door to the right. The key to that is under the wooden Madonna on the windowsill nearby. Lock that door again after you've escaped, and leave the key in the bucket of water you'll find there. I shall return that key, too. All you need do is climb over the wall and you are free. Good luck."

Sono sognatore? he asked himself. Am I dreaming?

"Why are you doing this? Who are you?"

"Silvio! Don't you recognize me? I am Maria Camastra. Gaetano Mancuso made a fool of my daughter, brought shame on my house. You gave me justice, when you were with Don Bivona. I say again, *Auguri!* Good luck!"

25

The events of the twenty-four hours that followed the acquittal of Vittorio Liotta and his mob have passed into history. At seven-thirty that evening, Harrison Parker met Angelo Priola at Pickwick's. Clarence Foley was not present on this occasion.

"You did well," Angelo said to Parker.

"It was your idea," the other man responded.

"It was Silvio's really. Is everything else in place?"

"Yes."

"Do you think it will work?"

"You're asking me? It's all we can do, given the verdict. Let's hope so. It *must* work."

Silvio dipped his hands in the wine and his fingers closed around the key. It was nearly a quarter past nine and the police station was as quiet as Maria Camastra had said it would be. There was no light save moonlight, but it was enough. He placed the tray just inside the door, dried his hand on his trousers, and inserted the key in the lock. It turned but made a grating sound. He froze, thinking back to that evening in Caltabellotta, when they had raided di Biondi's picture collection.

But Maria Camastra was right, bless her. The guard was at dinner and the peace of the police station was undisturbed. Silvio pushed open the door, went through, and closed it behind him. He relocked the latch, stretched through the bars, and dropped the key into the wine jug. There was a small plop.

He ran swiftly down the short corridor. The moonlight shone in through a window where the rounded silhouette of the Madonna stood out. He reached up and moved the statue to one side. His fingers felt for the key. *It wasn't there!*

432

Yes, it was. In the dark his fingers had been searching the wrong place. He found the lock—then stopped. He went back to the window. He had left the Madonna to one side. He moved it back to the center of the windowsill. He couldn't let down Maria Camastra.

He unlocked the outer door and went through. After relocking the door he waited a moment until his eyes had adjusted to the light. In front of him, he saw the wooden bucket with water in it. He dropped the key into the water.

The wall around the yard was about ten feet high. He chose his spot, ran at it, and gripped the top. But his fingers slipped and he fell back. He tried again; the same result. He was sweating, his heart heaving. He couldn't fail now. Please God, no.

He tried a third time. He ran . . . and jumped. His fingers closed over the far edge of the top of the wall, and his second hand followed swiftly. With his feet he pawed at the wall. This time one foot gained a purchase on the lip of a brick that stuck out a fraction; but that's all it took. He heaved, and although his foot slipped, he now had his elbow over the edge of the wall and could use that to lever himself up. He brought up a knee next, then heaved his entire torso horizontal onto the top of the wall. Without pausing, he threw himself down the other side.

He landed with a thud that made him wince in pain. His spine seemed to be squashed shorter. He waited a moment to recover himself and to listen.

Nothing.

Now what? The wedding was two days away and he had to get to Alesso before then. He needed to know what the couple's plans were in the interim—and he needed to know very soon.

There was only one person who could help.

Angelo was up early on the morning after the trial ended. He had his usual breakfast brought in by Anna-Maria, with the paper. An item on the front page caught his eye. He knew it would be there, but he wanted to study the wording for himself. It was a small advertisement that read:

MASS MEETING
All good citizens are invited to attend a mass meeting on Saturday, August 12, at 10 A.M. at Clay Statue, to

take steps to remedy the failure of justice in the Martell case.
Come prepared for action.

Angelo sat back, thinking. Around him the city was coming to
life. Down at the docks, ships were arriving or leaving, loading
or being unloaded. Over on Lake Pontchartrain, construction
workers would be arriving to start the day, reclaiming bit by bit the
shoreline of the lake so that more houses could be built on it. The
carnival costume makers, the ice makers in the refrigeration factories, whores all over the city were waking up to another day.

Every morning Angie had delivered the freshest Sicilian
oranges he could find. It was good to start the day thinking of
home. Except that Sicily wasn't home anymore. He thought of
Silvio and whether he was succeeding. In twenty-four hours
he, Angelo, would know whether Silvio's Cathedral Plan had
worked. Even if it did, would Silvio live to see victory? Angelo,
who'd never had a son, had come to look upon Silvio as his heir.
He himself wouldn't see the year out—but Silvio? Silvio might
have thrown away the prize at the very moment of victory. Not
exactly foxy. Angelo reached out and took an orange from the
vase on the table. He smelled it, closing his eyes in pleasure. After
all this time Angelo could still see the orange groves of Caltasinetta clearly. He dug into the skin with his thumbnail and
began to peel.

"Smeralda?" Silvio called across the darkened room. "Smeralda?"

Still sleeping, she stirred slightly. It was just dawn in Cammarata and he had walked all night. "Smeralda!"

She woke. Rubbed her eyes. "You! Get out!"

"Smeralda, please, I need your help. I was your son."

"No more."

"Please, Smeralda. I didn't kill those children. Surely Don Bastiano knows that."

"You are unnatural, Sylvano. *Disumano.* Annunziata is safer
with Alessandro."

"He is a murderer, a liar, and a coward. *Un codardo!* He
deserves to die. I need to know where he is today. I must find him
before the wedding."

"Why? Why bother? Annunziata will never marry you now."

"Why? Why not? What has happened? Has she changed?"

"She can tell you why herself."

Silvio was growing angry. He needed the information, that's why he had come back here. Smeralda had held her peace so far. She would do so again. But why wouldn't she help him? He grew more angry. Unfortunately, those *sbirri* had taken his gun, otherwise . . . He checked himself, ashamed. What kind of man had he become, to even think of threatening his own mother? *Sono serpente?*

"Smeralda, if you know where Alesso is today, why don't you tell me? If Annunziata won't marry me, what difference does it make? But you know Alesso deserves to die. For what he did to Bastiano, if for nothing else."

"Annunziata deserves to be happy, to have a proper family."

So that was it.

It was growing light outside. People were stirring.

"Smeralda, how can you be so sure I'm bad, and that Annunziata will be happy with Alesso? Zata could have chosen him above me, but she didn't."

"Save your sweet words, Sylvano. They're lost on me. I've shut you out of my heart."

Silvio was growing weary. Smeralda was stronger than he was.

A figure was moving across the courtyard, outside the window. "Smeralda?" called out a voice. "Are you awake?"

"I'm awake, Kostanza."

"Good. I was afraid you'd oversleep. What time is the rehearsal?"

Smeralda didn't reply.

"Smeralda? Is it eleven o'clock?"

"Yes!"

"Then we should leave no later than seven. I'll have breakfast ready in half an hour."

Smeralda stared at Silvio. He glared back. Daylight was filling the room now. Slivers of sunshine lit some washing on a line. It reminded him of flags on a steamboat. He suddenly noticed a clean dress hanging in front of a cupboard, and some new shoes.

"Is that what you're wearing to the wedding?"

She nodded.

"At the church of the Madonna dell'Olio?"

She nodded again. "Hundreds are going."

He couldn't kill Alesso at his own wedding. Not if he was to escape afterward.

Then he gasped. He had it. "*Il ripetizione!* The rehearsal. There's a rehearsal today, isn't there?"

He could see from the dismay on her face that he was right.

He knew all about wedding rehearsals. And one of the things he knew was that only a few people would be there, in the church. *Perfetto.*

At Clay Statue, on the corner of Canal and Royal streets, a crowd had begun to form. By ten o'clock there were perhaps nearly six thousand people massing near the monument.

Clay Statue was about thirty feet high. The figure of Clay himself stood about fifteen feet, above a pediment of about ten feet, on a base that rose some three or four feet from the roadway. At about five minutes after the hour, Harrison Parker climbed on the stone blocks that formed the base. He wore a dark frock coat and a wing collar. As he mounted the stones the crowd cheered, but he raised his arms and people were silenced so he could be heard.

"Gentlemen!" He had a soft voice, normally, but when he shouted it hardened. "Gentlemen of New Orleans. I stand before you today, not as your mayor but as an ordinary citizen, who has no desire for favor or prominence. But, like you, I am concerned—devastated—at the crisis which threatens to overwhelm this fine city.

"Affairs have truly reached a crisis when men living in an organized and civilized community, finding their laws fruitless and ineffective, are forced to protect themselves. When courts fail, the people must act! What protection, or assurance of protection, is left to us, when the very head of our police department, our chief of police, is assassinated in our very midst by the Mafia society, and his assassins are again turned loose on the community?

"Gentlemen, the time has come for the people of New Orleans to say whether they are going to stand for these outrages by organized bands of assassins, for the people to say whether they will permit them to continue. I ask you to consider this fairly. Are you going to let it continue?"

Parker turned first one way then the other so that all the people assembled could see his face. He raised his voice. "Will every man here follow me, and see the murder of David Martell vindicated? Are there men enough here to *set aside* the verdict of that infamous jury?

"Gentlemen! Fellow sons of New Orleans . . . follow me! I will be your leader!"

More cheers erupted as Parker finished his speech, and someone cried out, "Hang the dagos!"

Parker did not immediately get down from the statue, however, but instead helped someone else up. This was Thomas Whitgift. He, too, raised his arms, to quiet the crowd, to make himself heard.

"Friends," he said. "Many of you know me. I have lived in New Orleans all my life and I love this city as much as any man on earth. I cannot stand by and watch as it sinks beneath this mass of dago violence, corruption, and filth. Last night, I want to tell you, there was a celebration in the Parish Prison—and not only in the Parish Prison. In that part of New Orleans known as Little Sicily, there were feasts, with wine and good food, music and laughter. *Laughter!* Friends, I don't need to tell you that this is no laughing matter. Anyone who heard the Pinkerton agent give evidence in court knows what sort of people were acquitted yesterday.

"Acquitted!" And he spat. "Come with me and follow Harrison Parker. Come with us to the Parish Prison and do your civic duty!"

Parker and Whitgift led the way out of Canal Street and along Royal. The others fell in line, cheering and singing. As they walked along Royal still more joined in and women waved to them from the balconies.

At Bienville a second group of men was waiting for the first. These had been organized by Parker the evening before, and about thirty men had been provided with repeating rifles and shotguns by the local gunsmiths, Baldwin & Co. They fell in immediately behind Parker and Whitgift.

The procession reached Congo Square, in front of the prison. This was a predominantly black area, and many Negroes looked on. One old black woman was heard to say, "Thank God it wasn't a nigger who killed the chief."

Parker instructed the crowd to spread out and surround the prison, on all four sides. He waited while the people followed his orders.

Inside the prison, Governor Tucker looked grim. Some of his men had obviously been warned what might happen, because they had failed to turn up for work. He was ten short. Hearing the commotion outside, and seeing the crowds, he had immediately issued his remaining men with rifles and told them to man the two heavy doors of the prison, one on Congo Square, the other on Treme Street. Then he went down himself to stand by the Congo Square entrance, where Parker was.

"Tucker!" Parker yelled. "Tucker! Open up these gates."

"I can't do that, Mr. Parker. You know that."

"Open up! It's your duty."

"Don't speak to me about duty, Mr. Parker. Only the state governor has authority over me."

"Speak to the governor, then. He approves of what we are doing."

"I tried to telephone. He's away from his office."

"I won't stand all day talking, Mr. Tucker. We're going to force our way in."

Parker gave the order and a group of men from the crowd rushed at the gates of the prison. However, despite two further attempts, the gates held firm.

Whitgift, seeing that their campaign risked running out of steam, tugged at Parker's sleeve. "There's the other entrance on Treme Street," he whispered.

Parker nodded. "Come on." And he led the way quickly around the edge of the building, to Treme Street. On the way, Parker noticed a huge black man sitting on an old railway sleeper. "You!" he screamed at the black man. "Can you lift that?"

The black man nodded.

"Come on, then."

The gate on Treme Street was not as big as the main gate on Congo Square and it was clear from the very first thrust, with the sleeper being used as a battering ram, that it was a good deal weaker.

Inside the prison, as soon as he heard the smash of wood upon wood, Tucker dispatched his men to the Treme Street entrance. He himself again tried calling the governor, once more without success. He then went to the cells where Liotta and the others were held. He took out his keys. He spoke to Vito Liotta.

"The prison is surrounded by a mob," he said. "You must have heard. I'm releasing you from your cells. You'll never escape from the prison, but you might just find a place to hide—it's up to

you. Try the women's prison, on the third floor." And he went
from cell to cell, unlocking the gates.

Liotta led the others out. They had heard the shouting and were
growing agitated. They split into several groups of two and three,
some going upstairs, where Tucker had indicated, others going
outside, into the prison yard.

The Negro with the sleeper had others to help him. Five men, in
unison, battered the sleeper rhythmically against the gate. Each
time the wood of the gate gave way a little more. Then, finally, it
collapsed.

A huge cheer went up and the crowd surged forward. The
prison guards hesitated to fire on fellow citizens whom they would
have to live among later, so they stood aside.

Parker watched as perhaps fifty men entered the jail, more than
half of them armed. "That's enough," he said, turning to Whitgift.
"Keep a guard on this gate. No one goes in or out until I say so."
And he disappeared inside the prison with the others.

Inside, in the main corridor, Parker divided the men into three
groups, one for each floor. They soon discovered that the cells had
all been opened.

"Where's Liotta?" Parker addressed himself to a warden
standing nearby.

The man was too terrified to answer but glanced upward.

"Follow me," shouted Parker, rushing for the stairs. On the
second floor the cells were still locked, with ordinary criminals
inside. Parker continued climbing.

On the third floor, the women who were still locked in shrieked
and yelled at the sight of so many men with guns. Parker ran down
the corridor to the far end, where there was a door to the outside
staircase that led back down to the exercise yard. Tentatively, he
pushed open the door. There were three men halfway down the
staircase and another three in the yard itself.

"Yes!" he hissed, turning to the others behind him, and beckoning them forward.

As his group crowded down the stairs they saw another group
of men with guns emerge into the yard on the ground floor. Parker
shouted down. "Here!"

The others looked up and waited as Parker and his group
descended the stairs. By now, the six Sicilians had crowded
together at the far end of the exercise yard. Parker was relieved to

see that Vito Liotta was among them. He wore gray trousers, held up by braces, over a blue shirt. He hadn't shaved that day. The others cowered, but he stood up straight and met Parker's eye.

Parker returned his stare. Without looking at the men around him, the mayor didn't wait. "Do your duty, men," he said. "This is what we came for."

The rifles around him barked out—short, sharp sounds. The Sicilians were flung back against the wall behind them, their clothes spattered with blood. Some of them cried out, others just sagged as they were hit. They fell across one another.

Hearing the sounds of shooting, another cheer went up from the crowd outside the prison.

Parker stepped forward to inspect the corpses. He saw an arm move. "Finish him off," he instructed.

"I can't," breathed the man nearest him. "I feel sick."

Whereupon Parker took the rifle from him and placed its barrel next to the head of the man who had moved, Vito Liotta himself. He fired one shot into the Sicilian's head.

Just then they heard shooting from inside the prison. A second group of men had found another set of Sicilians. Parker walked back across the yard. He entered the building and climbed the stairs to the second floor, where the shooting had come from. He found the men, standing in front of three corpses. Except they weren't all corpses yet. Gino Fazio was still moving.

That gave Parker an idea. "Take him outside," he said to the men with the rifles. "Let the others see him, do with him what they will."

For a moment the riflemen hesitated.

"Do it," said Parker. "Then we can all go home."

When Silvio reached the church of the Madonna dell'Olio, it was deserted. To judge by the exchange between Smeralda and the other woman in the courtyard, he had two hours' grace. It was now just after nine and the rehearsal, he knew, was scheduled for eleven.

He let himself in and inspected the inside of the church. Like much else in Sicily it had hardly changed. The walls were still plain white, the apse was still undecorated, the attraction of the church lay in its uncompromising simplicity. The last time he had been here was that day when Annunziata had stormed out from a wedding, when Father Ignazio had denounced her relationship with Silvio.

His one problem now was his lack of a gun. The other men would certainly be armed. What if Alesso didn't arrive at all, alerted by the police in Santo Stefano? There was little he could do about that, but he had ensured that Smeralda and her companion would be late for the rehearsal, by stealing their carriage, abandoning it halfway, and then taking just the mule onward, for speed.

He chose his observation point. At the rear of the nave was a small gallery, reached by a wooden staircase. The gallery had a round window that afforded a view of the approaches to the church. He sat where he could see without being seen.

The minutes passed. He was so close to fulfilling his goal now that he thought he would be nervous. Yet he was strangely calm. Either it would work out his way, or it wouldn't. In any case he would see Annunziata and she would know he was doing all this for her.

He tried to put New Orleans out of his mind. He was so close to success now, here in Sicily, that he couldn't even imagine failure in America. He had to concentrate.

At about ten-thirty he saw people coming along the track from Bivona. Was it three figures—or four? As they drew closer he saw that it was three men and a woman—Annunziata! Soon after that he saw that one of the three men was a priest, but not Father Ignazio. What was going on?

The four people approached the church and entered: Alesso, Annunziata, the priest, and a man whom Silvio recognized as Alesso's guard. He was presumably also the best man. Despite what had happened at the auction, Alesso still walked with a swagger. Annunziata was as fair as ever, as beautiful as ever. That almond skin. No one looked up. Why should they?

Alesso and Annunziata sat in the front pew while the bodyguard sat on the other side of the aisle and placed his *lupara* by his side. The priest busied himself for a while, finding his place in the Bible, rearranging his surplice and his prayer book. Then he said, "I don't see your bridesmaid, Annunziata. Will she be here soon?"

"I hope so," said Annunziata. "Kostanza knew the time. Smeralda is bringing her."

It was the first time Silvio had heard her speak since he had left so many months ago. Her voice brought back those nights in the *bivio*.

"I think we'll begin," said the priest. "We won't wait for them. We want to be finished before it gets too hot.

"Now, I shall be here tomorrow, of course, although Father Ignazio will actually be taking the service. He's very weak, as you know, but insists on coming, so we shall make the service as short as possible. I hope you won't mind.

"Now, Annunziata, you stand here, and you, Alesso, there." He indicated a spot in front of where the bodyguard was sitting.

In fact, the priest now addressed himself to the bodyguard. "Giorgio, this is a wedding, a sacrament, and this is a church. No weapons, please. There's no need." He opened his prayer book and looked for the service.

Giorgio looked across to Alesso, who nodded. Giorgio picked up his *lupara* and made for the back of the church.

Silvio saw his chance. He watched Giorgio place his *lupara* in the shade of an almond tree near the church. Quickly, Silvio crept down the stairs from the gallery and ran to the back of the church, where the door was. He had just reached the end of the aisle when the priest raised his eyes from the prayer book and saw him.

"Hello? Hello there? Who are you? I say, what are you doing?"

It was too late. Silvio had reached the door, closed it, and bolted it with Giorgio still outside. He took the key from the keyhole. Now he had Alesso where he wanted. He turned to face the others.

Annunziata was the first to react. "Silvio!" she gasped. "Please God, no!"

But Alesso wasn't much slower. "Randazzo!" he cried. "My God!"

Silvio walked down the main aisle. As he did so he took from his pocket the object he had been careful to bring all the way from New Orleans. A garrote.

When he was about fifteen feet from Alesso and Annunziata, he stopped. Giorgio could be heard banging on the church door.

"Silvio," breathed Annunziata. "Why are you doing this?"

"Zata, how can you ask? He set me up. He betrayed us. *He* killed those children, Zata, not me. Thanks to him, Bastiano is in jail."

"It's not true!" cried Alesso. "He's lying. The whole plan was his idea."

Annunziata looked at Silvio.

"I talked to Ruggiero. There was a big meeting with the Liottas. They gave your fiancé Alia as a prize. The Liottas kept the narcotics. Alesso was to have been given Fontana Murata to run. . . ." Silvio looked at Alesso and smiled. "I found out about the geological survey, and the coal. I told Luca Mancuso."

Alesso looked shocked, but recovered. "You!"

It was the sweetest moment of Silvio's life. "And now I'm going to kill you." He moved forward.

The priest tried to intervene. "You cannot fight in a church."

More bangs came from the back of the building as Giorgio continued hammering on the door.

Suddenly Alesso rushed to the back of the apse. Pocketing the garrote, Silvio ran after him. On his way, Alesso grabbed the metal cross from the altar.

"No!" screamed the priest.

Barely had he done so, however, than Silvio snatched at one of the brass candlesticks. This time the priest just gasped.

Alesso and Silvio faced each other. The cross was longer than the candlestick, but heavier, more unwieldy. The jewels encrusted in its surface caught the light and glittered, like pebbles in a stream. Silvio moved closer to Alesso. He had a cold confidence about him. This is why he had come four thousand miles across the Atlantic; this is what he should have done long ago. At last, things were falling into place.

He lunged forward with the candlestick, but Alesso parried his blow with the cross. Silvio tried a second time—with the same result. They were warily circling around the apse. Giorgio was still banging on the door.

Alesso's breathing was calming down now as he adjusted to the situation. Silvio could see the expression on his face changing as he began to think of a way out. But Silvio's mood remained cold. He would outthink Alesso. There was no way out.

He lunged again—and Alesso parried again. But Silvio's lunge was a feint and he snatched back the candlestick as soon as he had pretended to swing it. Too late, Alesso realized what was happening—but now Silvio changed the angle of his aim, bringing the candlestick down on Alesso's wrist. He screamed in pain and dropped the cross.

Now, quickly, Silvio threw the candlestick at Alesso's head, making the other man duck while at the same time he nursed his injured hand. Silvio ran after the candlestick and hurled himself on Alesso. They fell to the stone floor, Silvio's hands searching for Alesso's throat. He was still perfectly cold. He had the upper hand; he knew what he was going to do. Alesso seemed to have gone limp. He was not resisting.

Suddenly Silvio felt a hot pain in his arm. Alesso had stabbed him! That's why he had gone limp: he had been quietly groping for his knife. The knife Silvio had seen in Alesso's boot that day at Fontana Murata.

Silvio rolled off the other man and got to his feet. Blood flowed down his forearm into the palm of his hand. Alesso couldn't have known it but he had sliced into Silvio's flesh in almost exactly the same place where he had been injured all those years ago on the *Syracusa*. The knife had missed the artery, so the bleeding looked worse than it was. But the pain was bad enough and now Alesso had the advantage.

Silvio stood for a moment, gripping his right forearm with his left hand, trying to stanch the blood. His mood was no longer cold. He was sweating, his heart heaved, and he was thinking hard.

Alesso got to his feet. He knew he had to press his advantage. He held the knife out and came toward Silvio. Silvio backed away. He ought to have remembered Alesso would have a knife. That had been a bad mistake.

They had by now traveled all the way around the apse and were again level with the altar. The priest and Annunziata were on the far side of the church, standing close together but not speaking.

Alesso kept coming forward. Silvio continued to back away, but he wouldn't be able to do that forever. Both his hands were sticky with blood. Alesso maneuvered himself near the altar, where there was another candlestick. He didn't need it now, but he was determined to make sure that Silvio didn't get it either.

But in doing that, Alesso had allowed Silvio near the lectern. Silvio saw his chance. He grabbed the Bible and held it in front of him, like a shield. It was heavy but it was large, and thick. He found himself thinking that it was probably bulletproof, let alone knife-proof.

He heard the priest mutter again. The cross, the candlestick, now the Bible.

Alesso had halted. Each man was trying to outthink the other, to surprise his opponent.

Silvio didn't dare look, but it felt as though the blood had stopped running down his wrist. The pain was still there, though, making him sweat. In fact, the sweat was running into his eyes. He would have to wipe them clear soon, but didn't dare do that just yet.

Now Alesso was coming forward again, the knife held out.

Silvio stopped backing off. Alesso stopped, too. Silvio glared at him, their eyes locked in a ferocious exchange. Then, before Alesso moved forward again, while both his feet were on the ground, together, Silvio threw the Bible to the floor.

Its heavy bulk landed on Alesso's toes and now it was his turn to scream in pain.

Silvio was on him, however, grabbing the wrist that held the knife with one hand and poking two fingers into his eyes with the other. Alesso screamed again as he was temporarily blinded. Silvio brought the other man's wrist down onto the back of a pew. But Alesso's wrist still held the knife. Silvio repeated the action. Still Alesso wouldn't let go. Silvio bent his head and bit deeply into the flesh of Alesso's wrist. The other man screamed again— and this time dropped the knife. Silvio kicked it away. Now they were even again, the way he wanted it.

But Alesso wasn't about to give up. He ran back toward the altar again and grabbed hold of the remaining candlestick. He turned to face Silvio. Before he moved forward this time, however, he snatched at the candle and pulled it away, revealing a long, four-inch spike. He brandished that at Silvio. Now he came forward again.

Alesso was thinking fast—Silvio had to give him that. How was he going to counter this latest weapon, the candlestick spike?

Silvio backed away. As he did so he looked around the little church. Not even Alesso's knife, supposing he could find it again, would be much help.

But the church was so plain. There was no decoration apart from the altar and the pulpit and there was nothing there—

Yes, there was! He turned and scrambled across the aisle to the pulpit. Alesso moved to follow, but Silvio was too quick. He ran up the few steps and found what he knew would be there: the incense burner. A small blue glass receptacle on a long chain. The priest, or the abbot, would swing this before and after services, but what mattered now was that the chain was strong.

Alesso stood below him, the spike of the candlestick pointing upward. Silvio held the chain. He began to swing it, in a circle. Probably his reach just outdistanced Alesso's, but Alesso might be able to parry the glass receptacle, or even catch it if he wasn't careful. Nonetheless the chain at least gave Silvio a chance.

Quickly he climbed onto the railing of the pulpit—and jumped down the other side. He stumbled as he fell, but Alesso had to run around a pew and by that time Silvio was back on his feet.

Alesso came forward relentlessly. He knew he had the edge. His weapon was longer, sharper, stronger. Silvio could swing the incense burner, but at some stage, unless he threw it at Alesso, he would have to get close if he was to win. And close up, Alesso had the undoubted advantage. Silvio had to outthink him.

Giorgio still banged on the church doors from time to time, shouting, "Alesso! Alesso!" He banged so hard, Silvio thought the lock must surely break.

That gave him an idea.

Alesso was still coming forward. Silvio was still swinging the incense burner, slowly, above his head. He backed away, down the aisle, away from the pulpit. He came to a break in the pews and moved to one side. Alesso followed, the spike of the candlestick all the time pointing at Silvio's heart.

Silvio retreated to the side of the church, passing one of the stone columns that supported the roof. Immediately he moved forward, back in the direction of the altar. There were no pews here, just a passageway to allow people to get to their seats.

As he moved forward his shoulder brushed the pillàr. It was perfect for what he had in mind.

Now he stopped.

Alesso, just rounding the pillar, stopped also for a fraction, immediately alert for any trick of Silvio's. But Silvio still continued to swing the incense burner slowly. He gazed into Alesso's eyes. Alesso's eyes were brown, like Silvio's, and wide open, taking everything in. *Perfetto.*

Silvio stepped backward. Alesso moved forward, his body now abreast of the stone pillar. In one movement Silvio took the chain of the incense burner above his head and swung it hard, very hard. At the last moment he let go of the chain and flung the glass receptacle at the stone pillar with all the force he could muster. He watched as Alesso's eyes followed the receptacle for a moment—and then Silvio saw no more. As the incense burner smashed against the stone pillar, he closed his own eyes and put his hands over his face.

The receptacle shattered into smithereens, tiny splinters of blue glass ricocheting in all directions. Silvio couldn't see, but heard Alesso scream in pain as his open eyes were caught by tiny fragments of glass that sprayed out from the stone pillar. Alesso was virtually blinded.

Silvio took his hands from his own eyes and leaped on Alesso. The other man had dropped the candlestick and was rubbing at his eyes, crying and gasping in agony.

In no time, Silvio took out his garrote and had it around Alesso's throat. At last!

It wasn't as easy as he had thought. His fingers were still sticky with blood and it proved hard to hold on to the garrote. Worse, Alesso, though still blinded, had found the chain of the incense burner where it had dropped after hitting the pillar, and was now wrapping that around Silvio's throat. Each man was trying to garrote the other.

And so it came down to a trial of strength. Who would give way first? Silvio's garrote was cutting into Alesso's neck; he could see the other man's face going red. But Silvio was growing weak, too, as the chain was pulled tighter around his throat. Worse, he felt his grip slipping as the blood on his fingers acted like grease, or soap. Alesso might be blinded, but he was getting the upper hand in this last—

Suddenly something warm and sticky spattered across Silvio's face and he felt the weight of Alesso's body slumped across his. The other man wasn't moving. At the same time the pressure on Silvio's neck had eased.

His eyes cleared. His breath came back and the strength began to return to his body. He looked up. Annunziata stared down at him. She was holding the crucifix. It was covered in blood.

Silvio threw Alesso's weight off him. The other man rolled to the ground and lay still. There was a deep gash in his skull and his hair was matted and caked with blood. His eyes were open. He was dead.

The priest stood a little way off. He looked terrified. Giorgio was still banging on the church door.

Silvio struggled to his feet. He was still weak. He put his arm around Annunziata. She dropped the cross, which clattered onto the stone floor for the second time. Her body began to heave as she sobbed and sobbed.

Silvio looked down at her and kissed her. Her lips were salty. "You are free to come to America. We are free."

But she looked at him as though she were terrified.

"Zata!" he cried. Then, more gently: "Zata . . . what is it?"

She shook her head. She was still sobbing.

"Smeralda said you would never marry me. But she wouldn't say why—what is it?"

Gently, she pushed him away. She wiped her eyes and her nose. She pushed her hair back into place. Eventually she composed herself enough to say, "Come. There is something I must show you."

Gino Fazio's body was lifted from the stone floor and carried down the stairs and out toward the shattered gate at Treme Street. A huge roar went up as the Sicilian's crumpled figure came into view. He was passed from the riflemen to the crowd, then passed over their heads farther and farther back. The roar seemed to follow the body as it was transferred from one person to another.

The crowd now extended to St. Ann Street, on the corner of which was a tall street lamp. Someone threw a rope over the arm of the lamp and made a noose. The noose was placed around Fazio's neck, and then he was hauled up to the top of the lamp. Blood dripped from his wounds sustained in the prison shooting and the rope bit into the flesh around his neck. His head sagged to one side.

The roar had begun again. Suddenly it stopped as Fazio came to and began to climb up the lamppost to the crossbar. He was aiming to free himself. This scene went on for several seconds as people watched in an appalled silence. Then a fusillade of shots rang out as men pulled their personal weapons from their pockets.

Fazio's body slumped and he hung down dead from the crossbar of the street lamp.

When Annunziata and Silvio reached Quisquina it was dusk. Throughout the journey he had tried to convince her to come away with him—after all, the police must be mounting a major search party by now. But Annunziata wouldn't listen. She was determined to go to the abbey.

Their route took them over much of the same ground as they had taken years earlier, after Nino had been raided in the *bivio*, when he had been captured by the Lazio Brigade. The slopes of Mount Catera, the gully of the Magozzolo River. But their mood was very different now.

When they reached the abbey, Annunziata didn't knock or pull the bell rope. She had her own key. She led the way across the courtyard to an inner door. Just as they were about to enter, a monk came out. He was tall and stringy looking: Luigi Garofali.

"Annunziata!" he cried in a soft whisper. "I was praying you would come." He turned. "Come with me, please. Father Ignazio's condition has deteriorated. I fear he doesn't have long."

"Oh no!" Annunziata stifled a sob and hurried after Garofali.

Silvio followed them at a distance as they walked swiftly along the corridor that lined the courtyard, the same corridor where Zata and he had waited all those years before with their grim message for the abbot. But this time the corridor was dark. Candles glowed at either end but the shadows were deep.

Garofali and Annunziata stopped at the far end. The monk gently opened the door. "I have given him the last rites," he whispered to Annunziata.

She went in. Unless Silvio was mistaken, this was Ignazio Serravalle's study. Silvio reached the end of the corridor himself. The door to the study had been left open and inside he could see Garofali and Annunziata standing over a figure lying in a bed. Father Ignazio's illness surely explained why Annunziata spent all her time here now. She had been nursing him. Was this what she wanted to show him? Was this why she wouldn't leave Sicily?

Silvio stepped into the room. The huge desk had been moved, to make room for the bed, but otherwise the study hadn't changed. The blue-green tapestry still covered one wall, the candelabra still stood on the mantel, dripping wax. The *tsk-tsk* of insects could still be heard through the open window. What had changed, however, was the smell of the room. It was no longer dominated by incense, or the mustiness of the abbey itself, and the abbot's books, but by hospital-like smells of medicine, disinfectant, body odors.

As he stepped into the room Silvio heard Father Ignazio speak. His voice was higher-pitched than Silvio remembered it, and he was clearly very weak. But it was still the voice of a forceful character.

"My child, is the rehearsal over?"

Annunziata murmured, "It is."

"Good." Father Ignazio paused. "Will you forgive me if I do not marry you tomorrow? I fear I am too weak."

Annunziata's eyes had filled with tears. She nodded, and murmured again.

The abbot's head turned toward Silvio. "But let me bless you both. Let that be my last act."

With a jolt, Silvio realized that the abbot had confused him with Alesso. Annunziata's hand went to her mouth. She, too, realized that the abbot was growing confused. His end must be very near.

Serravalle continued to look in Silvio's direction, beckoning him. He stepped forward and stood next to Annunziata.

The abbot looked at the couple with tired eyes. Garofali was speechless.

Father Ignazio began to speak in Latin. Weakly he raised his hand and made the sign of the cross.

This was too much for Silvio. "No!" he cried as softly as he could. "Father, I am not Alesso. I am Silvio. Silvio Randazzo."

The abbot stopped speaking. His hand fell back onto the bedclothes. His eyes focused on Silvio. Suddenly he was lucid and strong again. "You! Why have you come?" He looked to Annunziata. "Where is Alesso?"

When no one answered, he put his hand to his forehead and said, "No! Please God, no!" He looked at Annunziata, tears filling his own eyes. "Does he know about—?" Then his head fell to one side.

Garofali moved forward, closed the abbot's eyelids, and placed his hands over his chest, mumbling in Latin.

Annunziata turned to Silvio. In the gloom it was difficult to tell whether her eyes were sad or hard. "You should have let him think you were Alesso," she whispered. "*Bruto!* How could you be so cruel? He died crying, Silvio. He died *crying*."

Parker had fought his way out of the Parish Prison. Along St. Ann Street there was a streetcar that had been overturned by the crush of the crowd. Parker reached it and climbed on top of it.

"Friends," he yelled. "Listen to me!" He raised his hands for the noise to quiet down. People began to turn away from the corpse of Fazio hanging on the lamppost.

"Friends, our work is done. I will read to you the list of those who have died here today, the men who have, quite rightly, been executed by the concerned citizens of New Orleans."

He paused. "Antonino Siculo!"

A cheer went up.

"Girolamo Regalmici!"

More cheers.

"Biagio Gela!" Still the people found their voices.

One by one, Parker read out the names of the Sicilians who had been shot in Parish Prison. The people cheered after each name, until he concluded, "You see before you the body of Gino Fazio, which brings to eight the number of criminals we have . . . executed. And that only leaves one name, the biggest name of all, the leader of the Mafia society in New Orleans, the evil leader who has brought this fine city to the crisis we are now seeking to eradicate." Parker raised his hand and shouted, "Vittorio Liotta!"

The loudest cheer of all greeted these words. Men threw their hats into the air and one or two fired their handguns.

But Parker bade them be quiet. As the noise subsided he spoke again. "Friends, I called you together for a duty. You have performed that duty. Mob violence is the most terrible thing on the face of the earth. Now go to your homes, and if I need you I will call you. Go home, and God bless you."

"God bless you, Mr. Parker!" shouted several in the crowd as he got down from the streetcar and began to walk back to Canal Street. Slowly the crowds dispersed. No one took down the body of Gino Fazio. It hung there as flies began to feed on the congealed blood of his wounds.

Annunziata stood in the courtyard of Quisquina, sobbing gently. She had not cried when the abbot had died, but now her grief had caught up with her. Silvio stood close by. Each time he tried to embrace her she shook him off.

Silvio was confused. She had saved his life by killing Alesso. But she seemed in no hurry to come away with him, now that she had the chance. He realized that she had been fond of the abbot and that he, Silvio, had made a mistake in Father Ignazio's study. But wasn't honesty the best policy? And didn't she realize the danger he was in, the urgent need to move swiftly?

He tried again. This time she sagged into his embrace and he put his arm around her. He smelled her hair, kissed it. He kissed her on the cheek, then on the lips. This is what he had come to Sicily for.

For a moment she returned his kiss. Then she pushed him away violently. "No," she cried. "No!"

She escaped, and ran across the courtyard, pushing against a door and disappearing through it. He ran after her. Through the doorway was another corridor, dark and shadowy. He heard her crying again.

He moved down the corridor until he came to an open door. Annunziata was sitting on a bed, hunched up, nursing her knees. A solitary candle burned beside her. He stepped inside and stood over her.

This time he waited until she quieted down. Then he said, gently, "Zata, I'm sorry for what I did in Father Ignazio's study. But he knew there was cholera in Palermo, the time you sent little Nino. He didn't warn you. There has been so much deception, I had to be honest. That once." He paused. "I must be honest now. The police know I am here . . . in Sicily. I must leave. I can't go back to prison now—I would be lynched. I want you to come with me to America. We are free now. Smeralda says you won't come, but I don't believe her. Father Ignazio is dead. You saved my life. You must believe me, that I didn't kill those children in the orphanage. Come with me now. Please."

Annunziata looked at him and her tears began again. She shook her head. "I have deceived you, Toto."

He looked shocked but she quickly added, "Not in the way that you think." She sniffed and wiped her eyes with the ball of her hand. "I know that I was not loving during our last days together when . . . when you were here before . . . before Bagheria. Remember the day I left the church during that wedding ceremony?

How could you forget? You know I had been upset by Father Ignazio's actions, his threat to excommunicate us. But I was deceiving you all. What you didn't know, what he didn't know, what only I knew at the time was that I . . . I was pregnant."

Silvio swayed on his feet. Was this true? *Sono sognatore?* Am I dreaming? he asked himself. Of course it was true. Annunziata wouldn't joke about something like that. He felt elated. He had settled things with Alesso. Now this.

"You have a daughter, Toto," whispered Annunziata. "I call her Sylvana. But . . ." She hesitated, and looked down. Was she crying again?

"Zata? What is it? Zata! But . . . what?"

"But you will never see her."

The voice came from behind Silvio. He turned quickly, but he knew who it was, even before his eyes picked out the figure in the gloom.

He was lying on a bed, one arm bandaged in a sling. The other held a gun, a *lupara*. It was pointed at Silvio.

"Nino!"

There was silence in the room as the two men regarded each other. Nino looked older, much older. The color had gone from his skin. He was gray all over, as if he were made of stone.

Silvio broke the silence. "What happened to your arm?"

"I fell from a mule on my way here."

"I know about bones. Maybe I can fix it."

"Stay where you are."

"Nino, what—?"

"Shut up! I told you to stay away from my daughter. That's why you were sent to America in the first place, for God's sake. That's why she married Gino. You were warned—by Father Ignazio, by me, by Smeralda, by everyone. But did you listen?"

"Nino, listen to my side—"

"No!"

"But Annunziata loves me!" Silvio would not be silenced. "It wouldn't matter in America."

"Fuck America!" shouted Nino. "*Fotta! Fotta! Fotta!* Fuck! Fuck! Fuck! This is Sicily. Now listen," he yelled before Silvio could say anything else. "I'm going to tell you something I should have told you before. I tried to protect you; I felt it was for the best. I was wrong."

Silvio was silent. What was coming?

"Your father's death—"

"Yes?" hissed Silvio. "What about it?" What did Nino know? Did he know about Silvio's slow reactions? Please God, no.

"Your father was shot because he was with Aldo."

"Yes, I know. You told me yourself. Aldo had been interfering with Carcilupo business—"

"Wrong! That's what I told you to protect you from the truth. Aldo was shot by his cousins, the Bisacquino brothers. Shot because he had made their sister, his *cousin*, pregnant, and she had given birth to an idiot. She felt so guilty, so ashamed, that she drowned the child. Then she killed herself." Nino shifted his body on the bed. He pressed his lips together. Silvio remembered suddenly how, years ago, Nino had drummed his fingers on his mouth while he was thinking. "Now do you understand? You are repeating a pattern—"

"You mean . . . ?" Silvio looked from Nino to Annunziata. "You mean our daughter is . . . ?"

"No," said Nino. "She's fine. But no thanks to you. Thanks to you and your selfish obsession with Annunziata, three orphans are dead in Bagheria—"

"But that wasn't me. That was—"

"Who cares, now? You were part of it." Nino shifted his body again. "But we're wasting time. I'm giving you two choices, Silvio. Either you promise to leave Sicily immediately, and never return—"

"Or?"

"Or I shall shoot you, right here. Now. In this monastery. I'll finish it, where it all began. Aldo was never given that choice. I'm doing this for your father. He was a good man."

Silence.

Then Nino said, "Silvio, in case it makes it easier for you . . . I'm dying. I picked up something in prison. I escaped to spend a few weeks with Annunziata and . . . my granddaughter. It took all I had to bribe my way out of jail. I fell off the mule because I was already weak. So if I kill you, it doesn't change much for me."

Silvio looked at Annunziata. She looked sad but had stopped crying.

"You killed Alesso for me."

Now she did cry.

"Let that be your last memory." Nino was forcing the pace.

Silvio suddenly grew angry. "Can I not see my daughter, at least? *Sono orco?* Am I an ogre?"

Nino rested the gun on his knee. "No, Silvio. Believe me, it's better this way. I wouldn't have told you about Sylvana. If you see her you'll only miss her more."

"How can you be so inhuman?"

"Don't lecture me about being inhuman. You brought all this on yourself. But enough talk. Which is it to be? Are you going to leave Sicily, or do I shoot you?"

"You'd kill me, in cold blood? You used to say, be soft on the outside."

Silence. Then, "I'm not cock's-blooding, Silvio. I used to say that, too."

"How do you know I won't come back here, after you're dead?"

"Annunziata won't have you, if you break your oath to me."

"Zata . . . is this what you want?"

She had her hand to her mouth. Her fingers were wet with tears. She nodded.

He moved toward her, but Nino called out, "Keep away! I'll shoot."

Silvio stopped. He held up a ring. "I was going to give her this, for our daughter."

"No!" Nino glared at him. "The child will never know about you."

Silvio looked at Annunziata. Her arms now hung by her sides. Her eyes were closed.

He walked past her. As he reached the door he turned. "Goodbye, Silvio," said Nino.

Silvio looked at Annunziata. She was still crying.

Was this to be his last glimpse of her, tears streaming down her face? It would be an image that would haunt him for years.

He couldn't speak. He turned and walked across the darkened courtyard. He approached the door they had entered by, years before, when Annunziata and he had arrived to tell Father Ignazio that Nino—the Quarryman, Don Bivona—had been captured by the Lazio Brigade. He held open the door and paused a moment, smelling the familiar odors of the monastery, listening to the *tsk-tsk* of the crickets. He would never be here, in this peaceful place, again. He was just about to move on when he noticed a sound he had never heard before in a monastery. It was an infant crying.

PART FIVE

—◦—

Capo

26

After the lynching of Vittorio Liotta and his men, all hell broke loose across America. The Liotta case had been reported right across the country, in Italy, in Britain, where the *Times* took a particular interest, and throughout Europe. Anti-Italian riots broke out in several U.S. cities, the Italians withdrew their ambassador to Washington as a form of protest, and there was even talk of mobilizing the Italian fleet against the Americans. In New Orleans, a grand jury was installed to investigate the lynchings, but it concluded that the lynchers had been justified in their actions, pointing out that they had been led by the mayor, which meant that they were not just any mob but had included many of the most law-abiding citizens of New Orleans. The jury refused to hand down any new indictments.

Silvio made it back safely to New Orleans, but for a time, a long time, his heart was still in Sicily. He could not hear a child crying without coming close to tears himself. But he never heard from Annunziata again, or from his daughter, Sylvana.

Angelo reigned as the undisputed Capo of New Orleans for six months only, rather less than he had hoped. During the last six weeks his liver failure made him very frail. But he managed the transfer of power to Silvio with all his old dignity.

After the lynching, the Liotta family fragmented, at least in North America. One section remained in New Orleans, accepting a secondary role. Others, including the four defendants who had survived in the Parish Prison siege, fled north, to Memphis, Chicago, Pittsburgh, and New York, where they founded families of their own. Years later Guido di Passo successfully prosecuted the Pittsburgh Mafia.

Silvio attended Angelo's funeral in Metairie Cemetery, where

the Cataldos were interred, but two days afterward he received a
visit from Anna-Maria. Angelo had often said to Silvio, in that
final terrible year, that he half hoped Silvio and Anna-Maria could
now get married, and Silvio would not have objected. But Anna-
Maria had changed, and now, with her husband and father gone,
she was taking her mother and children on a European cruise and
tour, to forget New Orleans and maybe start again, somewhere
else. She was strictly businesslike in her dealings with Silvio.

"You were mentioned in Papa's will," she said. "He left you his
cigars." She held out the box.

Silvio was touched. He took hold of the box, but Anna-Maria
didn't let go.

"I'll miss you, Silvio."

"Then don't leave. We could get married."

She smiled and shook her head. "Remember that night on the
Syracusa? When I saw that gun you had? Remember how excited
I was? More than you, I think. I used to *love* that sort of thrill. Not
anymore. I don't blame you for Dick's death. If anyone's to
blame, I'm up there at the top. But I've seen what his absence has
done to the children. And I've seen what living with my father
has done to my mother."

She lightly kissed Silvio's cheek. "No, I'll go now, while the
good memories are close enough to keep themselves warm. If I
stayed it would all just run into misery, or blood. I don't expect
we'll come back from Europe. Good-bye." Then she turned and
went out.

Silvio opened the cigar box. Inside was a letter. The letter was
in old Angie's handwriting.

Dear Sylvano,
By the time you get this, I'll be gone. First, I want to congratulate you on that last maneuver with Liotta. A very impressive
piece of thinking. Real foxy. I was impressed by your great
scheme when you first outlined it in the cathedral, that Tuesday
when I went to confession. I wasn't sure you could pull it off,
faking the ambush, then making sure the case was dropped, all
as a way of setting up a vendetta between Liotta and Martell,
and making Liotta the natural suspect for Martell's death. I
knew you had to get rid of Martell, after what he did to you, and
that you needed to outthink Liotta, to prove that you were

smarter. But I never thought it would pan out just as it did. You were right on the button about Di Passo. He was so ill, so mad with Fazio and Liotta he lied his head off. That last finesse, instructing the judge to send them back to jail, even after they had been acquitted, was beautiful. Life is rarely so sweet. I salute you from beyond the grave. You arrived in this world too late; Garibaldi could have made a great general out of you. Anyway, you will make a great Capo. You should have some years of peace ahead of you, and you will become very rich. Sicily will be proud of you.

I am sorry you never became my son-in-law, but then I am sorry for many things, and it is too late now. You have all the *things* any man could want.

My only hope is that you find someone.

Angie

Silvio took out a cigar but didn't light it right away. He was thinking of old Angie saying he would have liked him as a son-in-law. Silvio had never had a father; a father-in-law would have been the next best thing. But that last sentence was the one that hit home. "I hope you find someone." Yes, indeed. *Sono orfano*. I am still an orphan.

In the years that followed, Silvio Priola laid the foundation of a criminal empire that exists to this day. It is ironic that Mafia businesses are called families, for this, the first of them, was never a family in the true sense. Just as Silvio was Angelo's heir but not his natural son, so those who came after Silvio were not his blood relatives either. He died in 1921, just before his sixty-second birthday, trying to fix the Jack Dempsey–Georges Carpentier world heavyweight title fight. A gold ring and an old fishhook were found in his waistcoat pocket. They were buried with him. The bulk of his fortune went to the Esplanade Street Orphanage in New Orleans.

The Birth of the Mafia
in North America

This novel is based on a number of actual events that took place in Sicily, North America, and Great Britain in the last quarter of the nineteenth century. Those facts are set out below, together with a number of references for further reading.

In 1879 an Englishman, John Forrester Rose, sometimes described as a priest, was kidnapped in the hills behind Palermo by a group of Sicilian mafiosi. Rose owned land in Sicily, on which sulfur mines were a prominent feature. His abductors were a mafioso bandit known as Leone and his deputy, Giuseppe Esposito. Leone sent a ransom note to Rose's wife, demanding £5,000. With his initial demand he cut off one of Rose's ears and enclosed it in the envelope. The British government was incensed and demanded that the Italian government do something to resolve the situation. This resulted in another letter to Mrs. Rose, containing her husband's other ear and part of his nose. The ransom was eventually paid, and Rose released. However, in the interim Leone's band raided another grandee and held an American artist. He was forced to write the letters in English to Mrs. Rose and made to sketch Esposito to prove that he was an artist. This sketch was mailed to Britain with the second ransom demand written on the back. It was allegedly sent by Esposito out of vanity, the mafioso regarding himself as very good-looking.

After Rose was released, the British demanded that the Italian government move against the brigands, and operating on inside information, a *brigata* of cavalry, artillery, and infantry raided Leone. He was killed in the shoot-out that ensued, but Esposito, though captured, escaped later on and fled to New Orleans, where he took the name Randazzo. In New Orleans he lived on a fishing boat on the river. He became involved in the importation of fruit through the docks, where his friends included one Giuseppe Provenzano. The Provenzanos were one of two families involved at the time in the importation of fruit into the USA via New Orleans. The others were the Mantrangas, led by one Joseph Machecha. On occasions, and very controversially, on Esposito's boat, the Italian flag was flown *above* the Stars and Stripes.

In 1881 the Italian government asked police forces in America to look out for Esposito. The New Orleans detective (and, later, chief of police) David Hennessy arrested Esposito. He was able to identify his man using a copy of the sketch that the American artist had made of Esposito during his capture and which had been sent to London with the ransom demand written on it. Esposito was put on board a ship, the *City of New Orleans*, bound for New York, where he faced extradition proceedings. Despite a concerted campaign by the Provenzanos (among others) to prove Esposito's innocence, he was found guilty and extradited to Sicily on an Italian warship. In Italy he was tried on eighteen counts of murder and one hundred counts of kidnapping. He was found guilty of six murders and sentenced to death, though this was commuted to life. He died in prison seven years later, of natural causes.

As a result of the Esposito affair, David Hennessy became a celebrity in America and eventually chief of police in New Orleans. He was a rumbustious character, himself accused of murdering a rival detective, though acquitted.

In May 1890 a group of New Orleans roustabouts belonging to the Mantranga family were ambushed at the corner of Esplanade and North Claiborne streets. As a result of the attack several members of the rival Provenzano family were arrested. The attack was the culmination of a war between the Provenzanos and the Mantrangas during the course of which, in one year, eighty-nine waterfront murders took place.

At the time David Hennessy and the Provenzanos were joint owners of a whorehouse known as the Red Lantern located near Hennessy's home. Before their trial could take place, David Hennessy was killed in circumstances that are still controversial. He was walking home on Girod Street, having had supper at Dominick Virgut's oyster saloon, when he was shot by a group of men from across the street. Before he died, he is alleged to have said, "The dagos did it."

At the subsequent trial of nineteen men from the Mantranga family, the word *Mafia* was first used in an American context. The head of the Mantranga family was still alleged to be Joseph Machecha, a fruit importer. Part of the prosecution's case concerned a certain Frank di Maio, an employee of Pinkerton's agency, who infiltrated into the Parish Prison to snoop on the defendants. He posed as a counterfeiter who had been arrested in Amite, upstate Louisiana, and he shared a cell with a highly disturbed defendant, Emmanuele Polizzi. By persuading Polizzi that he was being poisoned by the others, di Maio managed to acquire circumstantial evidence against the Mantrangas. However, he caught dysentery and eventually did not give evidence. (Later in his career he was indeed one of those responsible for the apprehension of Butch Cassidy and the Sundance Kid.) The rest of the evidence in the trial of those accused of the murder of David Hennessy was grossly contradictory and in fact either the great majority of defendants were found not guilty or no verdict was reached. Despite this, the judge in the case, Mr. Joshua G. Baker, refused to release the defendants, who, following their acquittal, were returned to the Parish Prison. The next day, a mob, led by several "concerned citizens," surrounded the prison, broke in, and lynched those defendants. They were either shot or hanged at the Parish Prison or just outside, in full view of a mob. One was hanged from a lamppost.

Later a grand jury investigated the actions of this mob but refused to hand down further indictments. The affair caused a rift between the American and Italian governments and, for a while, there were even rumors of war. These were soon quashed, but aggression and even lynching against Italians in other American states and cities continued for some time.

There is controversy to this day as to whether the Provenzanos or the Mantrangas were responsible for David Henessy's death and to what extent it was a revenge killing for his arrest of Giuseppe Esposito some years earlier. What cannot be doubted is that both the Provenzanos and the Mantrangas were recognized families in *both* New Orleans *and* Sicily as late as the 1990s. In January 1995 one Giuseppe Provenzano was sentenced to life imprisonment in Palermo for a Mafia murder. And the importation of fruit, before the age of refrigeration, helped to account for the highly organized nature of Sicilian gangs in New Orleans, ahead of anywhere else.

Further reading

All these references tell much the same story except for the book by Richard Gambino.

Adams, Margaret, *Mafia Riots in New Orleans*, Tulane University thesis, 1924.

Coxe, John E., "The New Orleans Mafia Incident," *Louisiana Historical Quarterly*, 20, 4, 1937, pp. 1067–1110.

Gambino, Richard, *Vendetta: a true story of the worst lynching in America, the mass-murder of Italian-Americans in New Orleans in 1891, the vicious motivations behind it, and the tragic repercussions that linger to this day*, New York, Doubleday, 1977. (The author, who is Brooklyn-born, of Sicilian parentage, makes the case that there was no Mafia involvement in the Hennessy murder, but that instead the Sicilians in New Orleans were "set up" by traditional American business interests. Otherwise, a good and full account.)

Harper's, "The Mafia and What Led to the Lynching," *Harper's Weekly*, 35, March 28, 1891, pp. 225–7.

Horam, J.D., *The Pinkertons*, London, 1970, Robert Hale & Co. See especially chapter 34, "Operative Dimaio: 'The Raven'."

Kendall, John Smith, "Who Killa de Chief?," *Louisiana Historical Quarterly*, 22, 2, 1939, pp. 492–530.

Marr, Albert H., "The New Orleans Mafia Case," *American Law Review*, 25, 1891.